FOX TALES ANTHOLOGY

Volume I

Dee Carey

Fox Tales Anthology I
Copyright © 2023 by Dee Carey

ISBN:
Paperback: 978-1639457441
ebook: 978-1639457458

All rights reserved. No part of this publication may be reproduced, distributed, or transmitted in any form or by any means, including photocopying, recording, or other electronic or mechanical methods, without the prior written permission of the publisher, except in the case brief quotations embodied in critical reviews and other noncommercial uses permitted by copyright law.

The views expressed in this book are solely those of the author and do not necessarily reflect the views of the publisher, and the publisher hereby disclaims any responsibility for them.

Writers' Branding
1-800-608-6550
www.writersbranding.com
media@writersbranding.com

Contents

MARK OF THE FOX

Chapter One 1
Chapter Two 10
Chapter Three 15
Chapter Four 26
Chapter Five 34
Chapter Six 41
Chapter Seven 47
Chapter Eight 53
Chapter Nine...59
Chapter Ten...70
Chapter Eleven...79
Chapter Twelve..88
Chapter Thirteen 96
Chapter Fourteen 104
Chapter Fifteen 113
Chapter Sixteen 123
Chapter Seventeen 132
Chapter Eighteen 139
Epilogue 151

THE FOX AND THE SWAN

Prologue 157
Chapter One 159
Chapter Two 167
Chapter Three 178
Chapter Four 190
Chapter Five 195
Chapter Six 198
Chapter Seven 208
Chapter Eight 220
Chapter Nine..228
Chapter Ten..231
Chapter Eleven...237
Chapter Twelve...240
Chapter Thirteen 249
Chapter Fourteen 254
Chapter Fifteen 264
Chapter Sixteen..268
Chapter Seventeen 286
Chapter Eighteen 296
Chapter Epilogue 300

What People Are Saying About
Mark Of The Fox

A romantic, yet dashing tale, of the knights of old, Druids, wizards, witches, and an enchantment that bespeaks the true nobility and romance of days gone past. If you want to walk the paths of the olde ways, then indulge in Dee Carey's worlds, and be swept up into the times of King Arthur, when chivalry ruled the lands, Druids foretold the future, and magic touched everything.

A truly delightful tale that could have come from an ancient tome. Dee Carey truly has the gift of transporting the reader back to a time of enchantment.

——Angela Verdenius
Heart of the Forsaken

To my husband, Bill,

my daughters, Casey (Derwood), Kelly

and my grandsons, Nik and Bill.

MARK OF THE FOX

Chapter One

Skree, the sharp cry pierced the morning quiet.

A quiet that up until the eagle's intrusion was so complete Ryan could not even hear the beat of his own heart. Yet, he knew that with each beat the magnificent creature drew closer. His heart thundered in his ears. *Today you are mine.* The eagle's wings cut the air without a sound, its feather tips slicing through the clear blue sky. *I shall be the most renown of all falconers.* How long he'd waited for this moment, this single segment of time that would earn him the fame he sought. It had taken him several days to excavate the pit. All was ready for the capture of the great bird. Inhaling, he picked up the scent of the fresh kill he'd prepared as bait.

Skree.

She drew closer. With trembling hands, Ryan placed branches over the opening. If she kept to her usual schedule, she would be here in moments.

He dared not breathe. He watched as she tested the air for scents and scanned the ground for any slight movement that would indicate prey. Ryan gently shook the tuft of fur he'd taken from the dogs. Long had he studied the eagle's habits, and he was certain she would mistake the piece of fur for a mouse. Slowly, she rode on the air currents in ever-tightening rings, then she suddenly stooped, diving with a ferocity he'd not anticipated.

She hit the branches with great force, and they gave way beneath her.

Heart pounding, Ryan threw a net over the opening. The great bird flew at him, her talons flaying his face. Tiny pricks of pain skimmed the surface of his skin and he felt the blood trickle from the cuts but he would have her at any cost.

Finally she calmed enough for him to sit and wait for her to recognize him as her new master. He sat there many hours, the net still around the bird. He sang and spoke to her softly, throughout the long day. Rocking her gently, as one would a child, he stroked her feathers. Finally, the eagle gave in to slumber. Gently, he wrapped her in the soft cloth he'd brought with him, being careful to secure her talons.

He raced to his tower, knowing his parents would wonder why he hadn't shown up for the evening meal. Placing the eagle on his bed, he noticed there was a great deal of blood on the bedding. He knew the talons cut his face, but there was too much blood for simple scratches. The bird's head lolled to the side, the eyes glazed over.

Ryan's heart sank. For all his care, he'd injured the great bird. His grand plan would be over before it even began if the eagle died. The dream would elude him. Turing the eagle's body over, he gently examined the bird. Then he spotted the cause for the blood. Her left wing was broken, the bone protruding the flesh. Hands trembling, he fashioned a crude splint from an arrow. Thankfully the bird seemed to be unconscious. He wrapped her in his bed coverings. Certain he'd made her as comfortable as possible, he hurried down the stairs to the kitchen.

Ryan went to the large barrel where Helga kept the salted meat and withdrew a piece. He moved stealthily, lest he wake the cook. To no avail. Though her hearing was weak, instinctively the old cook knew when there was someone in her kitchen.

"Who's there?" she cried, holding her lantern high.

Ryan stepped into the lantern's beam. "It's just me, Helga, I missed dinner, and I'm hungry."

"And how is it you missed dinner?" Helga asked, stepping around the table, bringing the light closer to see the lad.

"Great heavens, Ryan, what have you done? Did someone attack you? Your face is badly torn. I fear I will not be able to mend it without scarring."

Sorry he'd scared the woman, Ryan patted her arm. "Don't worry, a few scars will make me irresistible to women when I'm older." *Who I am is of greater importance, than what I look like. My woman will see past the scars to the man. She will know my soul.*

"Ryan, your parents would never forgive me if I leave you with scars.

Come, we will find Olyn. He will know how to treat your wounds."

Ryan prayed Helga could not smell the older blood. It would only raise questions he was not prepared to answer.

The bell Helga had placed at the entrance of Olyn's workroom pealed in the evening quiet. Olyn groaned. What could that woman want at this hour? With some difficulty, he slowly ascended the large, well-worn stair. The old cook stood outlined by the light from the hallway, her arm about young Ryan.

"Well, woman, what is it you need at such an hour?" Olyn demanded, somewhat angrily.

When he reached the top stair, he could see the boy's face, covered with blood.

"Great merciful heaven's, what have you done to yourself, Lad? No amount of salve will prevent scarring. Helga, fetch your sewing tools. This is going to upset Leigh."

Ryan wondered why Olyn mentioned only his father would be offended by any disfigurement. It was a matter of no concern, to him.

"Come on, boy, let's see if we can minimize the damage," the old wizard said, as he led him down to his workroom. They traversed the stair and Ryan began to falter. Suddenly he went limp and slumped against the wizard. Olyn swung him into his deceivingly muscular arms and carried him to the center of his worktable.

Grabbing a scrap of linen, Olyn began to clean the boy's face. He moved slowly as not to damage the flesh further. The tear was jagged and blood oozed from the ravaged flesh. The blood began to clot as Olyn pressed the square of cloth against the wound. The marks were wide and deep. Something or someone had done a great deal of cutting on this young face. The injury that would cause the most scarring was directly across the corner of his right eye. It was truly a wonder he'd not lost his sight. The gash continued across his cheek and down his neck into the hairline. There was no way he, nor even the greatest healer, could avoid the nasty mark that would cover much of the face of Ryan Longwurth.

Ryan came to, feeling Olyn's nimble fingers on his face. *Have I lost them both?* First the eagle and perhaps his perfect woman as well. He knew she would be greater than one selected by appearance, still comely looks were beneficial. And, he needed her at his side. This woman so perfect, Ryan feared of her existence. Still, her image pierced his brain. Scrappy, yet strong, hair of a brilliant copper, the eyes an entrancing green that could bore through the soul of a man. *She will share my life and dreams. If, in fact, I've not dashed them against the wall of wisdom.* He knew what he'd attempted would never be undertaken by a reasonable man. His dreams were more grand than those of a reasonable man. Long had this dream plagued him. First as a boy, when he'd found the inscribed stone, and now as a man with awakening passion.

He would have his eagle and his woman.

The woman carved on the talisman stone he always carried.

In her own tent, Ninaway felt secure in her abilities. Here she was the ruler, all the power hers. No one would speak a word against her. The animals were her friends. Though she'd hoped to have greater powers, the Queen of Briton greatly hampered her. She was well aware the English Queen was not enamored of her. Guinevere had tarred her with the same brush as her cousin Morganna, and had influenced her husband to decree Ninaway should remain forever in her own homeland.

It was a cold and blustery day. Few folks would be out on this day. All would be bundled at their hearths. Within this land, she could move about without fear of detection. She reached up to the branch that held the edge of her tent and her cloak. Wrapping the soft gray garment about her shoulder, she ventured out into the mist and noted the silver fog blanketing the moor. The path was barely visible. Good. She would not be observed on this cold damp morn.

She preferred no one knew of her comings and goings. With her cloak wrapped tightly around her, Ninaway made her way to the edge of a swift running stream. The chill waters rushed over the stones, thrusting the fallen leaves into the flow.

There, in the rapid current, was a family of foxes, a mother and three kits. Each of the kits smaller than the last. Without warning, a great rush of water tore the mother from her babies. The two larger ones gave themselves up to the raging torrent in an attempt to follow their mother. Vainly they pawed in the swift waters. Nothing could save them or their mother. Only the smallest female clung to an overhead branch. The smallest was certainly not the weakest. Valiantly, she fought the rushing current. Her tiny paws scratched bravely at the bank of the stream.

As she drew closer, Ninaway reached out and grabbed the tiny creature. Wrapping the mammal in the hem of her cloak, she began to sing to the tiny shivering fox. The animal was covered with mud, bits of grasses matting its fur. Its fear-filled eyes looked up at her.

Slowly, Ninaway climbed the bank and returned to her tent, unaware that the great wizard Merlin observed from a short distance. He shook his head at her actions. *What fool creature has she rescued this time?* Still, for some reason this woman had captured his heart. All the alliances he'd had throughout his lifetime paled in comparison to his feelings for her.

And it wasn't just her appearance, though she was beautiful. Her long blond hair fell free in cascading ripples of gold. No, for many other reasons this magical woman, who talked to the creatures of the field, held his heart captive. Eyes of softest gray, the color of a swan cygnet, seemed to drown in her ivory skin. Merlin likewise fell into the misty pools. He'd tossed aside reason and wisdom. Now, he was avoiding his duty, even hiding from Arthur, whom he trusted above all others. It had been several months since he'd conferred with the king. The chief advisor to the ruler of England spoke not a word to his regent, and affairs of state were in turmoil.

Ninaway smiled as she approached her lover. Though he was far older than she, the attraction was power, not comely looks. The tall, thin, white-bearded man possessed what she held most dear: control over all things.

As she drew closer, she extended her hand and offered the tiny bundle up to him. "See, Merlin, what the stream has given me this velvet morning. Is she not beautiful? Have you ever seen fur of this hue?"

Merlin swept aside the corner of her cloak that rested on his palm. Within nestled the smallest fox he'd ever seen. Clots of brown mud mixed with her mottled fur.

Merlin gazed upon the tiny creature with only the slightest admiration. The magic of Ninaway was more enchanting than any mere animal, though the creature was most unusual.

"Yes," he said to his love, "she is rather small. Do you think she will live? She's very nearly drowned."

Ninaway glanced at Merlin, smiled, and took the miniscule animal from him. "Have no fear, Merlin, I will restore her to perfect health."

Of that Merlin had no doubt. Ninaway would be able to accomplish the miracle the tiny fox would need to survive. He'd seen her heal the severest of wounds on her beloved animals. She had a natural talent that in many ways surpassed her skills as a witch. A true nurturer, she moved on to more practical matters.

"Come, Merlin, I need to warm this small one and to find some food for us to dine upon." She pushed aside the flap of the elaborate tent.

Within the confines of the tent, one seemed to be in a palace, the walls draped with the finest tapestries, gilded cages lined the parameter of a finely woven rug. The cages contained all manners of animals. There were cats, rabbits, dogs, and doves, living in harmony with one another. Though they lived in cages, there were no locks on the doors. They were free to roam and were never in contention with one another. Merlin was continually in awe of the magic of Ninaway. Throughout his lengthy lifetime, he'd never encountered another with equal skill.

Gently, she set the fragile creature in a soft woolen blanket placed on the edge of her elaborate bed and began to clean the fox. Her fingers moved with a tenderness that belied her usual nature. For the most part, the sorceress did not entertain compassion. The bed was big enough to hold countless numbers of bodies. In fact, many were already sleeping there. The tapestry enveloping the perimeter of the bed was spun with the finest of gold threads. He knew she'd conjured her possessions, yet the gentility of the collector was apparent. The cat stirred only slightly. The dog moved beside the newcomer and warmed the tiny fox. Perched on the upholstered headboard sat a pair of doves. They began to coo a soft melody and soon the fox was asleep. Clean and no longer fearful, the animal rested, and her slight, yet precise, breaths confirmed she would survive.

Ninaway watched the tiny being for a long time. "Merlin, have you ever seen a fox as small as this? I believe this particular fox is unlike any other in all the known worlds."

Merlin smiled indulgently at his love. "Yes, I'm certain of it."

The look in her eyes told him she knew he was humoring her. Though she didn't possess all the skills of a third-level wizard, she could read Merlin as clearly as any missive. "Have you ever seen fur of such a hue? It's so deep a red, almost like wine. What shall I call her?"

"How can you be so certain it is a she?" Merlin asked, feigning interest. Smiling, she said, "A woman knows another of her sex."

"Ah yes, the mystery of woman." He could deny this woman nothing. Whatever she desired, he would provide, even something as mundane as a name for one of her pets. "Ninaway, she is the color of fine wine. Why not call her Claret?"

"Claret? Yes, I like that. It is most fitting," she said, as she stroked the unusual fur of the now-stirring fox.

It should have been apparent to the wizard that this fox was different from any of her other pets. But he was so besotted with this woman, so unlike any other, his reason fled his mind. Her golden hair wound its tentacles around even the smallest confines of his mind. He could not resist, nor did he care to.

Ninaway softly crooned to her pets, adjusting her voice to that of the doves, matching the birds in tune and pitch. Unable to turn from the magnificent sounds, Merlin sighed. He was more than smitten; his very soul captured by the spell of Ninaway. He was bound as surely as any prisoner was in the deepest dungeon. He'd not even tried to keep his skills current. Likened to adultery, Ninaway had seduced him from his marriage to sorcery. A wizard could not actually lose skills with disuse, but the ability became dormant.

Olyn labored over the young boy. Once skin so perfect, now horribly scarred. It would be difficult to face Leigh. Leigh trusted Olyn to protect the boy, as he'd once protected him. The dangers were not as great for Ryan. He didn't live in an abandoned castle, and he had parents. Parents who trusted him to provide better care for their son than they had. Olyn had had some of his powers restored, but the worst had happened. His greater power, he would never again wield.

"Helga, sew the flesh around the eye. Use the finest of stitches. T'will cause less scarring."

Slowly and precisely the needle pierced the skin around the injury, and the tiny stitches drew closed the gaping wound. Her task completed, Helga looked on helplessly as Olyn prepared a balm to ease the scarring. Pulverizing a combination of herbs in a pestle, he added a dollop of wine. Ryan appeared unconcerned about the disfigurement.

"Olyn, don't worry. This will separate me from the dandies. I have no wish to be some fancy parading about court, hoping some foolish maid will notice me. What I have chosen to do with my life is not bearing upon beauty, but upon knowledge and skill. Please, stop fussing over me."

"Ryan, be still. At least I can reduce the damage," Olyn said, as he applied a foul-smelling substance to the face of the young prince.

"Lord almighty, that stinks," Ryan gasped, slipping from the wizard's grasp.

Helga grabbed the boy about the shoulders, then forced him around to again face the wizard. "Ryan," she said crossly, "you must allow Olyn to treat your wound, else there will be more to face than you are prepared to deal with."

"Helga," he whined, "it's just a scratch. I care not if it scars. Most falconers are scarred. 'Tis a badge of honor." He knew the woman in his dreams would not even see the scars. She would trust him and see into his heart. "You may feel it honors you, but in truth it smears both my honor and your father's as well." Olyn set the balm on his worktable, and turned to his Master Tome for assistance. Roughly, he turned the pages, hoping the answer would spring forth. Finding nothing, he slid into the chair beside the table and placed his head in his hands.

Ryan walked to the table and put his hand on the wizard's shoulder. Olyn abruptly brushed the hand aside. The boy's sympathy only served to open an old hurt.

"Olyn, I know you are concerned my appearance will offend my parents, but the matter is mundane. My mother will not care. Appearance means naught to her. Although my father is unscarred, I know many of his comrades are. It does not mean he thinks less of them."

"Oh, Ryan. Olyn doesn't mean you are less a person, only that you must be unmarked to serve the king," Helga said.

Olyn shot her a warning glare. The boy should not be drawn into a discussion involving royalty. His thoughts on the matter were well known.

"I told you, I have no wish to serve the king. Moreover, I have no wish to be a king. Now cover the wound and whatever scarring occurs, I will live with."

Olyn's anger turned to despair. "You foolish boy, what affects you affects the kingdom. Not only Arthur's, but others as well."

"I have no wish to be rude, Olyn, but I care not for kingdoms nor for court. You know well my feelings, please stop trying to change my course. With or without your help, I will become a falconer. The finest in all of Ireland." The boy stood firm, his arms crossed over his chest and his feet firmly planted.

Olyn sent him to his quarters and bade Helga to find Baylor the Black to look in on the boy throughout the long night.

Helga pushed her hair out of her eyes and gathered up Ryan's bloodied clothing. She hurried through the great hall, weaving between the long trestle tables. Nearly to the far end of the hall, she serendipitously discovered Baylor alone at a side table fashioning hoods from leather.

"Oh, thank goodness, I found you without going to the knight's quarters."

Baylor looked up from his task and smiled at the plump cook. Her round cheeks flushed red. "My lady Helga, do the men embarrass you?"

Briefly forgetting her mission, the old woman blushed. Gathering her senses, she said, "I'll pay that no mind."

"Well then, do you require my services this evening?"

"Olyn does. Please go to his workroom." The worried look again passed over her features.

He gathered up the materials he'd been using and stuffed them in his tunic. "I'm sorry I've dismayed you, Mother. Is there something amiss?"

"Yes, son, it's young Ryan. He's been injured. His face is horribly scratched. I fear he will be badly scarred."

"What is it Olyn wishes of me? I am not a healer."

"I'm sure Olyn knows which of your talents he will put to use. Please help him, Baylor," she said, touching her son's muscular arm.

Smiling at the woman he'd known as 'Mother' for such a short period, Baylor patted the old woman's cheek. "I will serve in whatever manner Olyn requests."

Chapter Two

Ryan looked about the tower room, with the odd sense he was not alone. On a tall perch, the eagle rested quietly. The right wing hung unnaturally, but the bird's eyes seemed clear and it was roosting comfortably. Ryan lifted his throbbing head from the pallet. A large man approached him. His vision blurred by pain, he didn't recognize his father's falconer.

"You, there, why are you in my quarters?"

Baylor crossed the room and stroked the breast feathers of the injured bird as he passed the perch.

"Rest easy, Ryan, you will undo my mother's handiwork. Olyn asked me to keep an eye on you."

Ryan focused his eyes and saw the one person who might be able to help him realize his dream. "Thanks, Baylor, I'm fine really." Ryan tried to sit, but the room spun before him. "Baylor, did you bring the stand for my eagle?"

"Yes, son, I did, but your bird needs more than a perch. The wing is badly broken, I fear it may never heal properly." The large man spoke softly.

Ryan's heart leapt up into his throat. The worst he'd feared had come to pass. Slowly, he lowered himself back onto the bed. Sighing, he asked his father's falconer, "Baylor, is there any hope Aqulia will recover enough to hunt? Any way at all?"

Baylor the Black smiled down on the disfigured boy. "It seems you are more concerned about your eagle than yourself. Frankly lad, you are a mess."

Ryan reached a tentative finger up to his face. Touching his eye and torn cheek, he flinched only slightly. "I guess I look pretty frightening."

"I've seen worse. People who work with birds are, for the most part, a scarred lot."

"How is it a Knight of the Round Table becomes a falconer?"

"I'd served the king for many years, believing I was a man without family or ties." The big man's voice caught. "I learned I have a mother and a brother. Arthur allowed me to return to Clare with your father when he was knighted. My mother is very old and the king graciously allowed me to spend time with her."

"How kind of him," Ryan said contemptuously.

"But, this still doesn't tell me how you became a falconer." Whatever it took, he would learn. He would be the most famous falconer in the kingdom.

"Since there is peace in Ireland now that your father is king, there is no need for a knight, so I turned my interest elsewhere, that I might be of service."

"How is it knights are so duty and honor-bound? Have you no wishes of your own? No dreams?" Ryan asked, incredulous.

"Young Ryan, you will learn to serve others is the greatest dream," Baylor answered with an air of regret. "Too many years passed, while I served the king for my own purposes. The reward is far greater to serve with dedication and zeal for a just cause."

"Ha," Ryan jeered, "I cannot believe all men feel this way. If this were so, there would be no need for rulers or laws."

"You are quite right, but fortunately there are such men as believe in right and honor. It balances those who have no honor and care not for right."

"I suppose you learned this from the English king, Arthur?"

"In part, I learned from Arthur, but honor and service are things I learned from my mother at a very young age. I hid from myself what I had learned, until I was reunited with her."

"Where's your mother now?" Ryan asked, hoping to draw the falconer into a friendship that would help him save his eagle.

"Here. She cooks for your parents."

"My Helga is your mother?" Ryan couldn't believe what he was hearing. Helga had been his alone. Not a person to share with others. She was the grandmother he would never have.

"How come she never told me she was your mother? Is she ashamed of you?" Shame was the only reason Ryan could think of that would prohibit the disclosure of such information.

Baylor laughed. "Well, lad, there was a time when that might have been the case. But, no longer. I'm sure if you asked her, she will happily acknowledge me."

Ryan grew tired of this casual banter. He wanted to know about his eagle. Glancing at Aqulia, he noted there was a falconer's hood over her head. Somewhat crossly, he asked, "How did that hood come to be on her?"

"I made it for one of my own birds, but when Mother summoned me and I saw your injured eagle I placed it on her. She will be easier to treat if she is hooded."

Ryan inclined his brow. "And do you propose to treat her?"

"Ryan, why are you so distrustful? You are so young to feel thus. I will help you with your eagle and try to repair her wing."

"Can you? Can you do such a thing? The splint I placed on her seems to be missing."

"I removed it and fashioned a smaller one that fits her more tightly. Barring infection, her bones should mend in several weeks."

"Several weeks? Can't you do something to speed the healing? I've not much time to train her."

Baylor ruffled the boy's hair. "And why is time so important to you? You are young and have a great deal of time before you. Do not rush your life away, young prince."

Ryan could feel the determination in his soul burning with a white-hot flame. He would be the first in all of Arthur's holdings to train a wild eagle. Such a bird was above his station, but he cared not. His well-muscled body could easily support the weight of such a bird. He'd forge ahead with his dream. Whatever the obstacles, he would overcome them. Determining humility would be a better tactic. Ryan shifted on his bed and moved aside. He patted the space next to him and bid Baylor sit.

"Tell me more about falcons. How many do you have?"

Baylor sat and began to tell Ryan of his birds. "In truth, I have only one. The remainder belong to your father."

"Have you no wish to own more?"

"I have found the more you own, the more things own you. I prefer to have fewer possessions and those are of the highest quality," Baylor said wisely. "Unus, a peregrine, is my only bird. She can out hunt any of your father's."

Slyly, Ryan replied, "You spend more time with her than my father's birds?"

"Ryan, that is not the case. I train them all together. Unus learns more quickly than the others do. She is the oldest, but the others will catch up."

Fearing he'd offended the falconer, Ryan said humbly, "I meant no insult. I merely wondered how much time is required to train a skilled hunter."

"I understand, Ryan, there is no set time. Each takes its own time. Should you like, I can see if your father would allow you to work with me. It will give your face a chance to heal, and he will know I am keeping you from harm," the big man said kindly.

Baylor was developing a fondness for the boy and wished to share his knowledge with someone who was as bonded with the birds as he was. The bird the boy had trapped was indeed a fine specimen. If the wing healed properly, she would be a valued hunter.

***

Ninaway smiled. The fox was now weaned and extremely curious. She no longer depended upon her for food. Smaller than most foxes, Claret continually discovered new places to hide. Another of the fox's pastimes was thievery. Bits of parchment, shiny objects, anything she put her teeth on, she stole and hid in one of her many secret dens.

Ninaway was more indulgent with the tiny creature than any of her other pets. Though she'd been very upset when she'd discovered Claret had purloined her love letters from Merlin. Understanding the power of the written word, Ninaway sought to control Merlin should he decide to leave her.

Ninaway searched the tent thoroughly. She moved each tapestry, lifted each rug, and threw aside each pillow on her giant bed. She found useless baubles, strips of cloth, but the letters were nowhere to be found. Aware of her pet's penchant for thievery, she was certain the fox had taken the letters. However, she said nothing to Merlin.

Claret wandered out to the meadow. Due to her diminutive size, she was able to hide easily in the tall grasses. Her stomach growled. She would have to search for food. Voles were her favorite meal and the meadow was home to numbers of them. Crouching her body deep in the grasses, she moved not a muscle. Voles resemble moles, however were capable of seeing. Claret preferred the somewhat plumper, though harder to catch voles. Her prey sighted, she remained still as death, not moving a muscle. The rodent came within a whisker-length of her snout. Swiftly, she pounced and dispatched the small animal.

After savoring her meal, the fox carefully washed. She groomed herself until she was satisfied every single strand of her fur was in its proper place.

Vainly, she viewed her own image in the nearby stream. Confident, she started her way back to Ninaway's tent. Leaping high into the air, she chased a butterfly, simply for sheer joy. The insect swooped down, then flitted back up high over the meadow grasses. Claret jumped within scant inches of the insect, certain she would be the victor, should she actually wish to consume the beautiful thing, then abandoned her mock hunt.

Preferring to enter Ninaway's tent by any other means than the main entrance, Claret poked her snout beneath the edge of the tent near the gigantic bed. Observing Ninaway searching frantically for something, she slipped under the coverlet.

Though she knew it was wrong, Claret derived pure ecstasy from the pilfering of Ninaway's possessions. She'd stolen pieces of jewelry, bits of cloth and her favorite, pieces of parchment. The crinkling noises the paper made fascinated her. Finding the parchment made different noises when it was crumpled, she grabbed a piece and shook it, dropped it and pawed it until it resembled a crude ball. Tiring of batting the ball with her paws, she turned her back on it and tossed it aside with her full tail.

The quick action of the white tip of her tail alerted Ninaway to her presence. Intrigued that another game was afoot, Claret lunged at her mistress then quickly retreated, eluding her grasp.

Chapter Three

Baylor stayed with Ryan throughout the day. Though the scarring was evident, none of the injuries seemed life threatening.

Ryan was anxious to be free of his bed. "Come on, Baylor, I'm fine, let me leave the tower."

The older, seasoned knight took the boy's chin in his hand and turned his head from side-to-side. Everything seemed to be on the mend, and there was no telltale redness that would indicate infection.

"Well, lad, it does seem you are mending well, but I want to speak to Olyn before you see your parents."

"All right, but please hurry, and do come back. I want to begin training Aqulia."

Baylor sighed. It had been too long since he'd felt impatient, eager to start a new venture. The knight stepped back and released the boy's face. "I shall return, young prince, but you must remember a bird that is injured must be healed first, before she can hunt."

"I know, I know, but I've heard you have to get them to accept you and the form of food they will hunt. Can we not start with that?"

"Quite so, Ryan. I believe you have the mettle to be a falconer."

"I will be more than a falconer. I shall be the greatest falconer in Ireland, maybe the best in the world."

"Mayhap you will, Ryan, but it all takes time. Training a wild thing is not like feeding scraps to the dogs in the great hall. The birds are very wary. They do not trust us. They have to learn we mean them no harm, before we can bend them to our will."

"But, you will show me?" Ryan asked, as he leapt from his bed and began dressing.

"I will, lad, but remember, do not leave the tower until I return." The man withdrew and left Ryan and Aqulia to begin a friendship that would make the boy a legend. At least, that was his intention. Legendary throughout the known worlds: Ryan, Aqulia, and his beautiful mate. He knew he would find her, just as he'd found Aqulia.

Baylor descended from the tower and headed directly to Olyn's workroom.

Approaching the door to Olyn's sanctorum, Baylor coughed loudly, in order not to startle the old man. Entering, he said, "Good day, Olyn, I've come to give you a report on Ryan's condition. There seems to be no sign of infection, but as you suspected, I fear there will be much scarring."

The old man dropped his arms to his sides in defeat. "Do you think time will ease the damage?"

"Time is a great healer, however, though the redness will disappear there will be a jagged line across the face of the prince."

"I agree. I must tell his father, though I do not look forward to the task."

"May I make a suggestion, Olyn? I believe 'twill be easier if you tell both parents at the same time."

Olyn wrung his hands over and over. "Perhaps you are right. I will see to it right away. No sense prolonging the agony."

"Do you wish me to accompany you? If it will make it easier, I will be happy to."

"Thank you, Baylor, that is most kind. However, I think it best if I face them alone."

Olyn tidied his work area, even dusting to avoid facing Ryan's parents. When he was unable to engage in any more meaningless chores, he slowly headed for Leigh's council room.

His heart fair to bursting with the sorrow he knew would pierce the souls of the two parents, he headed up the stairs. Each step became more and more of an effort. He reached the top and leaned against the cool stone. Stepping into the hallway, he saw Kit coming toward him.

"Olyn, are you all right? You look winded."

"I'm fine, lass. Age makes the stairs harder to traverse. Do you know where Leigh is at the moment?"

"Yes, he's in the council room. I'm heading that way now, will you join me?" she said, extending her hand over his arm.

Olyn smiled broadly and took her hand in his own. "You know, young lady, I miss the days aboard ship, when I was younger and adventurous."

"My old friend, I miss those days myself. When I had control of my destiny, not bound by any rules except my own."

Olyn lifted a finger to chide the former pirate.

Kit grinned, took his finger in her hand, and said, "Don't waste your time telling me I am happier now, and I would not have a son if I kept to the path I had cut for myself. However, Olyn, it would have been a great adventure."

He threw back his head and laughed, the sound seeming to come from his toes up through his torso. Shaking with glee, he nearly forgot his mission. The sobering thought hit him. He looked at the woman, the mother, his Kit had become. "Kit, I have grave news about Ryan."

Kit's eyes flew wide, her mother's instinct at the ready. "I've not seen him since yesterday. I thought to give him more freedom not to have his mother chasing after him at every turn. Has he run away?"

"No, child he's…" Olyn's voice failed him. He shook his head.

"Olyn, what is it? I demand you tell me." Eyes flaring, Kit said, "It is an order. I am your queen."

Despite the gravity of the situation, Olyn was amused by Kit's use of her royal status. "No, Kit, he is here within the castle, but he's been injured."

"Injured? How? Is it life-threatening?"

"At this point I don't think he is in any real danger. Helga stitched him up, and I applied salve to ease scarring and infection. I will clean the wound each day until he heals. He appears to be mending well."

Not convinced her only child was safe, Kit turned quickly on her heel and started back down the corridor.

Olyn grabbed her arm. "No, Kit, you must hear all of the tale, and I must tell you and Leigh together."

"Why? I am his mother. I will tend him. Leigh must deal with his kingdom," she said angrily.

"Please, just come with me and I will tell you everything, but Leigh must hear as well." The wizard put his arm about the shoulders of the lass he'd come to love as his own. They stopped at the door of the council room. Olyn tapped the open door. "Leigh?"

Looking up from a wooden table strewn with maps, Leigh smiled. "Come in, come in." Leigh leaned over, kissed his wife, and shook his hand. "What brings you two to the council room?"

Kit blurted, "Our son has been hurt and Olyn won't tell me how badly he's injured."

Leigh furrowed his brow. "It this so, Olyn? Is the lad in such danger you must keep it from us?"

"No, no, his injures are slight. He is in no physical danger." Warily, Leigh spoke. "And what other danger might harm him?"

"Leigh, he is not in any danger directly to himself, but countries may be in danger."

Impatiently Kit stamped her foot. "Tell me and tell me the whole of it now or, or... I'll hang you from the mizzen mast."

Leigh looked askance at his wife's choice of words. "We shan't hang you, Olyn, but you are trying my patience as well as Kit's. Disclose all now," he said firmly, drawing up chairs for them both.

Olyn sat and adjusted the folds of his robe. He hesitated, then began. "You know, young Ryan does not wish to be a king."

Leigh and Kit both nodded.

"He wishes to be a falconer," Olyn continued.

"A falconer?" Leigh replied.

"Why ever would he wish to be a falconer? As a king, he will have all sorts of comforts. As a falconer, he would face all manners of hardship. He cannot just decide to be a falconer. One must have the talent, as well as the time and patience to train the birds."

"You are quite right, but young Ryan feels he has the talent and the determination to learn."

Kit's nostrils flared. "What has this to do with Ryan's injury? I do not wish to hear what might happen, I want to know what has already happened. Furthermore, if I am not told at once, I will hang you, Olyn."

Olyn smiled wanly. "Ryan received his injuries trapping an eagle. He wishes to train the bird to be his first falcon."

"Train an eagle? Why that's like domesticating a... a..."

"... a fox, perhaps?" Leigh finished for his wife.

"Oh, don't be silly. That couldn't happen twice, could it, Olyn?"

"Perhaps, but I don't think that's what happened in this situation."

"Whatever the reason, I wish to see my son. Now," Kit demanded. Leigh nodded.

Olyn eyed the pair and said, "He's resting now. Baylor watched him through the night and he's with him now. The stair is too steep for me to climb. After Helga stitched his wound, I covered it with a balm and he went to his room."

Leigh and Kit shared a worried glance and started up the stairs to their son's tower room. Kit knew she was experiencing the pain of a mother whose child had been hurt. Though she knew every mother faces the fear at some time in her child's life, she'd never expected to even have a child, let alone endure the pain of her child in jeopardy.

Her husband's features were a studied mask. She could not read his emotions, could not understand how he seemed to be so dispassionate.

They reached the top of the stair and she immediately spotted Baylor sitting at the edge of Ryan's bed. He appeared to be talking softly to her son. Ryan's head lay on his pillow, but he sounded alert.

Baylor turned when he heard them enter. He rose and pulled up a chair for Kit to sit. She pushed aside the chair and sat on her son's bed. Forcing the concern from her tone, she said, "Well, my son, it seems you've done yourself quite an injury. Are you in pain?"

"No, Mother, I'm fine. It's just a scratch. Truly."

Leigh approached the bedside and looked down on his son's torn face. "Great merciful heavens, what have you done, Ryan?"

Baylor put a hand on his shoulder. "Leigh, have no fear. He will mend swiftly. The cut was sutured quickly, and there is no sign of infection."

"Baylor, I am sure you and Olyn gave my son the very best of care, but the fact remains he is going to be scarred," Leigh said dejectedly.

Kit stepped up to her husband. "Leigh, it matters not he will be scarred. He is royalty and will someday serve as a knight. Many, many knights are scarred. It will not affect his skills or his honor."

Leigh shook his head. "Baylor, please make her understand. If I try, I may regret what I might say." Quickly he turned and departed the tower.

"Kit, I know as a mother, you are concerned for his safety," Baylor explained, "But you must understand that all kings of Arthur's domain are to be unmarked."

"I understand, all right, I just happen to think it silly. A warrior can lead his troops, even if he is missing a limb or an eye. While I'm sure there are many duties I have no knowledge of, it can't be as difficult as fighting on a battlefield."

"You are quite right, Kit, but to rule for Arthur is a special privilege and only the perfect are to serve."

"And Arthur is perfect? If he were so perfect, why did his newly wed queen leave him for a foppish knight?"

Baylor squared his shoulders. "Truly, I do not know why she left him, or why it matters if royalty is unmarked."

"I know there is more afoot here than I understand. I will wait until Leigh is calmer then try to reason with him," she said, then leaned over her son's bed and kissed him on the forehead.

"I thank you, Baylor, for watching my son."

"Twas an honor, My Queen," he said, bowing low.

Kit giggled and cocked a brow at the knight. "An honor, My Queen?"

Again the opposing threads of love and duty tugged at Leigh's very soul. As a father, he loved his son regardless of his appearance, but he knew the duty to honor and the crown. His son's facial scarring was an accident. Surely Arthur and the Druids would understand. There had to be some way to make this aright.

With a heavy heart, Leigh began to pace the great hall. The high stone walls were cool with the afternoon shade, the tapestries blowing gently in the spring breeze. His heart was cold and still, Leigh paid no mind to the elegance that surrounded him. He closed his eyes against the inevitable and determined his best course was to confer with Olyn. Perhaps he would have some answers. Leigh would not defy Arthur or the Druids. Slowly, he descended the time worn steps feeling like a man walking to certain death. Though he'd faced many terrors in Arthur's service, nothing could compare to the dread eating away at his heart.

Far beneath the castle, the door to the workroom stood open. Leigh tapped at the casement. Peering in, he saw the old wizard stooped over the table in the center of the room. Only a single torch lit the cold gray walls. He cleared his throat to alert the old man. It became apparent Olyn did not hear him.

Time and girth had eroded the old man's senses. His hearing was most affected. Once able to hear the tiniest footfall of a scampering mouse, now even the loud scraping of the edge of the heavy door across the damp stone escaped Olyn's notice.

"Olyn, may I have a word with you? I need your guidance, old friend," Leigh said, crossing to the table and placing a hand on the wizard's stooped shoulder.

Olyn looked up, a tear in his eye slipping swiftly down his cheek. "I truly don't know how I can help you, Leigh. I've bungled the second chance I've been given. I should have watched the boy closer. I felt he had a better chance at life than you or Kit. Ryan has parents and a secure home. I have failed in my duty to Merlin, Arthur, and the Druids."

Leigh looked with compassion on his lifelong companion. "Do not judge yourself too harshly. There is no way you could have known the boy's wishes. What happened was an accident. Nothing more. It could not have been prevented no matter how vigilant any of us had been."

Olyn's tears flowed freely. "Would what you say were true. I could have had more power had I petitioned Merlin and discussed my reasons with him."

"Olyn, you were fortunate to have some of your power restored. I don't think Merlin would have given you unlimited power to control a rebellious child," Leigh said dejectedly.

Olyn stood and pushed himself from the table and slammed the large book shut. "There seems to be no answers, not even in the Master Tome. I do not know if I should contact Merlin, the Druids, or if I should trust the course of history to make all things right."

"At this point I think it would be best to follow protocol and start by contacting Arthur."

"Yes, I agree. Would you send Baylor? He is most familiar with Arthur."

"Baylor is a most reliable messenger. I trust him with my life," Leigh concurred.

"Leigh, time is of the utmost importance. This matter must be settled in the shortest time possible. How can we get Ryan to Arthur and find Merlin quickly?" Olyn said reflectively.

Throughout his short reign, Leigh had few decisions of this magnitude to consider. This determination would affect more than the people of the Isle of Clare. It would be felt on the mainland, throughout England, Scotland, and Wales. This was not the time for hasty judgment. He paced up and down the length of the workroom, back and forth, until he had a blinding insight. He spun on his heel and turned to face the wizard, stopping so suddenly he nearly collided with him. He caught Olyn as he was thrown off balance by his rapid change of course.

"Olyn, we must use the Travel Tunnel. It is the best solution. Time will not be a factor then. Perhaps at Camelot a healer with greater skills can be found. If we can get Ryan to travel with Baylor, we may be able to rid the boy of his scars."

"Your plan is a good one, Leigh, but I don't know if I can summon the Travel Tunnel without Merlin. No matter how I've tried, I cannot find him," Olyn said.

"Please, try once more. I must do all I can to see the Ordination is carried out. I promised Arthur."

Ryan became like a shadow to his father's falconer. Each step the knight made, the boy was on his very heels. He followed him as he trained the birds, mimicking all the tasks without complaint. Eager to absorb all the knowledge he could before he would be sent to Arthur's court. Baylor allowed him to bring the eagle with him to observe the sessions.

Aqulia roosted on the perch Baylor had provided. Ryan religiously cleaned the mews and inspected the tethers for signs of wear. Each morning he carried the eagle and the perch down to the training area. Ryan's injuries were rapidly fading. All that remained was the jagged scar across his eye and down his cheek. The lid of the right eye drooped but did not impair his vision. Usually a talkative boy, he spoke not a word during the long training sessions with the falcons. Baylor's own bird, the peregrine, was fast becoming the swiftest hunter of them all. Baylor was exceedingly patient with them, carefully smoothing their feathers and rewarding them when they performed well.

Leigh looked out on the courtyard and observed his son and his falconer. *It is heartwarming to see my boy learn from the best, but I must dissuade him from this path.*

Turning back from the window, he watched Olyn enter the room. The old man's pace was slow, almost as if he dreaded seeing his ward.

"Come in, Olyn. Were you able to find Merlin? Can we use the Tunnel?"

Tears threatened to spill from the wizard's eyes. He seemed reluctant to tell what he must. Each step appeared an effort. He kept shaking his head and wringing his hands.

"Olyn, what is it? Can you not find Merlin? As much as I know you dread contacting the ancient Druids, it must be done. Who knows what might befall the country if the Ordination is not carried out to the letter? We could very well be risking war."

Olyn raised his head with fear in his eyes. "By the heavens, do you think it could come to that?"

"You know better than I the power of the Druids. I'm told their power is boundless and can reach to the farthest corners of the known worlds."

"What you say is true, but I've had no luck in reaching Merlin. Do you think I can contact the Druids without his help?"

"You have no choice. You must try."

Slowly nodding his head, the old wizard turned from the king and shuffled down the long corridor. "I shall try, Leigh. I shall try."

Once again, he wished he had never encountered Arthur's sister, Morganna, the evil one who stole his powers. If he had been more vigilant and less tempted, using the Travel Tunnel would be a normal occurrence. As simple as saddling a horse and setting forth. However, such was not the case, and now he had to deal with the situation. Without delay, he must face the Druids and all their indomitable strength.

After what seemed like an endless journey, Olyn reached the door of his workroom. Slowly, he pushed it open, the wood scraping against the hardened dirt floor. The Master Tome was still in the center of the table where he'd placed it during his last try to reach Merlin. Reverently, he opened the ancient text and turned to the page where he'd first encountered the Mantle of Sorcery. Therein were directions for every imaginable task, but none for what he sought.

There was no written direction for contacting the Druids. *I can only hope they see my plight, have pity, and reveal themselves to me.*

He rolled back the sleeves of his cleric-like robe and leaned over the table, the book centered between his hands, then threw back his head and began to speak in some strange language of no particular origin. The pages of the Master Tome flipped back and forth, always coming back to the page concerning the Mantle of Sorcery. Slowly, a faint pink mist rose.

The mist became a thick pungent smoke, nearly choking him. His eyes watered and his throat constricted. Though his body was fighting the effects of the smoke-like mist, his mind centered.

Concentrating with every fiber of his being, Olyn read the chant from the Tome and repeated the words over and over in a seemingly never-ending litany. The mist concentrated and formed a cloak suspended over the Master Tome. Similar to the cloak when he'd first saw it, yet somehow different. It seemed to beckon him, drawing him within its folds.

He stepped up onto the bench at the edge of the table and stretched out his hand. The edge of the cloak formed into a gnarled hand and held him fast. Pulling him up into the core, the cloak spun at ever increasing speed.

What was happening? This was unlike anything he'd ever seen in his lengthy life. Around and around he spun, until he landed gently in a place with no apparent form. High behind a lofty podium, a group of beings looked down on the wizard.

"By whose authority do you dare to summon this assemblage?"

All the beings seemed to be speaking with a single voice coming from the center being.

Olyn froze. This didn't look like the same group he and Merlin had met with so many years earlier.

Rendered nearly speechless, Olyn stammered, "I—I… do not summon you, most revered priests. I simply need to inform you of an occurrence that troubles your Ordination."

"And, why is it your responsibility? Where is Merlin? He and he alone has the authority to summon the ancient Druids. By what misguided audacity do you now appear?"

"I assure you I call upon you out of the deepest respect. I need your help in restoring the full tenets of the Ordination."

"How have the tenets been broken?" Fear rose in Olyn's throat. If he were to alienate these priests, their power could endanger countless men and many countries. Should they choose, they could obliterate civilization itself. "The heir to the throne of Wales is scarred, his face torn by the relentless talons of an eagle."

"How is it a prince encounters an eagle? You were entrusted with his care. Does Merlin know of this?"

Olyn lifted his eyes, hoping to discern some features of the voice. "Sires, I come before you, alone, because Merlin is nowhere to be found. None of his usual companions knows of his whereabouts. I have tried on several occasions to reach him using the instructions he gave me, to no avail. I beg of you, please help Ryan restore his position as future ruler of Cymru. Can you not heal the boy as you have others?"

"Merlin must be found and appear before this board, or there will be a schism between Arthur's land, Ireland, Scotland, and Cymru. Unless the Ordination is restored the schism will remain forever thus."

At once, the voices ceased, and Olyn found himself again in the Travel Tunnel, passing swiftly over the seas and landing him back in his own workroom.

Chapter Four

"Ninaway, I need to practice my skills, else I will lose them. I must return to Camelot, to my workroom."

"If all you desire were here, would you not rather remain with me?" Ninaway asked Merlin, coyly.

"Of course, my love, I have no wish to leave you, but I owe others my loyalties as well," Merlin replied, using all the reason at his disposal.

Ninaway would have none of it. "You are to remain here with me. You know I cannot return to Camelot with you. No thanks to that damned Guinevere."

"I understand, my darling, but I will return as swiftly as possible. I must confer with Arthur. It is my duty."

"Your duty? Your duty is to be here with me, to love and protect me for the rest of our days. This duty is above all others. You will never leave my side." Her eyes burned with white-hot rage, her nostrils flaring like a spent horse. "You will never leave me. I forbid it!"

"I have no desire to be anywhere but by your side forever, but I need my work. It's part of who I am."

Her eyes softened and she lowered her long golden lashes and directed, "You shall have a workroom finer than any other you have ever seen. More grand than the whole of Camelot itself."

"How can this be, Ninaway? You have not the resources to build such a room. My texts alone are worth a king's ransom."

Haughtily, she looked at the old wizard. "Have you no faith in my abilities? I am a witch, you know, or have you forgotten?"

How could this enchantress believe he'd forgotten her power? He'd met first hand with her seduction. There was nothing he could do and in the face of her power, his own dissipated. Capitulation was his only option. "Whatever you say, my love. I am yours until the end of time."

Primly, she perched on a rock outside her tent. "I have something to show you."

Merlin felt adrift. He was giving up the prospect of ever seeing Arthur or Camelot again. The friends he'd made throughout his many years, he would never see again. And, so enamored of the witch, he cared not.

Minaway rose from her seat on the rock and took Merlin's hand in her own. "Come with me. I have a gift for you. I believe it will please you greatly."

She led him across the wide meadow and down a steep slope onto the beach. "Merlin, you must close your eyes. I will take your hand so you do not stumble."

Meek as a child, he allowed her to lead him, anywhere she chose. He could feel the cool damp air. Heavy, as if they were in an enclosed area.

Their journey apparently at an end, Ninaway bid him open his eyes. His eyes, not accustomed to the dark, saw nothing. Slowly it became clear they were in a cave.

"Why do you bring me to a cave?"

Ninaway's eyes danced with glee. "This is a very special place. I've made it all for you. There is not a single being in all the known worlds that knows of its existence." She ran ahead of him into the bowels of the cave. Lighted torches along the walls allowed Merlin to watch her as she ventured farther and farther from him.

Suddenly, she stopped and raised her arms into the air. What moments earlier had been a solid wall parted in the center and opened like two huge doors, revealing a vast workroom appointed like no other he'd ever seen. The high cavern walls were lined with more books than Merlin believed were in existence. Each volume bound in the finest of leather. The center table was comprised of solid marble, the top as smooth as glass. He walked to the edge of the table and placed his hand on the shining surface. Leaning over, he could see his own reflection. On the table in an elaborate hand-carved stand stood a most beautifully illustrated copy of the Master Tome. A very talented individual spent countless hours illuminating this book. The tome that laid open in his workroom at Camelot, though he prized it highly, paled in comparison to this marvel. Ninaway provided instruments and cooking elements, Merlin was sure came from all over the known worlds. In his wildest dreams, he'd never hoped to have at his disposal a full complement of sorcerer's tools. There was no single sorcerer who'd ever lived throughout the countless ages that had such resources at his disposal. Such a prize surely outweighed any other allegiances.

Olyn knew he had to report what he'd learned from the Druids to Leigh. Reluctantly, he rose from the spot in his workroom where he'd landed. Would that he could remain here lying on the cold dirt floor until all things were made right. He had no control over the Ordination, nor did he believe Merlin had such control. But, surely, someone had more power than he. He did not want the full responsibility of the Ordination on his shoulders. To share it with Merlin was a privilege; to bear it alone was too great a task.

Shaking the dust from his robe, he began to climb up his wide stairs into the council room Leigh had fashioned similar to Arthur's. Leigh's table was simple, triangularly shaped with seating for fewer persons than were accommodated at the Round Table. Knocking gently at the casement, Olyn saw Leigh pouring over numerous pieces of parchment.

The King of Ireland looked up, a worried look heavy upon his features. "Olyn, come in, I have some very grave news. A messenger from Arthur just arrived and tells me there is unrest in Cymru. Arthur fears war."

"Receiving such news from two separate sources surely confirms the validity of the information."

Leigh frowned. "What do you mean two separate sources? Have you received another missive I am unaware of?"

"As you requested, I contacted the Druids. I asked instructions to reinstate the Ordination. They offered no guidance for the Ordination, but did warn me if it were not set aright there would be war between your land, Scotland, Cymru and Arthur's."

Leigh placed his arm about Olyn's shoulders. "Cymru is another land separate from either Ireland or England. They are not presently at odds with us. I hardly think Arthur and I would ever be at cross points."

Not pacified, the wizard shook his head. "Never have the Druids foretold of an event that did not occur. We must do something to remove the stigma on your son."

"I do not think a simple scar should be called a stigma. Perhaps, if we can find Merlin, he can reason with the Druids. Somewhere, in the ruling of the many kingdoms of the known worlds, there was a scarred king. Disfigurement should not preclude the right of royalty."

Fear deep in his heart, Olyn nodded. "I am not sure I can control the course of the Travel Tunnel, but we must try to reach Camelot and confer with Arthur. Perhaps, within his castle walls, Arthur has a healer of extraordinary talent."

Ninaway felt confident Merlin would be absorbed by his new workroom and would not pay close attention to her comings and goings. Slyly, she slipped out of her tent and noted the soft glow coming from the beach below her. Merlin would be spending the first of many nights exploring his magnificent present. The only remaining flaw to the perfection of Merlin at her side for a lifetime was to secure her stolen letters. She knew the fox had taken them, and while she believed animals had more sense than most people gave them credit for, she was certain Claret had not taken them for any purpose other than a plaything.

The night was still, yet she could hear the gentle parting of the grasses, indicating an animal was prowling the moor. Ninaway held herself within her own arms, her velvet cloak wrapped closely about her body. The few remaining days of summer tended to have chilly evenings. Projecting her vision to include all of the meadow, she searched without ever moving. There, only several yards from her tent, she found what she sought.

Claret was rolling among the weeds. More particularly she was rolling with reckless abandon in foxmoor, a pungent weed native to Cymru. It could be found nowhere else on earth. Used to strange behavior of her pets, Ninaway smiled indulgently. She'd often seen her cats roll with the same joy in catnip. Nonetheless, she was unprepared for the next strange occurrence. The tiny fox rolled over and over, rubbing her snout then her belly, deep in the weeds.

Suddenly, Claret lifted her head, sniffed the air, and underwent a unique transformation. Where the tiny fox had stood, a young girl knelt in the grasses. Stunned, Ninaway studied the child. She appeared to be about fourteen or fifteen summers. Fair of face, her hair hung past her waist, a gently curling red-gold. Though her development led Ninaway to believe she was past puberty, her stature was diminutive. Whether the lass was displeased with her surroundings or the lure of the foxmoor drew her back down to the ground, Ninaway could only guess. Then the child rubbed the weed over her body and, within moments, she again became a fox.

"Olyn, Olyn," Leigh cried as he peered down the long stairwell to the wizard's workroom. "Have you found a way?"

"Leigh, my boy, I think I just may have. If I take the boy and Baylor, the tunnel will take us back to Camelot. Ryan is royalty and I am a wizard, if we encircle Baylor we will thus be transported."

Leigh nodded vigorously. "I'll tell his mother. If she feels he is going to be healed, she will not object."

"Will you come with us, Sire?" the old wizard asked.

"No, I gave my word. I am King in this land, but I will never leave without my wife."

"I truly hope your wife realizes how you honor not only your duty to the king, but your vows to her."

"She realizes," Kit said as she descended the stair. "I am well aware of the nobility of my husband, but I still feel Ryan's wishes should be considered. He is nearly fifteen."

"Kit, my love, Olyn believes Ryan's scarring can be greatly diminished by a healer at Camelot."

Kit raised her brow, in a skeptical expression Leigh knew all too well. "Olyn, you dare not deceive me. Is this so?"

"That is my hope, Kit," he answered carefully.

"Leigh, have you any other plans for my son other than being rid of his scars?"

He placed his arm about her shoulders, then bent down and nuzzled her ear. Whispering softly, he said, "Without our son, we could recapture the lust of our youth."

"If I were to believe your loins rule your head, I should have had my way long ago." Tossing her short red curls, she turned on her heel and quickly left the two to wonder what she truly wanted.

Baylor and her son met her as they were returning from the training field. Baylor held Aqulia and Unus on his forearms.

"Look, Mother, are they not magnificent?"

Reaching out to ruffle her son's hair, she laughed. "Yes, Ryan, they are quite beautiful. Is this what you truly desire? What you want for yourself as a man, not just a childish whim?"

"Nay, Mother, 'tis not a whim. It is a calling. Baylor tells me falconry draws people much the same as the priesthood. You have to have a love for it. And I do, I truly do."

"Well, Ryan, if that is the case you are going to have to heed your father's wishes and go to Camelot."

Turning his head and petulantly stomping his foot, the boy said, "But I don't want to go to Camelot. I want to stay here with Baylor and learn."

"By giving others what they desire," she said, drawing her mouth into thin line, "You receive your heart's desire."

Sensing his mother was saying something profound, he looked at her with a furrowed brow, a question in his eyes.

Turning from her son, she said to Baylor, "Is it not true the best falconers are at Arthur's court?"

"Quite so, my lady. I, too, hope to go there and learn more of the art," he said, deftly balancing the two birds on his muscular forearms.

"Mother?" Ryan said slyly.

"Could you not convince Father I would be doing his bidding by serving as a page and learning the handling of the birds? If Baylor were to go with me, then we should both benefit. Why, even Father would benefit. His falcons would have the best training and he would be fulfilling his duty to the English King."

"You learn quickly, son, but I must warn you behaving like a child will not work with your father. He is a man of duty and honor and attempts to trick him will be met with severe disapproval. If you truly desire to learn about the falcons, you must tell him straight out. Tell him you will accept the page's duty if you are allowed to learn the skill of falconry."

A short while later, Ryan paced up and down outside his father's council room, doing his best to look as mature and responsible as possible. Deciding he was ready, he firmly tapped at the door.

"Enter," his father's voice bid.

Ryan's heart rushed up to his throat, threatening to cut off his wind as he stepped through the door.

Leigh and Olyn were in a deep discussion and both looked up as he entered. "Ryan, my boy, Olyn and I have been considering how we might make you whole again."

Ryan felt the defiance rise, but he choked down his initial response. "Father, the scarring matters not. I will serve the king in another manner."

Leigh's mouth dropped open. "I don't understand. What has changed your mind? You were once so set against going to the court of the English King, now you wish to serve him?"

Olyn put a restraining hand on his father's arm. "Listen to what the boy has to say. Proceed, Ryan."

"I know my face is not unmarked, as you'd wished, and I accept the blame for that. That, I cannot change. I will, however, go to Camelot and study as a page, if you still wish me to. In return, I would like time to study the art of falconry, and I would like Baylor to accompany me. He, too, wishes to learn more about the art." *Moreover, I am certain I will find my predestined mate in another land.*

Olyn's eyes fairly danced with joy and relief. "Leigh, if it is possible to locate Merlin and he has an answer to the scarring of your son, the Ordination could be set aright. We could seek him in England."

His father rubbed his chin with his hand and paced across the council room. The lengthening shadows from the tall windows heralded the evening. "You do understand most of your time would be spent with the duties of a page?" he said, stopping directly in front of him.

Olyn rushed around the table and took Ryan by the shoulders. Nodding vigorously, the old wizard held him closely, frequently patting him on his back.

"Yes, Father, I understand. I will do as you ask, if I am allowed to learn falconry," the boy said firmly.

Leigh nodded. "Does Baylor know of your wishes? Is he prepared to travel with you?"

At the moment, all eyes turned to the open door. Kit strode in majestically, her skirts gently brushing the floor. The three men stood in awe, nothing breaking the silence, save the rustling of her gown.

"Gentlemen, have we come to an accord?" Kit asked.

"Accord, my dear? What do you speak of?" Leigh asked, knowing he might not like the answer.

"My son and your duty. Has he told you his wishes? Do they meet with the approval of the servant of Arthur?" Kit's eyes blazed, her tongue ready to lash out if need be.

"Kit, you well know I am not a servant of Arthur. I serve him as regent in this land, and in no other capacity."

Olyn stepped between the two. "Listen, Kit, you know Leigh has given his word never to leave this land without you. Now, we think we have a plan that will set the Ordination back in place as the Druids desire. Hear him out. You owe your son that much."

Her brow arched, she said, "I owe him that much? That is a foolish statement, Olyn, even for you."

"I apologize. I merely meant you must give the plan a fair hearing."

"Oh, Olyn, you always have everyone's best interests at heart. You are a good and fair man. I trust you, and my husband will do what is best for the boy."

"Will you please stop talking about me as if I were not present?" Ryan interjected. "This is my life we are talking about. My future, what I hope to do with my life. Can you not give me this small consideration?"

Chapter Five

5 years later

Ryan was content with the bargain he'd made. Here at Camelot, he'd learned more than he ever expected. Aqulia was prized among the hunters used in Arthur's service, and Ryan had earned a reputation as a skilled falconer. In the few short years he'd been at court, he moved from simple page to a valued squire to Baylor's brother, Dinan.

Though the scarring on his face was still very evident, no mention of the Ordination was made, at least not in his presence. He'd twice returned home. On the second trip, Baylor had returned and remained with his mother.

Ryan tended and carefully counted all the birds in Arthur's aviary. Several roosted on a long perch than held many numbers of birds. Neither Aqulia nor Unus was among them. Baylor had taken his bird with him when he returned to Clare. Aqulia often times was gone for long periods. A big bird, her territory range was greater than any of the other falcons.

Aqulia's keen eyes searched the ground for food. She'd not eaten in several days, so she needed fairly large game to satisfy her hunger. Around and around she circled well to the North of England over the land of Cymru. There, in a clearing above the bluff, she saw a quick flash of red fur. Smaller than a goat but far bigger than a mouse, she determined this morsel would be her next meal.

On the ground, the frightened fox saw the eagle circling, preparing to dive. Here in the open there was no place to hide. Quickly, she dove in the grasses. The weed was not particularly high and did not serve to hide her. Then she noticed it was foxmoor. Remembering the pungent odor and the resulting change, Claret rubbed her body deeply into the weed. Before the eagle could change its course, Claret transformed into a young lass. She stood on the grass, astounded to see the eagle had not varied its path.

Powerfully, Aqulia dove and only moments before what should have been the eagle's capture, she realized the creature was too big even for a powerful bird such as she. Quickly, she beat her wings in an effort to pull away from the creature. It was too late. Even as she pushed her talons in front of her to stop her assent, she collided with the naked girl. Ripping a huge gash in the shoulder and up through the neck, the talons cut deeply.

The girl fainted.

Ninaway walked the moor, as was her habit, early before the dawn. She liked the solitude and the quiet, often finding herbs that would retreat with the rising sun. Her desired find this morning was foxmoor. Like her fox, she'd found uses for the native weed. She used it as a poultice to heal certain festering wounds on her beloved pets.

Reaching the peak of the broad meadow where she'd found the weed before, she came upon the naked child, her back and shoulders deeply cut. Not a person usually moved to pity for humans, Ninaway found herself strangely affected by the sight of the bleeding child. She felt a kinship with this diminutive person. Carefully, Ninaway removed her cloak and wrapped the child in it. The girl's red-gold hair spilled over the edge of the soft gray cloak. The reason for her feelings became clear. She'd seen this very same child on the moor. The one who'd emerged from the foxmoor after Claret rolled in the weed. Stopping long enough to gather several clumps of the weed, she gently took the child and bore her back to her tent. Unconscious, the lass moaned as Ninaway held her gently within the cloak.

Sweeping aside the flap of her tent, she saw Merlin within it. Though her burden was light, she called to the wizard for assistance.

"What wounded animal have you discovered this time?" he said indulgently. Merlin had found it easier to remain with Ninaway, since she'd presented him with the enchanted cave workroom. He spent many hours reviewing ancient texts and distilling vapors of various substances.

"This time it is not an animal, but a wondrous child. I've seen her only once before. On that occasion, she vanished as quickly as I saw her."

Ninaway set the lass upon her bed. The animals moved a discreet distance, but still observed this newcomer carefully. Niaway rolled the inert body onto its side and began to clean the wounds. The blood was flowing profusely. Ninaway packed the wound with moss, hoping to staunch the flow. The blood began to clot and she moved on to the next wound. The second, not nearly as deep as the first, responded to simple cleansing. With her long slender fingers, Ninaway smoothed the red-gold hair from the face of the girl. Merlin moved to the edge of the bed and looked down on the wounded being, so tiny and vulnerable. He knew Ninaway could easily abandon her interest in the child, as she was not something she could make a pet. The witch preferred beings she could control, a creature that would perform tricks for her amusement. But this was a human being, no matter how small or how injured, and it was his duty to protect the wee lass. Stepping to the bed, he examined the dressings Ninaway had placed on her. They were clean and properly applied. He rolled the child onto her back and stared deeply into the face of the tiny female. Frightened, feverish green eyes looked up at him. He remembered that green, a green as clear as the Irish Sea. Could this tiny thing be another? It had not been that many years. What land was in danger now?

Out of touch with the affairs of state for far too long, he knew not what lands could be in jeopardy.

As he'd given his word to Ninaway not to contact Arthur, all he could do for the moment would be to keep careful watch over the girl.

Aqulia was not unscathed from her encounter with the child. The collision's force had re-broken her left wing. It was a long, arduous trip back and her wing gave her a great deal of pain. Fortunately, she was flying with the wind and not against it. She allowed the air currents to glide her safely home. As she came to the aviary's entrance, her wing drooped as it had when she'd first broken it. Painfully, she found her perch, and, clutching her talons around the cross piece, she rested.

Ryan heard the commotion at the aviary opening, the birds shuffling their wings and squawking a welcome to the incoming eagle. Aqulia made not a sound. She simply shifted her body to find the most comfortable position. Seeing his bird finally back at the safe roost, heartened Ryan mightily, but the bird's obvious distress frightened him.

She struggled to raise her weary head and shift her damaged wing. Gently, Ryan stroked her feathers and tried to assess the damage. He ran his fingers lightly over the injured wing, dismayed to find the wing severed in the same location of the initial injury.

Aqulia ruffled her feathers and moved away from his touch.

"Oh, great Aqulia, you have injured yourself again. Do not fear me. Somehow I will heal you once more."

He turned at a shuffling sound at the entrance of the training room. "Lad?" Olyn called into the dim light of the room, "I've news from your uncle."

"My uncle? Do you mean Uncle Aaron?" Ryan eagerly faced the wizard.

It had been too long since he'd seen his father's brother.

"Yes, Aaron is to be knighted, and awarded lands in the Kingdom of Cymru."

"I suppose that will please my father greatly, another of Arthur's puppets to serve from our family."

"Mind your tongue, Ryan. Arthur has been very good to you. He has overlooked your reluctance to mind your studies as a squire. You have been provided with the best training area for your eagle and have been allowed to learn intricacies of the art of falconry. Your eagle is a bird above your station. You have no right to disparage the king."

"Olyn, I mean no disrespect. I simply wish my father realized there is more than one noble profession."

"I'm sure he thinks there are many noble professions, but as King, he realizes the destiny of his family is to serve the crown. First as a page, then as a squire, and finally as a knight in the service of King Arthur."

"Since Uncle Aaron is going to be knighted, can he not take my place? If I were never born, he would be directly in the line of secession."

"That is so, my boy, but you were born, and it is your duty to serve. Aaron takes his proper place. Can you do any less?"

"Please, Olyn, I do not wish to discuss this matter right now. Aqulia has returned, and her wing is re-broken. Though the bone does not protrude the flesh, it is clear it is very painful. How I wish Baylor was still here."

"I'm certain the king's falconer could mend her wing. Why not confer with him, before you despair? Perhaps he would be willing to look at her."

"Oh, I'm sure he'd be more than willing. He resents me and would love to see Aqulia unable to fly," Ryan said, spitting out the words.

The old wizard shook his head. The boy had grown older, but not wiser. "Ryan, when will you learn the focus of the world is not centered on you? The falconer probably feels you have been afforded extra latitude in your service as a squire and he is quite right."

"That is not the heart of the matter. I am not so foolish or childish to think the falconer would feel I do not know my place. His resentment stems from my skills with the birds. My natural abilities and ease of handling the birds sticks in his craw like an oversized worm."

"Well, for the moment, make sure Aqulia is as comfortable as possible and I will have a look at her once your uncle arrives."

"Thank you. I'm going to splint the wing and hope for the best."

Everyone in Camelot appeared to be infused with the impending knighting. Tapestries were cleaned, walls whitewashed, and all bed linens were set in the clear morning fresh air. Preparations for the finest dishes and the lightest of trenchers were made. Arthur's best hunters brought deer and grouse to the feast. No expense was spared. This would be the grandest knighting since Leigh Longwurth. Aaron would then take his place at the Round Table, alongside his brother.

A horn sounded at the beach heralding a long ship pulling to shore. The boarding plank lowered. Sea swollen timbers creaked under the weight of the passengers. The railing ropes swayed with the rhythm of the lapping water. Ryan viewed the disembarking of his uncle and several others. Would he finally have to give in to the desire of his father and make the same trip himself? With Aqulia in danger, his future was plucked from his hands. Would his quest for the woman be in jeopardy as well? Though his dream of being a falconer was well known, he kept his desire for his ordained mate a secret of his heart. Eager to see Aaron, Ryan rushed down to the beach.

His uncle, a tall man, stood head and shoulders above the other travelers. The air filled with strange and conflicting odors. A fine lady passed nearby and wafted up the perfume of sweet jasmine, the fishmonger following close behind, emitted a less pleasant odor.

People all over the dock were yelling to one another, trying to find those arriving on the great boat. Merchants hawked their wares, yelling out the value of their goods.

Aaron stepped forward and grasped his hand.

"Ryan, my boy, it's wonderful to see you. How do you happen to be here?"

"My father sent me here to Arthur's court to see if a healer could be found for my scars."

The older man eyed him kindly. "Well, you are quite scarred. How long have you been here? It doesn't appear Arthur's healers have helped you. What treatments are they using?"

"In truth, Uncle, I have not been treated. I've eluded the healers and spent my time in the aviary, learning the art of falconry."

"A truly noble profession, but it is not the course destiny has prepared you for," his uncle answered wisely.

Ryan had no wish to hear his uncle tell him the same as his father had drummed into him for the last several years. The constant retelling of the tale made it increasingly unpleasant. Looking out to the sea, Ryan saw the freedom of the sea and sky. A man should be either a sailor or a falconer. No other callings afforded as much freedom. To be shackled to a kingship was scarce more than being a prisoner. Whatever the cost, he would be free, to hunt with his falcon, and to travel from land to land, in search of the woman.

Aaron grasped him about the shoulders and brought him into the procession leading to the castle. The many faces seemed to swim along the way as they made their way between two rows of armored men. Their suits sparkled in the noonday sun, lances crossed at the tips forming an arch. Aaron's men-at-arms followed them in the procession. There were twenty in all. As each group reached the stair, Arthur was there to greet them. He, in turn, introduced them to his queen, Guinevere, who graciously embraced each of them. The swish of her skirts the only sound heard. All was quiet and majestic.

Aaron stood to the side of Arthur; his men proceeded to the right, and left, alternately, of the raised throne dais. When all the men-at-arms were seated, two more persons proceeded along the pathway between Arthur's men. Ryan was astonished to see his parents. They walked arm-in-arm and warmly greeted Arthur and his queen.

When Leigh and Kit walked past their son, his mother reached up and kissed him. His father turned and clamped him on the shoulder. A gesture Ryan had forgotten, but now realized he missed sorely.

Each member of Arthur's court was anxiously awaiting the knighting service. The ladies brought out their finest gowns and the men made certain they were attired in their most luxurious garments. The Great Hall had been carefully readied. Even the golden dawn heralded the auspicious day.

Aaron spent the night in the squires' quarters with his nephew. The passed the long evening discussing their dreams and plans for the future.

"Uncle, do you truly wish to serve Arthur so far away from the home you have always known? To spend your days ruling people who are foreign to you?"

"These people are not foreign. They have the same concerns as peoples throughout the known worlds. If I can make the lot of any of Arthur's subjects better, then I have served him well."

"I have a problem with unselfish devotion to self-imposed duty."

Chapter Six

Heralds sounded the horns to introduce the king. A long red carpet was unfurled. Aaron's men-at-arms were seated on both sides of the carpet. An ancient bishop took his place beside the throne of King Arthur. The churchman's robes were of the finest crimson velvet and flowed about the frail bishop like ripples in the sea. In the center of the dais, Arthur sat majestically, his face devoid of telling emotion. His steel blue eyes looked to the end of the carpet. His robes of azure blue counter-pointed the red of the bishop's attire. Aaron nodded as his eyes met those of the king. Slowly, Arthur rose, pushing his fur cloak aside to greet Aaron Longwurth.

Aaron proceeded down the length of the carpet. When he reached the dais, he went to his knees and leaned forward to kiss the ring of the bishop. The bishop acknowledged the kiss and placed his hands on the head of the soon-to-be knight. The churchman then stepped back. Arthur stood and came to the edge of the dais. Drawing Excalibur from its scabbard, he placed the flat of the blade on Aaron's right shoulder.

"I dub thee Sir Aaron of Cymru," King Arthur said loudly, so that all gathered in the Great Hall could hear.

Aaron lowered his head, and Arthur moved the sword over the knight's head and placed the flat of the blade on Aaron's left shoulder.

Aaron rose and grasped the king's hand. Arthur drew him into an embrace. As much as he hated the pomp and pageantry of ceremony, Ryan found himself drawn into the majesty of the knighting. He felt pride in his uncle and in his entire family. They were all gathered here to witness this solemn occasion and to display the show of honor and duty to the crown. He had no desire to serve the same crown, but was pleased his family was so well respected, here in the presence of the rulers of so many lands. Someday, he, too, would be respected, not for his lineage, but for his skill as a falconer, and for the beauty and wisdom of his mate.

Leigh rushed forward to congratulate his brother. Kit followed close behind.

"Aaron, I'm so proud of you. I always knew you were one of the finest men I ever served with."

Ryan overheard his mother's comment. "How was it you served with Uncle Aaron?"

Kit and Aaron exchanged glances. "Well, son, it was very long ago and your uncle and I shared some adventures."

"Adventures? What kind of adventures? You never told me of serving with men. And, who were you serving?"

Leigh interjected, "Ryan, those tales are better left untold. Your mother was not always the dignified lady you see before you. In her youth she was daring and headstrong."

Kit's eyes flashed. "Is that to mean, that in my dotage, I've become dignified and manageable?"

Gently, Leigh embraced his beautiful wife and whispered in her ear.

Her expression changed from near anger to veiled sensuality, as she gently placed her finger on his lips. Gracefully, she approached the king and knelt before him. Arthur held out his hand and drew her upright. "Your son is a fine man. Someday he will be in the same place as his uncle." A tear escaped Arthur's eye. Kit knew he was thinking about Ryan's marred face.

Leigh noted the king's discomfort and drew him aside. "Arthur, I see Ryan's situation causes you grief. Is there nothing that can be done?"

"At one time I was not even concerned and was certain the matter would be set aright, by Merlin's hand. My wisest council has been gone from court nearly a year. I fear for his safety, as well as that of the land of Cymru."

"Perhaps Aaron's first quest as a Knight of the Round Table could be to locate Merlin?" Leigh speculated.

Arthur's eyebrows rose. "That is a very sizeable undertaking for a newly knighted man. Perhaps, though, I could send Olyn with him to survey his new lands and aid him in the pursuit of Merlin."

Ryan, alone in his quarters, pondered over the fate of his eagle. The bird was with him on the perch Baylor had made for him. Her wing drooped, even worse than it had earlier in the day. He had tried to find help for her. Gently, he stroked her feathers. She moved away, in obvious pain.

Feeling helpless, Ryan headed for Merlin's workroom. Olyn was there, his head deep in Merlin's copy of the Master Tome. Olyn's bald pate shown brightly in the lamplight, his gnarled fingers moving lightly over the pages.

Olyn raised his head and caught sight of him. "Ryan, my boy, come in." His eyes searched the face of the lad. "What is it that troubles you so? Are you not proud of your Uncle Aaron? He is truly a fine knight and Arthur is fortunate to have him in his service."

"Yes, Arthur is fortunate to have him serve blindly as all the others." Ryan sat beside the wizard.

"Ryan, why are you so bitter? Do you, too, wish to serve the king and resent your disfigurement as it bars you from service?"

"My disfigurement, as you call it, troubles me not. I am bitter because the fates have wounded my eagle."

"Well, young Ryan, what have you done to assist in her healing? Did you take her to the king's falconer?

"Olyn, I'm certain Baylor knew more about healing the birds than the falconer. Even I have more skill than he. Whatever is known to mortal man I have done for her. I need the skills of an animal healer, such as the one my uncle told me of."

"Aaron knows of an animal healer? Where would such a man be found?"

"I'm told it is not a man, but a woman. Some say a witch."

"A witch? You don't mean Morganna, the king's half-sister? She is evil, and I don't think she cares for animals except for use in her evil spells."

"The rumor is she is a witch in the land where Aaron holds property and is very reclusive. Some say she is so possessive, whoever or whatever falls into her grasp will never be free of her. She binds man and animal alike."

"If such is the case, why do you, who long to be free above all else, seek her out?"

"Trust me, Olyn, I am very wary. I need her skill, but I have no intention of becoming her prey."

"Will Arthur permit you to travel to Cymru?" the old wizard inquired.

"I have not petitioned him as yet, but I believe he will allow me to accompany my uncle to review his holdings. Arthur knows my eagle is valuable to him as well. She is a fine hunter. The loss of her kills will cut down on the meat served in the dining hall."

"I'm sure you're right, but it might be wise to mention the service to your family over the care of the eagle."

Ryan smiled. "I now realize why my father treasures your counsel above all others. You are truly a very wise man."

"Do you seek to flatter me, Ryan?" Olyn said, returning the smile. Ryan nodded, a foolish grin creeping over his features.

"'Tis no matter," the wizard acknowledged, "as the king asked me to accompany Aaron on his journey to Cymru. Aaron will inspect his property and I will search for Merlin. I think it will matter not if you accompany us."

"Truly, Olyn? Will you ask the king to allow me to join you and my uncle?" Ryan felt the longing to heal his pet arise anew in his heart. The feeling that her welfare could be controlled by the will of the king both frightened and angered him. He could not let his apprehension cloud his judgment. "Will you, Olyn?"

The wizard sat back in his chair at the table and pushed aside the Master Tome. The book slid smoothly across the worn table as it had made the journey before so many times. Prior to coming to rest, it turned itself, so when opened, the pages were facing the ancient wizard. The room became so still even breath halted. Neither Olyn nor Ryan moved even a hair. The book slammed open against the table and the pages fluttered. When the pages stilled, they opened to a passage entitled, "Veil of Obscurity."

Ryan leaned over the tome as Olyn began to read the passage. "What does it say, Olyn? Is it a message from Merlin?"

Olyn, so drawn into the pages, did not respond. Swiftly, he passed his gnarled fingers over the vellum, hand-written pages. The page grew warm, then hot. Olyn quickly removed his fingers. A mist so fine as to be nearly imperceptible slowly rose from the page. Like a gentle fog, a soft gray vapor reached out to him. He was entranced, Ryan reached out to shake him, to force him to tell what he was experiencing. But the lad's hand was unable to touch him, stayed by some invisible barrier.

Olyn looked to the ceiling, his eyes glazed as if in a coma. He could not hear Ryan's frantic cries, nor could he experience his environment in any way.

The lengthening shadows streaming in the last vestiges of the day greeted Olyn as he rose from the substantial, elaborately carved chair in the workroom. It had been early morning when he first entered Merlin's domain.

The passage of time was like a single instant.

Yet, impending evening shadows clearly showed the day had moved on without his knowledge. Dizzy, he nearly fell as he arose. He placed his hand on the table to steady himself. His hand grew warm as if in the grasp of another person. A whisper so soft and gentle he doubted its existence bid him release his conscious thoughts. Struggling to clear his vision, Olyn allowed his present thoughts to flow from his mind. He stared at his hand on the table. Covering his was the hand of a man older even than he. Merlin!

A voice, deep and resonant, yet curiously soft, bid him sit. Gently, Olyn lowered himself in the huge chair. Merlin's hand still covered his own.

"Is it truly you, Great Wizard?"

"Yes," the voice murmured.

"Why do you hide yourself?" Olyn asked, getting to the most desired question.

"I have given my word to the woman I love that I shall never leave her side. To contact you or Arthur violates my word."

"Why do you contact me now? Does this not break your vow?"

"You have summoned me using the 'Veil of Obscurity,' a matter I have no conscious control over. The Druids rule the obscurity and will not uncover the whole of a person so contacted. They allow the revelation only in times of great need."

"And, this is a time of great need," Olyn responded.

"Arthur is concerned about the land Ryan is to one day rule. He felt he could rely on you to mend the boy's scars that he might properly take his place as the King of Cymru."

Merlin's hand moved aside and turned the pages of the Tome. The index finger pointed to a passage written in a dark crude hand. The letters were overly dark and poorly formed. Not at all like the writing of Merlin, as was the rest of this book. Merlin had carefully and precisely written each word as directed him by the Druids. Truly this hand was that of another, even greater being than Merlin. The deep dark letters exuded a power of their own.

Olyn stared at the passage written in a language he did not comprehend. He looked at the hand, now resting on the edge of the book. "I cannot understand what is written. What am I to do?"

"You must join me in this land, and I will direct you to fulfill the Druid's Ordination."

Olyn sadly nodded. He knew he must do Merlin's bidding, but he had given his word to Ryan to accompany him and Aaron to Cymru. Resigned, he respectively inquired, "Merlin, what land do you now inhabit?"

"I am in Ninaway's land, the land of Cymru." At once the hand closed into a fist, rose, and dissipated in a burst of mist.

Chapter Seven

Confused by his meeting with Merlin, Olyn knew his duty was clear. He had to report to Arthur at once. Gathering his robes about his ample thighs, Olyn scurried along the massive corridor. The floors were highly polished and the surface was slick. His well-worn sandals slid beneath him. Nearly losing his footing, he found himself saved by King Arthur, who grabbed him about his broad shoulders.

"Thank you, Arthur, I very nearly fell."

"That you did, Olyn. These floors are not designed for racing. You should exercise more caution when you use the corridors." Arthur was duly proud of his marbled halls. There were few in existence and none to rival the beauty of Camelot's.

"Why are you in such a hurry? What can be of such import you risk breaking your neck?"

Breathlessly, Olyn responded, "I've found Merlin."

"Found him? Where? Did he say why he hides from me?"

"He said only, he remains apart from you and Camelot, because he's given his word to the woman he loves, to remain by her side. Contacting you would break his vow to her."

Arthur scowled. "Yet you have spoken to him. Surely he knew you would tell me of your findings."

Olyn closed his eyes and took a deep breath. He must inform the king without incurring his wrath. "I was able to reach him through the use of the 'Veil of Obscurity.' It is something over which he has no conscious control. The Druids set up the circumstances for me to locate him."

Growing increasingly impatient by the moment, Arthur glared at the old sorcerer. "Where is he?"

"Sire, he tells me he is in the woman's land of Cymru. He has given his word he will remain there with her. He did not say, but it is my belief he is enchanted by this woman, to the point he neglects his duty and vows to you, your Royal Highness."

"You are right, Olyn. We must rescue him from his own folly."

Olyn looked wide-eyed at the king. "Rescue him? How, Sire? He has far greater powers than mine. Only when the Druids intercede do I have any of the capabilities to accomplish such a feat."

"Fear not, Olyn. We will send Aaron to his new lands and he will help you locate Merlin."

Nervously, Ninaway paced her tent, back and forth, trying to determine what she might do. The lass remained in danger. Infection had set in, causing a raging fever. For all the powers and herbal healings at her disposal, Ninaway found herself unable to cure the fox child.

Jealously, she'd guarded her patient. She would not allow Merlin near her. His presence was becoming increasingly intrusive. Accustomed to having control of all things and beings within her interest, she resented a source of power other than her own. True, he now spent many hours in the magnificent workroom she'd given him. Still, he showed more interest in the injured girl than Ninaway felt was necessary.

Merlin was busy in his workroom and would be unlikely to observe her leaving the tent and scouring the moor for more potent herbs. Carefully, Ninaway covered the feverish child and bid her dog to oversee the girl in her absence. The dog leapt up on the bed and nosed the child gently with his snout. Claret stirred, moaned, and turned on her side. Ninaway slipped out the opening of the tent. Her tent was considerable and blended in with the surroundings of the wood. To the unschooled eye, the tent was not visible. Only a hunter, trained to search for well-hidden animals, would discern its existence.

Quickly, she gathered as much foxmoor and other healing herbs as she could poke into the cloth bag she wore at her waist.

Merlin observed Ninaway slip from her tent. He had been watching, waiting, for her to leave the child. So many things had gone awry since he left Arthur, Olyn's search for him, and now the discovery of another so like Kit.

While he did not intend to break his word, he knew it was his obligation to right the situations. He and he alone, on Earth, was responsible for the Ordinations of the ancient Druids' fruition. They must be completed as the Druids decreed. To ignore such a responsibility could very well ruin the entire world. The Druids could set their Ordination on another world. No one, other than they, knew how many worlds there were in existence. Merlin dared not risk wiping out civilization.

Olyn had contacted him once, using the 'Veil of Obscurity.' Perhaps he could do it again. Could Merlin signal him to the use of the veil, or must he wait until the other wizard realized the gravity of the situation?

Merlin went to the tent, high on the bluff, where the child lay. As he entered, the dog on the bed growled a warning, then moved aggressively to the edge of the bed. Merlin, annoyed, swept the dog aside. The animal offered no further resistance, instead jumping from the bed and laying quietly at Merlin's feet.

The child was awake. Her green eyes darted about the room. She spotted and her eyes went wide in surprise. Merlin saw that her eyes were clear, but vestiges of the fever still clouded her vision.

Merlin reached out and touched the tiny girl. As if by some primal instinct, she withdrew, grabbing the bedcovering and shrinking away from the wizard, her eyes never leaving his.

"Child," Merlin said gently, "have no fear, I will not hurt you, nor will I allow another to cause you harm. You are safe. Ninaway will see to your health and I will care for all other matters. Now lay back and rest."

The fear left the girl's eyes and she sank back onto the pillow. The dog immediately jumped up to his place beside her. Within moments, she was asleep.

Merlin swept the long red hair from her face. A face so tiny it seemed to be that of a doll rather than a real person. Her petite hands wrapped around each other, tucked beneath her chin. How the child's presence tugged at his heart. This poor motherless being, who could well be another whom the Druids had touched, was without family and had only Ninaway and him to care for her. Neither he nor Ninaway had any real experience with children. He was many centuries old and had never married. He'd never had the desire until he'd met Ninaway. But Ninaway cared more for creatures than people.

Yet, she was caring for the child with a diligence he'd not believed possible. Somehow, he had to contact Olyn and get a message to the Druids and Arthur. He peered out of the tent and spotted Ninaway approaching.

Quickly, he exited and hurried down to his workroom. He would go back up as soon as Ninaway settled in the tent and pretend it was his first visit of the day.

Ninaway entered the tent, her hands clutching fresh moss. Though she'd often used the foxmoor on her pets, she dared not try it on a human. She was unaware of the extent of the effect of the foxmoor and she would not risk losing her find. Though Ninaway cared not for others, she recognized the tiny being as a valuable commodity. She would use her as a pawn to further bind Merlin to her. How he studied the child troubled her. Perhaps he knew the formula for the transformation of the lass. This tiny child, so unlike any other Ninaway had ever seen. Perhaps this was the true key to binding him. With the greatest wizard in the known worlds within her power, her own magic would be boundless.

Tenderly she bathed the fevered brow of the child. So intent on her task, she didn't hear Merlin enter the tent. "Ninaway, how fares the child?" Merlin asked.

Eyes narrowed, Ninaway turned around and stared at the wizard. "She'll be fine. Just leave us. I'll take care of her. No one else."

"Ninaway, is that wise? True, you are without question the greatest animal healer in the known lands, but this is a person, and a very small one at that. She requires special handling. Perhaps I could help. For many years I healed Arthur's wounded men."

"How do I know you can care for a child? Warriors are much different from maidens."

"Quite so, my love, but they are more like warriors than dogs or rabbits."

Warily, she studied his face. Did Merlin even realize she was using the girl to weld him to her side for all time? "I shall concede you know a bit more about healing people than I. What would you advise? Her fever rages, though I've packed the wound with moss."

"Have you tried using the foxmoor? I know you have used it on several of your animals."

Enraged, she flew at him. "You tell me you know how to treat humans. Then, you ask if I have tried an animal remedy. What kind of logic is this? Either explain yourself or leave my sight forever."

He bowed his head. "You are quite right, however, this child is unlike any other. She is tiny and bears a strong likeness to another, who is of great importance to the Druids."

"What are you talking about? You speak in riddles."

Merlin knew he had to make the witch understand in terms that would force her to protect the child and not discard her as a forgotten amusement. His enchantment blinded him to her faults. While another woman might be concerned for the welfare of a child, such was not Ninaway's method.

Ninaway pressed further, standing and meeting him toe-to-toe. "How is it you feel foxmoor will help? It doesn't even grow in your land." Becoming more and more suspicious, she suddenly swept up the child and fled the tent.

Frightened, Merlin followed, calling to her as she ran over the moor. After many hours, she collapsed, still holding the child, in an exhausted heap. Merlin came upon her and eased her and her burden into his arms.

Ninaway was a substantial woman and no small weight, yet he swept her within his embrace with the grace of a young man. This woman he would treasure above all others, even this chosen one of the Druids.

Duty and honor tugged at Merlin's heart, all the while the love for Ninaway pulled in the opposite direction. Few men were able to serve two masters. Nevertheless, that appeared to be the course set for him, and he had no option but to comply. He must make sure the Druids were satisfied, and that the love of his life remained enchanted with him.

Carrying Ninaway back to her grand tent, Merlin set her and the child in the center of the bed. The other animals Ninaway tended for moved aside and allowed him to arrange the bedding about the two.

How beautiful Ninaway looked, lying there with the child. A child that could have been theirs, had they met centuries earlier. He wondered if Ninaway ever had thoughts of motherhood. Some tender feelings must have been stirred in her, as evidenced by her diligent care of the girl.

As her body warmed, Ninaway looked about and recognized familiar surroundings. She lifted herself up onto an elbow, careful not to disturb the sleeping waif. "Merlin, how do I come to be back here in my tent?" The anger in her tone gave him pause.

"Ninaway, beloved, you know I cannot live without you. I followed you and carried you back when you became unable to continue," he said, hoping to dissipate her anger.

Still wary, she said, "Would that you be so bound to me, I might never fear losing you."

"Enchantress, I know not by what power you bind me, but I am as connected to you as is my own arm. Nothing can sever the bond."

"Not even your duty to the king? You will stay with me for all time?"

Indulgently, he smiled. "Yes, Ninaway, I am yours even if the sun fails to shine. I will never seek to leave you."

"Then what is your interest in the child? Do you hope to send her to Arthur? She is my child, and she will never serve the king. Not Arthur, nor any other king."

"My interest in the child is not to cleave her from your heart, but to make sure she is given the proper care. It is my belief she is another chosen by the Druids."

Angrily, Ninaway swept aside the covers and sprang from the bed. "Never! The Druids shall not have her. The child is mine. I can give her all she might desire."

"I do not doubt your ability to care for her. I only know the fates of nations may depend upon her. Arthur and the Druids must be informed. I will remain with you, but you must release me," he implored. "I must speak with the king."

The amber fire in her eyes grew white hot. "Never, do you hear me, never shall you speak with Arthur again. If not for his ruling, I would be respected throughout the known worlds as a witch without equal. My powers would be used to enhance kingdoms. If dear, sweet Guinevere had not interfered, my life, too, would be one of service. She and Arthur robbed me of that station, now they must pay. You shall not contact them."

Chapter Eight

Though Olyn would have preferred a less arduous mode of travel, Arthur felt they should travel by conventional means since they were transporting the eagle and the king's falconer. He did not wish to reveal the Travel Tunnel to his falconer, as the man was new to Camelot, and Arthur knew not much of his background.

Exhausted after a full day's ride, Aaron found a place to camp until the early morning, when they would resume the journey. Aaron and Ryan pitched tents, while Olyn prepared a freshly caught rabbit. Ryan had snared the animal, as the eagle was unable to hunt with her broken wing.

Carefully, Ryan cut pieces of the fresh meat and gave it to the eagle. She showed no interest in the offering, only taking a small piece he'd pressed to release the blood.

"Soon, my girl, you will be mended and once again soar the skies."

"Why do you waste your time with that eagle?" the king's falconer said, in a tone that clearly suggested he had greater knowledge of falconry than Ryan. "Eagles are not meant to be falcons. She is too large a bird to control." The big man stood taller than any of the group. His head seemed to be oversized with his facial features grouped closely giving him the appearance of having the face of a child on the head of a man. His arms hung nearly to his knees.

Annoyed with the superior attitude of the falconer, Ryan turned his back on the man and continued feeding Aqulia. The bird pecked at the rabbit pieces and shifted her weight to accommodate the broken wing.

Olyn approached with the remainder of the prepared rabbit and some hard biscuits. "Come, lads, eat hearty, we will be on horseback another day. The journey will be more difficult if we are wracked with hunger pangs."

Stepping around Ryan and his bird, the falconer grabbed a greater part of the meat and two biscuits from the pot Olyn held out.

"See here, take a smaller portion, these rations are to last another day, perhaps two," Olyn chastised. "You are not the only man who requires nourishment."

"Morfran takes what he needs, and you would be well advised not to challenge me," the falconer said, as he bit a piece from the hind leg of the rabbit.

Ryan held the man in low regard. The two had been at sword points on more than one occasion. Morfran was a sneaky, opportunistic, devious man. Few at Camelot could even abide the presence of the man. He had nothing to recommend him for his post, save his skill at healing injured birds. He healed a severed talon on the king's favorite peregrine when all other healers were unable to treat the bird. However, he would not touch Aqulia. The bird herself distrusted the man.

"Falconer, I know not how you are treated at Camelot, but here on the trail, you have no more rights than the next man. You will take your fair share of the rations and no more. Do you understand me?" Aaron said, his hand resting gently on his sword.

Morfran contemplated the knight through narrowed eyes. "You foppish knights are all the same. Give you a title and you think you are better than others."

Sensing trouble, Ryan and Olyn backed away from the two men.

Morfran slid his dagger from his tunic, and advanced on the newest of Arthur's knights.

"You challenge me, fool?" he demanded, circling Aaron.

"I hardly think expecting a man to share a limited amount of rations is a challenge, but if you wish to best me, have at it." Aaron withdrew his sword, set it aside, and took up his dagger, watching the every move of the falconer. The hefty, lumbering man was slow, but his size gave him apparent advantage. Aaron suddenly advanced, lunged, and relieved the man of his weapon.

Stunned the knight had taken his dagger in such a rapid fashion, Morfran stepped back. "You are quite right, rations should not be a matter for challenge. I apologize. I let hunger hamper my reason."

Ryan and Aaron exchanged a meaningful look. Both men had felt the hostility fairly burn from the king's falconer.

"See to it your hunger does not place you in such a situation again," Aaron warned.

Aaron took the first watch. Olyn had advised that the strange behavior of the king's falconer warranted close scrutiny. Aaron disliked the man just on principal. Ryan shared his uncle's opinion and eagerly took the second watch. Morfran lay silently several feet from the campfire, his back to the others.

Olyn raised a finger to his lips and beckoned Aaron and Ryan to approach him. "Ryan, you have had the most contact with this new falconer of Arthur's. What is your opinion of the man?"

Ryan huffed and said, "When I first approached him about Aqulia's broken wing, he indicated he was the finest healer among falconers, and would be able to have her flying within a month's time. However, when I brought her to him, he refused to treat her."

Puzzled, Aaron asked, "What reason did he give for his refusal?"

"He didn't give any real reason, simply that she was not a falcon and he would not waste his talents on a bird that couldn't be taught."

"But, Ryan," Olyn interjected, "Baylor taught the bird with insignificant difficulty. The bird was already trained to hunt and return with its kill. His reason makes no sense."

"Her training was not difficult. She learned quickly," Ryan said. "I know she is a valuable hunter. I think Morfran has a personal reason for grounding Aqulia. He spends many hours coaching the smaller falcons and is particularly fond of peregrines and kestrels." Ryan glanced at the mound of bedding on the side of the fire.

Aaron remembered the trials an errant knight had placed before his brother. "He has the same demeanor as Lancelot. I do not trust him."

"I understand your feelings, but he must have impressed Arthur with his skill or he wouldn't have taken him on as the castle falconer."

Olyn drew the two further from the fire. "There is something amiss with this man. He knows this part of the world better than a native. Did Arthur say who recommended him?"

"It is well known Arthur relies heavily on Merlin's counsel. Perhaps, he recommended him before he left Camelot," Aaron concluded.

Olyn nodded and cocked his head in the direction of Morfran, who appeared to be moving. Lowering his voice, the wizard said,

"Tomorrow we set sail. We'll keep careful watch over him. If he gives us pause, we will dismiss him in Cymru."

At dawn, the camp was broken and the bedrolls strapped securely on the horses' backs. Before the sun stood high in midday, they reached the shore. There, moored in the bay, was one of Arthur's finest ships. A marvel of craftsmanship, the carved bow piece was a work of art. The sails were stark ivory against the blue sky. So brilliantly white, they rivaled the few billowing clouds overhead.

Aaron remarked, "What a fine ship Arthur has sent us. It is a vast improvement over the ship where his queen was held."

"I agree. It is even finer than Kit's ship, though she wouldn't agree," Olyn said, as he dismounted and removed his bedroll.

Ryan noticed the look exchanged by the wizard and the knight. "My mother? My mother had her own ship? But, she's a girl, I mean, a woman. How could she have a ship?"

Olyn smiled indulgently. "Your mother is unlike any other woman you will ever meet, young Ryan. Not only did she have her own ship, she was the captain and made a tidy sum pirating the shores of Clare."

"She was a pirate?" Ryan asked incredulously. This was just too much to be believed. He dismounted and slung his bedroll over his sturdy shoulder.

Morfran approached, then climbed down from his mount. "Well, this is a fine ship. The best I've sailed on."

"And, have you sailed a great deal in your lifetime, Morfran?" Aaron asked.

The falconer barely acknowledged the knight's presence before he deigned an answer. "I've spent a fair amount of time aboard ships."

"And, what land do you inhabit?" Olyn inquired.

The falconer withdrew, ignoring the wizard's question. How dare he?

Ryan started after Morfran as the falconer was walking up the plank to the ship. "You, there, have you no consideration for those in your company? A gentleman does not push ahead of others and answers when spoken to. What fool woman had the disagreeable honor of bearing you?"

Morfran spun around on the plank, his bedroll nearly toppling Ryan, and spat, "I never said I was no gentleman. I am a falcon healer, the best in the land, and as such I demand the utmost courtesy. You mind your place, squire."

Unused to such effrontery, Ryan felt the hair on the back of his neck prickle. "By what recommendation do you serve Arthur?"

"Who the king hires in none of your concern, boy," Morfran said, brushing him aside with a wide sweep of his long arm, nearly throwing him into the water.

Aaron stepped onto the plank and took Morfran by the elbow. "Morfran, I shall not tell you again, the rules while traveling are different from those at court. Here each serves the group. Do you understand me or shall I convince you in a stronger manner?" His hand once again settled on the sword at his side.

The falconer stepped aside and gallantly helped Ryan right himself. "You must be careful of your steps on this slippery plank," he said though clenched teeth.

"Thank you so much for your consideration," Ryan answered sarcastically. "Again, I ask by whose recommendation do you serve Arthur?"

Morfran smiled condescendingly. "I have the endorsement of Merlin himself."

Setting aside their differences and suspicions, the group boarded the ship.

The sails quickly filled with wind and the craft headed north to Cymru.

Morfran set himself apart from the others and remained on deck while the others went below to secure the rations. Ryan decided to watch the falconer closely and decided to stalk the man.

Older and wiser, Aaron reasoned the man couldn't escape their scrutiny while they were aboard ship. He and Olyn sat on the deck at the stern of the ship in the aftercastle, while Aaron stationed himself in a pile of rigging at the bow in the forecastle and watched Morfran.

Olyn handed Aaron a bit of salted meat as the two rested against the gunnels.

"Olyn, do you know why Morfran was sent with us to Cymru? It seems strange the king would send a new man to view my holdings."

"I questioned Arthur. He said little, save he was directed in a dream. Merlin told him to heed his dreams and Arthur felt the dream was under his direction."

"I guess I understand nothing of magic and dreams. Common sense should direct one to use caution in dealing with an unknown."

"I quite agree. I told the king to reconsider, but he was steadfast. You cannot argue with the king, he is king after all."

Aaron chuckled. "Yes, there is something to that. However, I trust my nephew's instincts. Ryan is wise to keep close watch on him. Morfran strikes me as a man of scarce principal. He will serve his own needs before that of another."

Suddenly, the ship tossed sharply to port. At once, the deck became perpendicular to the sea. Ryan and Morfran hurled down the deck to the gangway. Olyn and Aaron slammed against the stern wall. The sky, once clear and bright, now was as dark as ink, and filled with rage. The sturdy ship was tossed in ever-deepening swells. Four men clung to the sail lines and attempted to lower the sails. The wind grabbed the canvas and slapped it against the mast. Water raged in from the sea and down from the sky. Lightning crackled and split the mizzenmast, pulling the canvas over the slippery deck. To the stern, the bonaventure mast snapped like a twig in the wind. The bowsprit broke loose and pulled the breakhead free from the vessel. The captain shouted orders that rang familiar to Olyn's ears. As if he were Scilti once again, he aided the captain as he had so often done as a first mate for Kit.

The storm seemed to be losing force, but the ship suffered severe damage. What had been expected to be a short voyage would be prolonged as they were left with only two of the four masts. As the sea calmed, men scurried over the deck to clear the damaged sail and right the rigging.

Aaron cried out to his nephew. "Ryan, are you all right?"

Ryan pulled himself free from the tackle that fell from the mizzen and answered, "I'm fine, Uncle. Is Olyn safe?"

Olyn struggled to right himself on the slippery deck. "I am well, do not fear, Ryan. You shan't free yourself from my counsel so easily. This is not the first storm I've ridden out."

The sea took on a more comforting aspect. The white clouds danced over the gentle azure waves. Though they were two masts short and had only the main sail intact, they began to make their way along the shore.

Chapter Nine

Ninaway, alone with the feverish child, continued to bathe Claret with cloths dipped in cool water and mint leaves. The pungent herb caused Ninaway's eyes to water. Wiping them with the back of her hand, she began to determine how she could cure the child as she had so many animals. Did she dare try the foxmoor? Merlin would not recommend it if he felt there was any danger.

Carefully, she covered the child with a light woolen blanket. Making sure she was unobserved, she slipped out of her tent to the cave where she kept her medications for her pets. The foxmoor was secreted in a large basket designed to appear as a container of flowers. She extracted several handfuls of the herb and placed it in a mortar. Taking a pestle from the shelf above the basket she began to crush the foxmoor into the finest possible particles. Once the herb was ground as fine as sand, she poured it into a bottle. A cord wove around the bottle forming a loop for hanging on a belt at the top. Ninaway stepped out from the cave, looked over the moor and into the distant meadow. There, along the side of the meadow up from the shore, she saw a boarding party.

The limping ship pulled to shore and listed to port on the shallow sand bar. Aaron and Ryan pulled part of the gangway over the side for a disembarking plank. The plank was no sooner set than Morfran dashed down onto the beach, then quickly into the nearby wood.

"Morfran," Ryan cried to the departing figure, "get back here and help unload the supplies."

The pleas fell on deaf ears as Morfran continued his flight. Within moments, he was out of sight.

"Well, his disappearance is more satisfying than his presence," Ryan remarked.

"I like the man even less than you, Ryan, but I wish to keep him within my sights. His vaporizing into the forest troubles me. If he knows the land as well as I believe, why would he even wait for Arthur to send him here?"

Olyn shook his head. "There must be some connection to Merlin. We must find him, before we seek the healer."

Something nagged at Ryan's brain. Why was Morfran so eager to leave their company? Had he robbed them and fled to escape capture? If so, what might be missing? As far as Ryan was concerned, there was nothing of any real value aboard ship, save Aqulia. Could it be the falconer had purloined his eagle? It would be just like him, the foul bastard that he is.

Ryan set down the large trunk he carried from the ship and raced up the plank to check on the bird.

"Aqulia," he called half fearing she would be missing. The bird answered with a weak cry. He could tell she was in great pain. Carefully he placed her in a linen cloth and carried her off the ship.

"Uncle, we must find this healer at once, she grows weaker."

Aaron nodded, and Olyn approached and examined the bird. "You're right, Ryan. She needs attention and needs it quickly."

All the rations were taken off the boat and Olyn set a fire. Ryan brought Aqulia to the edge of the clearing and placed her on a thick branch of a fallen tree. He did not need to tether her, as she was too weak to fly.

"Olyn," Ryan begged. "Please do something to help her. I'm sure Arthur would want you to help her to fly once again."

"Yes, Ryan, I will do what I can. Leave me." The old man stared intently into the crackling fire.

Tongues of flame leapt higher and higher, as if stoked by brandy. Yet Olyn knew there were no spirits on the ship. There, within the golden yellow flame, hung a white-hot pulsating ball. Olyn stepped back from the sparks. At once, the flames receded into glowing embers. There, from the center, rose a blue-white hand. Olyn knew at once it was the hand of Merlin.

He reached toward the burning fingers. The heat caused him to withdraw.

A voice that seemed to blow in on the gentlest of winds spoke.

"Olyn, I will lead you. Bring the others. The eagle shall be cured."

"How is it you know of the eagle, Merlin? Our true mission is to find you and survey Aaron's lands."

"Olyn, how is it after all this time, you still question my power? I know all things."

Realizing he'd blundered, Olyn bowed his head and stepped back further. "Olyn, come here," the voice commanded.

"I am at your service, Great Wizard," he said, stepping forward. "What will you have me do?"

Moving as stealthily as possible, Ninaway drew down into the grasses to observe the men on the beach. She was not certain of their identities, but, from one of the men's garb, she knew one had to be a wizard. As she watched, the bottle of foxmoor secured at her waist, she heard a loud crashing of what only could be a person stomping across the moor. Hearing a rustle in the grasses near her, she turned and saw a hulk of a man coming toward her. She broke into a smile then stood and embraced the man.

"What brings you here, brother? Have they no further use for a bird healer at Arthur's court?"

Morfran extracted himself from his sister's grasp and in turn grabbed her beneath her arms and swung her high in the air.

"Ninaway, I've missed you. I've been sent here to aid the newest of Arthur's knights, to help him survey his land."

Ninaway narrowed her eyes and said, "Who does this king think he is?

This is my land and it is not to be portioned to any foppish English knight."

His large head shaking from side-to-side, her brother answered. "He says he's directed by a dream and it has something to do with the ancient Druids."

Skeptically, she replied, "It was not so long ago the Druids were part of my sisterhood and the brotherhood of the wizards. Now they claim dominion over countries? That is most thought-provoking."

Her brother nodded. "Yes, but that is not the most interesting thing. Young Ryan, a cousin of the Queen, travels with them as well. He has with him a stricken eagle and it is you he seeks."

"Arthur sent a wizard and a boy to find me? For what reason?"

Morfran reached out to touch her tresses with a tentative finger. "Your hair is so soft, like the finest down. You are magic, Ninaway."

Callously she brushed his hand aside. "Never mind that, I need to know all about these travelers who have come to my shore."

Morfran withdrew his hand. His sister had dismissed him and it hurt.

Trying to regain her favor he said, "I'll tell you all I know. I've been listening. Even when they think I'm sleep."

She gave him a tentative smile. "Thank you, brother, I'm certain your information will be most useful."

He smiled and followed her as she went back to her tent. She stopped at the entrance and waited for Morfran to pull aside the tent flap that she might enter. Majestically, she stepped into the magnificent enclosure. Morfran looked around in awe.

"This is much nicer than your last one. Can I sleep on the big bed?"

"I will find a place for you, but for now tell me what you know."

Drawing himself up to as serious a posture as he could, he began. "The wizard, Olyn, the knight, Aaron, and Ryan, the prince of Ireland, were sent by Arthur. At first just Aaron and Olyn were to come, but the prince asked Arthur to send him to Cymru so he could find you."

"Why would the prince of Ireland seek me?"

"I told you. His eagle needs treatment and Aaron heard you were here. I guess he knows you are a great healer."

"And, how is it you did not heal the bird? You have the skill. I myself taught you." Morfran forced his eyes shut and gritted his teeth. "I do not trust that damned eagle. It doesn't like me."

"So the king allowed this boy to come seek a greater healer?"

"Yes," he said meekly. For all his bravado on the ship, here in the presence of his sister, he behaved as a punished child.

"No matter, brother, you stay here and mind the tiny lass in the center of the bed. Do not touch her and try not to frighten her. I will return momentarily," she said, stepping out of the tent.

Hoping to find Merlin, she searched the area around the tent and, finding nothing, she headed for his workroom.

Before she reached the beach, she found him. Merlin was standing in the center of a small clearing within the thicket of woods. His head was thrown back, facing upward into a bright light. She heard him chanting. Unable to discern the words, she crept closer. So close, she could feel his breath, yet still she could not understand. What tongue was he using?

Ninaway settled back against a tree hoping she could catch the meaning by his manner. The bright light shone down on the wizard and where it struck the ground, a white-hot flame licked the air. Merlin thrust his hand into the flame. Instead of being consumed, his hand simply disappeared. His hand was no longer attached to his arm. Yet, he did not appear to be in pain. How could this be?

Frightened, Ninaway rushed into the clearing, certain the loss of his hand was her doing. The Druids must be punishing him.

Merlin, hearing her footfalls on the crisp leaves, turned and glared at her. "How dare you spy on me? What is your explanation for this intrusion? You have no right, woman." He shook the fist she thought was missing in her face. "It's you who have caused all this derision. You, who have placed lands in jeopardy. For you, I have neglected my duty to Arthur and the Druids. They may never forgive me for the wrongs you have committed. Now leave me."

"I will not leave you. Nor will you leave me. You must remain here in Cymru to care for our child."

"Our child? Claret is not our child. She is the child of no man or woman. She belongs to the Druids. Furthermore, it is my duty to see her presented to them. Her health shall be restored. I will treat her with the foxmoor."

"You shall not touch a hair on her head. She is mine and mine alone. I will cure her illness and she will remain here with me. No one shall take her from me. Not even your damned Druids," Ninaway said, gathering the bottle containing the foxmoor close to her body. She stepped around the many tiny cages she kept for her various pets.

Merlin started after her, but she eluded him, then raced back to the tent and her brother's protection.

Morfran was gazing down on the tiny child in the center of the large bed. He turned when he heard Ninaway enter. Looking back on the child, he said, "How can she be so tiny and still live?"

Ninaway shook her head in consternation.

"One need not be big in order to survive. However, one must be very clever or have the Druids oversee all."

"She has the protection of the Druids?" he asked incredulously. Morfran knew barely anything of the Druids, save they were most powerful, and his sister had warned him to avoid them. Gently, he reached out his large hand, touched the soft cheek of the child, and pushed the curl that had fallen on her face back into its proper place.

Ninaway knew her brother's tenderness was a weakness, but she saw a way to turn that weakness into strength.

"Morfran, you are to guard this child with your life. We are moving from this place, and no one is to know where we go. Do you understand?"

He nodded. He did not always understand his sister's directives. However, this seemed straightforward enough. It was his duty to protect the child and not allow anyone to know their whereabouts.

"Ninaway, am I to return to Olyn and the others, or do you wish me to stay with you and her?" he asked, pointing to Claret.

"For once you ask a good question, Morfran. For the moment, remain here in the tent while I treat the child," she said, pouring the pulverized foxmoor into a cup of broth. Gently, she raised Claret's head and bid her drink.

The girl drew in the liquid. Some of the substance slid out the corners of her mouth. Morfran reached down and wiped it clean with one of the cloths Ninaway used to bathe the child.

Ninaway smiled and nodded her approval. "Stay here while I seek Merlin. I will confront him once more and if he refuses my request, we will leave this place."

Her brother agreed and settled his body on a tiny stool next to the bed. Slowly, he stroked the child as one would a pet. He appeared to be enticed by the unusual child, as was she.

Drawn by the power of the Great Wizard's voice, Olyn followed the Merlin's directive and found himself in a small clearing in the center of a thicket. Merlin stood, shaking in rage.

"Damn her, how does she entwine me so?" The Wizard of the Third Realm to the High King Arthur appeared utterly furious.

"Merlin," Olyn tentatively asked, "Of whom do you speak?"

At once Merlin regained his senses, turned, and saw Olyn before him. "So you've found me. Come closer. We have much to do."

"I will assist you in whatever way possible." Olyn was frightened. He had never seen the senior wizard seem to be lacking in control. The ancient sorcerer seemed truly vexed.

"I am sorry, Olyn, it is personal, and like a foolish boy, I've allowed it to overcome all my duties. Are you alone?" the wizard asked, glancing behind Olyn.

"Yes, Great Wizard, I alone have come to your bidding. I did not feel you called the others. If I was wrong I shall find them and bring them to you at once."

Merlin shook his head. "No, no, you're all I need. Together we can right the Ordination. We must take the child, Claret, from Ninaway."

Anxious to find the healer, Ryan began his own search. Up from the beach, he saw a wide meadow with a small thicket to one side. Seeing no one, he walked toward the wood. Had he not been trained as a hunter, he would have overlooked it. So well hidden one could stare directly at it and not see. What appeared to be branches at first sight were, in fact, folds in a massive tent. He crouched down in the grasses and crept to the edge of the tent. The sound of an unaccomplished singer pierced the stillness, a voice unused to song, throaty and raspy. Ryan remembered the lyric as one his mother sang to him when he was very young. Carefully, he lifted the edge of the tent.

Inside, the lavish furnishings seemed fit for a castle. In the center sat a large bed with a tiny child in the middle. At the edge of the bed was a large man with his back to Ryan. Even though he was unable to see the man's face, he knew it was none other than Morfran. The giant seemed to be crooning to the child.

Ryan moved silently closer. As he approached, he noted the person in the bed, though small, was not that of a very young child. This girl was on the brink of womanhood. So perfectly formed, her budding breasts, taut against the gossamer gown she wore, excited Ryan in a way he'd never before experienced.

Enchanted, he pressed ever closer. He could see the burnished copper of her hair as the lamplight highlighted it. He longed to touch those brilliant tresses in the same way he caressed her image on the stone he carried.

Morfran turned from the bed and looked about the enclosure. Quickly, Ryan sank back between the group of cages at the edge of the tent. Strangely, no animal alerted the large man to the presence of another. Ryan was certain they knew he was there, but they chose not to reveal him.

Ryan watched as Morfran opened a trunk and extracted a loaf of bread and some cheese. Using the top of the chest as a table, the giant broke loose a piece of bread and sliced off a hunk of cheese. He settled back on the small stool and began to eat, washing down his food with vast quantities of the wine.

The girl stirred and the dog at her side emitted a soft low growl. Ryan took the dog's growl as a warning to proceed no further. Wishing to see more of the beautiful creature, he moved to the opposite side of the tent. Ryan knew he was risking discovery, but he was so enchanted he felt compelled to gaze upon this wondrous girl. His fingers itched with anticipation of touching her. By the heavens, he had never seen a woman more beautiful. His loins throbbed with desire. He had to take this magical person and make her his own. Claret moaned softly, and the dog stepped back from her, allowing her to turn to her side. Ryan bit back a gasp of horror. She'd been badly wounded. The long gashes on her back and neck were festered and swollen. He knew at once his mission! She needed Helga's sewing skills and perhaps the skill of a healer. Carefully, he crept from the tent.

Softly Merlin replied to Olyn's question. "She does not intend to harm the child, but Ninaway is not a person who always thinks rationally. She will do whatever she thinks right, even if it is not the best. I am certain she thinks this child is a way to bind herself to me. Ninaway suspects there is more to the child than simply an injured girl. Once she witnessed the change from fox to female."

Olyn gasped. "Can this be so? Is there truly another? What direction have you received from the Druids?"

"My word to Ninaway hinders me from contacting them. That is why you are so important."

"What am I to do, Merlin? Why have you bound yourself to this woman? She hampers you and your work," Olyn replied, shaking his head. How could Merlin entangle himself with a woman who wished to make him less a man, even less a wizard?

"I am reaching the limits of her enchantment. When I question my own reason, it is time to free myself from her smothering love.

Hers is not a love that has wings; it is as a shackle. I must be free, but, Olyn, I love her more than any other being in all the known worlds." Merlin dropped his head in his hands and began to weep softly.

"I am truly sorry, old friend. Love is so hard to find and the pain of losing it is excruciating. Would that I could spare you that pain." Olyn grasped the shoulder of the tormented wizard and patted it gently.

"I must return to her tent and make her see reason. She cannot hide the child from the Druids forever. They have ways of finding what they deem is theirs. Please come with me."

The pair went across the meadow to the small wood that held Ninaway's tent. Neither knew the other was a similar distance from the tent. Ninaway continued her journey from the tent as the wizards drew nearer.

Worried, Olyn asked Merlin, "Can you free yourself from this woman's enchantment? Or, does she bind you with a spell?" Olyn knew that in any event it was not truly what Merlin wished to do. Merlin would have Ninaway as wife and live in Arthur's land for the rest of their days. There was more to this tale than Merlin disclosed to his old friend.

"She binds me with the strongest thread in existence. Love is the true jailer of hearts." Merlin sighed. Each footstep toward the tent seemed more difficult to make.

"We are here. Please let me talk to her, before you come in. I need to prepare her, before we take the child."

Olyn looked on in wonder. They were standing near an ancient tree and suddenly he was alone. Merlin had vanished like the wind. He knew not where the senior wizard had gone. There he stood, wondering what would be required of him. How could Merlin convince this woman he loved that he must leave? And that he must also take the child she had come to claim as her own?

Hearing a commotion, Olyn reached out in front of him and placed his hands on a large gnarled branch. The branch gave way with no resistance, revealing a majestic tent.

Pushing the fold of the tent aside, Olyn entered. Merlin was leaning over someone on the bed and Morfran was snoring loudly on a stool, his head bent over on the top of a trunk.

Finding a stout rope, Merlin approached the sleeping giant. Quietly, he bound Morfran and sent him, still tied to the stool, outside of the tent. Morfran had consumed so much wine he did not stir. There, in the center of the meadow he sat, for all to see. He could be seen, but not touched.

Hurrying across the meadow, Ryan quickly returned to the boat on the beach. Crewmen were offloading supplies and making required repairs to the hull damaged slightly by the sand bar landing.

"You there, sir," he inquired of a man carrying a cask of pitch to the wounded ship, "Have you seen either of the wizards?"

"Wizards? I guess I knew one of them fellers was a wizard, but I only saw the one. There's enough magic around here without conjuring up more wizards."

Puzzled, Ryan said, "Magic around here? What do you mean?"

"I heard tell of a witch in these parts what can hide in plain sight. She makes her dwelling look like a tree or some kind of rock. Normal folks can never find her invisible tent."

Realizing he had seen this 'invisible tent,' Ryan returned to the meadow, where all seemed serene. The butterflies flitting over the grasses and the birds chirping softly in the warm sunshine reminded Ryan of long, hot summers back on Clare. Even the insects singing their cacophony of mismatched sounds and the stream of sweat trickling down his spine reminded him of home. As he walked over the rise in the wide meadow, he spotted Morfran, sitting in a chair. Carefully, he approached the unconscious man. He reached out to slap the giant into consciousness, but halted in mid-strike. He tried again. Something surrounded the falconer that prohibited anyone from touching him. Unable to sort out the puzzle of Morfran, Ryan returned to the strange tent and quietly lifted the flap he'd used to gain entrance the first time.

Therein, he spotted Olyn and Merlin hovering over the girl of his dreams. Rising from his crouched position, Ryan cleared his throat loudly.

Merlin and Olyn turned as one.

Ryan knew his father had once desired to learn sorcery from Olyn. He himself held no such desires, but he truly would like to know what part magic had in his life and that of the wounded girl on the bed.

Certain she was the maiden he sought, he asked, "Olyn, how is it you come to be here? Are you planning on kidnapping the girl?"

Olyn closed his eyes and raised his eyebrows. "Ryan, why are you so suspicious? People tend others without ulterior motives. Merlin and I are treating her wounds. And, yes, we do intend to spirit her from the witch who lives here."

"Is this the same witch who is the healer?"

Merlin answered, "Yes, she is. She is probably the most renowned healer of animals in all of the known worlds."

This pronouncement struck fear deep in Ryan's heart. "If you steal the girl from her, how can I attempt to have her heal Aqulia? From the gossip around the countryside, I have learned she is not always the kindest of witches."

Olyn's sad nod confirmed his worst suspicions. This sorceress was not one who would easily be crossed. Ryan feared both for the safety of the young woman and for the eagle. "Well, what are we going to do? Is she able to be moved? I can easily carry her wherever you wish." His heart longed to enfold the injured woman in his arms.

I will protect her from all harm, he thought, without considering how he would do so.

All he knew for certain was that hers was the image that lay as heavy on his heart as it did in on the stone his pocket.

Chapter Ten

The girl moved only slightly, seeming to melt into Ryan's arms. As he descended the meadow's slope onto the beach, he watched as Merlin indicated a cave's opening.

Olyn proceeded after Merlin, with Ryan close behind him. Once they were through the dark entrance, the illumination within was near blinding. Streams of light from no apparent source refracted countless numbers of times from the crystal walls. Rose and sapphire quartz stones were imbedded within the ice-covered edifice. Though there was no sense of cold.

Ryan still held the tiny girl. "Where shall I put her, Olyn? She's sorely injured and deserves the most tender of care."

Olyn looked on, worry on his face.

Ryan found himself disquieted to see the concern on the face of the wizard. If even the wizard feared the worst, the situation must be truly dire. Would his dream be shattered, before it was realized? First, his eagle in danger, and now the woman he'd searched for was gravely injured.

"Merlin, can you do something to help her? She looks so weak. Please?" Ryan implored.

Merlin seemed distracted. He was pounding something in a mortar and was using every ounce of his powers to pulverize the substance to powder.

Olyn approached the senior wizard and peered over the pestle.

"What are you grinding into sand? Is it something to help the child?"

"It is. Do you recall the manner Kit was able to transform?"

"I do, I thought it would be the death of me on several occasions."

Merlin smiled and held the substance aloft in a clear glass container. The light poured through it, casting brilliant green shadows on the crystal walls.

"Our next vixen changes as well, but in a far different manner. Only she can make the change occur. No one can force a change," the old wizard said. Ryan was becoming impatient with the slowness of the wizards.

"What are you two talking about? Enough of this nonsense. Simply cure her. You are wizards, aren't you?" Olyn met his gaze with somber eyes. "Yes, Ryan, we are wizards, and Merlin will use whatever methods at his disposal to right the Ordination. Have no fear, she will survive."

"Ordination be damned," Ryan huffed.

"Just save her life. Once she is well, I shall never let her out of my sight. I will be her protector."

Merlin sighed and took the powdered substance to the pallet where Claret lay. He placed it on a table at the side of the sleeping area and began to bathe her forehead with dampened clothes steeped in mint. It was a common remedy and usually sufficed to dissipate fever.

"Look," Ryan ordered,

"The damned witch did that much, can you do no more? Use some of your magic. You two don't understand. This is my woman. There is no other. She is mine." Olyn placed a restraining hand on Ryan's arm and bid him sit.

"Merlin knows, and has known far longer than you, the woman is destined to be your mate. He will take what measures he must. Neither question nor demand."

Frustrated, Ryan began to pace up and down the long room. He paused frequently to form a question, but, thinking more clearly now, held his tongue.

Olyn watched Kit's son and recalled a time when the lad's adventuresome mother was in a similar dire situation. Merlin had righted all things then, and he would do it once again. Olyn prayed with all his faith and strength. But the Druids must assist him, else she would perish.

Ninaway returned to the wood wherein she last saw Merlin. She found nothing and no one. Even the shaft of light was gone. Believing Merlin was repentant, she returned to her tent, thinking to find him there. As she came over the slope in the meadow, she spotted her brother sitting in a chair. She approached him and tried to touch him, as he appeared senseless. Her hand met with a rebuking shield.

"Morfran," she called out, "wake up. Why are you here in the grasses, when I ordered you to watch the child? Where is she?"

Slowly, Morfran raised his head. His eyes swam in their sockets. Blinking, he saw Ninaway before him. "Sister, please release me. I cannot move."

Angered, Ninaway shouted, "I cannot release you as I have not held you bound. Who placed you in the chair?"

Sheepishly, the giant hung his head. "I do not know. I was drunk on your wine."

"You fool. When will you learn? All things in moderation, my brother." Ninaway was certain none other than Merlin himself had bound her brother. No one else had the skills. Her mind raced. *How dare he do such a thing to me? I've given him everything a man could possibly want. Why has he chosen to turn against me?*

Leaving her perplexed brother alone in the center of a field, Ninaway hurried to the crystal cave, the only other place Merlin would go. She raced across the meadow, swiftly sliding down the slope to the beach. Voices came from within the cave. Soft, muted and unintelligible, yet she knew it was Merlin. It could be none other. She rushed into the mouth of the cave and hurried down the long corridor to the opening of the workroom.

Only inches from the opening, she found she could go no further. "Merlin, admit me at once!" she yelled. "This cave is mine! I shall not be barred! Do you hear me, wizard? Give me entrance at once."

Olyn and Merlin glanced at one another. Olyn spoke. "Have you barred her from the cave? Can she break the shield?"

"Have no fear," Merlin said with a sigh, "she cannot enter. Since I determined I must leave her, I thought it best to have a refuge. And, there must be protection for Claret as well."

"Claret? Is that the name of the child?" Olyn asked.

Ryan went to the opening of the room. "I can see the healer shouting in the corridor. Can she harm the girl?"

Merlin closed his eyes and drew in a deep breath. "Claret is her name, and Ninaway can no longer harm her. The girl is under my protection."

Merlin slumped then shuffled over to a long bench on the wall opposite the bed where the child lay. Carefully, he studied the light playing on the face of the injured lass. Her color was improving and she seemed to be more comfortable.

Ryan sat himself near her bedside and brushed the hair from her face. Merlin took note of the concern on the face of young Ryan. Here was a man committed. However young he might be, he had chosen and chosen well. Merlin was pleased Ryan's selection followed the tenets of the Ordination. Yet, the sorcerer's task was not completed. He must cure the girl and explain the position the two young people must assume. In view of Ryan's distaste for rule, this would be no easy mission. Ninaway's calls in the distance pierced his thoughts.

"Merlin," Ryan said, "What do you want me to do about this ranting woman? She seems to be daft."

"Daft?" Ninaway retorted.

"Daft? You fool. You think I have no control? I will show you just how much I control. This very cave will collapse and bury you all."

Merlin looked at the woman he loved so deeply.

"How could I have let my reason slip from me?" As the senior wizard looked on, Aaron appeared behind the witch. Gently, he placed his hand on her arm.

"Excuse me, miss. Why are you troubled so? Can I be of assistance?" The witch turned and pounced at the knight like a giant cat.

"I understand your duress," Aaron said gently.

"Perhaps we should reason with the wizards."

Afraid to trust this knight who seemed to have her interests at heart, Ninaway stepped back and observed him.

"Who are you that you understand? What do you know of this cave and the people who are inside?"

Aaron's eyes met those of Merlin, and indicated he would lead the woman from the cave and placate her.

"I am but a simple knight," Aaron stated calmly, "Drawn into this cave by the sound of your voice. You seem to need assistance. Are you hungry or cold, perhaps?"

Ninaway snapped, "I have no need of aid from any quarter. Merlin has dared to use his magic against me, and for this he shall pay dearly."

Feigning ignorance, Aaron replied, "Are you under some spell? Do you need me to find you some newts or another animal that you might rid yourself of a magic incantation?"

Ninaway fumed. Never in her life had she encountered such a fool, a fool who was apparently a knight. Foolish kings would knight anyone. She'd retreat and regroup. Once she knew what was at stake, she would act.

"Thank you for your kind words, good knight," she said, edging her way back out of the cave, "But this is a matter I best handle alone."

Aaron thought it best to allow the woman to go. She presently posed no danger to anyone. Should she act, he could appear to be her ally. Once she left the area, Merlin lifted the barrier, so that Aaron might enter the workroom.

"Thank you, Aaron," Merlin said.

"That was most expeditious of you. Ninaway needs to feel she has protection against me and someone to champion her cause."

"I only thought to defuse her anger. If it serves some other purpose, so be it." Aaron moved to the bedside of the stricken girl.

"How does she fare, nephew?" Ryan looked up at his uncle while he gently stroked Claret's forehead.

"She is very weak. Yet, they," he said, inclining his head to the wizards, "continue to do nothing." Aaron gently squeezed his nephew's shoulders.

"Do not be so hard on them. They'll not allow any harm to come to her. You must trust."

"All my life, I've been told to trust," Ryan grumbled.

"Trust that someone other than I, knows what is best for me. I grow tired of going only on faith, with no tangible results."

Olyn crossed the room to join them at Claret's bedside. "Ryan, you must suspend your disbelief. We are doing everything that can be done for the child. She will recover. You have my oath."

The three turned their attention from the tiny girl to Merlin, who had retrieved the powder from the bedside. He stirred the powder into a chalice of wine. Gently, he lifted the girl's head and pressed some of the liquid through her lips. Slowly, she began to awaken. She lifted her eyelids and the green within was as clear as the crystal cave itself. Her emerald orbs gazed quizzically at Ryan. He could lose himself in their depths. For a moment she studied his face so intently, his heart leapt into his throat.

"Thank God, you're better," he said, the joy in his heart as clear to all as if he were wearing a placard on his sleeve. He reached out his finger, tracing a line down her throat, nearly to the swell of her breasts that rose from the edge of the bedcovering. *Oh, that I could be as close to you as that fortunate linen.*

Frightened, she pushed him away. Fear once again flooded her eyes. She opened her mouth and emitted an animal-like cry.

"Please do not fear me. I would give my life for you." Merlin drew the lad from her bedside.

"Ryan, this is no usual young woman. It is my belief she has not been in this form on many occasions."

"Merlin, you make no sense."

"Merlin is right, my boy. We have no plausible explanation. The Ordination of the Druids works in many strange ways. And, we have no other option, save doing as we are directed." Angrily, Ryan rose to stride around the room to confront the senior wizard.

"Merlin, ever since I left my homeland, I've been hearing about the Ordination of the ancient Druids. What is this Ordination, and how am I to be a part of it? Have I no choice?" Merlin took the lad's elbow, steered him toward a nearby bench, and bid him sit. Impatiently, Ryan struggled against the wizard but Merlin held him fast. Olyn came to the bench and implored Ryan to listen to the senior wizard.

"Listen, boy, and listen well." The wizard's eyes blazed with the fire of a white-hot rage. Olyn drew back against the wall of the crystal cave.

"You are not the first to be touched by the Druids, nor will you be the last. However, you certainly are the most difficult. Nearly everyone wants to be a king, but not you. No, not you. Your precious reluctance may very well cause the end of the world as we know it. Have you no consideration for the people who share this world with you? Would you doom us all to extinction?"

Ryan took the wizard's hand from his tunic, brushed the fabric back into place, and said, "Merlin, I am certain I hold no such power. I have no desire to injure anyone, nor do I have the desire to rule. You and your magic will handle the matter."

Unable to contain his fury, Merlin let out a loud high-pitched cry, and the walls of the cave began to shatter. Shards of ice flew at many angles cutting everything in their paths to the floor, like a thousand knives. Wherever Merlin's gaze settled, the object ignited with yellow fire. Ryan noted that the leather-bound volumes Merlin had so treasured lay in a flaming heap. As if unable to control his rage, Merlin continued his path of destruction around the crystal cave that would never again serve another wizard.

What if Merlin set his sights on him? Or the girl? Heart pounding, Ryan leapt from the chair, brushed the shards of ice from his shoulder, then scooped up the injured girl and strode from the cave. As he left, he took the chalice containing the foxmoor and all the light within the cave with him. As he exited the cave, Ryan heard a wild cry, then silence.

A while later, Olyn righted the overturned bench he'd chosen as a refuge and looked about in the dim light for any signs of life. There, in a far corner, he found Merlin, motionless on the floor. Worried, he scurried over as fast as he could, picking his way through the shelving, tables, crucibles, and all manners of magic tools that surrounded the sorcerer.

At his side, Olyn extended a tentative hand to the magician's shoulder. Merlin flinched at his touch. His rage now spent, he sat quivering, trying to regain his composure.

"Merlin, we must flee," Olyn implored.

"The cave is destroyed. The overhead arches will not support the cave much longer. Come."

Merlin, now a scepter of evil wrapped in the Mantle of Sorcery, drew to an erect posture. A Merlin Olyn had never seen. So power-infused, the old wizard's height had increased tenfold. His shoulders crushed against the ceiling of the cave, forcing it to rend in two.

Ryan felt the ground tremble. Never missing a step, he carried Claret to a hollow in a nearby wood. He set her down gently on the moss. Drawing his tunic off, he covered her with the rough cloth. They were in a safe haven, hidden by the profusion of overhanging willow boughs. Making sure she was safely tucked out of sight, he left her side and went to get Aqulia.

When he returned, the girl was sleeping, untroubled by fever. It was clear the potion Merlin had pressed through her lips had hastened her healing. Though carrying the potion in the chalice had proven a difficult task, Ryan had managed to spill only the slightest bit. There remained a sufficient amount to cure both the girl and his eagle. He placed the bird of prey outside the willow branches and offered her some of the potion. Aqulia drank thankfully.

Ryan went into the willow bower and eased Claret to a sitting position. Slowly, he poured the healing liquid into her mouth. He could feel the warmth of the lass's body as he held her against his torso. His own body began to warm in response. Lovingly, he pushed her tousled hair from her face, caressing her as he did so. The girl looked up at him and smiled. The force of that smile could destroy a man's soul. Ryan eagerly awaited such destruction. Thick red lashes opened over deep green eyes. Never had he seen such beauty. In fact, he was certain there had never been such beauty ever before in the history of man.

Outside the willows, Aqulia began to squawk. Carefully, Ryan eased Claret back into a prone position, then covered her with his tunic. Her hand grasped his arm. He covered her hand with his own and bid her to rest as he reluctantly removed her slender fingers from his arm.

"I must leave you for moments only. My eagle is injured and calls to me. I will return quickly. Rest now."

Gratefully Claret closed her eyes. Every bone in her body cried out in pain. Yet, she felt somewhat restored. She could feel strength in the limbs that only a short time ago gave away beneath her. She would rest here in this cool dark place. Hopefully to regain the power and courage she needed. Needed? For what? *Who am I? For that matter, what am I? My fur is now smooth. I do not recall ever thinking about my body. Four legs and a tail, what more could one want?*

When she felt rested enough to venture from the willow bower, Claret rose from the ground and parted the branches of the large tree. She peered at Ryan. His back to her, he tended his eagle. Its cries struck fear in her heart. Her heart froze. Those sounds sounded familiar. Could it be the same devil thing that had attacked her?

As Ryan turned, the eagle came into her full view. Quaking, she recognized the bird of prey as the same one that Frightened, she fled, nothing covering her body. Naked, she ran seemingly without direction. Running until she could run no further. She dropped to the grass and smelled the familiar scent of foxmoor. This would be her salvation. She lowered herself into the weed, yanked great handfuls from the stems, and rubbed it all over her body. At once, her hands disappeared, and paws and claws appeared where hands and fingers had been.

Exhausted from her endeavors, Claret lay on the cool grasses. Panting to regain her energy, she rose and looked over the meadow. Her stomach growled. She would have to hunt. Her oversized ears twitching to catch the sound of a passing mouse or a tasty vole, she listened. A soft rustling indicated prey was nearby. Dropping into a hunting crouch, Claret sniffed the air, catching the scent of her favorite meal, a vole. From the sound of the parting grasses, it was a fairly large animal. In an instant, she pounced and caught the hapless rodent in her sharp teeth. Hungrily, she tore the meat from the bone.

Satisfied, she rested in the tall reeds on the open meadow. She knew her red fur blended with the tall dried weeds and hid her from view.

But Claret was not the only hunter on the meadow. The eagle needed food and with the power of the foxmoor, Ryan felt she was able to hunt for short periods. Swiftly, she rose above the grasses searching for a morsel. There, on the grass near the tall golden rushes she spotted a vole only seconds before it was captured by a fox.

Her efforts to soar above the meadow proved greater than Aqulia could endure. Her broad chest heaving, she came to roost on Ryan's sturdy arm. She would need more time to heal before she could hunt again.

Ryan stroked her breast feathers. "You are tired. Perhaps it is too soon for you to hunt. I'll snare a rabbit or mouse for you," he said, placing the bird on a thick, sturdy bough.

From the pouch at his side, he extracted a loop of leather. Reaching down to the scrub bushes in the meadow, he found a stick long enough to make a snare. Carefully placing the head of the loop near the end of the stick, he searched the open ground for a hole. He didn't care what animal might inhabit such a hole, a mouse, a vole, or even perhaps a rabbit.

Near a growth of rushes he spied a burrow that could only belong to a vole. Aqulia liked voles. Stealthily, he set the snare, covered the loop with grasses, and sat back to wait for the animal to emerge from its home.

Chapter Eleven

Claret felt the presence of the man so very close to her in the rushes. He made no sound. She observed he was directly in front of the hole where she had caught her meal. He stepped into view and she recognized him. He was the one who helped her escape the cave. *Does this man eat like animals of the field? How strange for a human.* When they hunted, they usually selected larger animals, and for some unknown reason, they cooked their prey.

Her ears pricked to attention. Something was exiting the tiny burrow. The rodent had no more than poked its pointed nose thorough the snare, than the loop slipped surely over the hapless vole.

Closing the loop, the man held the animal aloft for Aqulia's inspection. The bird shuffled in its position on the tree bough, demanding the morsel brought to her.

Ryan's foot was a mere whisker from Claret's snout. He did not see her, but she saw him. And, she saw the great eagle, the demon that had wounded her. *Why is the man so friendly to the bird? Does he not know what damage it can inflict?*

Conflicting emotions tore at Claret. She felt a yearning for, this man. He stirred her in a way she'd never experienced. Yet her fear of the bird could not be set aside. *Per*haps *this man would protect me from the great bird if I am a woman?* The woman he'd cared for so tenderly.

Crawling carefully on her stomach, she retreated to the foxmoor patch. There, she rubbed herself deep in the weed. Almost at once, she became a lass. Her red hair barely hid her breasts. Coyly, she covered as much of her body as she could with her hands.

"Sir?" she called out.

"Can you help me?" Not knowing what kind of help she might require, she stood puzzled before the handsome young man. His face was fair, yet marked with a long, jagged scar. His rugged countenance made him all the more attractive.

"What are you doing here? You're not entirely well. You need to rest," he said, approaching her with outstretched arms. Weakened from her endeavors she fell into them. He swept her up easily and carried her back to the willow, whistling for Aqulia. The bird flew to his shoulder and landed gently. The girl's eyes snapped wide in fear. Quickly, she threw her arms over her face and brought herself even closer to Ryan's breast.

"You need not be frightened, lass, it's simply Aqulia, the one I told you I must tend," he said, closing his arms about her more tightly.

Claret was not convinced there was no danger from the great bird. She'd seen firsthand what damage the eagle could inflict. Shuddering, she wrapped her arms tightly about Ryan's neck, attempting to remove the eagle from his shoulder. The large bird would not give way. She closed her talons more tightly about Ryan's shoulder.

Claret withdrew one arm and eyed the bird with suspicion. Frightened, but intrigued, Claret watched the handsome lad as he returned them to the willow bower, never taking her eyes off him as he found a perch for the bird. The bird shuffled its good wing and settled into a roost position. Aqulia's eyes met her, both eying each other suspiciously.

Ryan again arranged his tunic over the young woman and brushed her hair from her forehead. She would trust him, but not the bird.

"How did you come by the scar?" she ventured. Ryan tentatively touched the mark.

"It's an old injury. Aqulia scratched me when I first captured her."

His statement served to reinforce her opinion of the devil bird. This one, this Aqulia, was not a friend. She must be ever vigilant if she were to protect herself from the demon. The bird seemed to view her with less hunger while she was human than it did when she was a fox. *Now that I know how to change I can remain human while the bird is present.* Yet, hunting as an animal was far more satisfying than lying on the grasses waiting for someone to feed her.

"Merlin," Olyn encouraged, shouting up at the oversized older wizard.

"We have to get out of here." Olyn motioned for Merlin to follow him to the opening of the cave. He heard the crystal walls crashing down as they fled. The ice shards hit the ground like thousands of chimes. Olyn collapsed, taking Merlin with him as they exited the cave. With a final shudder, the cave completely closed. Merlin scowled as he looked back on what had been the only perfect workroom in existence. He would never know the like of it again. He cursed himself for his folly.

"How could I have been such a fool? Over the centuries, I have kept myself cut off from the wiles of women. I could always see the trap. Yet, I allowed this woman to ensnare me as easily as a fox snares a rabbit."

"Merlin, do not be so hard on yourself. Perhaps because you were not well acquainted with women you were easy prey. Moreover, you must remember Ninaway is not a mere woman. She has great powers. A man in love is easy to fool."

"Well, that certainly is the right word. Fool. I am truly a fool."

Panting, Olyn said, "There is nothing we can do here. We must find Ryan and Claret. The wrath of the Druids will be most fearsome if we are unable to locate them."

"The Druids will extract their pound of flesh, to say nothing of what will happen if Ninaway finds her before we do."

Brushing the final splinters of ice from his shoulders, the senior wizard now reverted to his former height. He shook his head and looked sadly at what he'd lost. The opening of the cave was littered with rock and dust. Here and there, a sparkle of quartz peeped through the rubble.

Olyn rose as well and brushed his robe free of all vestiges of the cave workroom. He'd been privileged to view it at all. Merlin took up the staff he'd saved from the cave and shook it in rage at the sky. As if in answer, the heavens rumbled. The firmament grew dark. Great rolling clouds raced across the sky. Lightning flashed, and the sea at their backs rose in great swells, the waves dashing against the shore. The wind began to whip their robes about their bodies, and they struggled to maintain their footing. Olyn held fast to the heavier wizard. Together, they trudged back up to the meadow. They would beseech Ninaway to give them shelter from the storm.

Merlin reached out to the bough that was, in fact, part of the woman's tent. There she sat in the center of the large bed. The very bed Merlin and Ninaway had shared for what seemed a lifetime. The tears that fell from her eyes were near as great in number as the drops of rain that fell from the sky. She looked up and choked back a sob.

"What are you doing here? This is my tent. You chose to leave. Now you have no reason to be here. Leave, at once."

Olyn touched Merlin's sleeve. "Remember she has powers beyond those of feminine wiles. Be careful of what you say."

Merlin nodded. "I know I chose to leave, Ninaway, but only because you were hampering my work. I must serve Arthur. It is my sworn duty."

She wiped her swollen eyes with the back of her hand, sniffed, and said, "I thought you loved me and would place me above all others. You betrayed me. I want an undying love, not a masquerade of devotion."

A trail of tears slid down Merlin's cheeck, "Ninaway, I love you with all I am capable of loving. You are my sun and my moon. No woman in any of the known worlds ever had a greater love. The failure lies with you. Your love is stifling, and you seek to bind with chains of possession, instead of the freedom to grow in that love. I gave you all I had, yet you never gave anything of yourself."

Jumping up, she stood in the center of the bed. Her footing unsure, she tottered from side-to-side on the soft mattress. Her eyes blazed with purple fury. She shouted, uselessly stamping her feet and shaking her fists at him, "You were privileged to be in my company. That is more than any mere man is worthy of. That is my gift to you. I allow you in my presence."

Merlin shook his head, pondering anew what could have caused him to allow reason to flee his mind. There was no prospect of making her realize he did in fact love her, but would not stay bound as a slave.

"Ninaway, my heart is breaking with the thought I must part from you, but I can no longer ignore my duties." He reached up to her as she stood wobbling on the bed.

She reached a hand to him. As their fingertips nearly touched, a lightning charge sizzled and a flame ignited in the scant space between their hands. Merlin quickly withdrew his hand.

"If you love me, how could you seek to harm me?" Merlin beseeched.

Eyes flashing, she spun several inches above the bed, so rapidly her body became a blur. And then, she was gone, leaving nothing of substance in her wake.

It seemed to Claret that she had always been a woman and always at Ryan's side. They together, complimenting each other in all things. Her joy was complete. Each day she lay at his side while he plied both her and the eagle with the foxmoor brew. They each grew stronger with each passing day.

Aqulia was now able to hunt for herself. Claret felt the same longings to hunt pull at her as well. Each morning she watched the large bird soar high above the hill and gently, yet ever so swiftly, swoop down a capture a tasty morsel. But Claret found herself growing restless, tiring of a life of indigent care. To be a woman and learn the ways of man was initially exciting, but the thrill was wearing off. She wanted to be free. Free to hunt her own food and not have to eat that pap that Ryan cooked for her.

Today would be the day she would escape, if only for a short while, and hunt in the tall grasses of the meadow, where she'd hunted her last vole. As the seasons changed, the voles grew fat. Claret's mouth watered just thinking of savoring the rodent.

Later that day, Ryan left her to take Aqulia to hunt high on the bluff to the far side of the meadow. Slowly she followed him, careful to remain undetected. When she was certain he was out of sight, she raced to the foxmoor patch on the meadow. No one was around to observe her. Lying gently in the tall grass, she detected the pungent foxmoor. What a heady perfume. She grabbed great handfuls and rubbed it all over her body. As swift as a summer shower, she became a fox, a creature so unlike any other, yet still similar.

Carefully she crept through the grasses, pushing her snout through the tall reeds near the entrance of the vole hole. She inhaled deeply, taking in the heady aroma of the vole's scent. Her meal was here. She could smell him, yet she could not see him. Intently, she stared at the entrance, moving not a whisker. The scent was becoming stronger. The tiny creature emerged only a fraction of an inch. Now! She snapped her teeth around the unfortunate animal. *Oh, it feels good to feel the crush of bone and the sweet taste of fresh blood. This is freedom.*

Overhead, she heard the sharp *skree* of the eagle's call. Though foxes were not usual fare for eagles, Claret knew her diminutive size and Aqulia's strength could easily make her prey. Reluctantly she returned to the foxmoor patch to effect the change.

As an accomplished hunter, Ryan's eyesight was nearly as keen as the eagle's. He watched as Aqulia soared above the meadow then followed her line of sight down onto the field where a tiny fox slunk along amongst the tall grass. So unlike any other he had ever seen. So small and so vivid red a coat, he didn't trust his own eyes. It had to be magic. Nowhere on earth was there such a tiny fox. Mayhap it was a witch sent from Ninaway. Ryan would put nothing past her. Quietly he crept to the area where the fox should be. He would do nothing to disturb the animal. Finally in his sight, he observed her stoop low on her belly and roll in the grasses. His eyes flew open in shock. Very nearly losing his breath, he could not believe what he'd seen. The fox became the woman he thought to be resting in the willow bower. The woman he felt was intended to be his own.

But he couldn't love a fox, could he? Could he detach his feelings from this odd creature, as this was surely the work of a witch? Though reason told him *yes*, his heart denied the possibility. Regardless of her form, he loved her. He simply loved her. There was no way he could leave her to fend for herself. This was his woman and he would care for her until the end of time. No magic or evil spell would separate them.

But how can we be together if she hides her alter existence from me? I must confront her. She must see I mean her no harm regardless of the body she inhabits.

Slowly, the young woman rose from the meadow and stood naked in the sun. Her beauty was so great, Ryan knew at once his selection of a mate was perfect. This was the woman he'd been searching for. The sunlight danced on her copper tresses, the reddish light bounced off the tallest reeds that blew gently in the wind. When she turned to face him, he drew in a great breath that nearly paralyzed him. So exquisite, so perfect, not a flaw to be found anywhere on her body, she stood proudly in the meadow. Slowly he rose, making no sudden moves, lest he frighten her. He stood and caught her eye. Claret smiled and walked toward Ryan.

He'd seen the change. *Will he be repulsed by my animal existence?* Her heart pounded as she moved toward him. She scanned his entire body. There was no hesitation in his step, nor did she perceive any reluctance to touch her. His eyes shone bright with acceptance. As their fingers touched, he gently drew her to him and held her tightly in his embrace.

"What is your name?" Ryan asked.

"Though I believe we are destined to be mated and I have cared for you for some time, I know not your name." Settling her shoulders and pressing her body close to his, she responded,

"I am called Claret."

"Claret? That is most unusual, who named you thus?"

"The witch," she answered.

Claret felt a wave of uneasiness pass through her. Would her pronouncement alienate him? If Ryan thought her to be the work of an evil sorceress, would he continue his care and feelings? She needed him to love her, in spite of, or perhaps because of her difference. Would he protect her from the great bird? Or, would he consider her simply a pet and keep her in some sort of cage? Would she be another of his menagerie? She knew he cared deeply for his eagle. The bird was most rare. As a tiny fox, she, too, was unique and thus valuable. Moreover, she felt special as a fox. Savoring her freedom and the joy of the hunt, it now became most important that this man love her. Love her above all others. More than simply a pet, she needed to feel the completeness of a love ordained.

He allayed her fears with a soft caress to her cheek and the tracing of his index finger along her nose to the tip. When he removed his finger from her face, he kissed her softly on the nose. Even though Ninaway had treated her well, Claret had never felt she really mattered. This man had made it clear; she mattered above all else.

"Claret, please allow me to introduce myself. I am Ryan Longwurth. My father is king of Ireland, and my mother is one like you."

"L-like me?" Claret stammered.

"How?" That there could be another being that inhabited two bodies was somehow comforting. She wanted to know more.

"What shape does she take with your father?"

"My father knew her first as a fox and only later in the relationship did he realize she was a woman as well."

"And, your father is happy with her as a fox as well as a woman?" Ryan laughed.

"I don't know. They speak little of themselves, but it is very apparent they are happy. His eyes shine when he looks upon her and she likewise lights up when in his presence." Claret smiled deeply.

"That is the kind of love I seek. I will settle for nothing less."

"Nor should you," Ryan said, briskly rubbing her arms as she was beginning to shiver.

"You're cold. We must find you some clothes."

Though clothing seemed unnecessary while she was a fox, now, without fur to warm her, she was indeed cold.

"Where will we find clothing?" she asked.

"We will go to the witch's tent. She must have something that would be suitable," Ryan said, tugging his shirt over his head and handing it to her.

Gratefully she took the garment and placed it over her head. She failed to position the lacings at the front of her body and was confused when the shirt seemed to choke her.

Ryan laughed, and moved to help her. In one swift move, he removed the shirt, spun it around, and slipped it back onto her body.

"Are all clothes this difficult?" she inquired.

"You'll get used to wearing them very quickly. They are handy for many reasons."

"I fail to see what real use they have other than as a replacement for fur." "In time, you will see they provide not only warmth, but beauty and power as well."

"Beauty? Am I beautiful?"

"Yes, my vixen, you are very beautiful and you are also well aware of the extent of that beauty," Ryan answered sagely.

She lowered her chin and smiled up at him through a thick fringe of red eyelashes. Having received the answer she sought, Claret wriggled out of his arms and raced across the meadow, his shirt just grazing her buttocks.

Ryan watched as the shirt lifted enticingly with each step she took.

Somehow Claret was even more tantalizing wearing his shirt than she had been nude. His heart beat so loud, he was certain it could be heard over the farthest hills. He raced after her.

Ryan saw Claret hesitate at the edge of Ninaway's tent, then touch the tree bough and enter. He wanted to cry out to warn her of possible danger, but he feared the warning would be heard by those most likely to cause the harm. Carefully, he entered the tent, hugging the sides of the structure, hiding from view. Claret did not take such precautions. Instead, she strode to the large cabinet near Ninaway's bed. Sitting on the edge, she nudged the dog aside and opened the cabinet. Many times, she'd seen the witch go to the cabinet and take out yards of clothing. Finding something to her liking, she pulled a bright green fabric, the very color of her eyes, from the cabinet. It appeared soft as she spun it in the air. Ryan began to step from his hiding place when he saw Morfran enter. Wisely, he slipped back into the space hidden from the view of the giant.

Chapter Twelve

Morfran saw the chance to redeem himself with his sister. The tiny lady was back. All he had to do was keep her. Loudly and clumsily, he reached for Claret as she admired the garment she'd taken from Ninaway's cabinet. Easily alerted to his presence, Claret jumped onto the large bed, rolled to the far side, and escaped his grasping hand.

"Come here, tiny one. Ninaway means you no harm. She wants you," the giant pleaded.

Thinking quickly, Claret rolled under the large bed and sought her hiding places, wherein she stored her treasures she'd stolen from Ninaway while a fox. Casting aside the metal and trinkets, she searched for something that Ninaway treasured above all else—the papers. Though here and there was a smudged entry, Claret knew this would interest Ninaway more than anything else. She remembered how upset the witch was when she'd purloined the letters. How she'd searched, turning the contents of the tent over and over. Though Claret couldn't read, she sensed the power of letters and somehow knew that Ryan would want to see them. From her vantage point beneath the bed, she saw him hiding in the corner.

At the exact moment she spotted him so did Morfran. The giant turned and grasped Ryan about the throat. Frightened he would be hurt, Claret dashed out from the bed and bit the larger man in the calf. Blood ran down his leg and into his shoe. She tore at the flesh as if she were in fox form, biting to expose the greatest amount of meat then pulling it from the bone.

Morfran yelled in pain, releasing his grip on Ryan's throat. Nearly unconscious, Ryan dropped to the floor.

Claret ran from the tent, hoping Ryan would flee as well. Exhausted, she sat on the ground outside the edge of the tent and waited for him to emerge.

Inside, the tent seemed to be spinning even faster than a Travel Tunnel. Ryan struggled to get his footing. Morfran held his wounded calf and cursed. He again grabbed Ryan and forced him to sit in a chair as he had been.

Carefully he tied the young prince many times more than was required to hold the man captive.

"Now why would that tiny lady bite me? She was like a wild animal," the giant said.

"If she cares for you at all, she will return and beg my forgiveness."

"Morfran, you will not live long enough for her to come to you for forgiveness." A look of concern swept over the giant's features.

"Did she poison me with her teeth?"

"No, you clumsy oaf, she simply does not require your forgiveness."

"But, she hurt me. You always say you're sorry when you hurt someone." Ryan shook his head. The giant was truly a contradiction. He thought nothing of inflicting pain on others, but when he was the injured party, he expected an apology. But Morfran seemed to truly be in pain. Claret had sank her teeth deep into his calf. Despite the severity of the situation, Ryan smiled, pleased his Claret had escaped and injured the simpleton. Now he had to get free before Ninaway returned. Though Claret had not poisoned Morfran, he feared Ninaway would not hesitate to poison him. The witch had powers Ryan didn't have the skill to elude. He had to trick Ninaway's brother, confuse him in order that he might affect his escape.

Turning his head, Ryan examined the wound and said, "That is a deep laceration. You could lose your leg."

"Lose my leg? You said she didn't poison me. Why would I lose my leg?" Ryan did his best to look concerned.

"Don't you know human bites are more dangerous than animal bites? It will become infected, and you will lose the leg at least to the knee, mayhap to the hip." The large man sank to the edge of the bed and moaned.

"What shall I do? Tell me. You know about these things. Save my leg."

"I can save your leg, but not if I'm tied to a chair," Ryan said sagely. "Release me, and I will help you."

Apparently fear of losing his leg frightened Morfran more than the wrath of his sister, Ryan thought, as he untied him. Though it had been his intent to rush from the tent as soon as he was released, Ryan took pity on the simple-minded oaf.

"Do you have any spirits? Wine or ale?" Sheepishly, the giant held his head low. "Not much. I drank most of it," he said, reaching into the chest and extracting a partial bottle of wine.

Ryan took it and dumped the contents over the wound. The giant yelped like a stricken dog.

"That burns," he cried. Ryan patted the giant's shoulder. Gathering several clean cloths, he wrapped the injury loosely.

"Now soak this with the wine each day," he instructed.

The giant nodded. "I thank you for your help. I will do as you say." While giant closely examined his wound, Ryan slipped from the tent.

Looking over the wide meadow, Ryan was unable to see Claret. *I hope that vixen has not chosen to change form again.* He knew his father dealt with a woman in two forms, but he was uncertain if he was up to the test. His heart beat with such force he feared it would leap from his chest. This strange, tiny, mystical being had so ensnared him, he found himself powerless to resist her charms. And, he had no desire to flee from her.

If his heart were held captive, he would gratefully accept the imprisonment. Glancing toward the tallest rushes on the far corner of the meadow, Ryan thought he saw movement that could not be attributed to the wind. Slowly he walked toward the rushes, straining his ears to perceive the slightest sound. Then he heard the sound, like someone spitting out an undesirable piece of food. He reached into the tall grasses and there, in the center of the reeds, sat Claret, regurgitating. Bent in half at her waist, she was wiping her chin with the back of her hand. Blood smeared over her face.

"Are you all right, vixen? He did not hurt you, did he? As I saw it, he got the worst of the encounter."

Continuing to clean herself, she looked up at Ryan while chewing mint to freshen her mouth.

"I am unharmed. That man has the foulest tasting flesh I've ever bitten into."

"What possessed you to bite him in the first place?" It was difficult to keep from laughing. The image of the giant hopping about on one leg kept popping into his mind.

"I did not consider any other option. I had my teeth, but I do not carry a knife, which would have been preferable. Besides, he will heal. I just wanted to get away."

"And, get away you did, leaving me to deal with a wounded simpleton," he admonished. His heart was bursting with pride. She was a formidable woman, one not easily duped. Clever as well as beautiful. Together, they would be able to realize his fondest dream.

She would travel with him throughout Europe. They would stage fabulous hunts with the eagle. Their tour of the known world would mark them as the most famous hunters in existence.

He knelt and using one of the cloths he'd taken from the tent, he wiped the blood from her face. As she was a meticulous animal, Claret welcomed the cleansing. She turned her head to the side, exposing the other cheek. Softly, he wiped it clean of all vestiges of the giant's blood.

Taking her face in his hands, he tilted up her chin and planted a soft kiss on the tip of her nose. The gentle kiss seared his lips with the fire of a passion, so great it could near consume him. He drew her up into an embrace, his arms about her tiny form. His hand covered most of her back. Her warm breasts pressed against his chest. Her lips sought his in an eager kiss.

Gently, he pressed his tongue into the warm cavern of her mouth. The action surprised her. She drew back, looked at him, then imitated the action. *Oh God, she's so perfect in every respect.* He had found the woman whose image he carried with him since he was but a lad. He'd never before felt he was a portion of something greater than himself. Joined with her, he was complete. Nothing else mattered. He could overcome any obstacles and realize his dream.

Moving back from her eager kiss, he placed his cheek against her copper tresses and drew in the sweet scent of her. Gently, he lowered her to the moss covered ground, an emerald carpet for his love.

The seduction of fame paled in comparison to the power of her enticement. The trees around them stood like a living cathedral.

Sunbeams shone through the giant pines; here and there a fern lifted its slender leaves, casting golden shadows on her face. So proud a face, one without compromise, a woman who could match him in all things.

As kissing was a new experience for her, Claret wondered how to proceed. He lay next to her, smiling as she reached up and traced her finger over his lips. As a fox, she was in season, as a woman, she hungered for the man at her side. She was certain instinct would have taken over for her first mating as a fox. Nevertheless, as a woman, she was unsure. Tentatively, she extended her hand over his broad chest. Her fingers caught like prisoners in the tangled mass of curls, she gently tugged him to her breast.

Eagerly, her mouth sought his. Her heart pounded, and she felt her temples pulsate with each beat. *Oh God, I cannot die, I've only begun to live. There can be nothing greater than this.*

For the first time in her existence, she felt complete. In the puzzle that was her life, this man was the piece that made the picture whole.

A dejected Merlin sat in his Camelot workroom, a magnificent room, but not nearly as grand as the crystal cave. The grandeur of that treasure lay in splintered shards and he knew there was no way it could be duplicated. Slowly, he raised his head and greeted his friend and colleague, Olyn.

"Merlin?" Olyn ventured.

"Are you unwell? You seem distraught."

"Thank you for asking, old friend, but the truth of the matter is I mourn many losses."

"Losses?" Olyn quizzed.

"You must mean the crystal cave. Or, is it the lady whose favor you have lost?"

Merlin sat at the long, thin table, his head held in his hands. Slowly, he passed his palms over his face, down to his chin and gently stroked his long white beard.

"If I've learned nothing else, I have learned to mourn only for oneself is a thoughtless endeavor. The loss I grieve the most is for Cymru, for the history of that nation, for Claret and young Ryan. Their lives will be ever troubled if I cannot make them see the right of the Ordination."

Olyn nodded in agreement.

"What you say is true, Merlin. But, how can you right the situation, if you know not their whereabouts? Somehow we must find them."

"You are quite right, Olyn. We must find them and find them quickly. Even now, Ninaway seeks them as well."

"You think she means them harm? What could she do?"

"In her present state, I believe she only wishes to have Claret returned to her, as she fancies the girl her own child. Only if she is thwarted will she become dangerous."

"How will we know if she feels threatened? We must find her before she approaches the two." Merlin, weary from the events of the day, drew in a deep breath and sighed.

"I must summon the full extent of my powers."

"Will that be enough? You must remember Ninaway is a witch." Merlin snapped his head up.

"You dare question the extent of my powers? She is a simple witch. She cannot best me."

Olyn heaved his large chest and answered, "I only seek to warn you, Great Wizard, when you let your pride get the better of you, your powers diminish." Contritely, Merlin nodded.

"Quite so, I have too often let my heart rule my head. I shall be careful. Thank you for the warning."

Aqulia rode majestically on Ryan's shoulder as the trio rode south into England. They secured mounts from an elderly farmer, who could no longer tend his farm. Ryan had saved enough coin that they were able to handsomely compensate the man.

Claret rode easily atop the plow horse, his large hooves sinking ploddingly into the dew soaked grass. Though overlarge for a lady's riding animal, the horse was well groomed with a soft white coat and a mane so shiny it sparkled like liquid moonshine. Claret bent over the animal's neck and caressed him. She felt an animal connection with him.

"I shall name this horse Moonshine," she called softly to Ryan who rode ahead.

"That is a fine name. He fits the part, but the names for our mounts are matters of no concern, compared to what we face."

"Exactly what do we face?" she asked boldly.

"We are leaving Ninaway's land. Who else seeks to harm us?"

Ryan slowed his mount to allow Claret to ride alongside of him. He reached over and took the reins from her.

"We are in grave danger. If the Druids learn we have no desire to fulfill their tenets, they may seek our deaths." Her large green eyes seemed to grow even wider.

"Death? Just because we want to be free? Why is the punishment so dire, simply because we are not rulers, but falcon hunters? Cannot they select someone else to rule? How hard can it be to be a king? Many would desire the position."

"Yes," he said, stroking the mane of his dark horse.

"Many would wish to be king, but the Druids have some all-encompassing power to rule the various countries of the known worlds, and they will not be ignored."

"Then let us confront them and tell them of our wishes. Surely, they would not want reluctant rulers. That would not serve the people they are to govern. Could you perhaps suggest someone more qualified to hold the post?"

"Come, I don't think we have that option," he said, handing her reins back and pressing his knees into his horse's side.

"I will think on the matter as we ride. We must get as far from Ninaway's land as possible."

"I shall miss her."

"Miss her?" he said incredulously.

"Are you daft?"

"Well, she did give me a home and she probably saved my life when she plucked me from the raging stream."

"I'll not say she was all bad, since Merlin was attracted to her. He would not choose a completely evil person as a mate, but of late, she is behaving strangely. I think we have reason to be careful."

"I believe it is wise to always exercise caution," Claret concurred smugly. Gently she tapped the reins against her horse's neck. The animal leapt to a brisk canter, and she pulled ahead of Ryan.

"Take it easy, Claret. Remember this is your first time on horseback."

"Ha!" She laughed, her hair dancing on the wind like brilliant copper streamers as she raced across the broad meadow. The grass rolled gently to the edge of a narrow slope.

Ducking her head close to her mount's neck, they slowed to a walk as she directed him through a green glade. There, in the center, was a waterfall flowing into a crystal clear pond. Throwing her leg over the animal's back, she slid onto the soft grass.

Swiftly, she shed the uncomfortable clothing and stood poised at the edge of the pond.

Ryan groaned. *Why does she have to continually test the boundaries of reason? Can't she understand we have to be careful?* He guided his mount into the glade following the sound of her horse's nicker. His throat constricted. Try as he would, he could not draw a single breath. There she stood, more perfect than the most unique statue that ever graced a magnificent cathedral. Her hair wafted above her ivory shoulders. His glance traveled down her exquisite form. She leapt forward, her body cutting the surface of the water in a single clean stroke.

Enchanted, he shed his clothing as rapidly as she had. Sure, strong strokes pulled him quickly through the silver water to her side.

"Claret," he murmured into the hollow of her throat as he drew her into an embrace. His hungry mouth found hers, their lips perfectly conforming to each other, welded together in a bond no man could sever.

Chapter Thirteen

Ninaway forced herself to project her rage in the area she could do the most harm. Her life was a shambles. Merlin had left, the fox was missing, and even her foolish brother had fled from her. It mattered not who was harmed, she needed revenge. She had been sorely wronged. This was all the doing of that spiteful Guinevere. That woman was simply jealous. *After all, I am the greater beauty and have powers.* Powers far more potent than the foolish queen's, stronger even than Guinevere's sister-in-law, Morganna, who was a talented witch. Even her powers paled in comparison to Ninaway's.

She knew Guinevere feared Morganna, but she also feared the Animal Healer to the North. This time, Arthur and his minions had gone too far. And they must be punished.

Using her ability to seek without being seen, Ninaway projected her sight as far from her tent as she was able, until she could see to the border of the barrier that she could not cross, either physically or by projection. The prince and Claret had fled the country. She would have to use her simpleton of a brother to extract the measure of vengeance she sought.

Again, she projected and found her foolish brother chasing butterflies over the meadow. He pranced and danced like an exuberant child on the first day of spring. She called to him.

Morfran spun around, seeking her but she had called him telepathically, without using her voice. Joyfully, he skipped back to her tent on the high meadow.

Ducking in order to enter the tent, the giant sat quietly awaiting orders from his sister. She turned, rage still visible in her eyes, and demanded her brother give her his full attention.

"Morfran, I have a task for you. It is very important. Do you understand me?" Morfran frowned, and Ninaway knew she would have to explain this plan to him many times over. She was not a patient person and resented the fact her brother could not grasp a concept in a single telling.

"Morfran? Are you listening? You simply must concentrate."

The giant nodded.

"I am listening, sister. I shall do as you bid." His attention wandered to the large bed, where the cat and dog were chasing each other. Around and around they circled, while Morfran smiled and watched them intently.

"Morfran!" Ninaway shouted.

"Pay attention. I have need of your skills."

"Skills? Which of my skills do you need, Ninaway?"

She was certain he would do whatever she asked. Like Merlin, Morfran was awed by the power of Ninaway. Moreover, he loved his sister and sincerely believed she was the most gifted of witches. She would prey upon his pride of being related to her. He would do whatever she required, and believe he was aiding a grand cause.

He sat straight in the chair and focused his eyes upon her. "Do I have to kill someone for you, sister?"

"No, you fool, you must simply bring to me the young prince and the lady who escaped from you the last time. Our lives depend on your skill. Do you understand?"

Numbly, he nodded and rose from the stool. Shoulders slumped, he asked, "Where are they to be found? I am sure they left the country."

"For once you are right, Morfran, they are out of the range of my projection spell. They have crossed the border into England."

"How will I find them? I have no horse, and I cannot walk all the way to England," he responded dejectedly.

"Do not concern yourself, brother. I will see you have a mount and perhaps some information as to their location. Hurry now and prepare for the journey."

Her brother shuffled from the tent and walked swiftly to a rock in the meadow where he kept his meager belongings. He reached under the stone and extracted a large sword. A fine German smith made it at Camelot. Morfran had helped his daughter who was injured, and as a courtesy, the smith awarded him the sword.

He held the sword aloft and marveled as the sun glinted off the polished blade. Again, Ninaway called him. He turned and entered the tent once again.

"What would you have me do, sister? I am ready. I can even slay dragons for you."

For a moment, only a fraction of a second, her heart softened toward her brother.

"I am certain you can slay all manners of evil for me. However, I do not require a death, but a life of service to me." The giant puffed up his chest.

"Ninaway, I live to serve you and none other. You know that well."

"Aye, brother, I do, and I have need of your service. I believe they are even now approaching Arthur's lands. If they leave the continent, it will be most difficult to locate them. You must hurry."

"I am ready. Where is my horse?"

Ninaway turned and flipped open the pages of a Witches' Directory and sought the page of conjuring. She ran her slender finger down the page until she found the paragraph entitled "Horse."

She read the incantation and, at once, a large, dappled gray horse stood before her. His saddle and tack was of purest silver. The reins were intricately braided of the softest leather. The animal itself was larger than most horses, standing at over twenty hands high. The mane of blackest hue was long and well groomed. The horse pranced impatiently on its large hooves. Morfran reached to the pommel and drew himself up into the saddle.

His sister reached up to him, handed him a sack of food, then produced a crystal on a silver chain. "Bend down, Morfran, that I might put this on your neck."

As the giant bent down, she placed the gift about his neck. "This will help and protect you. I have placed a projection spell on this object, and whatever you see, I can see as well. Do you understand?"

"You can see all that I do?" the giant asked warily.

"Can I see you as well?"

"No, you cannot see me, but you can hear me. I will tell you if danger approaches. I will be able to see as long as the crystal is unobscured. Always wear it on the outside of your tunic. I do not wish to see your hairy chest when I seek the prince and the fox."

Word the hunting trio was approaching flared through each township like wildfire. Wandering minstrels heralded their coming with exaggerated tales of their hunting prowess.

Aqulia flew ahead, swooping low over the heads of the townspeople. A sharp whistle from Ryan and the great bird landed gently on his muscular forearm extended over the head of his mount.

Claret sat upon the large workhorse, perched primly like a princess, and followed behind Ryan. She enjoyed the procession and continually marveled at the adulation they received in each new town. Her red hair cascaded over her shoulders and down her back, meeting the stark white of the horse's rump. The exhibition they staged mesmerized the crowd.

Claret majestically carried a small cage to the far end of a field. Within the cage was a large rat the townspeople had trapped to use as bait. As grain was harvested, the rodents moved in to claim their measure. Ryan called to her, "Release it." He circulated among the farmers gathering coin. "Pay no more than you think is fair, sir."

"'Tis worth a king's ransom to have our grain protected. I'll not begrudge you a fair price," a man declared.

Ryan stroked the breast feathers of the eagle and spoke softly to her. "Show them your mettle, Aqulia. We shall have fine accommodations this eve."

Aqulia quickly demonstrated her skill in killing the pests and thus proved her value to the peasants. The townsfolk set an upright log in the center of town. The eagle's perch, where she feasted on the bait rat, tearing the flesh with her sharp, hooked beak.

The townspeople were greatly impressed and led the trio to a two-story inn at the far end of the town, where they were served as grandly as a king. As evening fell, they were shown sleeping accommodations far more grand than the barren ground they were used to.

At the break of dawn, after a well-deserved rest, Ryan shook her shoulder, "Claret, waken, we have much to do today, if we are to earn our keep." Slowly, she roused herself from slumber, stretching her body like a cat.

"You make it sound as if you have an obligation to rid these farmers of all their rats. You owe them nothing."

"Claret, I have pledged my word, I would rid these folks of their vermin. It is my duty."

Not placated, but firm in the knowledge she could not alter his stance on duty, Claret dressed and readied herself for the hunt.

Ryan and Aqulia went to the granary wherein the village stores were kept. All the men of the town gathered at the front of the building, ready to assist the hunters. The fellow who indicated he would gladly pay a fair price led the men.

"How can we help you, lad? Though we are unable to rout the rats, we will assist you in whatever manner you wish."

Ryan looked over the crowd. He smiled, a thanked them, then dismissed them. Puzzled, the villagers drew back.

Claret was the pivotal member of the troupe. She went to the rear of the building, checking carefully to see she was not observed. Certain she was alone, she extracted some foxmoor from the pouch at her side. She removed her garments and secreted them along with the foxmoor pouch beneath a stone at the corner of the building. Meticulously she rubbed the herb over her entire body. Focusing on the core of her being and the task she was to perform, she underwent the transformation. The smell of rats nearby drew her attention. She pushed her snout into the narrow opening in the wall and forced her way inside.

At once the rats sensed her presence and fled toward the front opening. The moment they emerged in the morning's first light, Aqulia swooped down and grabbed two, one in each talon.

Claret circled around the interior of the granary ferreting out each and every rodent. Repeatedly, Aqulia dove at the fleeing rats, until not a single vermin remained alive. Since her kills were too numerous for her to consume, the villagers threw the carcasses into the center of the town square around the log erected as a perch. Confident she'd completed her part in the hunt, Claret again transformed and joined Ryan and Aqulia in the square. Ryan smiled as she approached.

"We have served these people well this day."

Claret smirked. "Service, duty—pooh. I do this because it's enjoyable."

"To serve is an enjoyment, but I am of the suspicion you mean it served your ends," Ryan responded, a twinkle in his eye.

He is able to read me all too well, she thought. *I should not give over the contents of my mind so readily.*

Pretending she cared not, she brushed invisible dust from her clothing and mounted Moonshine.

"Come on, you two," she said, cocking an eyebrow,

"There are more villages to *serve*."

Ryan smiled at her and mounted up, Aqulia roosting on his broad shoulder. Claret noted there was no difference in the height of his shoulders. He carried the large eagle with ease. An ease in which she took pride. Maybe life as a human would not be as restrictive as she thought.

Carefully avoiding Camelot, the three nearly reached the channel. Ryan did not want to risk discovery should they stop at Arthur's grand city. Too many knew them there. However, since Ryan did not think they were followed, he did not insist on speed. They set a good pace, but weren't driven by anything other than time and distance from Wales.

Another was also avoiding Arthur's holdings. Morfran had been warned not to appear anywhere near Camelot. Though she was not a skilled tracker, the trio were fairly easy to follow. Morfran had them in clear sight just moments before they reached the channel. He reached down to his neck and the crystal, holding it high the sun caught the image of the trio. At that moment, Ninaway felt a piercing in her heart. She saw what her brother saw. They were within reach, if only she could make sure that dunce could follow simple instructions. Why was she cursed with such incompetents?

"Morfran," she hissed, "Do not move too quickly, and wait until they board the boat to cross the channel. They will think they are safely out of England and will no longer exercise caution."

"Yes, sister," he answered meekly.

"I will do as you say. I shall not fail again." Ninaway sighed, knowing she should have better agents at her disposal than her foolish brother.

"Listen, and listen closely. The captain owes me a great boon. He will help you in their capture."

"What am I to do?" the giant inquired. Thinking he should remain out of sight, Morfran sank to the ground and began to speak to his sister in hushed tones.

"I'll make certain they do not see me until they are in my trap."

"Trap? Have you devised a trap?"

"No, well, y-yes," he stammered.

"I will dig a deep pit like I do for the wolves. When they step in, I will throw the net over the opening. She will not escape me again. You must give me stronger magic so I can change into something a fox fears." Ninaway signed. She could expect nothing less from the simpleton.

"Magic will not help. They are protected by the Druids. You must capture the fox alone. If you capture them together, each will aid the other. You must separate them. Keep each from the other."

The giant nodded. "How am I to do this? They are always together. Even the eagle sleeps in the same room with them. While they are on the road, when they rest, they are only fingertips from each other. The fox woman is never alone, except when she changes form."

"Then that is the time you must capture her. Make certain the change is complete, then trap her. But, I warn you, Morfran, do nothing to harm her. I shall have your head if she is damaged."

The giant meekly nodded. He would do as she bid. He quietly boarded the boat while Ryan dismounted and prepared to board. Ryan hailed the ferryman, who appeared to be talking to himself.

The old man caught sight of the trio and beckoned welcome. "Come aboard, come aboard," he called.

He seems overeager to have us aboard his vessel, Claret thought. *Many people must make this trip, and he should not be lacking for passengers.* She shook herself to rid her mind of suspicions.

As a fox, one had to always be on guard, and now, even as a woman, she had to be wary of the motives of others. Most people were devious and had a personal agenda.

Ryan led their horses up the plank to the old man's ferry, a mite more than a raft with an enclosed area to house the captain, should weather be inclement. The vessel sat low in the water, due to the weight of the large plough horses. The channel was quite calm, the crystal water bouncing the sunlight off its ripples. Claret sat atop Moonshine, watching Ryan conversing with the captain.

"Sir, just how long will it take to get across? I am anxious to be rid of England."

"Shouldn't take long. Probably be a mite sooner if I had sails. I thought about getting some, but it would just be something more I would have to care for," the ferryman replied. "I don't fancy mending sails. It's woman's work, and I have no woman."

Ryan smiled and looked at Claret. She met his gaze and knew this was the man time, providence, or Druids, she knew not which, had intended her. She was complete. If only he understood the wild pull that tugged at her soul. She loved him, but she needed to be free. It had been many days since she was free to roam as a fox. Hunger gnawed at her stomach as well as her heart. Ryan had done his best to provide meals for them. But she found the roasted rabbit and fowl unpalatable. She needed fresh meat, not skinned and cooked. The cooking took the flavor out of the meat. She found it a wonder they didn't starve, eating the way they did.

Claret found that she and Aqulia shared a fondness for fresh kills. The two had come to respect each other and often copied the other's skills. Aqulia often waited beside a mouse hole or rabbit burrow, in the same manner as Claret. Once the prey was spotted, the eagle pounced. Likewise, Claret would observe from as high a vantage point as she could find, sighted her prey, and descend upon it.

Alighting from Moonshine, Claret moved about the ferry and came to stand near Ryan and the captain. "Has he told you the length of our journey? Will we arrive before nightfall?"

The ferryman took off his hat and rubbed his forehead. Looking to the sky, he said, "Shouldn't be too long now, missy. We're nearly there."

Claret looked around the ferry, and her eye caught a movement within the weathered enclosure. Though her senses were not as acute as they were while she was in fox form, she caught the distinct scent of man. Could someone be hiding in there? For what reason? If it were a person, what would he have to gain remaining out of sight? Could this be someone sent by Ninaway?

Claret was not certain of the extent of the witch's powers. Nor was she certain the woman even wanted her. Ninaway would only seek to have control over her and the others. The others, they had become a part of her, in a way she was not certain she understood. Knowing only there was no force on earth that could separate her from Ryan and the bird. The bond between man and woman was understandable. She'd been in season and had felt the biological pull to mate. What she didn't understand was the feeling of being part of a team with both Ryan and Aqulia. *This is why wolves hunt in packs,* she thought.

Chapter Fourteen

Slipping unnoticed from the raft, Claret swam, removing her clothes as she did so. Ryan led the animals to shore and called softly to her.

"I know you're here, but right now we have not the time for games. Come and help me with the horses."

Playfully, she snuck up on him at the edge of the water and grabbed his legs. As she caught him off guard, he lost his footing and fell into the water beside her. She pulled his body closer and wrapped her legs about his torso.

"So, brave falconer, is it true you are the captive of the fox woman? You are my prisoner, you know." Ryan smiled.

"While it's true you have enslaved my heart, I still have control over my body."

"Oh, do you now?" She raised her body up to meet his, pressing against him just below the surface of the water. Feeling his hardened response, she entwined him with her arms as well. Placing water-soaked kisses all over his face, she nuzzled his ear. Whispering enticements, she fondled him.

"Claret," he moaned, "You can't do this in public. The ferryman will be scandalized."

"So, let him leave."

"Claret, my love, we are not like the wild creatures of the wood, who mate no matter the audience," he said, extricating his body. He shook, as much to rid himself of the water as to contain his desire.

She rose from the shore, coyly looking at him over her shoulder. Her glance held a promise. A promise he and he alone could fulfill.

Ryan mounted his horse and called to her, "Please dress and follow me. This is a foreign land and we should not be separated."

There was no way they could be parted, not by man, nor Druid, nor any other manner of magic. She dressed and quickly mounted Moonshine. As Ryan rode ahead, she admired the curve of his buttocks as he sat astride the large horse. His body flowed so naturally; man and horse seemed to be a single unit. So proud, he rode like a mythical centaur. The woman in her yearned to be with the man destiny had chosen for her. She found herself well pleased with the selection.

Moonshine's hooves pounded in sync with the beat of her heart, each beat drawing her closer. She could taste her desire, and it was sweet. Feeling the quickening in her heart flowing to the warmth between her thighs, she spurred the horse onward.

Just ahead in a clearing, Ryan saw a hunter's camp. A simple structure, just enough to shelter a man in case of a storm.

Ryan edged the large horse around the makeshift shelter and saw Claret approach, the look in her eyes so blatantly sensual, Ryan was relieved they were alone in the wood. For he was certain all could read the message, intended only for him.

He dismounted and assisted Claret from Moonshine. She seemed almost weightless in his arms. He held her to his chest, reluctant to part even momentarily. She reached up and entwined his neck, pulling her mouth to his ear, her legs wrapped around him as he supported her buttocks. He lowered his head to her breasts and inhaled the sweet intoxicating scent of her. So pleasant, no amount of honey or sweetmeat could entice him the same way as it had when he was a boy. This was confection beyond his wildest expectation.

"Claret," he moaned, his lips pressed into her throat. Her skin was so soft, so silky. He gently traced his finger over her shoulders to the rise of her breast. His tongue followed the same entrancing path ...... exciting her beyond measure. This was greater even than the thrill of the hunt. Being human might even exceed the freedom she enjoyed as a fox.

Alone in his workroom, Merlin contemplated the most recent pages in the book of his life. He had severed himself from the greatest love he'd ever known. His despair was in equal measure to the joy he once felt. For a certainty, the Druids were punishing him. With his vast experience, there was no comparison, no guide for him to understand the depth of his depression. So dark was the cloud, only the golden Ninaway could banish the gloom. Olyn knocked at the casement of Merlin's workroom.

"Come in, Olyn," Merlin said somberly.

"I have need of your friendship."

"And, what is it that troubles you so?"

"My life is a sham, a nothing. I have known few men whose honor I trusted and fewer women whose passion stirred me. I have long valued your counsel. Help me to make some meaning of my life."

"Me? How can I counsel you? You are certainly more worldly. I have lived a simple life. My friends, like yours, are few in number, but more the dearer in their friendship. I have never married, but raised two children and now consider their child my grandson. I once served the king, as did you, but with far less skill. Easily duped, I have paid dearly for my folly."

Merlin nodded wearily. "'Tis true, we are but victims of our own desire."

"Quite so, Merlin, but we must play with what we are dealt. We have a greater problem than our misspent lives."

Merlin shook his head and stroked his long white beard, as he was wont to do when he was contemplating a problem.

"The children must be found." He had freed himself from the lure of Ninaway, but nothing could sever the bonds that held him to the Druid's instruction.

"We must find them else nations are in dire peril."

"How are we to accomplish this? The Travel Tunnel moves too fast for observation and we are too old to travel on horseback at a full gallop." The older sorcerer smiled, noting his colleague's deferment to old age.

"You are quite right, but I shall use the simpler method of projection." Olyn hung his head, ashamed he had forgotten the extent of the powers of the Wizard of the Third Realm to the High King Arthur.

"I'm sorry, I failed to consider that option."

"No matter, old friend, what power we do not use ourselves, we tend to forget others have the capability."

Merlin drew to his full height and closed his eyes in the center of his workroom. From the ceiling that had no opening, a brilliant light shone down. Raising his face into the beam, he slowly opened his eyes. The illumination remained intense until he lowered his head. Then it vanished as rapidly as it had appeared.

"You have not found them, have you?" Concern grasped at Olyn's throat, as certain as a hangman's noose. There had to be a way to find the Druid pair. Though he knew his friend would be reluctant to return to Wales, Olyn knew the only personage who might have the solution would be Merlin's former lover.

"Though I am reticent to suggest this, perhaps we should consult Ninaway."

"The same thought passed through my mind. Like all wizards, I can only project to the boundaries of my homeland. If they are in Wales, she would have the power to see them."

"How would she receive you? Can you deal with her without being made a captive?"

"Olyn, Olyn," the older sorcerer clucked, "Now that I have set myself apart from her, she can no longer ensnare me. I don't know if she would be willing to aid us, but we have no other option. We must travel to Wales immediately."

The sun was rapidly falling across the pink-hued sky as Ryan shook the sleeping Claret.

"Come on, girl, we must get to the king's palace before nightfall." Slowly she raised her head from the crude pillow on the hunter's pallet.

"Will our accommodations at the castle be as comfortable as these?" she asked slyly.

He knew she was not referring to the luxurious linens they were certain to find at the palace of the king. His vixen wanted privacy to couple, now that she'd learned most did not consider mating a public activity. Though his experience had never before included sexual exploits, he was certain not all women were as eager for the act as Claret.

"Come on, roust your bones, woman," he said playfully, snapping his tunic in her direction. Reaching out, she grabbed his clothing and pulled him down to her.

"I'm not leaving until you feed me. I'm hungry," she replied, her mouth pursed and her tiny pink tongue emerging to wet her lips.

"Claret, we will eat when we arrive at the palace. I'm sure they will have every manner of treat to tempt you."

"You're the only one who can tempt me, and I hate cooked food."

"All right, I saved some blackberries I picked on the way here." He pressed the ripe berry to her lips.

She smiled and drew in the fruit with her tongue. The sight of the full pink lips stained with the berry juice mesmerized him. Some juice slipped out of the corner of her mouth, so he reached over and cleaned it with his own. Over his shoulder, Claret noted the ever-darkening sky. Gently, she pushed him from her.

"You're right. We best be getting to the castle." Ryan struggled to regain his composure.

"Why do you do that?"

"Do what?" she asked innocently.

"Tie my gut in a knot, then blithely delay our pleasure."

"I can do that?" Her eyes grew wide, totally unaware of the power of love or of the draw of sex.

Ninaway's tent stood solitary against the grove of trees, the same as when Merlin had left; the same, yet vastly different. Or, was it simply his perception had altered?

No longer blending into the landscape, the structure had lost some of its mysticism.

Merlin and Olyn approached and heard muffled sobs. Merlin raised the tent flap, and stepped into the domain of Ninaway. The animal cages were overturned and empty. None of her pets remained, and even the doves had flown.

Merlin cleared his throat loudly, hoping to alert Ninaway without frightening her. Despite all that had happened he cared yet for her feelings and did not wish her ill.

She sat in the center of the large bed, tears flowing down her pale cheeks. As he approached, she glared from beneath her wet lashes. The amber fire burned with a glow so intense it should have consumed the wizard. At one time, he would have been tempted to respond in kind, now he was tempered by mercy.

"You," she screamed,

"See what you have done. I have nothing. Even my pets seek refuge from me. Why did you choose to leave me thus?"

Struggling to retain his composure, Merlin spoke softly.

"The choice was yours, Ninaway. Your demands suffocated me. I only left because you drove me away." Olyn stepped between the two.

"Please, you must set aside your anger. It serves no valid purpose. Ninaway, we need your help."

Swiftly she wiped her tears with the back of her hand.

"Oh, the Great Merlin needs me? And, what do you need me for, most honored sorcerer?"

The bite of her words near drew blood, and Merlin withdrew as if he'd been wounded.

"Ninaway, please," he implored, "We have genuine need of your skills. Your sarcasm is not useful."

Slowly she turned, the eyes that only moments before burned with amber fire, now warmly glowed in contrition.

"You're right, Olyn, I have wasted far too much of my life serving my own ends and I've only found joy when for a brief moment I lost myself in you, Merlin."

Merlin shook his head sadly, closed his eyes, and sighed deeply. Ninaway crawled off the bed and walked into Merlin's open arms.

"How can I help you, Merlin?"

Though he was wary of the witch's motive, Olyn felt his hopes for his friend's happiness leap in his chest.

"Olyn, old friend, again I have need of your consul. Dare I love again?" Merlin asked.

"Since love is the greatest power in all the known worlds, not only must you dare, but you should do so with full abandon," his comrade replied.

Ninaway looked at the Wizard of the Third Realm to the High King Arthur, her golden eyes infused with understanding.

"The greatest wisdom is the epiphany of a fool."

A lofty white castle stood profiled against the red-hued sky. A structure so grand it rivaled the magnificence of Camelot. Ryan urged their mounts onward. Claret had mastered sleeping in the saddle and was dozing peacefully.

An ornate iron grill served as suspension for the white oak bridge over the expansive moat. White oak was nearly as durable as stone and showed hardly any evidence of the countless traffic the bridge had endured. Bits of quartz crystal glittered in the evening sky off the two circular towers on each side of the massive gate.

The sound of the horse's hooves clattering against the wooden bridge awakened Claret.

"Are we here?" she asked, stretching her arms.

"Yes, sleepy one, we are here," Ryan answered, smiling in wonder at her ability to sleep wherever circumstance found her. *We've come a long way, but finally we are free.* Ryan could still taste the salt in the air, though they were miles from the channel. His horse lifted its head nervously as they stood before the hand wrought iron gate. He reached up and pulled the cord to summon those who could give him entrance. A bell pealed in the evening quiet and the grill began to rise. It opened enough to allow a person walking to enter, but not enough to permit a man on horseback to proceed. A short nervous man came through to greet them.

"We thought you chose to remain in your previous town as the hour grows late. You are the hunters?"

"We are."

The man scuttled about and signaled another to open the gate completely. As they passed through, Ryan noticed the ferret-featured man was dressed in typical huntsman attire.

"Are you the castle huntsman?" The man glared at Ryan, acting as if he'd been offended. "I am, and I do my duty well. There is always fresh game at daily meals."

"Sir, I do not question your ability, I simply asked your function."

"Well, you'd best see to the muskrats and not mind my business of securing meat for the king."

"Muskrats?" Claret asked.

"What are muskrats?"

"They are the plague of the castle. Even now you can see them diving in the moat," the diminutive man said, pointing to the water surrounding the castle.

Ryan could hear the animals surfacing and diving, the sounds so numerous, he determined there were vast numbers of them.

"Are these creatures larger than rats?" Ryan inquired, shrugging his shoulder to determine if Aqulia could handle them as easily as she did rats.

The large bird shuffled, as if annoyed Ryan had disturbed her.

"Somewhat," the huntsman answered.

"They are a somewhat larger, but what makes them so troublesome is the fact they breed even faster than rats. For every one you see, there are ten you don't."

"What methods have you used to try to eradicate them?"

"We've used nets and baited traps. They chew through the nets and snatch the bait without springing the trap."

"So, they've outsmarted you?" Ryan said, arching his brow.

"How dare you impugn my honor, sir? I am the most respected hunter in all of France. Everyone knows the expertise of Phillipe LeBeau. Removing vermin is not my job."

"Thank you for your time, sir," Claret addressed the fletcher in the castle aviary.

"You're most welcome, young lady, I enjoy your company. Do visit me again."

Claret smiled, nodded, and moved to the perch that had been assigned to Aqulia. The eagle shuffled in greeting as Claret stroked her breast feathers.

"Well, my friend, can we do this without the Frenchman?"

Aqulia arched her neck and spread her wings, stretching them to their full extension.

Claret took the bird's reaction as affirmation. She untied the tether and found a falconer's glove. She fit her tiny hand in the leather glove. Though it was overlarge, it would serve its purpose to protect her arm from the eagle's talons. She presented her forearm to the bird as she'd seen Ryan do many times. The eagle would not leave the perch. Claret moved closer to the bird. Aqulia reached out one foot to nearly touch her shoulder. Claret nodded and smiled.

"You know you're too heavy for my arm. I understand." She laid the glove across her shoulder and the bird stepped onto her. Looking up at the large bird on her small shoulder, Claret was certain they were a comical pair. Aqulia moved closer to her neck to give her greater balance.

"Oh, are you the smart one? Don't worry, I won't be carrying you for long." She looked back at the feather mender and all about the aviary. The old man was busy at his task and there was no one else to observe them. Quietly, the two left the building.

It was nearly dusk and the shadows began to lengthen. At the side of the gatehouse, Claret perched Aqulia on a hollow log. Earlier she hid a pouch of foxmoor in the log. She shed her clothes and rubbed the weed over her body. Once again, she transformed into a fox. Slowly, she advanced to the edge of the moat. As part of the moat was in shadow, the muskrats were beginning to stir. One by one, they slipped from the water onto the grassy edge. Placing herself between the water and the castle wall, she herded them like sheep into Aqulia's talons. Two by two, the eagle caught them, squeezed the life from them, and tossed the bodies on the grass.

"Come on, Phillipe," Ryan directed. "We need to set these panels before the sun sets entirely. I don't want them to become accustomed to their reflections. Make sure they are in place, but leave them covered until it is dark and the torches are set."

"I will do as you say. Do you require more assistance than mine alone? I'm certain any number of the townspeople would be most anxious to assist you," the huntsman said, as he steadied the large reflective panel in order than Ryan might secure it.

"No, thank you. Your able assistance is all I need." Though Ryan did, in fact, appreciate Phillipe's assistance, for the most part he preferred to work alone. Alone, that is, save of the other two members of his hunt crew. He knew Aqulia was in the aviary getting a well-deserved rest, but he was unsure of Claret's whereabouts. Looking to the quickly darkening sky, he began to worry.

Turning his head, he heard a sharp squeak, clearly a rodent's cry. He lit the torch in front of the last panel he set. A streak of red passed in front of the panel, then the scurrying of a vast number of small animals, each crying out in distress.

"Claret?" he cried, hoping he was wrong, knowing in his heart he wasn't. Asking Phillipe's assistance had alienated her. She'd decided to do this on her own. As fearless as a child, she would try anything and challenge everything. He knew she was sly and cunning. What he had not considered? That she was also daring and inventive.

Overhead, he heard the soft beat of the wings of Aqulia. The two were hunting together. *They don't even need me.* The thought pressed a sense of loss deep within Ryan's heart. He needed them. Aqulia gave him recognition as a renowned falconer. Ryan was not only the youngest and most accomplished falconer, he was the only man to use an eagle as a hunting bird. Though such a bird might be considered above his station, no one, not even Arthur, had questioned it.

His need for Claret was greater even than the desire for fame. His heart ached whenever they were apart, even if the separation were moments only. So closely allied, her blood seemed to flow in his veins. He needed her, and fearing her in danger paralyzed him. His legs went numb.

Again he cried out, "Claret, Claret, oh God, where are you?"

Chapter Fifteen

Though the water in the moat was not actually frozen, it was a far cry from warm. Claret could not remember how many times she dove to herd the muskrats in their own element. Surprised to find an enemy below the surface, Claret watched as they scattered in various directions. Carefully, she chose the largest group and pursued them until they left the water. The frightened animals were easy prey for Aqulia.

As the night grew darker and colder, Claret began to tire. Just one last dive. Plunging in, she felt the chilled water etching her body with weakness. She could do no more, not this eve. Clawing her way up the grassy edge of the moat, she headed for the gatehouse. She needed clothing and the remainder of the foxmoor.

There, in the gatehouse, another watched her progress. She could sense the presence of man, the most deadly of all enemies. Cautiously, she sniffed the air and pricked her ears to hear the faintest sound. What she'd feared had come to pass. It was a man, the only man she truly feared. Though, in Claret's opinion, he was a stupid man, he was nonetheless dangerous. He blindly followed his sister's bidding. Claret felt in her heart that Ninaway wanted her back. Though Morfran was a simpleton, Ninaway was a witch who would sink to any level to achieve her goals.

Caret's mind whirled. Perhaps if she hid among the gate's mechanism she could rest and gather her strength. She shook to rid her fur of excess water and crept behind the largest wheel of the drawbridge's inner workings. Too tired to use the foxmoor to effect the change, she wrapped her full tail around her body and fell asleep. A sleep so deep she didn't hear Morfran approach her. Neither did she feel the net he'd thrown. Not until he'd drawn it close around her.

Ryan feared the worst. The only sound, his own frantic cry. No squeaks of dying rodents, nor beating of Aqulia's wings, not even the faint growl of Claret as she chased the animals to their deaths.

Carcasses of muskrats piled on the lawn above the moat gave evidence to her success. *Without Claret, I cannot continue.* To allow the king to believe otherwise would be a mockery. To play the man false would be against the strict code Ryan had set for himself. He had no other recourse. He must inform the king of his failure and return the hunt fee.

Ryan called out to Phillipe. No response, even the huntsman had left. He was alone. His only companion, the fear in his heart.

Reluctantly, he returned to the castle and went directly to the receiving hall. As the hour was late, there was not a soul to be seen. The king had few petitioners this day, as the villagers felt the foreigner would solve their greatest problem. How wrong they were.

Ryan left the hall and headed down the corridor to the quarters the king had assigned him. Pausing in front of a high, arched door with rich detailed carvings he noted that at either side of the arch were posted guardsmen. From their attire, Ryan knew them to be the French King's personal guard.

These men would give their lives for their king without hesitation. Ryan respected their loyalty and devotion. Perhaps, if *he'd* been more devoted to his king, Claret would still be with him.

As Ryan approached, the guardsmen crossed their lances in front of the large door.

"Please, good sirs, I need to speak with His Majesty. 'Tis a matter of grave import."

The guards stood firm, not moving their lances. One man reached behind and tapped the door. Several moments passed, an eternity to Ryan. The door opened a crack and a high thin voice addressed the guardsman.

"How dare you disturb His Majesty while he is dining?"

Softly, the guard spoke with the person on the other side of the door, though what was said was unclear to Ryan.

The door closed, and the guard addressed Ryan. "His Majesty will see you briefly, once he has completed his meal."

I hope he has already consumed a large portion, as waiting is not my strong suit. Ryan paced back and forth, as he pondered how he would petition the king to help him find Claret and Aqulia.

Well, it's this way, Your Majesty. This woman, she's not always a woman, sometimes she's a fox. Certainly, he'll believe that. More likely, he'll have me burned for heresy.

Ryan looked out over the moonlit sky. Suddenly a large bird seemed to block out the moon entirely. Could it be Aqulia? Ryan whistled. The bird ceased its circling and dove to the window where Ryan stood.

"Aqulia, thank God you're safe. Where's Claret?"

Though Aqulia could not speak, Ryan felt certain the bird knew the answer to his question.

At that moment, one of the doors opened and the man with the shrill voice bid him enter. Aqulia flew to Ryan's forearm, startling the man greatly.

"Oh, my word," he said, his voice a tiny squeak.

"That is a very large eagle. Will it stay on your arm?"

"You are in no danger from Aqulia. May I speak to his majesty?"

"What?" the man asked, his fear making him forgetful.

"Oh, yes," he said in a thin, reedy voice. "His Highness will see you now." Bowing, the man withdrew, and the king spoke.

"What is it of such importance it could not wait until morning?"

"I'm very sorry, Your Highness, I do not wish to disturb you, but I require your assistance."

"I instructed Phillipe to assist you. Has he failed somehow?"

"No, Sire, he has been of great assistance, but I am unable to continue the hunt." The king looked down his patrician nose and glared at Ryan.

"Young hunter, I have your pledge. You have been compensated. Do you not honor your pledge?"

"Sire, I will gladly return the hunt fee, if only you can help me find the woman who hunts with me."

"Ah, I see, your amour has found another. While France supports love, the purpose of my regency is not to search for lost lovers."

"No, Sire, you misunderstand, she has not fled from me. She has been taken. Kidnapped."

"You have received notice of ransom then?" the king inquired kindly.

"Your Highness, I beg your indulgence. This is a long and complex situation," Ryan said, struggling to find the words to obtain the king's aid.

Not fully rested, Claret felt cramped and stretched to ease her tired muscles. What? She was unable to move. A net closed around her tightly.

No! *I did not simply dream I was captured, I am a captive.* The net pulled so snug she was unable to see her jailer. But, she could smell him, he of the foul flesh. *I should have been more vigilant when I first caught wind of him.*

She knew the giant would be more watchful this time, as he was sure to have received a tongue lashing from his sister for his previous failure. Yet, Claret knew the simplistic sense of wrong and right Morfran possessed. He could easily be moved to pity. And, she would play on that weakness to affect her escape. Softly, she moaned and squeezed her eyes to make them tear.

The giant rose from the hollow log by the gatehouse when he heard her cry.

"What's the matter, tiny one? I did not mean to hurt you," he said, cradling the netted Claret in his massive palm. He peered at her, turning his head this way and that, his tightly clustered features giving him a comic appearance.

Claret began to shudder. The icy water in the moat had given her a chill. Now her moans were genuine. Her exertions weakened her and now she was, in fact, ill.

Morfran felt his chest tighten. He could see the wee one was in grave danger. Ninaway would have his hide if the tiny fox died.

Claret's body went limp, and Morfran went to remove the net. But the mesh of the net was strong and it cut her ear. The blood fell on the white fur of her muzzle. Morfran saw the red and panicked. Carefully, he cut the remainder of the net from her body.

Claret saw her chance. This was as she'd planned. Have him take pity, remove the net, escape. However, she had not the strength to flee. She lay cold, wet, shivering, helpless in the palm of his hand.

Morfran took her paw delicately between his thumb and forefinger, lifted the paw, then let it drop.

Even simple-minded Morfran knew she was sick. And, if she died from her illness, his sister would hold him accountable. He'd watched Ninaway tend her with the mint cloths. Scanning about the gatehouse, he found some leaves. He pulled a segment from his tunic, dipped it in the moat, and rubbed it in the plant. The pungent odor revived Claret slightly. By some miracle, Ryan was able to convince the king of his need for aid. His mention of the Druids gave his circumstance the urgency required.

The king dispatched five bowmen to search with Ryan. The men were instructed to bring back an unusually small red fox. Ryan felt she would most likely be in her fox guise. As an animal, she would have greater ability to flee her captor. Ryan and the bowmen set out across the drawbridge. The men were to scour the lands surrounding the castle. Atop Claret's horse, Moonshine, Ryan, and Aqulia rode forth. H

His heart thundered against his rib cage, hoping against hope his woman was safe. He could not bear the pain of temporary separation and if the separation were to be permanent, there would be no vessel great enough to contain his grief.

Ryan took the eagle from his shoulder to his forearm and spoke gently to her. "Aqulia, go and search. Seek out every river and valley until you find her," Ryan directed, his faith in the hoped-for miracle growing weaker with each passing minute.

Aqulia, soaring in ever widening circles, scanned the ground with her keen eyes. There, on the grass at the edge of the gatehouse, lay her hunting companion. She dove low to confirm that it was, in fact, Claret. When certain it was Claret, the eagle returned to Ryan's forearm.

"Back so soon?" he asked, his heart in his throat.

"Do you tire or, have you found her?"

Ryan had ridden quite a distance from the moat and had not bothered to look back. Aqulia flew back in the direction of the castle. Turning his horse, Ryan, too, headed back the way he'd come. This was the miracle for which he'd hoped and prayed. Aqulia had found her. *Oh, please, let her be well and free of injury.*

He pressed his knees into the horse's sides, urging him forward. Each beat of the animal's hooves drew him closer and closer.

Nearly to the gatehouse, his eyes widened. He froze in terror. A bowman was drawing a bead on the tiny fox.

Morfran, too, had sighted the bowman and threw his arm in front of Claret to protect her. Ryan cried out, his words outdistanced by the arrow that sank in Morfran's arm. Ninaway projected to every hill and vale, every cave and wood. The Druid's pair was nowhere to be found. Exhausted from her extensive search, Ninaway sank onto the large bed.

"Merlin," she said tiredly, "I cannot find them. In all of Wales, there is not a single trace."

Olyn, who had been standing nearby, approached the bed.

"Merlin, could they have crossed the channel? Would they risk the undercurrents?"

"Olyn, the boy is young, not foolhardy. He would not chance crossing on horseback, but it is a strong possibility he would engage a ferry." Ninaway looked up wearily.

"Is the boy strong enough to protect Claret? She is tiny and could easily succumb to sickness, if she is not properly cared for."

Softly, Ninaway began to weep. Her shoulders shuddered with each sob. Merlin gathered her in his arms and held her against his chest. She buried her head in his shoulder and hiccupped. Unable to control the spasms, she wept anew. Merlin patted her back gently and bid her to relax.

Gathering her inner strength, she calmed herself and the hiccups ceased. She pushed herself away from Merlin and looked kindly into his eyes.

"I'm so sorry I treated you in such an uncaring manner. I now realize what a folly it was. I missed my chance for true happiness by believing possession was love. You cannot fathom the depths of my despair."

"Let us not waste time on what might have been. We will simply use the present to better advantage," Merlin said, again embracing her.

No sooner was she within his arms, than she cried out in pain. Quickly, he released her.

"Have I hurt you, Ninaway? What's wrong?"

"No, no." She struggled to catch her breath.

"I'm not injured, it's my brother."

"You can feel your brother's pain? How can this be so?" Olyn queried. Merlin smiled. "Ah, my love, you remember the old ways."

Tears fell softly down her cheeks.

"I use the old ways, Olyn, as I am not skilled in the new ways. I was too absorbed in my possessions to learn." Merlin comforted her, joining her on the bed and taking her hands in his own.

"Tell me, Ninaway, did you use the Crystal of Observance to see what Morfran sees as well as what he feels?" Numbly, she nodded.

"The pain in my arm is so severe it could only be a deep wound from a sword or an arrow." She looked down on her arm. A narrow trickle of blood traced a delicate path to her hand. Never before had she experienced compassion, the need to assuage another's pain. Her brother was injured and she, too, felt the sting. Not only did she feel the pain in her arm, her heart was pierced as well.

"Morfran, brother, do you hear me?" The giant looked around. Like before, there was no one, save him and the fox. He took the crystal from his neck and held it high in the air.

"Do you see me, sister? My arm is hurt."

"I see you, Morfran. Do not fear. I will tend your wound. How fares the fox?" Ninaway asked carefully. She was newly concerned for her brother and did not wish to offend his tender sensibilities.

"How can you tend me? I am in France, sister. I cannot walk home," he responded, fear evident in his voice.

"Don't trouble yourself. I shall come to you. Stay where you are. Do not leave and keep the fox with you."

"Yes, sister, but will you be quick? How can you come to me in time? I don't want to bleed to death and the fox is really sick." With those words, Ninaway knew her brother was genuinely concerned for the fox's welfare.

"Rest easy, Morfran. Merlin, Olyn and I will come to you in the Travel Tunnel. It moves very swiftly," Ninaway said, confident the wizards would assist her.

The giant nodded and sat down on the hollow log to await his sister and the sorcerers.

He looked over the meadow and saw a man on horseback rapidly approaching. The man was shouting at another man who was on foot.

"You fool, the fox must be alive. You are to find her, not murder her."

"Foreigner, when the king tells me to get an animal, the assumption is he wants its pelt, not its company," the man screamed at the rider.

"Be gone, you are of no further use."

Morfran recognized the horse before he sighted the rider. It was the dappled, white horse the lady had ridden. The very same lady he now held in his hand.

Ryan watched closely as the giant tenderly stoked Claret's fur with a single finger. He dare not demand Morfran turn over the fox, as at any given moment the simpleton could undergo drastic changes and become a danger to her. But at this time Morfran was tenderly caring for Claret and she was safe in the giant's hands. Carefully, he approached the log. Morfran looked up.

"You cannot have her. Ninaway will make her well."

Warily, Ryan said, "Could I please hold her? I will do nothing to harm her."

"I know you love her, but you do not keep watch over her. You don't care for her safety." Morfran clutched her closer to his chest. "Ninaway wants her. She will see the fox is always safe."

Damned if he isn't right, Ryan realized. *I should have made certain she was in no danger before I set the panels with Phillipe.*

"Don't you come any closer, young prince. My sister is coming to heal me and the fox."

"Your sister is coming here to France? To heal you? I know your sister, Morfran. She is in Wales and has no way to get to you."

"Yes, she is too coming. She's a witch, you know, and the wizards are with her."

"The wizards? Merlin and Olyn?" Somehow Ryan felt certain Morfran was not capable of duplicity. The giant spoke simply and stated only the facts. "Did she say how they were coming to your aid?"

"Yes. She said she was coming in a tunnel. And, she will."

"Still it is a long way from here to Wales. Are you certain she can come so far?"

"Yes. She promised. My Ninaway said she will be here quickly. She will not leave me here to bleed to death."

Ryan looked at the clotting wound. "The arrow struck no vital organs. I am certain you will not perish."

Morfran looked at his arm, put his finger into his mouth, then tentatively touched the injury. "I guess it's not too bad. It's got a scab. See," he said, holding his arm so Ryan would have a better view.

"You are very brave, Morfran. To take an arrow intended for another takes great courage."

Morfran puffed with pride. "You will tell my sister how I saved the fox?"

"Gladly, sir. You are a man of great valor."

Morfran appeared to bask in Ryan's lavish praise. Ryan turned his head. He'd heard something. Louder and louder, like the beat of the hooves of ten thousand horses.

Morfran cupped his ear with his huge hand. The sound grew louder still.

Could this be the sound of the Travel Tunnel? Ryan had never heard the tunnel from the outside. From within the swirling mass, he recalled no sound.

Morfran initially appeared intrigued, but as the tunnel came near, his features contorted in fear.

"Fear not, Morfran, this is how your sister comes to us," Ryan answered, confident Merlin, at least, would soon appear before them.

"Are you certain, Prince? I wish nothing to harm the tiny fox."

As Ryan nodded, the tunnel quieted. There, on the grassy slope of the moat, stood Merlin, Olyn, and Ninaway.

Eagerly Morfran ran to his sister, clutching Claret to his breast. "She's here. I told you she would come for me," he said, glancing back at Ryan.

Within the giant's grasp, Claret moaned. All thought of fame and notoriety fled Ryan's mind. All that was important was Claret, the fox woman who was the very reason for his existence. Celebrity without her was as dust in his mouth.

"Please, Morfran, let me take her to Merlin," Ryan begged.

"No. Ninaway is the greatest healer in the known worlds. She will tend her." Morfran thrust the sickened fox into Ninaway's arms.

"The boy is right," Ninaway said, tenderly holding the fox. "I will help to cure her, but Merlin will direct me."

"And you agree to this?" Ryan asked the wizard incredulously, sensing Ninaway had other designs on the tiny fox.

Merlin moved to Ninaway's side, placing his arm about her shoulders, then carefully examined the fox with his other hand. "There seems to be no injury or broken skin. She suffers from an illness. Her fever is very high. We must get her some foxmoor." The wizard turned to Ryan. "You must have some with you. Where is it?"

Frightened, Ryan stammered, "I-I have only enough for a single transformation. Claret took most of it when she decided to hunt the muskrats on her own."

"She must have taken some to return to her woman form," Merlin replied, his eyes drawn to ominous slits. "Search," he demanded.

Ryan looked among the drawbridge gearings and found her empty pouch. "Merlin, sir?" he said reluctantly, "I've found her pouch, but it is empty."

Morfran looked on, eager to help his newfound friend. "I used it to soak the cloths, like Ninaway did."

"Fool," she cried out. "You used it the wrong way."

"Ninaway," Merlin chided, pressing her close to his side.

At once, she nodded contritely. "I'm sorry, brother. You would not have known."

Looking up at Merlin, she said, "We have no other choice. The weed cannot be found on French soil. We must return at once to Wales."

Chapter Sixteen

Once in the tunnel, the moments passed so rapidly Ryan was not certain time had passed, until he stepped out of the tunnel outside of the invisible tent in Wales. Back and forth, Ryan paced, wearing a path in front of Ninaway's tent. The three wizards were attending Claret. They only allowed Morfran to observe as his sister cleansed and bound his wound.

Ryan ran to Morfran as he emerged from the tent. The giant rubbed his arm and smiled at Ryan.

"Morfran, is she safe? Can I please see her now?"

"You cannot see her. Ninaway said."

"Then why are you smiling? Is she still in danger?"

Morfran sobered somewhat and said, "She needs rest and foxmoor. Ninaway said I was brave and helped save the country. Me. I saved the country."

Anger raged in Ryan's breast. He should have been the one to save her. It was, after all, his duty. D*uty? I care not for duty. Oh, God, make me see the right of it.* Nervously, he raked his hand through his hair, as if the furrows created, channeled strength to her. Would that willing it would make it so. He'd taken Claret far from her homeland, where the source of her power and strength resided. The trust was broken.

She had every right to expect his protection. And, he'd let her down. Failed. Now he must pay the price. Did one dare implore the Druids? Those very beings he'd defied. Would they help or cast him and his wishes aside, just as he'd cast aside their directive?

Was he even worthy of the love he knew she held for him? To never again lie within her arms and feel the desire that was above all other needs. Truly, his childhood dream of being a renowned falconer was as nothing compared to the joy he'd found with the tiny fox woman. He'd been taken by surprise by the depth of his feelings. This was a gift from the gods. A gift he wasn't willing to relinquish.

Hesitating moments only, he reached for the flap of Ninaway's tent, nearly colliding with the emerging Olyn.

"Olyn," he exclaimed. "How does she fare? Please, tell me through some use of your magic she will survive."

"It will take more than my magic alone, more, even than Merlin's. This will take the influence of the Druids, Ryan. You must persuade them by agreeing to adhere to their tenets."

Again, he raked his fingers through his hair then wiped them across his brow. "Her life is more dear than my own. I will do as the Druids direct. Anything they require. Please tell them, Olyn, so that my love might be safe and well."

The wizard wrapped his arm about the young man's shoulders. "Ryan, you've made the right decision. Merlin and I shall inform the Druids. Merlin," Olyn called, "young Ryan will agree to keep the Druids wishes. Is that not splendid news? Surely, it can only help her."

"Your current reason in the face of so much folly may have come too late."

Once could almost see the heart within the chest of the young falconer rent in two. His anguish was palpable. "By all that's sacred, in all the known worlds, I shall not lose her now," he said, shaking his fist at the darkening sky.

Slowly, Claret's lashes fluttered as she opened her eyes ever so slightly. The room was swimming in circles. She closed her eyes and forced down the rising tide of nausea.

Outside, she heard Ryan's voice at one with the rumbling thunder. The heavy rain pelted against the canvas tent. Ninaway scurried about lighting lamps to push away the impending gloom.

Ryan and Morfran entered, dripping water on the once luxurious carpet. The rug, like all the other tent appointments was dirty and discarded. Ryan was aware of the value of the rug and moved the giant aside that he might save the carpet for future use.

"I've told Olyn I will do whatever is necessary. My life without her would be a fate worse than any imprisonment. If I must rule to save her, I have no other option. I shall do as the Druids decree."

Claret fully opened her eyes and looked up at Ninaway. "Are all men so easily ensnared by love?"

Ninaway smiled and glanced at the senior wizard. "They are when the love is true, my dear. Now you must rest in order to regain your strength."

Ryan neared the bedside as Ninaway rose to yield her place to him. The young falconer sat and wrung out a fresh mint cloth. Gently, he mopped her brow. Many hours he sat and tenderly wiped the fevered sweat from her forehead.

Gratefully, she sighed. She was loved. Never having experienced mother love as a child, the emotion nearly overwhelmed her.

Minute after minute, the hours slipped into endless days. Ryan stayed at her bedside marveling at his own fortune to have found her and praying the fates would continue to keep her at his side. Never ceasing his ministrations, he remained steadfast. No power on earth or in the heavens could entice him to leave her side. He would protect her. It was his duty. A responsibility he would not shirk.

Olyn came upon the pair and softly touched Ryan's shoulder. Startled, Ryan looked up quickly.

"Olyn, have you another potion I can treat her with?"

"Do not fear, Ryan, it will take time, but she will recover."

"Can you promise me that? Is it a certainty?"

"She will recover, Ryan. It simply takes time. You must be patient."

"Patience is not something I can count as a virtue."

"I am well aware of your eagerness in all things. However, this time you have no alternative. You must wait until the foxmoor can do its work. Come," the wizard said, leading him from the tent, "You should go and wash and find something to eat."

"If you're certain, Olyn. It's been several days, and even I am growing weary of the stench I emit."

Olyn smiled wisely, nodded, and said, "A sweet smell might do more to rouse her than the odor you presently carry."

Playfully, Ryan tapped the old wizard on the shoulder. Olyn responded by ruffling the young man's hair.

As Ryan left, Merlin emerged from the tent. "She wakes and is fever-free," the wizard declared. "Come and see her, Olyn. It seems she is even more beautiful than before. The Druids are wise in their selection. Where is the falconer?"

"Merlin, he's not left her side for nearly two days. He goes to bathe and eat."

"Very well, while she sleeps let us inform the Druids of Ryan's compliance."

Both Merlin and Olyn felt far less trepidation facing the ancient Druids on this occasion. The Travel Tunnel whisked them swiftly to the place without walls wherein the Druids held court.

Merlin addressed the august body, speaking loudly, as he was proud to impart the news Ryan would comply.

"Sires, much has transpired since we last spoke. Young Ryan has agreed to adhere to your tenets, and will serve as the King of Wales."

"And, what of the fox woman? Will she serve beside him?"

"The Ordination covers them as a pair. One without the other is of no value." Merlin stepped back meekly. He had not considered Claret might object.

He should have thought the matter through completely, before seeking the company of the Druids. Olyn pulled at his sleeve.

"Come, Merlin, we must return and make certain all the requirements of the Ordination are met." Olyn seemed anxious to be out of the presence of the all-powerful ruling body of the Druids.

"Olyn, you are quite right. I should have given the matter more careful consideration. Perhaps I am falling fool to Ninaway's new enchantment." Olyn smiled widely.

"I am certain that is not the case. The woman truly loves you. You are the most fortunate of men."

"Again, old friend, you are right. My failures are of my own making. There is no other being that deserves the blame." Olyn shook his head and laughed.

"You always look for the gloom in matters. Search for the light. Only there will you find the true answers."

Ninaway smiled tenderly at her charge. She reached down to draw the red gold curls from the face of the sleeping Claret. The touch, though gentle, wakened the girl.

"Ninaway, thank you for your healing skills. Once again you have saved me."

The witch smiled widely. "It's you who should be thanked. Your presence in my life has changed who I am. It's made me a better person."

Claret grinned, her green eyes twinkling with glee. It seemed ages had passed since she'd felt this fit, strong and eager to resume her life as a fox and a hunter. She looked about the tent and noted the giant sitting in a corner.

Claret sniffed the air. Smells of cooked food filled the tent. Though not fond of cooked meat, her hunger was so great she cared not.

The giant, too, appeared tantalized by the cooking odors. He rose from his stool in the corner of the tent and approached his sister.

"What are you doing, sister? I've never seen you make food before."

"True," Ninaway responded, "Tis a not-often-used skill, but, in fact, I am quite an accomplished cook."

"You must be." Morfran nodded.

"It smells wonderful. When do we eat?"

Carefully stirring the pot, the sorceress looked kindly upon her brother. "First, we must feed our charge. She's not eaten for several days and needs to rebuild her strength."

The giant approached the pot holding a tiny bowl in the palm of his hand. "Morfran," his sister admonished, "You must wash before you eat."

The giant looked at her, pure wonder in his eyes.

"Why?"

"Because you must. You don't want to get sick do you?"

"Washing won't keep you well," he said, pointing at Claret.

"She's always washing and she got sick."

"Nevertheless, before you eat, you must wash."

Setting down the tiny bowl, the giant threw his hands up in the air and skulked from the tent. "Wash? What good is it? I washed last winter and it was nearly the death of me," he said as he retreated.

Claret laughed as Ninaway shook her head.

"Ninaway," Claret inquired, "Is the giant truly your brother?"

"Yes, he is, but it's only recently I've appreciated the relationship." Claret sniffed.

"He seems gentle enough even though he is very big. He may mean well, but he tastes awful."

Ninaway wrinkled her brow. "Whatever do you mean? Have you actually tasted him?"

Claret was well aware she'd caught the sorceress off guard. "I bit him, when he captured me," she said, offhandedly.

Ninaway clapped her hand over her mouth, stifling a laugh.

Claret became aware that, as the giant had changed and the witch had altered her demeanor, so, too, should she renounce being a thief. "Ninaway, so many times you've come to my aid. Had you not swept me from the stream or saved me when I was ill, I would never have known love. Thank you."

"My child, I, too, have learned the value of love. And, it was you who taught me to value people above possessions."

"I'm sorry," Claret said. "I stole things from you when I was a fox. I would like to return them."

"Claret, the trinkets are of negligible worth. In fact, I left them about to amuse you. Sometimes I would watch you purloin them, taking them in your mouth then hiding them beneath the bed. The letters, however, I would truly love to have them back."

"Why are they so important? I watched you read them over and over. Surely you must know them by heart?"

"Oh, yes, I know each and every word. Though many are beyond my comprehension."

Puzzled, Claret pressed the witch further. "If you cannot understand, how do you know the words?"

"When he wrote them, he would read them to me and I listened very carefully and committed each word to memory. I practice my art slowly. The spell book is illustrated and I can easily follow."

Claret knitted her brow trying to decipher this strange course of events. "If you know the words and can use the spell book, why do you need the letters?"

"For several reasons. First," she said with a smile, "Is because the man I love wrote them. Secondly, they are my learning tools."

"Merlin wrote them?" Claret responded.

"That I understand. But why do they become instructional?"

Ninaway closed her eyes and spoke very softly. "I am trying to become the woman a wonderful man like Merlin deserves."

"So you are learning to read to impress your lover?"

Ninaway blushed like a shy child presented to a stranger then turned back to her previous task.

Claret moved about the massive bed and took a packet of letters from beneath the edge of the mattress.

"Ninaway, here are your letters. I kept them carefully as I knew you prized them. I was going to use them against you, but now find you to be an ally, not a foe."

The witch put her head in her hands and wept. When she could control the tears, she reached out, took the extended packet, and pressed it to her breast.

At that moment Morfran returned, soaking wet from head to toe. "What have you done, brother? I told you to bathe, not swim."

The simple-minded man shrugged his shoulders and replied, "No matter. Swim or wash, you get wet."

Resigned this would be the only concession to cleanliness, Ninaway bid him bring her the bowl for Claret.

Happily, the giant proffered the tiny vessel along with another four times its size. He extended the hand with the larger bowl first.

Ninaway sighed. "Morfran, we must feed the lady first, then you shall have your fill."

Still tired, but refreshed, Ryan headed back to the witch's tent. As he'd only eaten a piece of bread, the odors of Ninaway's cooking drew him. Reaching to the bough that served as an entrance, Ryan looked in the enclosure. He was certain no changes had been made yet it was somehow different. There was no longer the sense of impending doom. The air felt lighter, almost festive. He searched in the dim light for the cause of his elation. There, in the center of the bed, sat Claret. Sitting up and eating.

Ryan had never thought such a simple act could give him so much pleasure. His heart beat with such a force he was certain the earth shook beneath his feet.

Ninaway turned and smiled. "Come in, Ryan, join us. I've made a stew, and there is plenty for all of us."

Morfran pouted. "You said I could have my fill after she ate," he said, pointing to Claret.

"Morfran, there is enough. You shall not be deprived." She laughed as the giant rose and rushed to the serving pot before Ryan even found a bowl.

Ryan's eyes glistened with tears of joy as he moved to the edge of the bed. He'd never before realized the depth of his feelings for the tiny fox woman. The desire for her love and companionship was greater than any other he'd experienced. Truly, without her, his life was as nothing.

Ninaway placed a bowl in his hand, and Ryan looked at it only briefly, before setting it aside. His hunger was not for food.

Morfran quickly devoured all that was in his bowl and greedily reached for Ryan's. His sister reached out to restrain him, but Ryan nodded and handed the bowl to the giant.

Quickly, the simple-minded man looked from Ninaway to Ryan and back to confirm he could have Ryan's portion.

Ryan smiled. "Take it, friend. My present need is not for mere nourishment."

Ninaway nodded, and took her brother's hand to lead him from the tent. "Wait," the giant said, "If he doesn't want food, maybe she doesn't either." He reached across the bed for Claret's bowl.

Claret grinned, her eyes brimming with mischief. She extended the bowl, then quickly withdrew it, and drained the remaining stew from it.

"That's not fair. It's not nice to tempt folks," Morfran whined.

Ninaway and Morfran slipped from the tent. Ryan paid little heed to their leaving. Consumed by his desire, Ryan tried to moisten his lips in prelude to her kiss. His throat constricted as lust fused his body with fluids. Tenderly, he leaned across the big bed to trace her jaw with the back of his hand. She reached up and held his hand. So gently, did she touch him, yet the sensation caused him to shudder. He'd never known such a slight touch to have a force, such as that he experienced as she drew his hand to her breast. Her skin felt so soft, yet he could feel the strength in the tiny face. This was the woman destiny choose for him. He felt an indescribable pride for her beauty, intelligence, and skill. His belief in her abilities exceeded his faith in his own. Together, they were the finest hunting team England, or any other land, had ever known.

However, at this moment he was not thinking of hunting. His prey lay before him on the witch's bed. Her red-gold curls drew him to her like a moth to a flame. Moving close to her, his body molded to accommodate hers.

"Claret," he said, murmuring her name into the curve of her neck as her body, taunt as a bowstring, strained to meet his, the soft curves of her slender body molded to the hardened muscle of his.

Her softness was as eider down, and he felt himself drowning within her velvet folds. Nowhere else on this world nor on any other had any man known such joy. He felt a completeness he'd never believed a man could possess.

Though she'd never mated as a fox, Claret was certain man's way was definitely preferable. To see the face of a lover and watch his expression was surely a gift from the gods. Feeling his power over her tiny body excited her to desire more. She sniffed in Ryan's scent, fresh from his bath, and it was good. Her own smell was simply of mint. She preferred the scent of the foxmoor. However, that scent could only be released by rolling in the herb. It would be some time until she was able to frolic on the meadow and press that odor into her fur. *Will I retain the scent when I turn woman, or will it not cling to my skin as it does my fur?*

The questions filled her mind as her mate filled her. This was all that mattered now. The time for questions would come later, once their lust for one another was satisfied. This time.

Chapter Seventeen

With each passing day, Claret found that her strength increased, as did the desire to hunt. She needed to run free on the high meadow and find food more to her liking than what Ninaway prepared. Ninaway had done her best to provide her with nourishing and rejuvenating food, but it lacked the flavor of the fresh kill. Too, she wanted to renew her hunts with Aqulia. It had been far too long since they'd ferreted out rodents. Then guilt stabbed at her heart. She'd never even inquired after the eagle's well-being.

For the moment, she was alone in the grand tent. Ninaway was off securing herbs with her brother, and Ryan was seeking the wizards. Feeling strong enough to venture from the bed, Claret fairly leapt from the mattress and landed gently on the soft pillows Ninaway placed all about the floor of the tent. As curious a woman as she was as a fox, she decided to explore beneath the huge bed. As the bed was high as well as wide, she had no trouble crawling under it. There she found all manners of bounty, silver balls, scraps of ribbon, a tiny trinket fashioned of gold and letters. Then she remembered why she'd taken the letters. To aid Ryan, yet he no longer needed protection from Ninaway. She was glad she'd returned them to the witch.

Carefully, she crept backwards from beneath the large bed. Only her buttocks protruded from the coverings.

Ryan entered the tent. She heard him laugh as he spied her exit from the bed. "Well, now that's a pretty picture, your bottom wiggling enticingly from across the tent. What if it hadn't been I who entered? Do you tantalize all who enter here?"

"I am not tantalizing. I'm finding more things I once took from Ninaway."

It is time they were returned to her."

"That's considerate of you. Ninaway has changed, and it is only right you treat her with renewed respect. She did save you. That is a matter that cannot be set aside. Ninaway is truly a good witch now."

"Many people change over time. I was once afraid of Aqulia. Now she is a treasured hunting companion. Is she well? I've not seen her in so long."

"She is fine, Claret, though I suspect she would like to see for herself that you are on the mend."

Claret's eyes grew wide. "On the mend? I am as fit as you are. Let's go find her and have a quick hunt."

It was clear she was up to the chase. She showed no signs of weakness. Lovingly, he looked upon her as she tugged at his arm, leading him up the hill overlooking the meadow. Fear and doubt crossed his mind. *If we hunt together, are we violating the Druid Ordination? Will it even matter once they realize I am scarred?*

Claret raced to the clearing where their horses were tethered.

Today Aqulia's weight felt heavy on his forearm, but not nearly as heavy as his decision to follow the tenets of the Druids. *I wish I had listened when my mother told me of the power they wield. Do we dare try to change the directives?*

Looking around, he saw Claret approach on the farm horse, Moonshine, leading his mount, Black. She dropped the reins and his horse stood firm. Gently, she stroked her horse's mane and urged it forward with her knees.

"Claret," he said sadly, "are you certain you are strong enough to hunt? Can you make the change without rolling on the ground? It's damp, and you may catch a chill. I promised the Druids I would look out for you. I really think we ought to wait a day or so."

"You are such a timid mouse. Without risk, there is no life. Come on, live with me." She tossed her curls and urged Moonshine to proceed at an even greater speed.

Ryan mounted and pounded his horse into a full gallop. Closer and closer, they came. Once he was abreast of her, he reached over and took the reins.

Claret's eyes sparkled with a mischief that, as yet, he was not yet fully acquainted. Deftly, she snatched them back and headed for the foxmoor patch. Only a few yards separated them, but it was enough for her to roll in the weed and effect the change.

He watched the transformation and marveled anew at the extent of her skills. *She is so clever. Perhaps she can find a way we can obey the Druids and not have to rule.*

Quickly, she slipped through the grasses and found a vole hole. Signaling Aqulia with a wave of her white-tipped tail, she blocked the entrance of the vermin's home. The animal retreated and exited at the rear of his den. Aqulia grabbed it with a swift clutch of her talons. Though the bird was hungry, the two had learned to share their kills. Aqulia gently laid the dead vole at her paws. Claret took the offering in her teeth and sank back on her haunches to sever the animal into more manageable pieces. She gave the biggest piece back to the eagle.

The duo savored their meal then meticulously washed themselves. Aqulia preened with her large hooked bill, carefully aligning the splines of her feathers while Claret's rough tongue smoothed each individual hair of her fur.

Once their ritual cleansing was completed, the two exchanged glances and raced across the meadow. Aqulia rose high in the air as Claret sped through the grasses. She succeeded in flushing a quail. At once, Aqulia descended on the hapless bird.

Ryan observed the spectacular event, envy clawing at his heart. He, too, wanted to be free. Free to roam the fields, free to hunt and be unfettered by the trappings of royalty.

Just then, Aqulia returned to her master's forearm the quail in her talons. Ryan gently took the kill from her and brushed her breast feathers with the back of his hand, well pleased with the hunter his eagle had become. It was due to his training and the bird's own natural skill. This was his dream, this magnificent eagle, and the woman whose beauty was unrivaled, together forming the hunting party without equal throughout the known worlds.

I cannot give this up. I have worked too hard, for too long, to relinquish it without a thought. Surely, the Druids can understand the value of this team to England and the other lands the Ordination affects. Why cannot they see the wisdom of allowing me to help the country by serving as the hunt master to my uncle as King? Aaron would have been chosen, had I not been born. Why does my birth change the course of a country? I am but a single man unprepared for court and all its trappings. I prefer buckskin to silk, and hunting to prancing around drinking watered wine.

Rayn sat tall and proud gazing at the sun setting over the broad meadow. Aqulia perched on his shoulder. He was certain Claret would soon be at his side.

Only the smallest shafts of sunlight remained and still Claret did not appear. Fear clutched his heart in a vise grip. She was only days from her sick bed. Had he taken too great a risk? Slowly, he dismounted.

The hair on the nape of his neck stood rigid. He could sense something, or perhaps someone? Darkness surrounded him. The sun had disappeared beneath the horizon. Then, without warning, someone's hands covered his eyes.

The faint odor that he'd never smelled on any other woman enveloped him.

"Guess who?" Claret chirped.

Confusion clouded his mind. Should he berate her for scaring him or do what his nature wanted? Gratefully, he turned and swept her up into his arms. "Please do not do that to me again. I cannot bear the pain."

"I hurt you by covering your eyes? What manner of disease is this?"

"No, you did not cause me harm by covering my eyes. The pain is the separation. I need to be with you. When I cannot see you, I fear for your safety."

"But, Ryan, 'tis you who say you must be free. How can you be free if you are shackled to me?"

"The bond between us is not of man's making. I need not be chained to you. I simply need to know you are always with me."

She shook her head, the green eyes clouded with the paradox. "Then we must hunt again. On the hunt we both have freedom and we are together."

Ryan closed his eyes and breathed deeply. "Claret, I promised the wizards I would do as the Druids direct, if they would spare you."

"Why did you make such a bargain? You knew the foxmoor would cure me. You sold yourself too cheaply."

"Perhaps, but the Druids are all powerful. Had they not secured my vow, you would have died," he said, resigned.

"Then we must convince them it would be folly to have a reluctant ruler. Surely they would know a good ruler must enjoy the task."

"Claret, don't toy with me. These are all-powerful beings. Their directives cannot be set aside, simply because we dislike the task set before us. They could do us and our homelands grave harm."

"No one shall harm you while Aqulia and I draw breath. We can protect you," she said, entwining her arms about his neck and running her tiny pink tongue over his lips.

Ryan steeled himself against her seductive onslaught, but all for naught. Unable to resist, he slowly submitted to her enticement. What frightened him more than the force of the Druids was the danger to Claret.

But, here and now, the only danger was his own desire gnawing at him like a hungry wolf. He was afraid the force of his uncontrollable lust would damage her tiny body. The strength was his, the delicacy hers. Yet, he knew deep within his heart her strength could surpass his own. The Druids had chosen them both. One could not supplant the other.

His eyes heavy lidded with sensuality, he held her gently in his arms as they both fell back on the soft grass of the meadow. He pushed aside her copper curls, tucking one errant coil behind her ear. Running his hand slowly over her face, tracing down her neck then cupping her breast, he sighed. *Whatever she desires from me, she shall have. I can deny her nothing. All her dreams are my dreams, whatever she wishes, I shall grant.* His head swam with the contradictions. *Which master shall I serve? I love her beyond infinity.* Her kisses melted his reason. Nothing mattered, save the lovely woman before him. Swiftly he removed his chausses and tore the simple shift from her body. He needed to feel her skin against his own, the fiery flesh that seared his soul. The soul not charred with the promise the Druids extracted. But, even this, mattered not. Again and again, his mouth sought her breast, tenderly suckling the nipple. His hands glided over her body, so beautiful laying there on the meadow. Slowly, he entered her. Then soon became lost within the confines of their lust.

Unbeknownst to him, the meadow was home to other eyes as well.

Merlin, too, was on the high grassy slope above Ninaway's tent. Though Merlin saw nothing wrong in their coupling, their words disturbed him greatly. Petition the Druids to find another to rule the lands they had been chosen to rule? How dare they? Their simple desires were as dust to the Druids. They must comply. They will comply.

Merlin ranted and railed against the clear blue sky.

Without notice, the heavens opened and rain poured down with such a force it created a river in the deep valley between the high meadow and the slope by the tent. Swiftly, it rushed through, taking all in its path with it, down through the gully to the nearby stream. It was clear the pair heard the onslaught of the rushing water. They stood up and quickly dressed themselves. Thinking they were unseen, they showed no modesty.

"They shall be the death of me, I fear," Merlin said as he frantically waved his staff at the heavens. "Stop, stop, I say. You must make them obey, but if they drown they will most certainly not comply."

Merlin had never felt such betrayal. The boy had given his word and the lass had been spared. Now he must live up to his bargain. At the waters receded, the ancient sorcerer waded across the newly formed river, using his staff to secure his footing. When he reached the other side, the pair was completely clothed and extended him welcome.

"Hello there, Merlin," Ryan said. "Did you see the water near engulf us? We are fortunate we did not drown."

"Fortunate? You fools. You have no comprehension of the fortune that has befallen you. The Druids' gift is beyond measure," he shrieked. So angered, the venom spewed from his mouth like foam from a rabid dog.

Within the tent, Olyn felt the ground shake. He'd felt this only once before and knew it was Merlin's doing. Swiftly, he rushed outside, calling breathlessly to the senior wizard.

"Merlin, Merlin, you must hold your rage."

The Wizard of the Third Realm to the High King Arthur spun about and glared at the interloper. "And by what right do you chastise me? You have been broken of your powers once. Shall I strip you of them entirely? Be gone, you have no rights in this conversation."

"Merlin," he gently chided, "A conversation is not usually held at the peak of one's voice. Calm yourself. If you are not careful, you could very well bring the wrath of the Druids down upon yourself."

"So," the wizard screamed, "It matters not. If the boy doesn't honor his vow, all the worlds will pass away. Then I shall happily pass with them."

Ryan drew near the two, holding Claret, his arm about her shoulders. "We do not choose willingly to defy the Druids. It is simply our nature demands that we be free."

Olyn nodded, shaking his head up and down as if it were on a child's rag doll. "I understand, Ryan, I truly do. But, you must honor your vow. Else, your freedom is all you will have. No fame as a falconer, and no Claret to share it with you."

"How?" Ryan asked, his eyes brimming with unshed tears. "I cannot leave her, and she will not follow me as a queen. Only as a hunter."

Merlin bore down on the pair. "How do you know this to be true? Did you ask her plain and tell her she would be a queen, to help govern her homeland, and protect it from rampage? Or did you assume she would accept no other life?"

Ryan stumbled backward. He had not actually put the question to her in quite this manner. "I ... No, sir, I haven't. But have you forgotten she is part animal? Foxes need to be free."

Claret stepped from Ryan's hold. "Why must I be either one or the other? Does Ryan's mother still roam the fields of Ireland as she wishes? Or is she kept in a cage within the castle walls, so no one will know of her animal existence?"

Olyn felt his heart swell with pride. This chosen one of the Druids was of the same mettle as the first. "My child, you are quite right. A compromise can be struck."

Chapter Eighteen

"Ninaway," the giant cried, "Did you do that?"

"No, Morfran," she replied calmly. "Not my doing, but most certainly the work of a sorcerer." Deep within her heart, she knew not only was it the work of magic, but also that Merlin was wildly enraged. Her feet and legs still felt the tingle from the violent shaking of the earth.

Carefully, she and Morfran approached the tent, where the flap had been thrown open, exposing the contents to anyone who might pass by. Merlin knew the flap was to remain sealed, as did Claret. Why would either leave her home thus exposed?

At the far edge of the meadow, the voices of Merlin and Ryan shook the air.

"Merlin, surely you can understand. Your life, too, has been altered by love. Can anything less satisfy me?"

The wizard glowered at the young man.

"I am not bound by oath or Ordination. You are."

"Ryan," the wizard yelled.

"By your vow she was spared. Your life for hers."

Ninaway approached the shouting pair, her hands in the air. "Please, you must stop this. Some arrangement can be made to accommodate all."

Merlin looked at the woman who had changed so much and wondered at her wisdom. "Perhaps you are right. Have you any suggestions?"

Claret, angered by the interchange between the sorcerer and Ryan, said, "It matters not how plans can be altered to satisfy the Druids or anyone else. Even if Ryan gives up his freedom, I shall not. There is a reason I have the ability to change form and until it is clear to me, I remain unfettered. Do what you will. I am free."

Olyn shook his head, then turned his attention back to the others. Ninaway was talking softly to the wizard and his countenance seemed to soften. "Merlin, you of all wizards, should know anger only embroils the issue. You must look at all the possibilities."

Ryan stood silent, unable to speak. Olyn's eyes met his as they both realized Claret was missing, gone without a trace.

Only a single pair of eyes watched her exit. As Ryan approached her and extended his forearm, she flew, not to him, but high and away. Aqulia circled once then landed on a big stump near the edge of the tent. Ryan again approached her. She ruffled her feathers and turned away from him.

"The damned bird knows where she is. Go and find her and bring her back," Ryan begged.

Olyn looked at the bird that had once considered Claret a meal and realized a bond had been forged between the two. "Ryan, Aquila is not going to assist you. We must find her on our own."

Merlin looked up to see the pair departing and said, "Where are you going? We have plans that must be made."

"We go to find Claret. She is gone," Ryan said, the catch in his voice clearly indicating his fear that Claret might be lost forever.

"Gone? Where would she go? Doesn't she understand the power of the Druids?" Merlin retorted.

Ninaway nodded knowingly. "Not only does she not understand, she cares not."

Olyn smiled wryly and asked, "Merlin, do you remember how we tempted Kit? Perhaps we can do the same to Claret. Ryan, she does like sweets, doesn't she?"

"That is the only prepared food she does like. Honey on biscuits is a particular favorite."

Olyn gave a soft smile, remembering another so like Claret who had the same weakness. "Very well, we will tempt her with her treasured treat."

The three returned to Ninaway's tent wherein they found the giant eating biscuits.

"Morfran, do not eat all of those. I need them to find the fox woman."

"Where'd she go?" he asked, crumbs dropping down the front of his tunic.

Ninaway took the remaining biscuits from her brother, looked to the shelf of her cooking materials, and extracted a pot of honey, ignoring his question.

"But we don't know how far she's gone. Can she even smell it so far away?" Ryan asked, convinced the plan would fail.

Olyn placed a comforting hand on his shoulder. "I am certain Claret's nose is as keen as your mother's, and she always found the biscuits. Claret will do the same."

Merlin smiled confidently. "Olyn is right. She will come for the biscuits."

So quietly had she slipped away, Claret felt certain no one even noticed. She hurried across the broad meadow to the foxmoor patch. She inhaled deeply, drawing the scent down into her lungs. A scent so comforting, she felt what she had chosen was the right path. Dropping to the ground, tearing her clothes from her body, she gratefully rolled in the fragrant weed. At once, the transformation took place. She marveled at how quickly the change was effected.

In her fox guise, she felt safe and free. No one to tell her what was expected of her. Yet, there also was no one to care. Had she bargained too cheaply? Was the freedom enough to sustain her throughout her solitary life? She was not certain. A single tear slipped from her eye down on her snout. Forcing herself not to dwell on what she would never have, she lifted her head and set out in search of food.

Though not really hungry, she felt she should hunt. Crouching low in the grasses, she sniffed the morning air. It wasn't her favorite game, but it was something she savored as much as voles. Biscuits with honey? Who would make biscuits out here?

She walked in the direction of the tempting odor, carefully hiding in the tall grasses. The scent was stronger now. Slyly, she slipped into the clearing near Ninaway's tent. There, on a clean linen cloth, sat the enticing biscuits. She leaned as far as she could into the clearing without exposing herself completely.

Suddenly, a loud flap of wings broke the silence. Aqulia swooped down and plucked the biscuit from the cloth. Confusion clouded Claret's mind. She and Aqulia had learned to share kills. Why would the bird suddenly steal from her? At once, the clearing filled with people; Ryan yelling at the eagle, Morfran laughing along with his sister. Merlin and Olyn stood dumbfounded. The eagle had made fools of them all.

That explains Aqulia's petty thievery. Relieved her companion had not turned against her, Claret retreated further into the high brush.

She watched the eagle soar high into the air then swoop down to an area the pair used as a retreat. Hurrying through the tall reeds, Claret quickly joined her hunting companion.

Aqulia sat on the ground, one talon covering the pilfered biscuit. As Claret entered the small clearing, Aqulia lowered her head and pushed the biscuit toward the fox's paw.

Gratefully, Claret broke the biscuit and pushed the larger portion back to the eagle. The eagle reached out, took her piece, and broke it with her sharp, hooked beak.

Claret's keen ears pricked up at the sound of footsteps moving swiftly through the grass. They were close, and growing closer still. Aqulia raised high in the air and headed out to sea. Claret followed the eagle's direction and headed for the shore. Faster and faster she ran, trying to outdistance the footfalls of those giving chase.

Near a mound of debris sat Morfran. His feet and legs seemed to be missing. What manner of magic is this? Claret wondered.

Drawing nearer, she could see the giant's feet and legs inside a hole in the earth.

Though Morfran was a simple man, his vision was keen. He spied the fox and extended his hand with a small remainder of honeyed biscuit in his palm. "Come here. You want some, don't you?" he said enticingly.

Claret would not be fooled by that ploy again. She raced around his back causing him to turn quickly. As his body twisted, he slid into the earth.

Carefully, Claret peered down into the opening. There, she saw the giant, horrified, as he held his bleeding hands aloft. "Help me," he cried. "You're magic. Get me out of here."

Claret thought of the change in Ninaway and reasoned the giant had become kinder as well.

Giving a sharp bark, the fox looked down into the opening, turned, then ran back to the foxmoor patch. Aqulia circled around and around, keeping a vigil on the helpless giant.

She could hear voices only steps away from the foxmoor patch. Quietly, she dropped to the ground, rolled in the weed, and found her discarded clothing. She looked up to see Ninaway crying and running toward her.

"He's hurt," the witch screamed, blood running from her hands.

Close behind, Merlin tried to console her. "He can't be injured badly. The wounds are superficial. Please calm yourself, and we will find him." Claret stood up in the clearing, allowing the witch to see her. "Ninaway, he's not hurt badly. He's scratched from the ice and crystals. Though not in any real danger, he is simply frightened."

Ninaway blew out a shaky breath. "I hope you are correct, Claret. Now that I have learned to care, the pain is great."

Ryan and Olyn caught up with the others. Nothing else mattered to Ryan but Claret. Olyn stood beside Merlin as they contemplated the best course of action.

"He must have fallen in the hole I made when we were trapped in the falling crystal cave. I can think of no other explanation."

Claret humbly hung her head. "I fear I am the reason he is in the cave. When I saw him without any feet or legs, as I was a fox, I became curious and raced around his body. When he tried to capture me, he fell into the hole. He begged me to help him."

A surge of pride shot through Ryan. At one time, Claret would have never considered the plight of the troublesome giant. Now she would be his rescuer.

But he needed to know how Claret felt about *him*. Would she stay with him if he asked as Merlin had suggested? Or, would she simply prefer her freedom?

"Ryan," Claret directed, "find some rope. It is not going to be easy to lift him from the cave. He is a very big man. Moreover, he is frightened and most probably will not aid us in his rescue."

Ryan closed his eyes and took a deep breath. Perhaps working to save the giant would remind her of the link between them. Forcing down his own need and focusing on the giant's predicament, Ryan turned to see her rushing across the meadow to the edge of the cliff overlooking the sea.

"Claret, wait, I will fetch a rope, but it is going to take more than a rope to raise that giant."

She looked to the wizards for assistance. Ninaway was overly concerned for her brother's safety. "Ninaway, Ryan will go into the cave and place him in a sling with some pulleys I have with me."

Olyn looked puzzled at his comrade's statement. "How is it you are always prepared for any situation?"

Merlin smiled, confident the heavier wizard admired his skills. "Olyn, I have been a wizard for many, many years. One learns to always be prepared." As Ryan approached with a rope, Merlin handed him the pulleys. Ryan and Claret quickly set up the pulleys and tackle, binding one end of the rope about a stout tree.

Claret attempted to sit in the sling and lower herself down into the hole. Ryan took the tackle from her. "You are not going to risk getting lacerated with those ice shards. I am already scarred. I shall go."

She placed her hand over his and said, "Ryan, the giant is no concern of yours. I owe his sister my life. I will go."

How the pain of the sting of her rejection seared his heart. *Does she not realize her debts are my debts?* He gathered her into his arms. "Please, let me do this, if not for the giant, then for you. It is the least I can offer you."

"If you wish. I will get your horse to pull you up," she said, sprinting across the meadow before he could argue.

There was so much more he wished to give her; like his name, his possessions, and dominion over his heart.

He looked down through the opening over the cave and saw Morfran crying profusely.

Ryan called down to the giant. "Morfran, be still. Cease your cries. We will save you. I am coming down to pull you up."

Terrified, the giant screamed, "You cannot hold my weight. I am far bigger than you are. Only Ninaway can help. She will use a spell and I will be out of here in the blink of an eye."

An equally tearful Ninaway stood at the edge of the opening. "Do not fear, Morfran, Ryan shall save you. You are too heavy for my magic alone."

"Please," the giant wailed, "only you can save me. You built this horrible place."

Claret returned with his horse, Black, and secured the tackle about the saddle horn. She tossed the rope and pulleys to Ryan and mounted the large animal. Ryan placed himself in the sling he fashioned and indicated Claret was to ride slowly toward the hole.

Carefully, Ryan lowered his body into the opening. He immediately noticed that the walls were covered with sharp shards of ice crystals and bits of quartz. As he came nearer and nearer to Morfran, the frightened man flailed his arms and tried to force him from the cave. "Go away, you'll ruin the spell and I shall never get out of here."

Ninaway yelled to her brother. "There is no spell. I cannot undo what I have not done. Ryan will save you."

"I don't believe you. You are mad because I lost the fox and you put a spell on me, and now I am cursed to remain here forever."

Ninaway lowered her head and wept.

Merlin took her about the shoulders and drew her back from the opening. "Talking to him only confuses the poor man. Step back. Let Ryan and Claret do what needs to be done. He shall be safe. I promise you."

Ryan was nearly on the floor of the cave when Morfran pushed him from the sling. He fell against the cave's sharp walls. His face was lacerated by hundreds of the ice shards. Blood streamed down his face. He felt the warm blood trickle down his cheek, touched it and drew back his finger and saw the red.

When Morfran saw what he had done to the only person who had ever praised him, he became even more frightened. "Please, Ninaway, you must save me. Only you can rescue me. See what I have done to my friend?"

Ryan shook himself and stood beside the giant. "Have no fear, Morfran. We'll get you out of here. Be still and sit in this sling," he said, helping the terrified man into the apparatus that would carry him to safety.

"Claret," Ryan yelled, "pull back as far as you can. When he is clear of the opening, hold Black steady while Merlin and Olyn free him from the sling."

Claret nodded, clicked her tongue, and urged Black backward at a smooth and steady pace.

"I know you're scared, Morfran, but don't flail about so, it makes it harder to pull," Ryan implored.

His eyes glazed with tears, the giant looked down on the face of his bleeding companion, nodded gently, and endeavored to remain as still as possible.

Ryan's sturdy horse easily pulled the giant from the depths of the earth.

Strange, Claret thought, how a man so muscular, could be so frightened. She gave Black the command to remain in place and dismounted to assist the wizards.

"You're safe now, Morfran. You can get out of the sling," Olyn said.

But the terrified man would not let go of the straps supporting the sling.

His fingers were white at the knuckles and his eyes as wide as saucers.

Ninaway stepped toward her brother and gently pried his fingers from the straps. "You're safe now, brother. No more ill shall befall you."

"You promise, on your sacred word as a witch?"

"I do so solemnly swear. No harm shall come to you, but you must help and not be so foolhardy."

"I didn't want to fall in the hole. I was trying to get the fox back for you."

Ninaway smiled. "I know, Morfran. I no longer desire the fox. She has her own destiny to fulfill."

Claret listened, and wondered if there was something that called her to a duty she did not comprehend. *Could it be the Druid's plan is truly the right path for me? Why would they make my nature wild if I am to conform to rules that stifle freedom? A wild thing should, above all else, be free.*

Ryan! He was still in the hole. She gathered her wits, took the sling from the wizards, and again lowered it through the opening in the cave roof.

"Come on, Ryan, get in. Black and I will pull you up. It will be easy for him, as you do not weigh twenty stones."

Once again, the horse performed the maneuver with ease. Black was another perfect member of their hunting team. He responded quickly to orders and could be depended upon to carry them out to the letter.

How safe it felt to be part of a team that functioned so well. This was the ultimate freedom, to practice your skill in tandem with others to achieve the common goal. Though she was usually in fox form when she hunted with the others, she felt the same sense of achievement as a human.

Ryan sat in the sling as Black and Claret pulled him free of the hole. His hands and face flowed with blood. He could feel the clearer air, and once above the opening, he drew in great breaths. How cleverly she tied the tackle and mounted the horse. She was the woman of his dreams and more. If he were to search all the known worlds, he would never find a more perfect mate.

Lifted from the earth, Ryan tried to free himself from the sling. His loss of blood rendered him weak. The wizards and Morfran hurried to Ryan's side. The giant scooped him up and carried him to Ninaway's tent. Merlin circled the bed where the wounded falconer lay. The cuts on his face were deeper than the wizard had first believed. His hands and arms peppered with lacerations bled profusely. The veins on his wrists were very nearly severed. It would take a near miracle to save the lad.

Olyn sat at the edge of the bed, tears flowing freely from his eyes. "Merlin, we must do something. Even if he never agrees to the Druid's conditions, he must be spared. This boy is near a son to me. I cannot lose him."

Claret moved to the side of the bed next to Olyn. "Olyn, did you forget he did agree to the Druid's conditions if I were spared? Cannot I do the same for him?"

The old wizard looked to the fox woman, moisture glazing his eyes. "I do not know, my dear. Perhaps... perhaps."

Morfran approached Ninaway, who worked at the far end of the tent preparing some herb cloths to staunch the flow of blood. "Sister, can you contact the ancient Druids? Do you know where they live? I need to talk to them."

"You, Morfran? Why?" his sister asked.

Merlin stood abruptly crossed to them. "It is worth a try. Morfran, you are right. We must try to get the Druids to understand."

"No, not you. I will go to them. I owe the falconer my life. It is my duty," the giant said bravely.

Ninaway moved to the edge of the bed and placed her hand on Olyn's shoulder. "Olyn, have you heard what is being said? Morfran wants to petition the Druids to save Ryan."

Merlin sighed deeply and closed his eyes. "You are a brave man, Morfran. However you have no place in the court of the Druids."

"Well, *you* can come with me," he said, matter-of-factly to Olyn. "They know you."

Olyn hung his head. "No, Morfran. They do not know me. I have only seen them at the behest of Merlin."

Quickly, the giant turned and nearly collided with the senior wizard. "Then you must take me," Morfran directed. "At once."

Claret was secretly pleased the giant had spoken on Ryan's behalf. But, deep within her heart, she knew she was the only one who could save Ryan. *He sacrificed for me, can I do any less for him? I love him with all my heart, one that would no longer beat, if not for him.*

Merlin approached her, the power within the ancient sorcerer so strong it near drove her to the edge of the tent. "Claret, you know your duty is clear. You and you alone can spare him. He has lost a great deal of blood. I only hope it is not too late."

Angered by the wizard's statement, she cried, "Too late? If it's too late, you are the one at fault. You cannot lay the blame at my door. If I had my way, we would be far and away from this place, hunting and loving together as we planned."

Olyn tried to temper her anger. "Please, child. Be careful. It is not wise to incite Merlin."

"Do you think I give even a fragment of concern for the ire of the wizard? My only concern is for Ryan, injured only due to his soft nature that would not allow the giant to suffer, though the man's predicament was of his own making."

Ninaway approached her former pet and placed her hand on Claret's shoulder. "Please, Claret, do not blame my brother. He is simple, but he means well."

"Yes, I understand, but, we must save Ryan," she said, shuddering at the possibility he could not be saved.

Merlin walked from the tent to be alone with his thoughts. In the cool autumn air, he smelt a strange acrid odor. From over the hole of the crystal cave rose a pillar of red-hued smoke. As the smoke became more concentrated, the unmistakable odor of foxmoor permeated the entire meadow. In the center of the smoke pillar, a shaft of brilliant light formed. Merlin threw up his arms to protect his eyes from the blinding light.

"Merlin," a deep voice boomed. "We are gravely disappointed in you. Over countless ages, you have done as we bid. Why do you now fail us?"

Olyn rushed toward the light. "Sire, please, Merlin did not defy you. He simply—"

"Cease your prattle. Do not dare to speak unless you are so directed." Ninaway moved slowly from the opening.

"Witch, come here." Frightened, Ninaway froze unable to move.

"Come here, woman. Now!"

An unseen force propelled Ninaway to the edge of the pillar. She stammered, "W-what do you wish of me, ancient Druids?"

"Do you understand the properties of the weed foxmoor?"

"I do, most revered priests. What would you have me do?"

At once a shower of green spewed forth copious amounts of the weed from the opening in the ground.

"Ninaway, you must brew all of these leaves in a kettle and render them down until a thick porridge is formed. You will rub this over the face, arms, and hands of the young falconer. The poultice must completely dry, then be removed. Continue to do this for three days, no more, no less. Three days, do you understand?" Speechless, she nodded.

Ninaway tended Ryan as the Druids directed. All kept a constant vigil. The wizards and Claret each prayed silently.

On the eve of the third day after the poultice had been removed, Ryan slowly opened his eyes. Ninaway lifted the cloth she'd used to clean the dried foxmoor from his face. Claret rushed to the bedside.

"Well, it's about time you awoke. You had us worried," Claret said, reaching down to kiss him on his forehead.

He pulled her into an embrace, placed his lips against hers, and kissed her deeply.

Olyn laughed. "It seems you are well enough not to need our constant supervision. Perhaps, it would be best if we withdrew." He herded Ninaway, her brother, and Merlin from the tent.

As Claret drew back from Ryan's kiss, she noted his scar was gone. "Ryan, what has happened to you? Your face is unmarked."

"Unmarked? How can that be? I've worn this mark for many years. Why now would the flesh be unblemished?"

Claret searched the tent and found a looking glass. "Here, see for yourself."

Ryan peered into its surface. Reflected was the face of an unscarred man. His eye was straight and true. He was as his father, fair of face with eyes of clear blue steel. This was a man who could be king, an asset to the crown.

Claret threw her arms around him and fell onto the bed. Ryan laughed and nuzzled her neck.

"Ryan, that feels so good. You cannot know how I've missed being with you."

"Missed being with me? From what Olyn said, I gather you have been with me every moment of the day."

"Keeping vigil over a sick person is not the same as making love," Claret replied, removing her clothing.

"Then it was my body you missed, eh, vixen?"

The pungent odor of the foxmoor seemed to blend with their bodies creating a perfume so fragrant it was intoxicating. Her red hair tumbled over her shoulders and across his face. He drew in the heady scent. His mouth moved over her shoulders and down to her breast. Gently he caressed the sweet mound and eased the nipple to his lips.

Drawing back, he saw sensuality smolder in her eyes. "Oh, Claret, thy name is woman, and you complete a man."

She pressed her tiny hands over his chest and down to his waist. Glancing down she saw evidence of his desire and pressed her body tightly up against his. He rolled onto his side and held her hips. Slowly and completely, he took the woman destiny had chosen for him in the dance as old as time.

Epilogue

Ryan stood proudly overlooking Camelot. The spires pierced the sky like golden needles. Claret stood at his side, dressed in a gown of red silken splendor. At her elbow stood his parents, Leigh and Kit, the King and Queen of Ireland.

Today would be coronation and wedding of another royal pair. All who had touched the lives of Ryan and Claret were present. Every member of his family was there, including his newly knighted Uncle Aaron. Helga stood, her hands nervously kneading her apron, with her sons at her side. Even Ninaway, who had been banned from court so many years ago, was welcomed.

Merlin approached the group and extended his arms. "To see you all here is most gratifying. The Ordination of the ancient Druids has come to fruition. Ireland and Wales are well protected and will prosper. It has been so decreed. Are you comfortable with your decision, Ryan?"

"Yes, Merlin, I could not have selected a finer mate, even with the wisdom of Solomon."

"Does this mean you would have me clove in two?" Claret said, nudging him in the ribs. "Would you have me as I am now, as a woman or as I can be a fox?"

Leigh stepped forward and placed his arms about Ryan and Claret. "You have chosen a difficult path, my son. This woman is like no other, save your mother. I can only tell you the trials are well worth the rewards."

Ryan smiled, confident his father spoke the truth.

What They Are Saying About
The Fox And The Swan

Dee Carey has spun a magical web that makes one suspend reality and cheer her morphed characters on. Although this is not the type of genre I personally read, I found myself swept up in the storyline that was peopled with strong characters that formed a complete population of essential beings —not one too many and not one too few.

The Fox and the Swan is a story where the stepmother truly is a witch. The plot, the arranged marriage of a young girl to a curmudgeon to save her family, is one that is tried and true but definitely has a different twist with sorcery and religion becoming compatible.

The transition of humans to animals was so believable one never lost faith in the story and I had to read it to its conclusion in a short time. Dee Carey keeps you wondering about the outcome all the way through. The setting in Scotland rings so true you are visually whipped across the sea and live the Highland life while the story unfolds. Recollections of Narnia crept into my mind as I was reading as it certainly carried that flavor of magic and the struggle between good and evil.

Whether you read fantasy or not, I recommend *The Fox and the Swan* as a good love story that plays out blending fantasy and reality that makes you believe in it and its characters.

Mary Jean Kelso, Wings-Press and Whiskey Creek Press
The Homesteader, Goodbye Is Forever, The Homesteader's Legacy, Blue Coat.

Dee Carey has a flowing, somewhat unusual style, and Fox In The Mist moves quickly. Her descriptions are simply fantastic, and I had no trouble picturing every single element—from the prancing of a tiny unicorn to the thrilling sensations of a single romantic touch, to the idealized sweeping vision of Arthurian castles. What a lovely, lovely book. I look forward to more unusual magical tales from Dee Carey.

— 5 Unicorns, Enchanted In Romance

To Bill,

my love for always,

my daughters, and grandsons.

With special thanks to my critique

partner, Steve Yates.

THE FOX AND THE SWAN

Prologue

Rory "Tag" MacTaggert

I had to dig quickly. My paws were raw, so furiously did I scrape the ground. If the Grail were discovered, she would be lost. I would never know love and thus remain a fox for the remainder of my life. Though my claws were torn and bleeding it was little sacrifice to save her. It was for her my heart beat. If I were never able to win her love, to know she would be safe because of my doing would assuage my guilt. Oh, God, how I wished I could draw back the words, that they had never been spoken.

It seemed so long ago I found her. She was beautiful beyond compare, her eyes a crystal blue, which rivaled the brilliant skies over Scotland. Skin of finest alabaster, she was as perfect and clean as freshly fallen snow. Her voice sang to me even now. Now, that she was forced to fly through the skies as a swan and perhaps never regain her true form. The priest said it was done to protect her, but still I doubt his wisdom. Might it not be better to send her to another land than to relegate her to being a bird? Swans mate for life and how devoutly I pray Fionna will not find one she fancies. I must have time to free us both from the prison of animal guises.

The hard packed ground finally yielded and I thrust the vessel deep into the hole. Free from prying eyes and greedy men, the Grail would be safe, as would Fionna.

Initially, I did not mind being a fox. I was seventeen and it seemed a lark. I thought the witch's curse folly. Why my father was attracted to her is a mystery to me. Though comely, her eyes held a sinister glint.

Her first and only thoughts were for herself. My father was a wealthy man and newly widowed. Burdened with a young boy, he sought someone to care for the child. I was that child and now I may never become a man. Still I hear her screams ring in my ears.

"You whelp. You'll not rob me of my due. I endured your insufferable crying and messes for far too many years to realize nothing."

I scurried as fast as I could to escape her ranting. Halfway across the meadow, I noticed I no longer ran on two feet, but four. She really was a witch. Other children taunted me with the epithet thrown at my father's wife. The mother of my friends avoided her. The only time she appeared in public was to attend church services. Other families would crush themselves into narrow pews to avoid contact with her. My father, relieved to have someone to raise his son, noticed nothing.

Only when I felt the pangs of true love did I desire to be human. Ah, Fionna, the fair, how could I have brought you so much pain?

Chapter One

Rory "Tag" MacTaggert—in the beginning

Evan MacTaggert was a careful and prosperous businessman. He oversaw every part of the production of the wool. I followed him to the warehouse, the mill, and on this fine day, down to the river. Hundreds of bleating animals jostled each other for space. The sheep, not fond of swimming, boarded the low-slung barge reluctantly. Here and there, a brave lamb dared to push its way along side of its mother, crying loudly for food and comfort.

After much jostling, a hulky hunched man secured them on the flat-bottomed boat. Sullivan worked for my father for many years before I was born. Faithful and tirelessly, he labored. I tugged at my father's coat tail, as I watched the old man herd the sheep on the unstable vessel.

"Can I go with you? I want to see where the sheep go."

"No, my little tagalong, you cannot. Even Mister Sullivan does not go the entire way."

"B—but," I stammered, "Why?" Da shook his head.

My father would not be won over by whining, so I determined it would be the better tact to bide my time, until he was in a more receptive mood. He put his muscular arm about my shoulders. I felt protected, and no one, or nothing could harm me. All little children should feel as safe as did I.

My father led me through the narrow streets to the edge of town, where he'd left our wagon. With ease, he lifted me high up onto the wooden seat and wrapped a blanket around my lap. It was not cold, but Father took no chances. He was a very deliberate man.

A misting rain worked its way up to a torrent. Da lifted the blanket up and over my shoulders in an attempt to keep me dry. The rain snaked its way down my neck, chilling me. I shuddered, and Father held me close. The sky cried with a sense of impending doom. We rode in silence. Da spoke not a word, but hugged me to his side.

The sturdy horse guided us through the mud-filled road, its hooves plodding through the thick ooze. Overhead everything was gray, the clouds rumbled ominously, lightning flashed through the darkened skies. In the brief flashes, I watched my father's face. He wore an expression I'd never seen before and was clearly frightened. Of what, I could not comprehend. He was a brave and courageous man. Mere thunder and lightning would not cause him to cower with fear. Furthermore, why did I feel the fear as well?

Shortly, we arrived at the house. Father lifted me from the wagon and set me on the step in front of our door. The groom, who awaited our return, took Father's horse saying, "There's not much time."

My father left me abruptly, not bothering to retrieve the blanket or to assist me from my wet clothes. He raced up the winding staircase. The house was still. Even the canary my mother kept in the sunniest room of the manor had ceased its song. No bustling of servants, no sound from the kitchen, nothing broke the silence. Even a young boy was able to sense there was something wrong.

I stood in front of the narrow staircase still in my wet garments. Looking up, I saw my father descending, each step he took heavier than the last. Slow and deliberate, as if he were avoiding reaching the landing. His longish gray hair stood out from his head like a band of serpents. I'd never seen him thus. This man was a stranger. His countenance, that of a man who'd waged a monumental battle and lost. As he drew close to me, I noticed tears streaming down his face. He made no attempt to brush them away or to hide them in any fashion. Dropping to his knees, he embraced me, crushing me against his massive chest and forcing the breath from my lungs.

"Father." I struggled. "What has happened that saddens you so?"

"Tag, I'm afraid your mother is gone."

"Gone? Why? Where did she go? Why didn't we go with her?"

"My son, were it in my power, I would have gladly gone with her. You have a full life ahead of you. Even she would not have wanted you to leave."

"Da, you make no sense. What happened?"

He stood and stiffly brushed his clothes. "You are not to worry, lad. I will find a housekeeper straight away. You will be cared for."

Nearly five, I did not need a nursemaid. Though father deemed it necessary, I didn't want anyone strange in the house. I wanted my mother. Quickly, I raced past him up the stairs and into my mother's room. I threw open the door before he was able to catch me. Then I saw her, white, not moving.

"Rory MacTaggert," Father screamed, "Come back here this instant."

My father never yelled at me. He came to the bedroom door and quickly stood in front of it so I could not enter.

The maid appeared from nowhere and brushed past me and Da, saying not a word. In her arms, she carried some sort of material. The fabric was different from the sheets on our beds, but it, too, was white.

Father scooped me up and let loose a primal cry. I'd never heard the like of it before. He wailed loud and deep, like a wolf in a dark forest. Then he seemed to return from his pain and noticed he held me so tightly he was hurting me as he carried me down the stairs. I'm sure he didn't mean to harm me, but his hold would leave bruises on my young arms. He released me and set me back on the floor near the entrance of our manor.

"Oh, God," he said, as he noticed the bruises forming.

"You are all I have left and I treat you thus. I'm sorry, son."

Though the marks on my arms were tender, it appeared he suffered the greater injury. "It's all right, Da, they'll go away. I know you didn't mean to make them."

"There are so many things I did not mean to happen and now I can never make it up to her." He brushed his hand through his unruly hair, and turned away from me.

Faithful as a pup, I raced after him. But he eluded me and ducked into the study, firmly locking the door behind him. I pounded on it with my fists. I remember no more of that terrible day. It is probably best that way.

Fionna Sullivan

I watched as the lad tugged at his father's coattails. He was a funny little boy. Though we were the same age, he seemed to me to be much older, even though he followed his father like a clinging girl. It was something in his eyes. They were a soft green and seemed to discern your every secret with a single glance. He never looked at me in scorn, as did so many others. They called me *witch* and *changeling*. As if my white hair was somehow otherworldly. Sometimes, when I was alone and feeling strong, I chose to believe it made me special, as a favored child, one whom God looked upon kindly.

But I knew the truth. I was nothing, a deformed being, even though my body wasn't twisted or grotesque. My stark white hair set me apart. Only my brother Sully and the boy called Tag treated me as equals. Often times Tag and his father would come to our island. When his father and mine discussed business, we played and raced across the wide meadow on the top of the bluff that surrounded the magic valley. I, alone, was the only one allowed to venture into the hidden place. Not even my father, any longer, went through the channels of the underground river. When I was very young, he'd fallen and injured his back. Until that time, my father was the only one who took the sheep to their special grazing area. The sheep would not stay alone on the raft and would simply jump off and drown. We lost a full year's wool, until Papa noted how the sheep responded to me. Maybe it was my hair or the sound of my voice, but when I rode the barge with them, none drowned. It was not the most comfortable of journeys. I had to crouch and lie among the frightened creatures as they bleated. Their cries echoed off the cavern walls. Sometimes as the boat scraped across the narrow bottom, I had to get out and push. The sheep did not like me to leave them. While I was in the water I had to sing to them softly lest they perish. Quickly, I learned how to placate the most nervous and then took them to the valley. I took pride in this God-given talent to lead the sheep.

***

Tag

The housekeeper, who in her own mind became my mother, was not the most desirable of women. When Da hired her to look after me, it seemed a workable situation. After all, I was not an infant and required little more than supervisory care. Initially, she was kind and capable, and the fact she was comely did not escape my father's eye. Within two short years they were married, and the glint in her eye became more and more sinister.

Father turned the financial matters of the family over to her, and Hagga responded cleverly. She found slight discrepancies, nothing glaring, but enough for my father to allocate the entire process to her. She carefully accounted for every penny and eagerly showed him the records of each week. He was proud this woman had a greater facility for figures than my mother. I did not feel the same way. That evil glint told me there was more to this Hagga than my father realized.

She provided me with food and clean clothing, nothing more. I was never read to, nor tucked in at night. Within my heart she would never replace my mother, who'd played with me and had offered comfort at every injury, whether imagined or an actual scraped knee. Hagga had no compassion, none. Not for the youthful child in her care, nor for anyone. The puppy my mother had given me for my fourth birthday had been banished from the manor and was forced to remain chained in the stable. Neither was I allowed to go and play with him, as my clothes got dirty and I smelled of animal whenever I went to visit the pup.

Frequently, to force the hag from my mind, I would recall better things. Like the first time I saw Fionna. She was sitting on the edge of the dock when her father was loading the sheep onto the river barge. Her hair was so white when the sun hit it you were nearly blinded by the brilliance. She sat so primly, unlike her unruly brother who was to become my best friend. Da always allowed me to follow him when he went to the island. Hagga did not like me to go, but permitted it as it kept me from the house and she did not have to bother with me. She resented me having fun, but rather than refuse she urged me to go with my father as a way of demonstrating her so-called kindness. I did not care why she allowed me to tag along as long as I could be with Da and visit Fionna and her brother.

The first time I saw Fionna sitting on the dock, I felt my heart flutter. Of course at that age, I placed no particular significance to the phenomenon. Her eyes were even bluer than the sky above us. And when she laughed, birds twittered along with her. She was beautiful and joyous. She had a majesty unlike any other I'd known.

Her older brother, Sully, was not as agile as his sister and frequently fell over his own feet. Fionna would assist him and never taunted him for his clumsiness. She possessed every good quality I'd ever known, reminding me of my mother. Certainly not in appearance, though my mother had been a beautiful woman, Fionna had the same sense of consideration and the same quality of joy.

Whenever I fell into despair, I thought of Fionna. She became my shining beacon of hope. Oftentimes, I would lie awake in my attic room thinking of the white-haired maiden rather than wonder why Da had allowed that woman to banish me to the attic. Hagga turned my sunny room into her private sewing and accounting room. As he believed it helped the business, Da did not protest.

As the months turned into years, Hagga gradually took over more and more of the business. Yet, Da never allowed her to come to the river and see the lambs go to their secret grazing. I think she resented me even more as she realized Da did permit me to go with him. It wasn't his company, but his business she desired.

They were together nearly four years when my father became ill. He became weaker and weaker, barely able to eat and was abed for longer and longer periods. When it came time to take the sheep to the grazing, he was too frail to go to the river.

That evening when I went to visit him as I always did, to tell him of the progress at the mill, he bid me close to the bed.

Da turned over to me more responsibility for running the business than perhaps as lad of my years should undertake, but I was up to the task, much to Hagga's chagrin. Resentment rose in her like a high tide of bitter bile.

She tapped at the bedroom door and inquired, "Evan, would you like some tea? Perhaps it would help you to rest."

He lifted his half-hooded eyes, begging me to send her away. I went to the door and opened it a crack.

"Hagga, my father needs to rest, but perhaps a cup of tea would be restoring." I knew Da had something of grave import to tell me and knew if she were not given a specific task she would listen at the door.

My father lifted a weak hand and motioned me closer to him. "Rory," he said, smiling, "Tag, I am afraid the time has come when you must take over the business. I know you are young, but you are also wise beyond your years."

He stopped speaking and coughed, rising the phlegm in his throat. Again and again he coughed, unable to breathe. I lifted him gently from his pillow and gave him a drink of the water at his bedside. Swallowing, he seemed more comfortable and again began to speak.

"Son, I've noticed of late, the tallies for the wool do not match the accounts Hagga presents to me weekly. I fear I was wrong in marrying her."

Though this was perhaps a revelation to Da, I knew the same four years earlier. "Da, do not trouble yourself. I can handle the accounts. I've studied the books when Hagga goes to market. I was about to tell you of my findings."

A firm tap at the door alerted us both of Hagga's return. I could hear the soft clatter of the cup against the saucer as she balanced it on the tray. As I started for the door, Da reached up and grabbed my sleeve. "Rory, take this," he said, thrusting a ledger in my hand. "It contains the true records. Protect it for me, son."

I hid it beneath a chair cushion and went to open the door. I nodded politely and tried to take the tray from Hagga.

"No," she said, "it is my duty to care for my husband's needs." She brushed past me and set the serving dish on the side table next to my father's reading chair.

"Hagga," Da requested, "Please allow me some time with my son. We have much to discuss."

"Don't be foolish. Whatever could you discuss with a mere boy?"

I reached out and firmly grabbed her by the elbow and steered her to the door. She wrenched her arm from my grasp and turned.

Facing my father, she said, "I'll not leave until you consume that tea, every last drop. You hear?" Hagga then sat firmly on the chair with her arms crossed. It was the very chair where I'd secreted the ledger. I prayed she would not notice the difference in the cushion.

"I'm waiting. I can sit here all night. If my husband cannot show me the courtesy of drinking the tea I prepared especially for him, I will remain here forever."

Da coughed, and I reached for his water. "No, Rory, bring me the tea. I'll drink it. Every drop, Hagga, I promise. Now please leave me with my son."

"Not until I see you drink from the cup."

"Damn you, you witch," I muttered under my breath, as I took the cup and passed it to my father.

As he put it to his lips, she rose and left the room. The moment she cleared the threshold, I jerked the cup from my father's lips.

"Tag? Why did you do that?" he wheezed.

"Believe me, Da, I have very good reason." I smelled the unusually dark tea in the cup. Though I couldn't identify the contents, I could tell it wasn't just tea in that vessel. "From now on, Da, I will prepare your food. I don't trust Hagga. She put something in your tea."

"Don't be foolish, son. What would she have to gain? She knows the business will turn over to you, next year."

I shook my head. Da did not believe anyone would be so evil as to commit murder, certainly not the woman he wed. But I knew there would be many teas between now and my eighteenth birthday. I would have to watch out for him, since he refused to do it for himself.

"Just be careful, Da, she's not to be trusted." I took the teacup and emptied the contents into the potted plant by the window.

"All right, Rory. Once I am well, I will eat with the herders."

"Good, Da, and while you are still in this room, do not eat what she brings you. I will feed you after she leaves. If she insists on seeing you eat something, pretend to bite a tiny portion and when she leaves, spit it out."

"Tag," he said with a sigh, "Surely all this is not necessary. She knows well I have provided for her and the business will go to you. What would she want with a business to worry over?"

"Hagga is not like other women, Da. She craves power, not merely the security most wives desire."

Sighing deeply, my father, a shadow of the man he once was, laid his head back on the pillow. "I will do as you say, Tag. You are wise beyond your years. I trust you as fully as I did your mother."

It gave me a faint hope that he did not trust his present wife as fervently as he had the first. I prayed he would be strong enough to resist Hagga's efforts.

Chapter Two
Fionna

My Uncle Elidor was as dear to me as my own father. My mother's brother was a kind, unusual man. He'd studied many years to become a Druid and was a master of his craft. When my dear mother died, he returned to our island to help my father raise my brother and me. When we were very young, he kept a close watch on us. As we grew older, he provided us with an education that could not be obtained anywhere outside of a Druid tutelage.

Elidor was my uncle, my friend, and my most trusted confidant. He was always able to answer questions I dared not ask of my father. We talked long hours of my mother's childhood. To speak of mother to Papa wounded him so, I did not trouble him. But Elidor was more than eager to tell me of his sister's childhood exploits. You could tell he and his sister were very close as children. It seemed he regretted the time he spent studying, away from his sister.

Uncle believed family was the most desirable structure for the preservation of all that is good in mankind. He revered all life, human, animal, even the plants were held in high esteem. If he were to come across an injured animal, he would tend it carefully until it was strong enough to return to its home. Though he cared for many animals, none were caged. They knew they could rely on Uncle Elidor to do his best for them. Passing his love of creatures on to Sully and me, he taught me how to communicate with the birds and oftentimes I could get them to sing along with me.

Times were becoming meager for us. The loss of a full year's wool and Mrs. MacTaggert's accounts were straining on our family's finances. When Mr. MacTaggert handled all the funds and we had a slim year, he would extend funds against the following year. Mrs. MacTaggert, however, was not so generous. She hoarded every penny. It was my belief she told her husband she extended the same courtesy, as did he, then pocketed the difference herself.

Papa worried that he could not provide for us as he always had. I was of marriageable age and he thought to find me a husband who could provide for us all. Not considered a beauty, he sought out older men, who would not be offended by my unusual coloring.

We owned three quarters of the land at the rim. The remainder belonged to a man new to Scotland. He was a Briton of some royal heritage and my father thought him to be a fine match.

I did not like the man. He frightened me. When Papa told me he had betrothed me to Laird Arwan Pheland, I fled to the comfort of my brother and Tag. Surely, they could come up with a remedy for this terrible mess.

The boys were fishing at the edge of the island's rocky coast. As I approached, I heard Sully taunt his friend, "So you think my sister is pretty? Jeeze, I love her, but that white hair separates her from the beauties."

Tag turned abruptly and cuffed my brother. "Don't you say another thing about Fionna. She's perfect just as she is. Her white hair does not separate her from beauties; it elevates her. She has a beauty that surpasses all others."

Though I was truly upset about my betrothal, Tag's words made my heart sing. To know someone treasured me provided some comfort. I loudly cleared my throat to alert them of my presence. When they looked up at me, Tag's face quickly turned crimson.

Even as I smiled at him, my tears began to flow. Soon I was consumed by my crying. They both rushed to me. My brother, angered, wanted to murder the one who'd harmed me. Tag, however, had made the quick assessment I was not physically injured, merely gravely offended.

He rushed to my side and placed his arm about my shoulders. Rubbing his sleeve across my face, wiping away my tears, he asked, "What happened? What have you been told that alarms you so?"

"Papa wants me to marry Laird Pheland."

"Pheland, that pig?" Tag replied.

"He's so old and ugly in a strange sort of way. Why would he offer his daughter to a man old enough to be your father?"

I let myself slide to the sand on the narrow beach and covered my eyes. "We're so poor. He needs the bride price to pay off our debts."

Tag looked truly puzzled. "Why are you poor? My father pays you no matter if it is a good year or bad."

Sully gently lifted me from the ground and brushed the sand from my skirt. "Yeah, your father did, but that witch won't, and she is the one in charge now. Since your father has been ill, she even refuses to allow us some mutton from time to time."

"But why? What is one sheep more or less? Through the bounty of the valley we have more sheep than any other herd in all of Scotland." Tag shook his head. It was clear the witch had reached farther than the manor with her evil.

"Did you tell Papa how you feel about this man?" Sully knew Papa would do nothing that did not please me. However, I knew it was my duty to save our family, so I said nothing. I had no other choice.

"When?" Tag asked.

"When does this foul thing take place? How much time have we?"

Struggling through my tears and hiccups, I replied, "After the herd is taken to the summer grazing."

Tag nodded, then closed his eyes and pounded his fist into his palm. "We need a plan and a way to hide you."

"Hide me?" I cried.

"Where can one hide on an island? There are no woods or vast structures that no one inhabits. It would be impossible to hide here. Though no one could find me if I stayed with the sheep, how would I eat? Where would I find shelter?"

Tag paced up and down along the beach. Finally he turned and said, "You will stay with me. I can hide you in the stable and bring food to you every evening. No one will find you there. I trust the groom, and Hagga hates the place. She says tis putrid."

Tag

Spring all too quickly blended into summer. The time for the sheep to be taken to the hidden pasture drew near. Sully and I spent long hours pondering how to save his sister.

I'd been able to convince Da to turn the business accounts over to me. As time passed and he became weaker, he relied on me for the truth of the state of his company. Hagga resisted at first, but when Da told her that as a woman, she would not be permitted to conduct business she acquiesced, albeit reluctantly. Each evening as I visited my father he seemed to grow smaller. His once broad shoulders now were thin peaks of bone and his eyes were sunken. He dared not eat anything Hagga prepared for him and sometimes had to wait until I returned from the island before he had any proper food.

Fearing her scheme to poison my father might be completed, I created a business relationship for my father with the groom. Though Hagga questioned the presence of the man at the manor, she did not confront the groom nor forbid him into our home. She feared my wrath and the condemnation of the servants. Always aware of servants' tales, she was careful, lest she give them fodder for their gossip mill. When I was unable to bring Da's food, the groom would sneak bread and mutton to him.

As I fed my father the evening before the lambs were taken to summer grazing, he smiled wanly and pushed away the spoon.

"No more, Rory. It is done."

"No, Da, you must eat to regain your strength."

He shook his head. "No, son, I can endure no longer. Now I know you can handle the wool and the sheep, I can rest. My soul will be still, knowing you will carry on the family tradition. Someday, you too will raise a family and carry on the business for your son."

"I understand, Da, but stay with me until the sheep go to the hidden meadow." Though my heart protested, I, too, knew it was time.

Fionna

Though I enjoyed my special privilege of accompanying the sheep to their summer grazing, this year my heart was filled with dread.

Once the journey was over, I would have to wed Laird Pheland. I prayed Tag's plan would free me from my father's promise. Within my soul I would do anything to save our family, but to wed such a despicable man frightened me to the core. I dared not tell Papa my true feelings, as he would then break the betrothal, which would plunge my family into ruin. If only I could have some time to reason over the problem.

I stuffed some clothes and my hairbrush into a bag and headed down to the dock. Sully was already there, waiting for me. Papa had herded the animals onto the dock and my brother was about to load them. When he saw me he motioned me back. For some reason, he did not want me to be seen. I drew close to the bales of straw used to soften the floor of the barge.

Sully rushed to my side. "Be careful, sister, Laird Pheland is speaking with Papa. If he sees you with that bundle, he may conclude you wish to flee. Even he cannot be so arrogant as to believe you would desire this match."

"Desire? My God, Sully, the very thought of him turns my stomach, near to retching."

"Give me your bundle, and I will pass it to Tag. He'll know how to handle Pheland."

Tears crept slowly down my cheek. "Though I hate the thought of marrying him, how else can I save our family?"

"Hush, lass," Sully said, "I will speak with Uncle Elidor, once you are safe at the MacTaggert's, he will find a way, the responsibility for the Sullivans lies not on your shoulders alone. He will make Papa see reason."

He drew me to the loading dock, where Tag was waiting.

"Sully, Fionna," he said, inclining his head to the holding pen where Laird Pheland was speaking with my father.

The boys blocked the view, and Sully passed my package to Tag.

The sheep appeared nervous and frightened. Though the grazing in the valley was sweet, they feared the river and the dark cavern. Sully walked among them and petted the most agitated. Deep within his heart, my brother loved these creatures. He led them onto the barge and nearly fell into the river as he moved aside so the tiny lambs could be near their mothers.

Tag caught his arm and saved him from a dunking in the cool waters of the river.

"Sully, you are the biggest bumbler I ever met. Tis a wonder how you function without a nursemaid."

My brother's face grew flushed. "I know, I just don't pay attention to what I'm doing, only the sheep."

My father and Laird Pheland approached, as I was ready to step onto the barge. My father smiled expansively and introduced Laird Pheland to me.

"Fionna, my dear, this is Laird Pheland. This will be your final trip, as when you return you will become his wife."

"My final trip? Who else can handle the sheep? Please, Papa, do not take this from me, too." Quickly, I covered my mouth as I realized I'd said too much. Apparently neither man noticed my slip of the tongue, as Papa smiled and held my arm as I boarded the barge.

I picked up the pole and waved to Tag and Sully as I headed the raft to the cavern. This could not be my last trip. If my brother were to take over the journey, there was a good chance the sheep would not be the only ones drowned.

The opening of the cavern seemed a gaping mouth ready to devour me. The swift current took us for a while, until the water became shallow. There was little light in the tunnel and the sheep drew their comfort from me. As I slipped into the cool river water, I sang softly to them. The animals became still and it was easier for me to push the barge along the channel. I'd made this trip so many times I did not need light. I knew each rock in the river and every turn of the tunnel. I could not imagine my clumsy brother making this trip. The underground passage was slow as the river twisted and turned and broke the swift current of the larger river outside. It would take me two days to bring the sheep to summer pasture. Toward the end of the journey, they would be hungry and frightened.

There was fear in my heart as well. I, too, was tired and it would be so easy to give myself up to the river. Yet, though I would rather die than be wed to Pheland, I could not make my father and brother suffer.

I could now see light at the end of the long channel. The skies were clear and the smell of sweet clover enticed the sheep. The sunny sky would not be so for long. Soon the Scottish mist would settle over the valley. The constant vapor over the grazing field was the very reason the sheep were brought here. The air, constantly filled with moisture, caused the fleece of the sheep to grow thick and nearly waterproof as their bodies acclimated to the humidity. Their fleece was a national treasure. No other Scot produced finer wool.

Tag

Fionna would not return until tomorrow and I hoped her Uncle Elidor would offer some assistance. Sully and I searched the entire rim, even trespassing on Arwan's land. The Druid was nowhere to be found. Finally, when we were near to giving up the search, we found him, leaning against an ancient oak and muttering to himself, his words slurred and difficult to understand.

It became clear to me the man was drunk. Though why he would be in such a state was a puzzle. Neither Sully nor I had ever seen the man consume any beverage other than spring water.

As we approached, I noted he was crying as well as rambling.

"Ah, Sully, what are we to do, my boy? She cannot marry this monster. I cannot make him understand this is not a fortuitous match."

Sully knelt down beside his uncle and said, "You are right, Uncle Elidor. We must, somehow, stop this madness. Tag plans on hiding her at his family's stables for a short time until we can come up with a better plan."

"But how? Pheland will be awaiting her return. He's vowed to wed her at once. He's even planning on the Bishop being here to perform the ceremony. The man arrives no later than tomorrow at dusk."

Elidor was doing his best to gather his senses. He wiped his tear-stained face and stood. "My friend, Joseph of Armithea, is arriving today. Perhaps he could help. He has given me a great charge. Maybe through his intervention, I can find a way to protect Fionna until another more worthy suitor presents himself."

Sully yanked at my arm and gestured with his head that I was to tell of my desire for Fionna. However, I knew, though we are the same age, Fionna may be ready for marriage in the eyes of her father, but he would not consider me worthy. I was as yet an untried youth. The fact that I loved her was of little consequence.

"Who is this man of such great import that he would visit a single Druid priest? Is he a Druid as well?" I asked.

Elidor laughed. "He would find it humorous you think him to be a Druid. He is a follower of Jesus Christ, the Christen leader."

"And this Holy Man has given you a charge?" I asked. "It would seem the man would seek other members of his own sect to carry out whatever this mission is."

Elidor smiled, the corners of his mouth curving slightly. "Well, boys, like Sully I have a certain degree of blumbleness that would draw covetous eyes away from the mission and protect my charge. Joseph is truly a wise man and uses all of God's gifts, whether they are apparent to other men or not."

"While I am happy you have received this honor, Brother Elidor, I fail to see how this can help Fionna."

Again the tears threatened within the uncle's eyes. "I am not certain it can, but I must ask. My niece is very dear to me and to see her unhappy distresses me, to say nothing of her feeling compromised by her family finances. Whatever I learn, I will tell you immediately, as we must come up with a solution before Fionna returns."

Tag

I went into my father's room just after dusk. The groom had been there and brought food for him. Owen was cleaning the table as I arrived.

"Tag, your father has eaten well this evening. He seems in fine fettle. I leave you alone to visit. I'll come back for the plate and cup later."

"Thank you, Owen, but there is no need. I'll bring the service to the stable. I need to discuss something with you, so I will be coming there anyway."

The thin, middle-aged man bowed his head slightly and withdrew.

Da was sitting up against freshly fluffed pillows. His eyes were unusually clear and his color good. I prayed it meant his health was improving.

"Well, Tag, today was the day the sheep were taken to pasture, was it not?" he asked.

I moved to the side of his narrow bed. Hagga had replaced the master bed with a single, as she felt he did not need the room. While it was true he was shrinking, it would seem a man should be allowed to be sick in his own bed. Her rules and regulations were stifling both Da and the staff. She had ordered my room in the attic not be cleaned along with the rest of the house. I kept it tidy myself, and often noted my things were not where I had placed them. Her telltale heavy perfume clearly indicated she'd been in my room.

"Yes, Da, today was the day. It went fairly well. The sheep were loaded without mishap, although I thought Sully was going to fall into the river." Da smiled.

I could tell he wished he could have been there to see Sully stumble. Not that he wished Sully any ill will, but he recalled how comical Sully was.

"You seemed troubled, Rory, what is the problem? Did we lose any sheep?"

I scowled, thinking of the mutton that was denied of the Sullivan's. "No, Da, not a single head. We even had a greater lambing this season than last."

"So what is on your mind has nothing to do with the wool production?" he inquired, his perception unerringly clear.

I dared not tell him of Fionna's troubles. "Da, you never mentioned why the herd is kept on the riverside, off the island for a portion of the year and spends the remainder on the island. Why is that?"

"Come, Rory, you know the sheep are taken to the hidden valley to take advantage of the mists."

"Yes, Da, but why cannot they pasture within the valley the entire year?" If, in fact, they could be within the valley for the full season perhaps our yield would increase.

"I know what you are thinking," he replied. "When I arrived here with a small herd, I tried to pasture them within the valley, but the mists grow so heavy in the winter months the animals find the air too thick to breathe. I lost nearly every head that first year. It was only by chance I learned from an old shepherd how to make best use of the mists."

"Well, if that is the case I will just have to find a better way to bring them to summer pasture."

"Why would you need a better way? Portus tells me his daughter has taken over his duties of accompanying the sheep on the journey through the underground river."

"That's true, but she is a woman. Soon she will marry and must do her bridegroom's bidding."

"Do I detect a note of despair in your statement? Do you wish his daughter for your own?"

Da's perception was as sharp as an eagle's vision, yet I dared not reveal my feelings. I had too many issues to deal with before I could think of Fionna as my wife. Preventing her from being someone else's was far more important at the moment.

I closed my eyes, hoping to hide the emotion that was surely displayed for all to see. After much inner consideration on the matter, I opened them. "Da, my feelings are secondary to the business. You taught me that. Besides, I am too young to marry."

Da smiled. I knew he was thinking of his marriage to Mother. He'd been even younger than I when he'd wed.

"I understand, my boy, you are most wise. The business is far more complicated than it was when I started it. Today, five sheep would not even be considered a herd."

I threw back my head and laughed. "Five sheep? You never told me that was the beginning herd."

"I started with fifteen, but lost ten that first year. With the help of that shepherd, I was able to turn three ewes and two rams to a sizeable group."

"You were extremely lucky you were not left with either five ewes or five rams."

"Tag, I am certain the good Lord had something to do with that. I was so frightened that year, I wore thin my knees as I prayed for guidance."

"What was the urgency? Surely, you knew it would take time to rebuild a herd."

"I knew, but I did not have the time to take. Your mother was pregnant with you, and I needed funds to provide for her."

His face softened as he broke into a wide grin. "You should have seen her, son. She was as big as a house and glowed with an inner fire that rivaled the sun. How beautiful she looked."

At that moment, I heard a rustling outside of the door. Quickly, I rushed to open it. I spotted Hagga's skirt rapidly whip around the hall corner. God, couldn't she give the man some peace with his pleasant memories? What did she hope to gain by listening at my father's door?

"Never mind her, Tag. It won't be long now and she will be gone."

"Why is that, Da? Is she planning some sort of trip?"

"No, son, the trip will be mine."

"Yours? Are you strong enough to travel?" I asked, dreading his answer. "I cannot stave off the reaper any longer. I've made my peace with the Lord and with you. Nothing else remains to be done."

Suddenly the door burst open and Hagga stormed in. "Nothing left to be done? What about me? How will I be provided for? You've taken the business from me, what have I left? This dungeon of a home? I want what is my due."

My father gazed at her with deep regret, unable to hide the loathing in his eyes. "You will be taken care of, Hagga. You will not have to remain here. Rory will live in the manor. You may go wherever you choose."

Unable to be civil, I pushed her out of the room, closing the door against her screams. I would not allow her to mar my father's last moments on earth with her ranting.

"Never mind, my son. I am going to be with your mother. I feel badly you must remain with that witch. Contact Laird MacDonald. He will handle all the affairs."

I rushed to my father's bedside and knelt beside him. "Da, please don't go." I whined like a child, for at that moment I was just a boy losing his father.

He took my hand in his and grasped it tightly. Though gaunt, his grip was still powerful. I closed my eyes and breathed deeply as I felt my father take his last breath. Then I was alone.

Chapter Three
Tag

Losing my father was relegated to the same painful place in my mind as my mother's passing. I preferred not to dwell on the hurt, but instead turned my thoughts to prevention of another injury, one that could cut more deeply. Each of us, in some corner of our consciousness, realizes we will probably outlive our parents, but I was not prepared to live the remainder of my life without Fionna.

She was living in Owen's quarters, but could not do so for long. Hagga had ordered the groom off the premises, as she told me she was certain the man had poisoned my father. She had no authority to order the man to leave, but she was beginning to build a plausible defense, as she knew I would accuse her in the misdeed.

Each evening as I brought Fionna her food and a change of clothes from her brother, I could see the confinement was wearing on her. "Fionna," I begged, "you must go out during the day. To remain within this stable is not good for your health."

How I longed to take her in my arms and profess my love. Once the estate was settled and I could offer her more than my devotion, I would declare my intentions.

Laird MacDonald informed me the will was to be read publicly, as it was Da's intention to spread his wealth as widely as possible. My father had been very generous to his workers and he wanted them to know they would be protected in the same manner by his son.

Fionna peered up at me, her brilliant blue eyes full of trust. "Tag, I would love to go out during the day. I tried to leave for a brief ride yesterday and was no more than free of the stable when I saw Arwan sitting on a dark horse above the ridge. I fear he searches for me."

"You're probably right. I'm certain he's questioned your father. The poor man is beside himself with grief. Arwan is likely to use your absence as leverage to sell the rim and the valley to him. He does not know I own the valley."

Fionna fell to her knees, crying. "What are we to do? I cannot live here forever. With Owen gone, Hagga will search the stable."

I knelt beside her and placed my arm about her shoulders for comfort. I dared not offer more. "You're right, but we have at least till the end of the week when the will is read. She won't come down here until she is sure of her place. I will meet with Sully and your uncle. We will find a solution. You have my word. I shall not fail."

Quickly, I turned so she would not see the fear in my eyes. I had not even the glimmer of an idea how I could save her, but save her I must. As I left the barn, her scent remained with me. Mingled with the smell of the clean straw, it was headier than any perfume devised by man.

I headed for the lambing shed, as I knew I would find Sully there. He would be cleaning the pens that had just been vacated by the sheep Fionna took to summer pasture. He was whistling and sweeping in a strange sort of off-beat rhythm.

Sully was a man of unique qualities. He truly believed in the goodness of man. It was difficult for him to believe one person would harm another. Unfortunately, he'd been forced to accept that all men are not filled with the milk of human kindness. Arwan Pheland was the epitome of evil. So like Hagga, one could almost believe they were cut from the same cloth. Today, whatever else I may accomplish, I must find a way to protect Fionna.

Oblivious to any concerns other than the pens' cleaning, Sully did not hear me enter. I grasped him by the shoulder to get his attention.

"What?" he started. "Great heavens, Tag, are you trying to separate me from my wits? You scared the devil out of me."

"Would that it were the devil were that easy to rout. We must find a solution for Fionna. Today, Sully, we are about out of time."

Sully leaned the broom against the side of the shed. "I have been trying to convince myself there is not a problem, but even my bumbleness cannot accept allowing my sister to be wed to that pig."

"The only one I can think might be able to help is your uncle."

"Elidor? He's as much a bumbler as I. How can he help?" Sully asked, his eyes imploring me to provide an answer.

"I don't know, but we have to ask. Come on, let's find him."

Looking back to see all the pens were ready for the next season's lambs, he nodded and fell into step beside me.

Together, we followed the narrow path to the top of the rim in silence, each hoping to come up with the answer. I stepped along with my head down.

Suddenly, Sully placed his arm in front of me. "What's wrong? Why did you stop me?" I asked.

Placing his finger to his lips to indicate I was to keep silent, he pointed to a copse of trees. There were scant places on the rim that supported many types of vegetation. I was surprised I'd never seen it before.

"Look," he whispered, "there's some sort of shrine in there. See the stone that looks like a table?"

I did see the table. What's more, I saw Sully's uncle draped over it, a goblet loosely held in his hand. The man had clearly had too much spirits.

We were about to enter the grove, when I saw Arwan approach. This grove was on his portion of the rim. "Well, you fool priest, what are you doing on my property? This section of the rim is mine."

Elidor lifted his head and smiled drunkenly. "I'ss knows that. This shrine was constructed, long before you and me ever existed."

"You think that matters to me? It's just a silly pile of rocks. I will tear them down and build a mansion for Fionna once we are married."

"Oh, now you want to do something for the girl? Not just take advantage of her to acquire more land?" The wine was losing its hold on Elidor. It was apparent he, too, thought Arwan cared not a wit about Fionna.

"Once I receive fair compensation, the girl may do as she chooses. She's so damned ugly I wouldn't bother to rut her."

My heart cried out. I wanted to throttle the man. He'd no right to call Fionna ugly. Her father had chosen Arwan because he thought the older man would appreciate her unique beauty. It was clear he did not. Sully had to use all his strength to restrain me. I gathered my senses, realizing to confront Arwan would alert him to our desires to free Fionna from her father's promise. To thwart him, he could not be aware of us.

Elidor stood and faced Arwan. "Sir, if you simply desire wealth, I have something so valuable, its worth cannot be measured."

"Oh, you do? Well then, why do you not pay off your brother-in-law's debts?"

"I cannot, as the item must not be sold. Its worth is in power, not money," Elidor replied, carefully avoiding naming any specific object.

"You bumbling drunk. I want you off my property within the hour. And don't bother to return. I shall have these stones removed and hauled away. Now leave."

Arwan turned and left the copse of trees. "Elidor," I called softly, "is he out of sight?"

Sully's uncle turned, slightly confused. "Who's there?" he asked.

"It's just us, Uncle," Sully answered. "What are you doing here? I never saw this place before, and I thought I knew the entire rim."

Elidor struggled to regain his wit. "You've looked at it many times, Sully, but you have never seen it."

Sully turned his head and asked, "Does this have something to do with your being a Druid priest?"

"It does, my boy, but I must say nothing more. Merlin will be angered enough with me to know I allowed Arwan to view this place."

I failed to comprehend how someone who was not present could be aware of the situation. I'd thought Merlin to be a myth. Yet, Elidor referred to him as if he were alive today. If I remembered the tale correctly, Merlin was a wizard. If in fact he was, this could be the answer to our problem. "Can you call him, Elidor?"

"Call him?" the Druid asked, seemingly bewildered by my request. "Merlin appears at his will, and his alone. If he comes now, he will be here to punish me. To reveal a Druid grotto to those who would seek to destroy it is truly a most dire occurrence."

"Look on the bright side, Uncle, if he comes, perhaps he will help us."

"Help us?" Elidor asked, his eyes half glazed over.

"It's no use, Tag. He cannot aid us in his present state. Let's leave him to sleep it off and find the solution ourselves."

"Sully, we've not the time. Fionna will be back at dusk. We must have a plan in place before she arrives. Pick him up. We'll take him back to your father. Perhaps he can sober him up quickly."

We'd walked not one hundred feet, when a tall man in a flowing crimson robe approached. I'd never seen him before, but he had an air about him that made me recognize him as an ally.

"Excuse me, gentlemen, I believe the man you carry is a friend of mine." The man leaned heavily on a long staff. His gray beard curled softly about his chin.

Sully stepped forward, his hand extended and said, "This man is my Uncle, sir. Who might you be? Are you Merlin?"

The corners of the man's mouth curled upward and then he laughed, very softly. "No, young man, I am no wizard. Anything I accomplish is through the power of the Lord."

Not to be deterred, Sully further pressed the man. "If you are not Merlin, who are you?"

Bowing slightly, the old man introduced himself. "I am Joseph of Armithea, a follower of Christ."

I could not reconcile the apparent blending of faiths. How could Elidor, a Druid, be a companion of a Christian?

The old man leaned over and set his staff aside. "Allow me. I have some tea I carry for any injuries that may beset me. It will quickly restore Elidor," he said, taking the Druid from us and laying him on the ground, leaning against one of the taller stones.

Within moments after he pressed the teacup to his lips, Elidor sat up straight. "Oh my God, what have I done?"

"Did you reveal the location of the Grail?" Joseph asked.

A bewildered look passed over Elidor's features. "I do not know."

I knew. "Laird Armithea, he did not reveal the location of anything. He simply alluded he had something of great value. He did not say what that might be."

The old gentleman sighed deeply.

"Truly the Lord does protect us from our own folly."

Tag

Knowing our presence was not required, Sully and I withdrew. Silently, we headed for the beach.

"Tag, do you think the Holy Man can help?"

I had prayed as hard as I was able, that such would be the case. Yet, I hesitated to give rise to false hope. "I do not know. We must find a way to stall Fionna's return. If we meet her at the beach before dusk, perhaps we can hide her so Arwan does not know she has returned."

"It's risky. He will be anxiously awaiting her. But, unless Uncle Elidor can persuade Laird Armithea, we have no choice but to try."

As the sun grew lower and lower in the sky, so did my hopes sink. As the appointed time grew near, we went to the dock. A purple haze settled over the water, and there appeared not a ripple in the surface, as if it were made of glass.

Joseph of Armithea

I was a stranger in this land, where my dear friend resided. Though he was beside himself with grief for revealing he knew of some precious treasure, I knew it was in God's plan. Somehow, something good will come of his apparent misdeed.

"Fear not," I said, "I fully trusted you with the Grail, and continue to do so. Though you fear what you call your bumbleness has been your undoing, it is in fact the very reason you were chosen for this."

Angered, Elidor replied, "I fail to see how my failure can be an instrument of God."

I knelt beside him as he sat against the ancient oak that served as a symbol of his faith. "God uses each of our gifts to his best advantage. What others believe is a fault, God counts as a virtue."

"You mean I am worthy in the eyes of the Christ?"

"Yes, you are, Elidor, and He counts you as one of His own."

"He accepts me even though I am not Christian?"

"He died for all our sins. All of us, not a chosen few."

"If this be the case," Elidor said fervently, "I, too, will be a Christian."

At once, a startling darkness overtook the Grotto. The table within split down the center with a horrific crash, sending shards of stone flying everywhere. And, from the breach, a tall man in a blue robe emerged, his eyes charged with fire. Though I knew the Lord would protect me, I grew fearful, for I had never experienced such an occurrence. It was not unlike the day at Calvary.

The man spoke. "How dare you set aside your vows, Elidor? You studied long and hard to become a Druid. Are you telling me your training was simply a whim?"

My friend struggled to find his tongue. "Great Merlin, you know I am devoted to the teachings I labored so long to learn. I simply would like to be a Christian as well."

Merlin softened his countenance, nodded, then spoke slowly. "Perhaps that is what was intended all along. Joseph, what must be done to make my priest one of the followers of Christ? From what I understand of your faith, there is no ceremony involved, except the immersion of the person in a body of water. Is this not correct?"

"It is, Merlin, I believe that is who you are. We call the ceremony baptism. It is symbolic of the purity we have as children and the love God has for us."

"Do I understand correctly that the basis of Christ's teaching is love?"

"You do, Great Wizard. While I know only a little of the Druidic instruction, from my friend here, he tells me your faith is respective of all living things, which I equate as love. Thus the apparent difference is, in fact, a similarity."

The stern Merlin lifted his chin and looked at me with crystal blue eyes. His white beard swayed gently as he contemplated my statement. Stepping from between the severed table pieces, he tapped the base of his fox-headed cane on the earth, and what had been wrought asunder became whole.

"Gentlemen, the matter of my being Christian can be dealt with at a later time. My love for Christ will remain constant. For the moment, I must help another I love as well. Fionna, my niece, is being forced to marry a man not of her own choosing."

I looked at the forlorn Druid, but was unable to discern why this matter was unacceptable. Marriages were frequently arranged without thought of the persons within the bond knowing one another. "Elidor, I fail to understand why this is a matter of concern to you."

Elidor faced me, his eyes swimming with tears. "She has been betrothed to a man simply to save her family from financial ruin. He has spoken to me and made it clear he finds her ugly and has no intention of honoring the marriage once he has secured the land that is offered as a bride price. And Fionna is so noble, she will not allow another to bear the burden."

The Druid's body trembled as if he himself had taken on the burden of this child's life. It became apparent to me that the priest loved her as much as if she had been his own offspring. To be compelled to marry a person who had no intention of honoring the marriage vows was wrong. I could not allow this to happen.

Merlin, who had been listening closely to Elidor's statement, moved close to my side. "Neither of our faiths can tolerate this abomination. I know of the man Elidor refers to. He is greedy and devious, and he hopes to gain control of this very isle. It is my duty to protect our grotto and the island. Such a man must be handled with cunning, not outright confrontation."

"Who is this man, and how can we protect the girl? If her father has pledged her, how can we dishonor this betrothal?"

Merlin paced up and down the narrow grotto. Then he paused, lifted his head, and placed a long, slender finger to his lips. Suddenly, the Druid sanctuary became flushed with a brilliant light that washed over us like a tidal wave. The illumination dimmed then settled a narrow beam onto the old wizard.

"The woman cannot marry if she is no longer a woman."

It was as I feared. The sorcerer wanted to resort to magic. I had been able to accept the man's presence, even the blinding light, but to trick a child of God was unacceptable. "Do you plan to turn this child into a frog?" I asked.

The ancient wizard threw back his head and laughed, as if my interpretation of his power was ludicrous. I'd simply related what little I knew of such beings.

"No, Laird Armithea, I will simply give her a guise in which to hide until we are able to convince Arwan that this is not the proper course for the child."

Elidor stood, then leaned heavily against the old oak. "To convince Arwan of anything would take longer than it did for this oak to mature. He will stop at nothing to achieve this island. He believes once he secures the rim, the valley will be his as well, and he will then have control of the wool production this isle is famous for."

I knew many cultures offered a bride price to a prospective groom, but to hand over the source of a family's income made no sense to me at all.

Merlin interjected, "I realize it is hard to fathom the ways of the Ancient Druids, but trust me, friend Joseph, what I intend will protect both the girl and the wool."

"How? What can you do, Merlin?"

"With your friend's help, we will transform the girl. The guise must be an entity that can perform the duties she now undertakes. If not, the wool cannot be protected." Abruptly the wizard turned and paced once more. Back and forth he walked, each trip to the end of the grotto becoming shorter as he paced faster and faster.

I reached out and took the old man's arm, halting him. He raised his head and surprised me with a smile. From the little I'd seen of him, a smile seemed out of place, both for the man and the situation.

"Fionna will become a swan on this very eve. She will still be able to take the sheep to the summer pasture, yet Arwan will believe she has vanished. There will be no trace of her in her human form."

"I can see that this will protect her for a time, but we cannot relegate her to being a bird for the remainder of her life."

"Quite so, Christian. That is your part."

"M—my part?" I stammered. "I cannot perform magic. What do you expect of me?"

"I would use your Grail as an instrument of protection." The sorcerer raised his long arms, causing the sleeves of his robe to bunch at his elbows. The man was so thin his gauntness was almost comic, though I knew the man was far from humorous. He had a great problem to solve, and I also knew it was my charge to assist him.

"Great Merlin, I will do all I can to aid you, but I cannot compromise the Grail." I feared trivializing the most sacred cup.

The wizard moved closer to Elidor and grabbed the man roughly by the front of his robe.

"Elidor, have you forgotten Tivannia?"

The Druid turned a puzzled face to Merlin, tears forming in his eyes. "I'll never forget her. I love her with all my heart."

"She will come to aid us and protect her daughter."

"How?" the Druid cried.

"She died when her daughter was born."

"Elidor, have you forgotten Tivannia was a priestess? She did not die. She simply moved to another plane."

Elidor sighed deeply and slipped down to the sparse grasses outside of the Druid sanctuary. "I thought she was playing a game, when she said she was a priestess. Only a very special few are so chosen and all reside in Avalon. Not here on this tiny isle within a river."

"Fool! Perhaps it is better you become a Christian. They are not required to know the whole of their faith. Priestesses live wherever they can be of service. You sister is here, on this very isle, protecting the sheep, the isle, and her daughter."

"But how? I myself saw her pass from this life."

"Perhaps if you lingered longer instead of being about mourning at once, you would have seen the second passage from this existence to the realm of Hydon."

***

Rory "Tag" MacTaggert

The shadows grew longer as Sully and I made our way down from the rim. Each of us knew there was little hope of saving Fionna. As we walked, I slowly recounted the passages I'd endured in the past. My father's death still fresh in my mind, I wondered what he would have done in the same situation. One thing I was sure of, he would not wander about aimlessly hoping for a solution to drop in his outstretched hands. I had to do something, to take an active role. Even if the attempt were thwarted, at least I would have made that attempt.

"Sully," I said, grabbing his clothes and leading him quickly along the path. "We are going into the underground river. If we can reach Fionna before Arwan arrives, we can hide her within the cavern."

Sully was hesitant, probably because he didn't know how to swim, but I would not let him refuse. Once we were on the narrow beach, I searched the top of the rim and any other route Pheland might take. No one was about.

The waters of the river were cold even in the summer evening heat. Once, when I was much younger, I'd stolen away from my father and entered the underground river. The waters within the cavern were much colder, I remember that chillingly. But nothing must stop us now. We had to rescue Fionna from such a cruel fate.

Sully followed behind me into the bone cold water, hanging on to my tunic for dear life.

"Ease off, Sully, the water is only knee deep. You can walk. You don't have to swim."

His teeth chattering, he replied, "H—h—how do you know it won't get deep in a hurry?"

As on my single previous trip I had not ventured far, I did not know exactly how deep the waters grew, but I wasn't going to tell him that. "Relax, underground rivers are never very deep."

Apparently he concurred, as he plunged ahead, unmindful of the depth.

Clumsy as he was, his step was determined. He knew this might be the only way to keep his sister from the evil man her father had chosen for her to marry.

The cavern twisted a few paces ahead, the walls overhead lowered, and we were forced to crawl in the river, with only our heads above the water. The curving wall cut off all of the outside light. We had to feel our way along the riverbed.

I grew increasingly fearful. It seemed to me we should have reached Fionna by now.

Elidor the Druid Priest

I was glad the boys had left. It was my fault and the responsibility was mine. I'd been chastised by the Great Merlin, rather an honor, if you choose to believe in his power. The many years of study were not serving me well. I'd not the merest hint of an idea of how to save my niece. Yet, through whatever means, I had to pluck her from this terrible fate. It certainly wasn't of her doing, save the fact she would not tell her father of her true feelings. I know Portus would have found another answer for the financial dilemma and not have permitted his child to be forced to marry a man she feared, but she would do so for the sake of her family.

Merlin and my friend Joseph stood outside the grotto and were conversing intently when suddenly the sky grew an odd shade of green. Now, Scotland is a very green country due the frequent rains, but this was a green I'd never seen before. It was a sparkling emerald so infused with light I found the color blinding to look straight at it.

I watched my friend and Merlin staring at the column of infused green light. How, I wondered, were they able to look at the intense light without shielding their eyes? Within moments, the glare softened and I was able to see my sister within the radiance. The sister I'd thought long dead.

I rushed forward to greet her and noticed she did not seem to be of the same substance as Joseph and me. The iridescence was as Merlin's. Truly my blessed Tivannia was here with me. If not in body, surely in spirit.

"My dear sister, do you know what is happening to your daughter?"

Tivannia moved to embrace me. I could smell her essence, but could not feel her arms about me. "Yes, dear Elidor, I know, and with the help of your friends, we will protect her."

"But how?" I whined.

"Arwan watches every moment at the mouth of the underground river. He is not an easy man to fool."

Chapter Four
Tivannia

It was wondrous to see my dear brother again. He'd changed little since I'd left. Of course, I followed his daily being, but not on the same plane. I watched the daughter I'd never held, as well. She was a beautiful child and my heart filled with pride to see the way she handled the family, even riding with the sheep to the summer grazing. This terrible yoke would not be laid upon the shoulders of my precious daughter. Only my dear Portus knew I'd been a priestess of Avalon, but I am certain he questioned my wisdom in allowing the situation to go this far. He would wonder no longer. Today with the help of my brother and his friend, Merlin and I would save the lass.

"Gentlemen, this is how we are going to protect my daughter and this holy isle."

Both men looked at me, expectation clear within their eyes. Elidor did not know here on the Hydon Isle was a tiny sanctuary where the "Old Ways" were kept much the same way as within "The Mists of Avalon." The valley is home to the Scottish priestesses as well as the summer pasture for the sheep. We, too, take advantage of the mists to remain hidden from those who would seek to destroy us.

I could see my brother's friend was skeptical; most Christians do not believe in the old ways and fear their power. But this man seemed strong in his own faith and was certain nothing could compromise him. Yet, he said, "Mistress, I am unsure of not only your presence, but how can I allow the Cup of Christ to be used in a ritual that does not adhere to the tenets of the religion it represents?"

"Fear not, Master Joseph, the cup will be unharmed, and I believe you will realize in time this was as your God planned long ago. Have you forgotten, we Druids foretold the coming of your Savior?"

Elidor stepped forward and clasped his friend by the shoulder. "Do you not remember, Joseph, when we first met, I told you I found mention of the very same in my Druid instruction?"

The older man remained unconvinced as was evident by the hard line of his chin. Then Joseph sat back on the ground, leaning against one of the massive stones, and stroked his beard, nodding as if he'd had an epiphany. Awkwardly he rose, briefly inclined his head at me and said, "Mistress, as I think over many of the conversations I've enjoyed with your brother, I do recall he mentioned such was the case. In any event, I daresay should this be wrong, Christ will not permit it to happen."

Merlin grew angry. "You think what I propose would in any way compromise the teachings of your church? In my lifetime I've known many of your sect and most were not boastful of their God, but simply strived to serve him."

The two robed men were squaring off like combatant youths. I must keep them on track if I am to save my daughter." "Gentlemen, enough. Merlin, please come to my side and Elidor, take your friend to the opposite stone of this sacred circle." One did not usually chastise the Great Merlin, and I feared angering him further, but to rescue Fionna I would dare anything. "Please, Laird Armithea, may I hold the vessel?"

"Mistress, I trust you will not abuse the power of the Grail, but can you tell me exactly how you will use it?"

"As I present it to the Mother Goddess, the Grail becomes a sign of the promise that my child will be restored once the danger has passed. Once the Goddess sees it, the cup will be returned to wherever my brother has secreted it."

"You do not wish to have it in your possession?" the skeptical Holy Man inquired.

"Master Merlin, have you not told Joseph my brother is to be a bridge between our faiths as more come to accept the Christ and our world of the Fey will pass from sight? Your anger draws you from your duty, sir," I chastised the wizard lightly.

"Tivannia, I apologize for my behavior. We must consider the consequences not only for your daughter but the isle, and the vessel must be safeguarded as well," Merlin directed.

"Quite so, Master Merlin, the three are tied inexorably to one another." My brother left the clearing and went into the grotto. When he returned, he had a silken pouch, which he placed in the hands of the Holy Man.

Joseph of Armithea extracted the vessel and placed it carefully in my outstretched palms. He then took my brother's extended hand and moved opposite the Master Druid priest and me. The cup itself was plain, a vessel for a man of the people, produced by a simple craftsman.

I raised my arms and called upon the Great Goddess to use her glamour to protect my child, the Isle of Hydon, and the Cup of the Christ. It took all of my strength to raise my arms and hold the cup. No matter how great the effort required, I must aid in the projection with the Mother Goddess. I could feel my substance growing evermore faint. Laird Armithea drew the greater measure from me. As a new believer, he had much to discard. His faith in his God was greater than his newfound belief in beings who transported from other realms. Yet, he did his best and when he saw what his doubt was doing, he refrained from staring at me.

The azure blue of the skies gave way to brilliant reds and golds as the rain emanated from each wisp of cloud, and the wind blew with the force of a gale. The men joined hands to prevent being swept away. My bare feet were planted firmly on the holy soil, so I did not feel the force of the wind. Lightning slashed the crimson firmament. The Goddess had served us well. As I lowered my arms, I noted Merlin's smile. I knew the deed had been done.

***

Tag

The water was rising within the cavern. I had all I could do to keep my head above water. Sully was panicked, stretching his neck and yelling for me to save him as the water lapped at his chin. Suddenly

I heard a strange noise. I stopped and Sully bumped into me. Taking hold of his tunic, I indicated he was to hold silent. I strained to hear. It sounded like the flapping of the wings of a large bird. But how could a large bird get into the underground river? There was barely enough room for a small duck to land.

We crept along on the sandy bottom, till the cavern ceiling rose and the water grew warm. There, in front of us, was a pure white swan. Its feathers were as glistening a white as Fionna's hair.

"Fionna."

As soon as Sully said the words, I knew he was right. The magnificent bird was his sister. He rushed forward. His action startled the bird and it flapped its wings furiously.

I whistled softly, a tune Fionna and I had often used to call the wild birds on the rim. Apparently, she recognized the melody, as gracefully she brought her large wings to rest on her back. Around her long slender neck was a silver collar studded with green gems. From the collar hung a fine silver chain, the end tethered to the low barge. The chain was so finely wrought; it seemed not to be strong enough to pull the empty barge. Yet the vessel moved along smoothly over the underground river. She was as regal a bird as she was as a woman.

"Look," Sully cried, "That's my mother's choker and chain. I used to play with it when she held me. I remember."

I'd only seen his mother on one occasion, and I did recall her unusual jewelry, a unique piece that stuck in my mind. It was the same choker. I was certain of it.

"Fionna," I cried, "please let me know it's you." I felt certain she could not speak, but if it were, in fact, her, she had to give me some sign.

The swan extended its long neck then dipped its bill into the water, finally drawing the neck back as far as it would stretch. My heart leapt. It was Fionna, there was no doubt. She would be safe. But how? Had Elidor used some Druid magic?

In truth, I cared not one wit as long as Fionna was protected. But for how long would she remain thus? Would I never know Fionna as a woman?

As we neared the river entrance, the swan slowed its pace. Using her wide feet she propelled herself forward so effortlessly I found myself caught up in the sheer majesty of the bird. Once in the brilliant sunshine, the light refracted off the bird's feathers drawing all eyes to her. Yet Sully and I held back. I wished I had held the end of the chain. Somehow it became untethered.

Fionna unfurled her great wings and I spotted the chain cascading behind her as she took flight. Higher and higher she soared then circled over the edge of the rim up and out of sight.

At the highest edge of the rim, Arwan Pheland sat atop a massive black stallion. The bird flying overhead drew his attention momentarily. I prayed he was not smart enough to realize the bird was, in fact, his intended. As I was not certain how the deed was accomplished, I did not know what knowledge the fiend might employ. Could he have some magic evil powers we were unaware of?

Chapter Five
Tivannia

I'd used nearly all my strength to transform my daughter. I was weak, unable to return to my spirit state. Alone on this isle among the Scottish Priestesses, the charge to protect the "Old Ways" was mine alone. Most of the other women within our sanctuary were from other lands. I was the only native born. The day I became a priestess was as fresh in my mind as if it were yesterday. The Lady of the Lake herself had come to initiate me. It was there she gave me the extreme honor of remaining in my homeland. Most priestesses spend much time in Avalon learning the old ways, but the lady told me I had a natural proclivity for the sacred rites. I suppose the fact my dear brother was a Druid, who studied long and well, may have had something to do with her decision. Only four years older than I, Elidor had approached his studies with zeal. He would spend hours telling me of the ancient lore. I believe the lady knew neither of us would do well without the support of the other.

Merlin, seeing my distress, had come to my side and eased me to the ground where I leaned against the sacred oak. I drew my strength from the mighty tree and once again marveled how Elidor had managed to hide it from unwelcome prying eyes. But, on this day, he'd done the unthinkable. He'd revealed the grotto to one who would seek to destroy the faith, and all those who practice it. His friend Joseph seemed untroubled about the hiding place for the Chalice, so who was I to judge? Merlin, too, seemed unconcerned.

Gathering my growing strength, I rose and then dematerialized from Elidor and his friend. It would be sometime before I would see my brother again.

Tag

As Fionna flew in swan form over the rim, I felt my heart rent from my body. She would carry it with her until to the end of time itself. I prayed she knew she was the custodian of my dreams. Who could have performed this wondrous deed? Arwan would never think such a thing could happen. I knew, though, he would accuse Sully and me of kidnapping Fionna. Sully, for all his clumsiness, believed the swan was his sister. He was so relieved she would not have to marry Pheland I feared he would reveal the mystery of the swan. I would have to be his constant companion at least until the time came to return the sheep to the winter pasture. It would be three long months until I would again see the woman I love, or I should say, the swan. For I was certain she would remain a bird until the time for the return trip of the sheep. If only she did not find other swans and assimilate to their ways and forget she was actually a person.

Sully and I stepped out of the water and made our way to the dock. The empty barge seemed to know where it was moored for the summer, as it glided soundlessly to its proper location.

Sully secured the vessel and then fell back as the sudden appearance of a nearly transparent woman startled him. She was very beautiful, so like Fionna. Her hair hung from her head in long graceful curls. She smiled at us and drew nearer to Sully. I could see her stroke his cheek, much like a mother caressing her first born.

"M—mother?" Sully stammered. "How can this be you? You died so long ago. Surely your spirit resides in heaven. Why have you returned?"

The woman stepped back, though her feet did not touch the dock. "My child, how I have missed you. I've never left this isle and I am with you always, to protect you and your sister."

"Was it you who transformed her into the swan? Or has some evil fiend stolen her away? Please, tell me Arwan Pheland has not the power to do such a deed."

"No, my son, he has no power liken to mine own. His only force is his own insatiable greed."

I moved to Sully's side and addressed the glowing transparent visage. "Madam, are you truly Sully's mother? How can this be? He told me you'd perished giving birth to my Fionna."

The woman smiled, her eyes seeming to discern my every thought. "Yes, Tag, I did lose my existence on the same plane as you and other mortals. I am a priestess of the Hydon Isle and thus moved to another type of existence."

"Did you know your daughter was in danger? Is that why you have returned to us? How can we assist you? I love your daughter with all my heart and will be unable to rest until I know she is safe."

"Fear not, young Rory, I shall hide her in swan form until after the return of the lambs. Then we face an even greater danger. Once she is again a woman, Pheland will want to hold my dear Portus to his promise."

Sully stood before her, his mouth agape. He knew without a doubt this was his mother, but was overwhelmed by her unusual presence. "But, Mother, how can we save her? If Pheland holds Papa to his bargain, he will be duty-bound to offer Fionna as a bride."

"I understand, my son, but fear not, three months is a long time. Much can happen between now and then." At once, the woman disappeared, as rapidly as she'd arrived.

Chapter Six
Tag

Hagga treated me with an exaggerated courtesy, which belied her true nature. I'd nearly forgotten the will was to be read by the end of the week. It was clear Hagga had not. She'd even ordered my room cleaned. What she hoped to gain by pretending concern for my feelings was a mystery to me. I had not anticipated Da's death would fill my coffers with riches. But she was determined she would get her due, even if it meant allying herself with me.

I dressed carefully on the appointed day. Laird MacDonald's offices were in the best part of the village. A respected barrister, his offices were well appointed. He'd always handled any legal problem my father's business encountered. I assumed he would do the same for me, now that I had charge of the business. Out of consideration for my father and his business associate, I dressed accordingly.

Hagga called up the stairs to me as I finished. "Son, are you prepared for the will reading? And do dress properly, not in your usual shepherd's clothing. We mustn't keep Laird MacDonald waiting."

Son? She'd never called me that while my father was alive, so why now? It was clear she planned to wrest the business from me by pretending I was in need of a guardian. But a few months from eighteen, I was a man both by experience and circumstance. I'd been running the business for nearly a year and needed no guidance from the likes of her. Father had prepared me well. I knew the operations and responsibility of the company. No one employed by my father would receive any less consideration from me than they did from my father. I would carry on the business and hopefully pass it to my son one day.

I hollered down, "I'll be with you in a moment, Hagga." I wanted to retort with a sarcastic "Mother," but I dared not risk her rancor. Not that I feared her anger, but this day would be trying enough without dealing with a hysterical woman. I was certain she would not give up the business without a fight. However, she knew she could not conduct business alone, and that she would need my compliance. And compliance was something I was not prepared to give.

She was waiting in the carriage as I stepped through the door. "Come, Rory, we will be late with all your dawdling."

I raised an eyebrow and glared directly into her narrowed eyes. She lifted her chin and faced straight ahead as Owen drove the elaborate carriage she'd rented for this occasion. I certainly could have ridden in the wagon and I'm sure Owen would have preferred driving it in his regular clothes. Hagga, however, had ordered him wear a coat and top hat to parade her through the streets.

In front of the three-story office building, Hagga directed Owen to stop. I stepped down and offered my hand to her to assist her from the carriage. She gave me a look that clearly showed she didn't expect any courtesy from me. However, I would not shame my deceased mother by exhibiting bad manners. Once Hagga was standing in front of the building, she folded her elaborate parasol and strode ahead of me. She opened the door to reveal a formal sitting room where one could wait for Laird MacDonald to come from his office and welcome you. We sat no more than ten minutes when Portus Sullivan, his brother-in-law, and his son also came to the sitting room.

Hagga hissed at me, "What are those peasants doing here? They have no right to be present at this will reading."

At that moment, Laird MacDonald emerged and heard her comment. "Hagga, you are mistaken, they have every right to be here. There will be some others, as well."

"Why?" she demanded. "Rory and I are his only family. Evan's will should concern no one other than Rory and me."

Laird MacDonald was a rather hefty man and too gruff for the likes of some. But my father trusted him implicitly, with good reason. "Evan MacTaggert has dictated who is to be present, not you."

Hagga bristled and swept her voluminous skirts onto the narrow horsehair couch. She drew her mouth into a thin line, as if threatening the attorney with her authority. In fact, she had none. Da's will had been carefully instrumented and would be carried out to the letter of the law.

"My secretary would be happy to get you some tea, if any of you would like." Laird MacDonald looked from face to face about his sitting room.

Sully found a chair next to me and leaned over.

"Why are we here? MacDonald sent a messenger we were to be present but did not say why. Do you think that witch is going to order us from our home?"

Placing a hand over my mouth, I turned and whispered, "I am certain that is what she would wish, but have no fear. Da would never have permitted it and MacDonald is here to see my father's wishes, not his greedy widow's, are carried out."

"I hope you are right. Pheland was at our door early this morning demanding my father present Fionna."

"What did your father tell him? Did he say she's vanished?"

Sully turned and said, softly so no one in the room other than me could possibly hear him, "No, Elidor overheard him and rushed to Papa's side and told Pheland Fionna is ill."

Fear washed over me. "She's returned then? Is she very sick?"

Sully closed his eyes and said, "No, you fool, Elidor was buying time. The only strange thing about it is Papa offered no contradiction. And Arwan Pheland believed every word of it."

Several other people I recognized from the mill entered. Hagga eyed each of them suspiciously. I could almost see the functions of her mind. She was calculating the division of my father's worth.

Laird MacDonald ushered all of us into his spacious office with fine leather chairs, enough to accommodate all of us, and a shiny silver tray set with biscuits and scones.

Sully, who always considered his stomach first, reached for one of the scones and carefully ladled the provided honey over it.

Laird MacDonald smiled. He'd known Sully all of his life and often seemed amused by his childlike behavior. The well-fed man circled his massive desk and sat. He clasped his hands in front of him and stared down at the papers on his desk.

"Ladies and Gentlemen, we are here today to learn of the intent of the deceased, Evan MacTaggert. Evan was a careful businessman and has trained his son to be the same. I will first address the issues, which pertain to those who are employed in the mill. None of you will lose your positions, nor can the present owner alter any of your wages."

At this, Hagga snorted. Clearly she'd intended to fire many and cut the wages of the remainder.

The barrister continued. "Evan further states, while the mill is presently running at a modest profit, raises cannot be offered at this time. However, he has set up a fund to aid widows and orphans of those workers who through injury or death are not able to provide for their families."

At this, Hagga grew incensed. "How can that fool of a man harass me from his grave? The mill and all the land are my due. It was through my careful management of those profits that they increased. I will have a say in this matter, mark my words." After she made her pronouncement, she rose from her chair and started for the door. As she reached for the knob, the door opened and there stood Arwan Pheland.

"Sir, you were not invited to this proceeding," Laird MacDonald said. "You have no business here. Please leave."

I swear I smelled sulfur, so sinister was Arwan Pheland's presence. Glaring at the attorney, Pheland lowered his head and said, "MacDonald,

I have every right to be at this proceeding. I am here to represent the rights of my sister."

"Your s-sister?" I stammered, staring at Hagga. Apparently my intuition was correct. Not only were Hagga and Arwan alike in demeanor, they were related as well.

Hagga marched back to her seat. Arwan dragged a side chair from alongside of the wall and sat next to her. Hagga managed to force a single tear to flow from one eye. I know she seeking compassion, but here she would find none. Again I marveled how my father could have been so easily misled.

"Very well, sit if you must, but you will be powerless to change anything in this will, as it was carefully drawn with much consideration."

"All I desire is to see that my sister is given her due," Arwan retorted in clipped tones.

MacDonald continued. "The mill will be run by my son, Rory MacTaggert. As will the summer pasture. The manor is his as well. Though he is a young man, he is fully capable of handling all the business affairs. On a personal note, should any mill worker have a problem, rest assured my son will solve it in the same manner as I did."

Pheland rose and threw the side chair against the wall. "My sister is to have that mill and the pasture. She put in her time caring for him and his fool son. I cannot believe such an astute business man would not compensate his widow."

"Sit down, Pheland," the attorney said, his tone baring further interruptions.

"My widow," MacDonald read, "will be provided for with a monthly allowance of ten pounds, which should allow her to live very handsomely. She has indicated to me she does not like the manor and would choose to live elsewhere. Accordingly, I have provided her with a housing allotment."

Hagga shifted in her seat and crossed her arms in front of her body. I could tell she was not pleased, but she knew here was not the place to voice any objection.

Laird MacDonald read on. "Rory, my son, will continue to live in the manor and all those servants will remain in their positions, until such time as Rory chooses to do otherwise."

Pheland leaned on the barrister's desk. "How is it a son, a very young son I might add, is allowed discretion in matters and a wife, who practically ran the business, is given no authority over her own estate—however meager?"

"Sir, if you choose to remain at this reading, you will conduct yourself in a manner that befits a gentleman or I will have you ousted."

Both Sully and I rose, eager to eject the interloper but Laird MacDonald shot us a restraining glance. Pheland picked up the thrown chair and sat upon it his eyes drawn, like those of his sister, into narrow slits.

The attorney rose and shook the hands of all the mill workers. "I do thank you for your time. Should any have need to access the widow and orphan fund, contact me at once and I will expedite the process." He then led them to the door. As they left, Hagga let out a deep sigh and drew her arms more tightly about her body.

I could smell the danger emanating from her. She would not sit idly by and see me have the running of the business. Perhaps, this was what she'd been planning all along, she and her brother. If she owned all the land on the isle and the mill, Pheland could do the business and she would be the power behind the man. Even as a young boy, I'd noticed her thirst for power, and over the years, her thirst had not been slaked. I would have to be wary.

Bidding my friend Sully goodbye, I headed back to the manor. No doubt Hagga had gone there as well. I dared not leave my father's business papers unattended. Now that I knew Pheland was her brother, I couldn't allow her to know the true workings of the company, as with her brother's aid she could steal my birthright.

As I approached, I noted a light in Da's study. Hagga was definitely searching for the ledger. I could only pray she would not expect to find it beneath a chair cushion.

I knocked loudly at the door, startling her. "What are you doing here?" she asked.

"What am I doing here? This is my home. According to Da, you have no love for this manor. And, if I recall, none of your belongings are in this den."

She glared at me and drew in a great breath. Holding that air within her lungs, she was clearly considering her options. She expelled it in a rush. "This is my home. I've lived here for many miserable years and my imprint is on every room within this manse."

I devoutly hoped what she'd said was not true. I hoped to eradicate everything that spoke of her. "Hagga, you know that is not the case. This room was Da's and his alone. As I now own the manor and the business, you no longer have a reason to be here. I will have the servants pack your belongings have them taken wherever you wish."

Suddenly she pounced at me with the ferocity of a lioness protecting her cub. She dove over the desk and from God knows where, she brandished a knife. The blade was double-edged and clearly sharp as the light refracted off it. Within moments, she flailed at me, the edge of the dirk pricking my neck.

I shrugged my shoulders and managed to elude her. Then I pushed her to the ground and, grabbing the hidden ledger, I fled.

She raced after me, cursing me in some strange tongue. Faster and faster, I ran. Though I was stronger than she, I did not want to risk her injury, as her brother would use it to his advantage. As her final words rung in my ear, something about her due, I became fleet of foot and only then did I realize I raced on four feet not two.

My heart froze. What had the witch done to me? I held the ledger tightly within my teeth. Glancing at my feet and legs, I noted they were covered with black fur. My chest was white, as was my tail. Looking over my back, I saw more fur of a red hue.

***

Fionna

Arwan Pheland was behaving like an unruly child, throwing rocks at the shore birds. Fortunately his aim was poor and none were injured. His ire appeared to increase as he searched for bigger prey. I was swimming near the river's edge next to the water reeds when he sighted me. At once, he began pelting me with pebbles. Few struck me, causing me little discomfort. My apparent non-reaction angered Pheland as he reached for larger stones. One stone struck me in my neck, breaking my chain and crushing my windpipe. Pain wracked by body. I quickly hid deeper within the reeds as I needed time to heal. Finally, bored with his destruction, Arwan left.

I peeked out from the reeds and spotted a fox at the opposite shore. The animal was carrying a book in its mouth. Craning its neck as not to damage the missive, the sleek animal leapt into the water.

I felt the blood trickle down my neck. My wound must be deeper than I thought. I watched the fox step from the river as I passed out.

I know not how long I was unconscious. When I came to, the fox was over me. Were I a natural swan I suppose I would be frightened. Yet, not only was I not afraid, the presence of the animal gave me peace. The fox tore at the necklace attempting to remove it from my injury. The pressure was intense, and I made a sort of bleating sound. The fox, seeing my discomfort, stopped tugging and began to lick my neck. Not as an animal cleaning its own wound, but tenderly, more like a caress. I felt certain this was no ordinary fox.

As I had been transformed, so had Tag. Our minds melded at once. I understood his very thoughts. His ministrations to my wound were those of a lover. He drew back his mouth and exposed his sharp teeth. Applying them to the choker, he tried to wrest it from my throat. The action caused further bleeding, and I fought to remain conscious. To no avail.

***

Tag

Finally I found her, and now I may lose her for all time. *If she dies from this injury, I'll kill that Pheland myself, even if I have to steal into his bedroom and crush his windpipe.* I'd seen him throwing pebbles at the birds as I neared the water's edge. The stone that had struck Fionna was much bigger and had done severe damage.

Perhaps, if I dragged her to higher ground I could find her some help. As a fox, I was useless to aid her. Not wishing to harm her further, I pulled gently at her breast. I could not grasp a wing or her neck as my strength was limited in comparison to her body weight and yanking on an appendage would result in a greater injury. A swan was a massive bird and I was a small fox. I had not considered how I would again become a man, but someone must have the answer for it. For Fionna to remain a bird, and I a fox, was more frightening than any thought I'd had of hell.

Finally I was able to hide her among the bulrushes and weeds. She was still within a deep sleep. I knew if I tried to remove the choker she would wake and cause herself further damage. I softly licked her bill and stole away, confident she was well hidden.

I had to find her brother to get her help. I searched the narrow beach and found Sully, whittling on a narrow branch, whistling a birdcall. I barked and drew his attention. He stared at me intently, as one does when trying to recall the name of an old acquaintance. He did not know me. I suppose it would have been expecting too much for him to recognize me, as did his sister. I barked again and took a short run down the beach, hoping he would follow. He did not. I again ran up to him and barked as loudly as I could. This time, though he did not know me as his friend Tag, somehow he understood I needed his help.

I ran alongside of him, having to stop frequently as the bumbler fell over his own feet several times. Each time he fell, I felt the thought connection grow stronger. I felt he completely understood me when we reached Fionna. As he swept the reeds aside and saw the injured swan he turned on me with the ferocity of a wolf.

"You fiend," he screamed. "What have you done to my Fionna?" Tenderly, he removed the crushed choker from her neck and wrapped a cloth he'd found within the pocket of his tunic, about her cut. I stepped back and watched, hoping he would realize, not only did I not cause the injury, I was trying to save her.

The bird stirred, opened its eyes, and gazed at me. So intent was Fionna's scrutiny, her brother began to question himself.

He crossed the short distance and approached me. Extending his hand palm up, he jumped slightly as I placed my wet muzzle in it.

He drew back his hand and scratched his head. Looking from Fionna to me, several times, it became apparent he knew I had done her no harm. Kneeling down on his haunches, he petted my head.

"If you are my friend Tag, move your tail," he requested.

Though Sully was not fleet of foot, his thoughts raced to the proper conclusion. I wagged my tail as furiously as possible. He nodded.

"Well, my friend, now we have a greater problem. If you are a fox, how can you run the business? Hagga and Arwan will win," Sully lamented.

I could not allow him to fall into despair. For no action was far worse than a wrong action. I tugged at his tunic with my teeth and indicated the rim above us.

He understood at once. "You're right. Elidor will have the solution. If not he, then his friend Joseph will have an answer."

I glanced back at the swan. Though the choker had been removed, she still needed care. She was again bleeding through the cloth.

I yipped at Sully and he ran back to Fionna. He removed the soiled cloth and rinsed it in the water. Again he held it firmly to her throat. The bleeding had stopped but she still needed constant care. As an animal I was unable to tend her, but if I were to go for help, who would understand me? I cocked my head quizzically, hoping Sully would discern the burning question.

"Tag, you must stay with her. Hold your muzzle against her throat and do not lessen the pressure. Do you understand?"

Quickly, I moved to Fionna's side and did as Sully directed. He turned to climb to the rim and find Elidor.

Within an instant, a near-blinding white light blocked his way. The Lady Tivannia again appeared.

"Who is responsible for this foul deed?" Kneeling down, she held the swan's neck, applying the pressure as I had done. "Sully, go and find my brother. Tell him nothing, but bring him here at once."

She directed her gaze at me. I was certain she would know what had happened. "It looks as if the witch has finally learned of her powers," she said, cradling her child gently in her arms.

Sully heard her statement and turned back. "Mother, what do you mean? Does Tag's stepmother possess evil powers?"

"Sully, never mind, I will handle the witch. Go, do as you are told."

As my friend ascended the trail to the rim, his mother spoke softly to me. I believe she did not want to concern her injured daughter. "Well, Tag, it looks as if she changed you in a fit of rage. Has she ever done anything like this before?"

I shook my head no.

Tivannia smiled. "I thought not. She may have the power, but she lacks the skill. Without one, the other is useless and dangerous."

Chapter Seven
Elidor

As I sat alone and discouraged within the grotto, I pushed the wineskin from me. I needed to clear my head if I were to be of any use to my beloved niece. I'd never before in my life relied on drink for courage and found it ill- equipped to instill bravery. Through its consumption I'd failed. Failing Merlin, embarrassing my friend, and no longer the strong advocate for Fionna as I had always been. The girl relied on me for protection and understanding of her mother's passing. I'd always be able to relieve her fears with a story of Tivannia's youthful pranks. But no story could erase the image of that evil man.

I then recalled, with hope in my heart, her mother was, in truth, still with us. No doubt with her, my friend Joseph, and the vast wisdom of Merlin, the child could be saved.

Clear in purpose, I rose from the bench and saw my nephew rushing toward me.

My heart sank. What could be worse? I thought the direst of circumstances had already befallen us, yet Sully's urgency indicated an even greater danger. "What is it, lad? Please tell me nothing more has happened."

"Oh, that I could, Uncle. Fionna is injured and Tag has been enchanted into a fox. You must come at once."

Truly the bowels of hell must have opened else this could not have occurred. Were there even more evil forces at work here?

Sully motioned at me and together we raced down the steep path to the beach. Due to the slope, we ran faster and faster. I collided with the boy and the two of us fell onto the narrow beach. I saw my sister holding the swan as tears slipped down her translucent cheek. Going to her side, I assessed the bird's injury. Though she bled, there was evidence of clotting. She would not perish, but would be sore for some time.

Tivianna handed the swan over to me while she searched for some moss to aid the clotting. I looked deep into Fionna's crystal blue eyes and did my best to reassure her with a Druid chant. A simple phrase, much like a lullaby for a troubled babe.

I felt the child relax and give herself up to slumber as I laid her gently on the reeds the boys had flattened for her. Though, in fact, only my nephew was a boy. Tag had truly become a fox, but with my Druid training I was able to recognize him as the boy I once knew. I gently covered her with my cloak, as it would become chilly as evening drew near.

"Tag, how has this happened to you? Tivannia, surely this was not your doing?"

My sister sat on the bench, her hands seemingly helpless in her lap. "No, Elidor, it was Hagga."

"Hagga? From where comes her power? Is she a witch?"

"She is, dear brother, but as yet has not learned the extent of her aptitude. She has the talent, but not the skill."

I had not considered any force, other than pure avarice, would belong to the evil pair of Hagga and Arwan. This would complicate matters further. It was a situation that required greater wisdom than either Tivannia or I possessed. We would have to summon Merlin and find Joseph.

**

Merlin

I seldom speak in chronicles such as this, but I must decry the depravity of these foolish mortals. They rape the meadows and pillage the trees, then expect nature to be kind.

Watching the imprudent priest as he struggled with the demon spirits, I wondered at the folly of men. Elidor knew well the Druid teaching that extolled sobriety.

True, there are forces here he cannot fully comprehend. That Hagga is a witch is small surprise to me. However, Elidor would have no way of knowing. A simple man, he trusts everyone and everything. This time to his own detriment.

Lo these many years have I avoided meddling in the affairs of mortals. 'Tis for me a foolish endeavor. For no matter when or how I set things aright, men plunge back in and once again drown by their own efforts. However, I cannot allow past situations to color my thinking on the matter. I weary of mine own admonition. All too often I am called upon to intervene in the affairs of men. As they will not understand, the result is quite frequently war.

This mortal or, if truth be told, immortal, required my services. He would save all of mankind, or so his followers believed. He'd allowed his messenger to seal a sacred Ordination of the Druids with the cup He had held to His lips at His last meal. As I will honor all faiths, even if they differ from mine, I will once again try to set man on the right path.

I know not how much longer the two worlds will endure, but feel deep within my heart the Realm of the Fey will one day pass from this world and move to another.

I've grown so weary my eyelids flutter and I feel the need of a bed. There, before me, running pell-mell up the steep incline are Sully and a sleek red fox. The lad is running with much more grace than he usually displayed. Was this a hallucination? Dare I trust my weary eyes?

Sully cried out. "Merlin, you must save her. Though she is enchanted, she has come to real harm."

"Who must I save? I've enchanted no females in Scotland in many centuries." While what I'd told the lad was accurate, I'd had no true hand in the making of the swan, but without question I knew he meant Fionna. The need in the boy's eyes was enough to break my heart. Though I've lived many lifetimes, the rare love between these siblings was something I do not often encounter.

The fox began to growl. His display of temper was calculated to stir me into action.

"Please, Merlin, you must come. Even Tag wants you to help."

That, I well understood. The urgency of the fox was even more compelling than the compassion of the brother.

"Where is she? Is she sick or injured?" I asked, hoping my calm tone would relieve their fears.

"She's on the beach with my mother. Her neck is cut," Sully stammered. "Please, Great Wizard."

"She's been attacked? Who would do such a thing? Even if she weren't enchanted, what kind of a fool would harm a swan?"

"We're not certain."

At once, the fox growled and circled as if giving directions. I understood he meant the man from the rim. The very one the swan was supposed to marry.

"Very well, lads, I will see what I can do. Lead the way."

***

Tivannia

Sully and the fox returned with Merlin. I prayed the wizard had the skill to save my only daughter. I lived in a time when daughters were prized in the same manner as sons, and I was unwilling to see the child suffer. Though she is a majestic bird, she feels weightless in my arms. I'd never held her as an infant and my arms around her felt the loss of her childhood.

Though in the enchanted guise of the fox, Tag retained the loyalty he'd always had for my children. He'd been unaware I watched as he championed for my little girl, never allowing even her brother to taunt her for her unusual hair color. I could tell he was in as much anguish as I. Though I've never seen an animal cry I was unsurprised to see the little fox weep. So much in pain for his love, he howled in the manner of a wolf.

Sully and Merlin arrived behind the fox.

Sully fell to his knees beside his sister and cried out, "Merlin, you must save her. I'll do whatever deed you wish, just save my sister. She is a good person and she doesn't deserve to suffer because she does not want to wed an evil man. No woman should endure such a fate."

"I agree, lad, however she is enchanted not only by the intervention of your mother, but the seal of the Church is upon her as well. I, alone, cannot remove the spell."

I tugged at the wizard's garment. "Then you must find my brother's friend, at once. I fear I cannot mend her while she is a swan. Once she is returned to her human form, I can treat her wound."

The wizard turned and glared at me, and I released his robe. "Madam, I will do all in my power to bring your daughter to the treatment she requires, however, do not ever again touch my robe."

"I most humbly beg your pardon, Great Merlin, but I will dare anything to save my daughter."

"I understand, but remember ruffling my feathers will not hasten the shedding of your daughter's," Merlin said, his chin held high.

Duly chastised, I bent over my daughter. Her breathing was shallow and faint. "I fear she has lost the will to live. She will not fight for herself. Merlin, we must give her some hope if she is to survive long enough for Joseph to return."

Tag padded over to me and nuzzled Fionna. Briefly, she opened her eyes. Her lashes fluttered as Tag licked her bill. "Mother," my son implored, "please help her make her see how life can be with Tag and not the terrible fate she faces with Arwan."

Merlin clapped Sully on the shoulder. "Well, lad, that is an excellent suggestion. If she sees the better portion of life, she will fight to survive. Tivannia, lay the girl on the reeds and come with me."

"Oh, please, Merlin, I cannot leave her. She is my child, the one I never held to my breast."

"Nor will you never again feel her embrace, if you do not do as I bid."

Reluctantly, I set her softly on the reeds and went to do the Master's bidding. I dared not put my daughter at further risk.

***

Sully

I watched as my uncle held my sister and sang the songs he used to sing to us when we were children. The songs had always brought peace and comfort when we were afraid. I prayed they did the same for Fionna now.

Each time she fluttered open her eyes, Tag licked her bill and moved his muzzle to her wound.

Though I did not want to leave her, I knew the only way she could be saved was the presence of the Holy Man.

"Uncle Elidor, we have to find your friend." He raised sad eyes and begged me not to ask him to abandon the swan.

Promises were made to be kept, and he'd given his word to my mother.

"I know you promised not to leave her, but if you do not, she will die in your arms."

Elidor nodded. He turned to Tag and said, "Lad, you must stay with her and allow no one to harm her. You know I have no desire to leave her, but if we are to save her, I must." Turning back to me, he directed, "Sully, she must be moved to a safer place. It is too open here. She may be discovered."

I agreed and followed him in to a concealed area deep within the water's reeds. "Uncle, I will make the area more comfortable for her and you can go back and carry her."

Tag knew how grave the situation was, and I was equally certain he wished that witch had not changed him into a fox. No matter his form, he would guard my sister with his life.

Neither my uncle nor I owned any horses and we would need the swiftest mode of travel possible. "Uncle, we have no mounts. How can we even purchase them when we have no coin?"

My uncle smiled widely and said, "We have none, but Arwan has many. Surely he would not object if we borrowed a couple to save his betrothed." Stunned, I stammered, "You mean you will ask him for horses?"

"Not exactly. We will borrow them and return them unharmed, but we won't tell him we are doing so."

I could not believe my ears. Elidor, a Druid priest, would advocate stealing horses. But he had, and it certainly seemed the only way to save her, therefore, I would not quibble.

"How long must we leave her, Uncle? Can you assure she will be safe?"

"Yes, Sully, you are right, we may be gone a long time. For Fionna, each moment counts. I will place her in suspension until your mother returns. Tivannia will know what to do."

Afraid for Fionna's safety, I asked, "Are you certain? We cannot harm her further."

"No," he replied, "I would not place her more in harm's way. The suspension will hold back time as well as protect her and Tag from discovery."

Confident we did all was possible to ensure Fionna was guarded and protected, we set out to secure horses from Arwan Pheland. Swiftly we climbed the trail to the top of the rim. Surely we were blessed as neither of us exhibited our usual clumsiness. Once at the top, Arwan's stable was in clear sight. No one appeared to be around anywhere. Most likely Arwan was plotting with his sister on how best to secure Tag's holdings. He would be on the mainland.

Still, we took precautions not to be discovered. As well liked as Pheland was, I felt even if we were discovered by someone in his employ, they would aid us rather than turn us over to their master. The Briton had few, if any, friends on the island.

Elidor hitched his robe up and crawled along side of the barn. I followed silently. At the far end of the stable were two stalls, each holding a sleek horse. These were not farm horses but animals bred to be raced against others of their kind. They would be perfect for our journey. I crept up to the door of the first stall and crawled in. Slowly, I stood beside the animal. It did not appear to be frightened in the least, as if he were waiting for me. Looking over to the second stall, I saw my uncle was experiencing the same reaction from that horse.

To descend the rim, we chose the longer, safer path. It would do us no good if the horses were injured by taking the steeper path, even though it was swifter.

Once on the beach, we moved to the ferry barge to take us to the mainland. The barge was small and manned by anyone who chose to use it. A sturdy system of cables and pulleys was used to move the conveyance. So little was the boat, Elidor had to remain on his mount while I worked the pulley system. We crossed without incident.

***

Tivannia

It seemed we walked forever and none of the land we'd traversed was familiar to me. Merlin, though very old, seemed tireless. I felt each step I took was as if I were carrying a millstone. To me, we were wandering aimlessly, but I knew each step was purposely taken. Merlin knew exactly where we were going and why.

Though the terrain we trod was unfamiliar, it did resemble the average meadow and wood, until the wizard stopped suddenly and raised his arms to the heavens. At once the skies darkened. 'Twas as midnight on a moonless eve. And then, through the blackness, shone a beam of light so brilliant it was beyond description. From the center of the beam, a tunnel formed.

Merlin took my hand and led me into the passageway. Everywhere I cast my sight was a radiance the like of which I'd never seen. As my eyes became accustomed to the illumination, I noted the walls consisted of millions of tiny crystals.

Gently, I pressed upon the wizard's hand. He glared down at me with a stern expression. I smiled, knowing I had not violated his rule of not touching his garment.

"Well," he asked, "What is it you wish to understand?"

"Can you tell me how we have come here and for what reason are we here?"

I could feel his exasperation at my questions, but I had every right to know why I was here and if my presence here would aid my daughter. I would not back down.

Merlin nodded and stroked his long white beard. "We are within the Cave of Crystals. It houses the fates of each and every soul in the known worlds. By showing what can or will happen, we can reveal to Fionna the joys she will experience if she fights to live."

I looked above and around me. Everywhere images were refracted by the crystals embedded in the walls. I could discern no clear image of anyone. "I think I comprehend what you are saying, but if this is so, why cannot I see even one single undistorted image that should be representative of one person?"

"My child, you cannot because you have not been granted permission to do so. Only the Conclave of Ancient Druids can grant that."

"And where is this Conclave?" I begged. The constant delay worried me. My daughter needed help now, not at the convenience of some ancient priests.

"I will summon them and request audience." Merlin drew himself to even greater height and stretched out his arms.

At once the heavens darkened, a deep midnight blue as dark as an angry sea. Suddenly a single beam of light appeared. Merlin stepped within its radiance. Speaking in a tongue incomprehensible to me, he chanted. Within a moment he was gone, leaving nothing but a thin wisp of crimson smoke.

It seemed as eons, though I am certain it was moments only, until the wizard reappeared. He carried with him his cane and a fair-sized dark rock. Though the stone was certainly heavy, Merlin carried it with ease. His strength had to have come from his power, as his fragile frame could not have done so alone.

He set the heavy stone on the ground and struck it with his cane. At once the rock divided into two pieces.

I cleared my throat loudly to draw Merlin's attention to the half of the rock on the left. His present view was of the right side of the stone. I coughed slightly until his gaze followed mine. There, on the smooth surface of the rock, was the image of my brother and son. Why had Elidor left her? He'd given his word.

The sorcerer raised his hand as he studied the image. I was then able to hear their conversation.

"Sully, do not fear, we will find Joseph. He is a good man and will sense our need. Somehow, either through Druid intervention or the grace of the Christian Lord, Fionna will be saved."

"But, Uncle, how shall we find him? He could be anywhere from Ireland to Rome or anyplace in-between the two."

Elidor nodded. "I think it best to go to the court of King Arthur."

"How can Arthur help?" my son asked.

"Arthur's knights travel far and wide, they will know the most likely routes."

They were riding fine racehorses and were traveling swiftly. But would they find the Holy Man in time to save her?

I prayed silently their journey would be swift enough to save my only daughter.

Merlin responded, though I'd said nothing aloud. "I will compress time and they will arrive at Camelot within moments."

Assured the wizard would handle the problem, I glanced at the other segment of the dark rock, the surface of the stone as smooth as a mirror. "Merlin," I called.

He glared at me but nonetheless turned his attention again to the right side of the severed stone.

He tipped the stone so the surface was parallel to the ground and then knelt beside it. Using the dark stone as a scrying mirror, the venerable Druid showed me the crystals more clearly than they appeared overhead. He selected a single crystal and enlarged the image until it covered the entire surface.

My daughter, no longer a swan and her chosen mate no longer a fox, were in the MacTaggert manor. The home she'd made was very like what my dear friend had created for her husband. It was once a warm and welcoming home. Hagga had added no personal touches while she resided there and it warmed my heart to know my daughter would be a perfect hostess and loving wife. The scene played out as Rory MacTaggert returned from a day's work at the mill...

The door of the manor flew open as Tag called out, "Fionna, where are you? I have something to show you."

I gasped as a beautiful young woman, my daughter, Fionna, descended the stair and rushed into his arms. He caught her up and swung her about in a circle. She nuzzled into his neck, and he threw back his head and laughed.

"Are you getting all lovey so early in the day, my dear?" Fionna smiled as he set her back on her feet. "I am lovey all the time, dear husband. I merely wanted to take in the scent of you."

Tag grinned, swept her up once again, and tugged at the ribbons on the front of her dress.

I felt the intruder on such a private moment and turned from the image on the stone. Merlin did the same, but allowed the scene to play out. It was clear this should provide incentive for Fionna to remain alive to live out the lives portrayed.

Tag picked at Fionna's laces then shucked off his shirt and threw it onto the floor. He then grabbed his wife's arm and raced toward the stair.

Fionna, very much the new bride, blushed charmingly. However, this was no timid handmaiden. With equal abandon, she shed her clothing leaving a trail of garments along the stairway as he carried her to their bedroom.

The room was bright and airy. Fionna opted to have fewer pieces of furniture in the room as she felt the room to be a haven for her and her husband, not a showpiece to influence people.

Lightly, Tag placed her in the center of the opulent king-sized bed. The bedding was of the finest linen and embroidered extensively. Tag was neither impressed nor intimidated by the splendor of the marriage bed. The only thing that took his eye was the beautiful woman on the mattress. Fionna grabbed a corner of the sheet and attempted to cover herself. Tag leaned over her, balancing himself on his hands, and took the offending sheet in his teeth. He shook his head and growled softly.

"Oh, you wish to still be an animal?" his wife asked.

He cocked an eyebrow and tilted his head. "Well, you do bring out the animal in my soul. I become a ravenous beast when confronted with your bounteous beauty." She laughed and took the sheet from his teeth and placed it in her own.

Leaning over his wife, Tag kissed her nose and removed the cloth from between them ...

As I heard my daughter's moan of satisfaction and the obvious sounds of mating, I averted my ears as well as my eyes. I was certain Merlin would not intrude on the pair further, but only leave the scene to play out for Fionna. I smiled and followed him as he led the way from whatever place we were in.

***

Fionna

I could never have imagined my mother's choker could do such harm. I found the pain endurable only because Tag was with me. He pressed firmly against my wound. The blood no longer flowed and still he held firm. Always my champion, though still a fox, he retained the loyalty he'd possessed as a man. I knew he would never abandon me, no matter the danger to himself. I was so tired. Fighting to survive seemed to me to be a vain effort. Allowing myself to relax, I fell into a slumber, unlike any other I'd ever experienced.

Tag knelt over me in our four-poster bed wearing nothing but a smile. He jerked the linen sheet from my teeth and softly nuzzled my neck. How, I wondered, could anything be more perfect? And, within a heartbeat, he showed me. His hands were like magic. Everywhere he touched me seemed to melt beneath his fingertips. Soon I would be a soft pool of compliant flesh. Gazing up at him, I could see the strength in his shoulders, the muscles flexing as he held himself over me. He slid beside me and allowed one leg to hold me captive. As he brought me close to his chest, I could feel his warm breath on my cheek. Slowly, he turned my head and placed his lips upon mine own. His kiss made my heart sing. I'd never known the human body could contain such joy. A joy I will gladly share with him forever.

As I awoke, I saw the broken choker and silver chain lying beside me. When my mother had removed it, I'd begun to hope I could survive this foul deed. Everything vile and evil I'd encountered had found its home in the vicious souls of Hagga and Arwan. Somehow we would best the heinous pair. I know not from what well I drank the cup of courage, but I was feeling stronger. With Tag holding my wound, my brother and uncle seeking the Holy Man, I was confident right would be restored in my little corner of the world.

The dream I'd just witnessed gave me the true picture of what a life I would have if I did not abandon hope. Hope is so often a timid and tenuous thing. The origin is usually unknown, yet mankind cannot survive without it. The wizard must have realized how tenaciously I would fight, if I were shown the fruits of the battle not yet begun. And fight I will, with all that is within my being. I shall not surrender to despair, as the life I will have with Tag is worth any effort, no matter the toll it takes. I willed my strength into my battered body, down to the last feather of my wing.

Chapter Eight
Elidor

Though we were on the road only moments, at once we were within sight of Camelot. Surely, Merlin had a hand in this. If I'd thought the magnificent castle was only a short ride away, I'd have made the journey long ago. To say the structure was grand only told half the story. Within our view, a panorama was displayed, of truth, honor, and the true kindness of men for one another. Though these things were not tangible, they were nevertheless present. I was certain Arthur had spared no expense to build the wondrous castle. However, the grandeur was not in mortar and stone, it was in the sense of justice that permeated the very air. Arthur was known throughout the land as a fair and just ruler. Most men knew to become one of Arthur's knights of his fabled round table was a worthy goal. Many aspired to be his champion just from the tales told by wandering minstrels.

Sully appeared equally surprised by our swift journey. He sat upon his horse, or rather Arwan's horse, and looked about, simply taking in all the magnificence of Camelot. "Uncle," he called, "look to the highest spire. Even there is a pennant with the king's standard. I wonder who climbed so high?"

I smiled. I knew though many craftsmen were employed to build the monumental structure, the impossible touches were done through the magic of Merlin. However, I am certain he would not count this endeavor as true magic.

"Uncle Elidor, we must tarry no longer."

I quickly followed his lead. We were headed down a slope into a green valley just below the castle. Nearly to the bottom, I spied another rider.

Unable to see clearly, as the sun shone in my eyes barring my vision, I held silent.

The man called out, "Elidor, it's Joseph, answer me."

As we descended deeper into the valley, the sun became shielded by the hill and I was able to see my friend clearly. Shouting to him, I indicated my surprise at his presence. "Joseph, what brings you back so quickly? When you left you told me you would not see me again this year. What changed your plan?"

Joseph easily moved his mount alongside mine and extended his hand. I took his hand and shook it vigorously.

"Elidor, I, too, am glad to see you, but do not shake me apart. Why my plan is altered is not fully known to me. For some reason, I felt compelled to return. Though I usually am able to discern the word of God, this directive was different. I feel I am but a landmark on another's journey."

Sully, now more self-assured, had regained some of his clumsiness, and slid from his mount. He fell to his knees. "Maybe," he said, "Merlin summoned you."

Quickly, he brushed the dirt from his knees and looked to me for confirmation. It could be possible. Merlin has powers far beyond my imagination.

"Sully, you could be correct, Merlin would know of our predicament and, as it affects not only our family but the economy of the country of Scotland, he might well intervene."

I could tell Joseph felt disconcerted by this information. He was always true to his God and feared offending Him.

"Fear not, Joseph, Merlin would do nothing that did not follow the guidelines set by your Jesus."

"I'm sure that is the case, Elidor, as the Lord would not have permitted the summoning from Merlin, if it were wrong. It seems I have been directed to do something. For what reason have you come to this place? As I recall you were reluctant to travel so far to Camelot."

Smiling, I replied, "Quite so, old friend, but in this instance, the journey was not lengthy. Merlin somehow made the journey far more swift than it would ordinarily be."

"I am sure you will enjoy your visit as Arthur is a most gracious host. I only wish I could remain with you. Yet, now I see you safely here at Camelot, I must pursue the Lord's journey," he said, slapping the reins against his mount's rump.

I was disconcerted by my friend's actions. He'd never before abandoned me when I was in need of his guidance. Perhaps the Druid interference frightened him.

Sully remounted Arwan's horse and turned the animal. Tugging on the reins, he maneuvered his position ahead of Joseph and me. "Come on," he called. "We cannot waste time. Fionna needs our help and she needs it quickly."

Sully obviously did not believe Joseph to be of any value in our search.

Perhaps it would be better to seek the king without Joseph's guidance.

Sully's comments jarred me into action. I spurred my horse, and we raced onward toward the imposing structure as Joseph headed west. So quickly, he was out of sight within moments. I feared we'd erred in allowing Joseph a different route. We'd failed in our mission. But there was no other choice. We must go on to Camelot. Joseph was on a divine mission. We would find aid in another quarter. Perhaps Merlin would be there and would help us.

***

Arwan Pheland

I always knew she had the power. She thought I was just flattering her because she was my pretty little sister. Of course she is very dear to me, but her power is truly present. It was a force I wanted for my own, but I was denied.

When she was just a tiny girl, Hagga made her dollies dance in the air. She sublimated her talent when she discovered boys were fools for her comely looks and thus easily manipulated. Druids drove us from our land so long ago because Hagga was a witch. As a child, she killed the baby lambs for sport. The Druids banned her entire family from the isle, but as there was no proof the isle even existed, there was no recording of the document that banned us. I shall regain our heritage.

Only when she became extremely angry did she discover her true calling. We could have whatever we wanted. And have it we shall.

She'd transformed her stepson as he fled the family manor. It was only a small beginning, but I was grateful she'd told me straight away. She would need much practice, if she were to perfect this talent to a finely honed skill. I awaited her on the narrow beach below the rim. Killing time by throwing stones at shore birds, I caught movement within the rushes at the shoreline. Quietly, I parted the grasses and peered upon a very interesting scene. A small fox and a large swan were resting among the reeds. The fox had its muzzle upon a wound on the neck of the large bird. Could it be the same swan I struck with a rock earlier? If it were, could this fox be Hagga's stepson? I cannot accept the two animals would be allies unless they were enchanted. Could the Druid priest I'd found on my land have something to do with this circumstance? I was certain Hagga was not the only one on this strange island with unique powers.

As it was clear the bird was gravely injured, I dared leave it and return to my sister. Hagga was pacing her old bedroom in our family home on the peak of the rim. Soon she would regain her rightful title of Lady of the MacTaggert Manor as well as our family home.

"Hagga, I've learned something that could be of great value to us. Remember I told you I hit a swan the other day? Apparently, I injured the bird more than I thought. I found it today among the reeds. And the strangest thing, it was with a red fox."

My sister stopped and turned abruptly. "A fox, you say, and did it have green eyes?"

"I don't know. I wasn't that close, but for certain it was not the usual variety fox. Foxes and swans are not frequent companions."

Hagga sat at the solid oak desk she used to handle our household accounts before she married that fool MacTaggert. She drummed her fingers on the well-polished top. Over and over, she drummed, until the monotony nearly drove me insane. "Hagga, tell me what you are thinking. How can we gain from this situation?"

"Oh, dear brother, we will gain. And we will gain even more than my dear departed husband had. We shall have it all; the island, the manor, the business, and the respect of all of Scotland."

"But, Hagga, there are but two of us. How can we accomplish all that?"

"For a smart man, sometimes you are a fool, Arwan. We have both come to the same conclusion. I am a witch, but I need to perfect my skills."

"Oh, splendid, and what are you going to do? Go to witch academy?"

"Precisely, dear brother. I will use Uncle Mordred's spell book."

I vaguely remembered the well-worn missive I'd found when I first returned here. It held no specific significance for me as I was without power. But Hagga did have the power, and the ancient tome would be our salvation.

I remember the last time I saw the book. The day I arrived on this small isolated island, the local caretaker showed me thorough my father's house. An impressive, imposing structure, most certainly the largest on the island.

As we stepped through the main entrance, the chill that filled the air seeped right into one's marrow. Many years of vacancy had left the mansion bleak and unwelcoming. The caretaker had rushed me through then quickly left. The very moment the man was clear of the door, the house began to warm. He was an outsider, and the mansion would not welcome him. I, however, was family and truly belonged there. As I wandered through the long dark halls, I'd remembered the few times our Uncle Mordred had visited.

He was my father's brother, though there was no family resemblance. A recluse, Mordred had rarely ventured out of his home. My father had never said his brother was a warlock, but Hagga knew he was. Once, when he visited, my sister and I followed him as he placed a tome in one of the hollow panels in the library. It remained there to this very day. Now Hagga would once again use the ancient volume. She directed me to the panel.

The panels were very tall and my sister was not able to reach to the upper portion that opened when struck. I reached over her and opened the panel. Within lay a large volume covered with a thick gray dust. I tried to blow off the offending covering, and Hagga told me not to brush away the powder.

"Arwan, everything that touches this book has function." She extended her hands over the tome and at once the dust seeped directly into the volume. "You see? Even the dust has knowledge. It was present for many years and absorbed the teachings of its surroundings."

"And now it's become part of the book?" I asked incredulously. It seemed strange to me that my baby sister would have this vast knowledge, when I'd attended the same schools as she. Yet I, a man, was powerless. I envied her that, but as I loved her, I would not challenge her for her hidden strength.

She'd stood by me when I was forced to leave London and flee to our family's only remaining home. Always comely, Hagga quickly found a young widower who needed a governess. Her credentials were impeccable as she served as nursemaid to one of the country's best-known families. So she did not live with me and rarely visited, as we did not want the family she worked for to know of our relationship.

"It feels good to be home. There is much power within these walls," she said, embracing herself. Hagga was tall for a woman and had a look some would call haughty. But her looks were deceptive. Long, curling blond hair and soft gray eyes led one to believe she was merely a pretty piece. But there was far more to my sister. She was smart. My father turned over the family accounts to her when she was only seven. She could have easily run a large company, only the fact she was a woman prohibited her from doing so. Not one to be easily deterred, she'd found another way.

I helped her lift the huge book onto the library table. Reverently, she brushed all else from the table, until the tome itself was alone. As she extended her hands over the book, smoke rose from its depths. Hagga began chanting in some language I did not comprehend. As she spoke, the smoke turned crimson and began to take on the form of a cloak, as red as burning coals. The hem flicked with fiery tongues as they reached out toward me.

"Be still," Hagga directed.

For cripe's sake, I thought, I'm paralyzed. I couldn't move if I wanted to.

Suddenly, all was still. Even the tall clock at the entrance of the library ceased its chime. Then there came a voice, soft, yet terrifying.

I stood frightened, and grew more so each passing moment. In an ominous whisper, the male voice spoke from deep within the voluminous folds of the cloak. "How dare you use this tome, Hagga Pheland? This is the spell book of an ancient warlock. You do not have permission to use this book."

Hagga laughed. "Permission? You old fool, I need not permission. I have the talent, and I will use whatever I wish to gain my desires."

The voice then shouted, "You are not the first witch I've destroyed."

***

Sully

I'd never seen a place so magnificent. Each blade of grass had its place, and the lush shrubs stood as sentinels along a carved stone walkway. As we entered the courtyard, a neatly attired groom took the horses. I'm certain he wondered what manner of men we were, as our mounts were the better groomed. Yet he cheerfully directed us to Arthur's chambers. Once inside the castle proper, I began to feel uncomfortable. As meanly dressed as we were, it became clear we did not fit in. It was as if dirt were outlawed. The very walls shone a glistening white, and thin silver tendrils swirled through the marble and highly polished hallways gleamed in the sunlight that shone through the beautiful glass windows.

However, my discomfort fled in the hospitality of the king. Arthur rushed forward and took my uncle's extended hand.

"Welcome to my humble home," the High King of Briton said.

If this was what he called humble, how grand could heaven be? I bowed awkwardly. My tongue became lodged behind my teeth and, try though I would, I became speechless. My uncle spoke for me.

"Your Highness, we are here on a mission of grave import. My niece, the lad's sister, was enchanted into a swan to protect her from having to marry a most unsuitable man."

"I see, and how can I assist you? I am merely a king, not a wizard," Arthur replied, as he picked an offending piece of lint from his robe.

His action seemed dismissive to me, and I resented it. Perhaps this grand king was not what I believed him to be. "Just because you are a king and I am just a man, you have no right to imply the situation is beneath you."

Elidor grabbed me and hauled me back. "Sully, that is rude. The king would never imply the fate of one of his subjects is beneath him. Arthur is the most fair of all the kings, of all time. All he meant was in this instance he alone is powerless."

"What are we doing here? I though he was to help us."

"Apparently, you have forgotten, Sully, all we ask of the king is the destination of my friend Joseph and if any of his knights would know the quickest way to find him. I fear we should have gone with him on his quest. He might have known how to help Fionna."

I had forgotten. I'd been so concerned with my sister's fate and that of my friend. My mind was muddled. I thought Joseph was returning to his homeland. I should have detained him when last we met.

"Arthur, do you know of his planned destination?" Elidor asked.

The king rubbed his hand over his neatly trimmed beard. "All I know is he set out to find you and direct you to me. Why he thought I might have knowledge to aid you, I do not know."

My uncle often found solace in thinking of concepts others could not grasp. If Joseph were to aid us, why did he flee in another direction? Elidor turned and spoke as if he'd had an epiphany.

"Joseph wants us to pray for guidance, and not rely on magic alone. That is why he left to reveal our own hearts that we might heal the stricken girl. I'm certain he will return to aid us if he is truly needed," my uncle said with an undisputable conviction.

Chapter Nine
Tivannia

Once again, I was alone. It was clear to me, though the wizard was physically within my sight, his spirit had fled to another plane.

His features contorted and he flew into a rage. "How dare you?" he demanded of someone not visible to me.

Whoever had raised his ire had done so by a far more grievous fault than touching his robe. Something of monumental value was at stake.

Suddenly, his manner changed, as if the problem at hand had been settled to his satisfaction. The wizard turned and directed me back from the crystal cave. I was hesitant, yet I knew there was reason behind his every action.

We stepped from the cave back into the strange tunnel that had brought us. Merlin held firmly to my hand and we were swept up into a swirling funnel of air.

"Where are we going now?" I asked.

"I told you not to question me. Is this too difficult a task for you, witch?"

I found myself unable to understand his demeanor. I'd never treated him with anything other than the deepest respect. He spoke to me as if he were dealing with a miscreant.

Within a heartbeat, we landed in a palace far more grand than I could have imagined. Marble halls, sculpted walls and tapestries of such intricate design, I could only wonder at the skill of the maker.

So this is Camelot, I thought. *Will my problem even matter to a King with such abundance?*

Our presence was not apparent to the others within Arthur's council room. My brother and my son were conversing with the king. Sully seemed vexed and angry, but Elidor was calm and apparently far more reasonable than my son.

Elidor looked up at King Arthur in respect. The king was nearly a head taller than my brother. "Your Highness," he said, "this is not merely the fate of my niece, but one that affects the economy of the entire nation."

This piqued the interest of the regent. After all, this could affect many within his realm. Merlin and I hovered over the fabled Round Table, its polished surface gleaming up at us.

At once, the people below us seemed to diminish in stature. The tabletop grew longer, its surface seemed as a scrying mirror, dark and faultless. As the ancient wizard peered deeply into the mirror, it grew clear that Merlin was no longer on the same plane as I. The lesson should have been learned not to question the Great Merlin, but my daughter's life was at stake. I shook his arm, demanding his attention.

"This is important. Why do you dwell on something that is happening elsewhere? Why is my daughter, my temple, and the Hydon Isle not first and foremost in your mind?" I shouted and quickly realized this was a grave error.

For some reason, Merlin displayed uncommon restraint with me. Gently, he explained, "It is not yet the time. Joseph will tell us at the appointed hour."

I grew impatient. "Fionna is now in grave danger. I cannot wait."

Merlin drew himself to his full height, which was considerable, and ordered me to look into the table's surface.

Therein I saw Hagga ranting, "This book is mine, bequeathed to me by my Uncle Mordred and his uncle of the same name before him. I shall use it as I so desire."

Then Merlin became part of the tableau displayed upon the table. He responded angrily, "Another, far more talented than you, challenged me. You know where that foolish sorceress resides today?"

He took up a gilded chain he wore about his middle and shook the small cage attached to it, until the creature within squeaked in protest.

I, of course, had heard tales that the Great Merlin wore about his waist the cage of Arthur's half sister, but until now I was not certain if this were a minstrel's song or an actual fact. The squealing mouse confirmed the validity of the tale. Now I knew, and would never again dare to question. Merlin's motives may be a puzzle to me, but I shall never try to countermand what he deemed proper.

Chapter Ten
Tag

I fear, though it is certain she will not die, Fionna has a long way to go toward complete healing. The blood no longer flows. I find it is caked upon her throat and my muzzle. I eased away from her gently as not to disturb the forming clot. She did not awaken, though I am certain she feels the soft whisper of my fur leaving her feathers.

After making sure she was safe and comfortable, I went to the water's edge to wash. I heard voices, angry, anxious voices. Quietly, I drew back into the reeds at the edge of the water. Crouching low to the ground, I observed Hagga and her brother.

"I tell you, I saw the bird right here," Arwan said.

"Well, she may have been here, but she is not here now," Hagga said, exacerbation in her tone. Though she was the younger of the two, it was clear she thought herself the wiser. "We have to find the bird and the damned fox."

My heart froze. I could not allow them to find Fionna. Hurrying back to her side, I prayed she was strong enough to help me to hide her. I wished Hagga had changed me into a larger creature, that I might carry my beloved to safety. She must have heard me approach as she raised her head in greeting.

Hello, Tag, she said, forcing her eyelids open and communicating through our melded minds. *Where have you been? I did not believe you would leave me alone.*

I only went to wash. Within a heartbeat, I would appear at your side, should you need me.

I know, she replied, and once again closed her eyes and tucked her bill beneath her wing.

I poked at her with my snout. *You cannot sleep now. We must take you to a better hiding place. Arwan and Hagga are just the other side of the reeds.*

Slowly, she withdrew her head from her wing. Her eyes were flooded with fear. It seemed to me she was far more timid as a bird than she was as a person. She was never fearful making the long lonely trip to the summer pasture. Why had being enchanted changed her personality? Would she ever again be the joyful lass I'd fallen in love with? Even if she were returned to her former guise, would she still be fearful for having had the experience? The many questions flooded my mind, but I could not let my own fear to place her in further jeopardy. Again I nudged her.

This time she stood and padded behind me as I went deeper into the reeds and bulrushes. Though there was some firm ground, the footing for a human was quite treacherous. I knew they would follow only as long as they had sure footholds.

I could hear them plodding through the marsh.

Arwan cried, "For cripe's sake, you're a witch, do something. Conjure them to us. Why should I have to traverse these ridiculous bogs?"

Hagga hesitated, as if thinking his statement had merit. After all, what was the good of being a witch, if you have no abilities to aid you in problematic situations? At least that was what I believed she was thinking. I'm certain she wasn't planning to use her skills for good. I wonder if there was ever a time in her life when she had been a good, happy person? She wasn't from the moment I first met her, and over the years, little had changed. In fact, she'd became more and more bitter with the passage of time.

She turned to her brother and said, "You're right, we will not pursue them further. I must study Uncle Mordred's book and learn how to bring them to us. I vaguely remember seeing the book when our misfit uncle visited us. He was reading about a projection spell. At the time I thought it a wonderful tool. Let's go home and let them enjoy the cold and dampness alone."

I guess they had forgotten that we were creatures not accustomed to comfort. Being alone in the swampy area of the river was little inconvenience for us.

Fionna appeared extremely tired. A swan spends little time on land other than nesting and running through river rushes and weeds took a great deal of effort. I found a little cubbyhole cut into the riverbank. The roots of an ancient tree had been slightly eroded by the water and when exposed formed a tiny haven. Quickly I wove sticks and reeds into the roots to hide her from view. The area was small, but enough for the two of us. Fionna relied on me for protection, and at the moment she was so terrified she could not reason for herself.

I prayed when this is over she would be the same woman of courage I so loved. Leaning against her broad wing, I examined the wound on her neck. Though some of her feathers were missing, the wound itself was closed tightly and healing well. If in truth she would have further need of feathers, I was certain they would return. If it were up to me, she would never again have need of wings or feathers and I would have two feet instead of four, but wishing would not make it happen.

Once again fatigue forced her to sleep. Though in my heart I would never leave her, for her own safety I had to lead Hagga and Arwan away from her. Slowly, I lifted my head from her wing and stood. The ground was soft and muddy so my tracks would be easily seen. I had to be as cunning as fox was considered to be. Trying to leave only the slightest of tracks I then found an area that might appear to be a hiding place for Fionna. Perhaps too obvious, but I was not dealing with a skilled woodsman. I circled around, making a bed of the grasses.

Then I stomped away, leaving deep impressions in the earth. Again I approached the area and set off in another direction. I did this many times taking various routes. There were tracks in every course. The untrained eye would deduce that there were many foxes in this location. I knew Arwan did not spend any time in the usual manly pursuits such as hunting and fishing. I felt certain she would again send him to find us.

He would then report to his sister that the river's edge was overrun with foxes.

Elidor

Having learned little from Arthur's court, we left to return to Fionna. Again, time compressed and we were quickly alongside the Hydon River. Our view was obscured by the soft gray misting rain. Like a velvet shroud, it hung over the river. The air, though, smelled clean, as the scent of water lilies hovered over the wet grasses. A soft breeze pushed the water's surface gently like the lapping of a kitten at a milk bowl.

The near silence was pierced by plaintive sobbing. So deep a grief, one would assume a soul had been lost to the devil with no hope of redemption.

Tivannia parted the rushes where she heard the crying and therein saw massive crystal tears falling from the dark eyes of the swan. Quickly she rushed forward and embraced the bird. Fionna ceased her cries and sought the comfort of her mother's arms.

Mother, she implored, *help me.*

Tivannia smoothed her feathers and said, *Fear not, my child, we will locate Joseph and he will tell your uncle the proper ceremony to remove the seal placed upon you.*

Nay, she wept, *'tis not the guise that grieves me so, 'tis Tag.*

My sister knelt beside her daughter and asked, *Tag? Why, what has he done?*

Oh, Mother, he's left me!

Left you? Tivannia responded. *Fionna, he may not be here at the moment, but I am certain he will return.*

Sadly, Fionna shook her narrow neck. *No, he waited until I slept and stole away, like a thief in the night.*

Nothing I could say or do would salve this wound. The boy must be found. I was certain he was leading the evil pair away from Fionna, but she was in no mood to listen to reason.

***

Tag

I felt as if my very heart was ripped from my chest. I had no desire to leave the woman I love, yet to save us both I had to betray her trust. I knew she would believe me false, yet there was no other option. If I stayed, Arwan and Hagga would find us both. Better they find only me, and not to be certain it was me they found, than to capture Fionna. Though I knew the Grail seal could not be broken by the likes of them, evil so often finds a way and I dared not risk it.

I was several hundreds of yards away from the area where I'd hid my beloved, when I heard them tromping through the reeds along the riverbed.

Arwan cried out, "I see tracks. This has to be him. There cannot be that many foxes on this island."

Hagga pressed forward and peered at the multitude of marks I'd left in the soft mud. "Well, what I see indicates there must be a vast number of them. Tracks lead in every direction. Though foxes are said to be clever, I doubt a single fox could have made all these prints."

I wondered if Hagga regretted turning me into a fox. Perhaps she should have chosen a larger and more visible animal, an elephant perhaps? I quickly covered my muzzle with my paw, as I was convinced they could hear my laughter. I probably did not make a sound, yet in my mind I howled. The pair of them was the most unfitting duo to use tracking skills.

"Hurry," she directed. "Set those snares and box traps. We'll catch the lot of them and then I will determine which is Rory."

Arwan rushed to do his sister's bidding, though he grumbled with each trap he set. "Why do I have to do all the work? Can't she just poof them into place? What's the good of being a witch if you can do nothing?"

I watched from the cover of the river rushes. To my surprise, I noted many pairs of eyes staring at me. They were like my own, with a green glint shining through. As they advanced, I saw they were foxes, a far greater number than the island could have supported. There was not enough of a food supply for that many foxes. Quietly they advanced, then, as if ordered, they stepped into the traps and snares. Only one trap remained un-tripped. I knew not what compelled me to do the same, yet I did so, without hesitation. The box trap fell over me and enveloped me in complete darkness.

I heard Arwan's whoop of success as he heard the last trap fall. "You were right, sister, there are many. And we've captured each of them. Now, with your witch powers, you can sort out which is your stepson."

Hagga snorted. "That whelp was never as a son to me. I'll show him a mother's love when I find him. He'll wish he never trifled with me."

I winced as I thought of my mother. It would tear her heart to see what I've become and how Hagga drove my father to an early grave. However, now was not the time to ponder past wrongs. I waited until I heard footfalls at the side of the box. It was my plan to run as soon as the box cleared the ground. Yet, when I saw daylight, I dared not. Each trap was filled with a fox, the exact duplicate of me. There was more than fox cunning at work here. This was the work of either the Divine or the Druids. Or perhaps both?

Chapter Eleven
Elidor

I knew the only way I could save my niece would be to call upon my friend Joseph. He and he alone could save her. What we learned at court would bring us closer to the Holy Man. Several of Arthur's champions set out with the mission of finding Joseph of Armithea, and then dispatching him to the Hydon Isle. Now that I realized he left us only that we might seek the Lord for aid.

Merlin would assist him in his journey once he was located. The wizard was unfamiliar with the tenets of the Christian's faith, yet he, too, was aware Joseph was the child's only hope. The Holy seal must be broken in order for Tivannia to heal her daughter.

"Tivannia," I said, "leave the child with me."

Though I knew to summon the Great Merlin risked incurring his wrath, I had no other option. I'd spent many long hours learning the Druid craft and now I must call upon that knowledge. I remembered well the honor bestowed upon me when I was given the final rite of summoning. Not all Druids were so blessed. It was presented to me as a token of my dedication to my craft. I was an apt pupil and quickly learned the highest of powers. However, I also recalled the stern admonition at the presentation.

"The honor of The Summoning is given with due consideration of the Sect's Elders. You must always honor this gift, for if it is used frivolously, it will be snatched from you."

I'd never used the gift, as other aspects of my training had always served me well. *Had I never used it because I was uncertain of the degree of skill I possessed or because I feared, more than death itself, the rancor of Merlin?*

I placed a soft binding spell over the swan to prevent her injuring herself further. Then I cleared a wide circle around her. Carefully, I trod down the rushes and grasses. When I'd finished, the grasses laid precisely, so that not a single blade disturbed the perfection of the pattern. At the circle's edge a soft gray mist rose, hiding the swan and the summoning circle. The mist was thick, so dense as to near have substance, like a velvet curtain shutting us off from the rest of the world.

I stood as close to Fionna as possible and extended my hands over her. As I did so, the top of the curtain formed into ribbon-like segments rising to the sky. The ribbons wound themselves together, forming a tightly braided canopy over the entire circle. This was a Druid tent. Though I'd not said the words, it was a spell I'd used many times over. I am certain it was an unconscious thought put to action. My sister returned and seemed unsurprised to find the tent and entered quietly.

This final ritual I'd never before employed. The risk of failure was far too great to undertake this summoning lightly. Certain we were safe from prying eyes, I lifted my arms and slowly, softly, chanted The Summoning Rite.

Nilrem, emoc, emoc ot em ssorca eht seiks fo eht tsav esrevinu.

Nilrem, Nilrem, I ma ni deen fo ruoy modsiw.

Nilrem, Nilrem, reah dna emoc.

It seemed a vast amount of time passed as I chanted over and over, more times than I could count. Though it probably was but an instant, my arms grew heavy as the top of the misted tent parted and allowed the evening sky to be seen.

The North Star glowed with an intensity I'd never before beheld. It seemed the star was created for me alone, as its splendor focused on the narrow opening at the top of the tent. So brightly did it shine, I had to shield my eyes. And, from within the brilliance, The Great Merlin appeared. The greatest sorcerer of all time had heeded The Summoning.

THE FOX AND THE SWAN

***

Merlin

Once again, I find myself compelled to speak in this chronicle. Never in the multitude of centuries I've lived through have I ever encountered a problem of this magnitude. Of course, never since the dawn of time itself have the Druids and Christians entered into a covenant to protect a compromised human. Furthermore, I am certain it would not have occurred in this instance if it weren't for the reverence of the Priestess of the Hydon Isle. Tivannia is quite unlike any other woman among the protectors of the "Old Ways." A teacher not only of the rites of her faith, but she taught her priestesses the physical endurance needed to live under such trying conditions. Even the famed sheep could only manage the climate for the warmer months. Her followers had not only endured, they thrived under her tutelage. She studied long and hard to learn the true responsibilities of her faith and craft. Tivannia had created a haven here on a tiny isle within a narrow Scottish river. Her name was revered not only in her own land, but in Avalon as well. The Elders had decreed her request would be honored as recompense for her devotion.

The child, Fionna, made a beautiful swan, but the Lady of Avalon herself had given her seal the swan would again be a human. And I would not see the Lady's seal compromised.

The Christian Joseph of Armithea is a man of strong principle, and I respect that. However, his vision in this instance is limited.

Suddenly I was dragged from my own thoughts by a force so little used I'd forgotten its power. I was being summoned.

Chapter Twelve
Tivannia

The circle encompassing Elidor, Fionna, and myself seemed to grow smaller. Then I realized another person was within the Summoning wheel. Though I had no premonition of his coming, the Great Merlin appeared. He seemed disoriented, quite unlike the great wizard's usual demeanor. As if he was unprepared for his own presence. Something outside of his vast power drew him to this circle.

"Welcome, Merlin, your presence is much welcomed. Can you offer some solution to our dilemma?" I asked.

The wizard blinked, then smiled as he acknowledged me. "I believe I can, Priestess," he responded.

My heart rushed to my throat as I dared to hope my daughter would soon be restored. Elidor stood silent, his arms hung loosely at his side. He seemed unable to speak. Gently, I took his arm and shook him.

"Elidor, Merlin is here. He's come to help us."

My brother seemed to have awakened from a deep sleep. At once he slightly bowed to the ancient wizard.

"Great Merlin, you came," he said, his tone full of awe.

The frail elderly gentleman stepped from the circle and returned Elidor's greeting.

"Forgive me, Great Merlin, I am surprised the summoning worked. I'd never used it before, as you well know. It will take me a few moments to gather my senses to tell you why you are needed."

"There is no need. I came to the same conclusion only moments before you summoned. Joseph must be found. It is the only way the child can be transformed."

I was eager for the sorcerer to help my daughter and tugged at his sleeve. He glanced at my hand on his garment and glared at me. I could tell this was only a mock anger, as he quickly smiled.

"Mistress of Hydon, together we will find the Christian. We will use the most base of our powers to discern his location. You, project to the edges of this land and if you find him not, I will project unto the edges of my land. He cannot possibly have gone further than our vision."

It was difficult for me, as I had nearly depleted my energy being on the same plane as my children. However, I summoned all my remaining strength to do the wizard's bidding. I searched every crevice of Scotland, every hill and vale. No corner escaped my scrutiny. Joseph was not anywhere in Scotland. I hung my head and reported, "Great Merlin, I've looked everywhere. He's nowhere to be found."

"Fear not, Tivannia, I'll locate him."

Merlin seemed untroubled that I had been unable to find the Christian. His lack of apprehension gave me hope. If the greatest wizard of all time was unperturbed by the current situation, my faith dictated I should not be concerned. To be lacking faith in Merlin was unacceptable.

Merlin extended his hands and led my brother and me from the circle, leaving Fionna to rest surrounded by the binding spell Elidor cast.

Merlin looked up to the top of the mist tent through the opening he'd used to enter. He held my hand in his right hand and Elidor's in his left. As he projected, we, too, were able to see as he saw. Over hills and meadows he searched, and finally near the cliffs of Dover, Joseph of Armithea rode upon a small donkey.

The Holy Man had a strange pallor, and it grew clear he was ill. Slowly, he slipped from his mount, apparently losing consciousness. He would need medical attention or he would surely not live another day. I looked to the wizard and silently begged to be allowed to heal him.

"You may, my child," Merlin said, and at once I was swept up and landed gently at the stricken man's side.

He'd fallen from his mount and lay upon the rough ground. Quickly, I removed the blanket from the donkey's back without the animal's knowledge, and arranged it on some soft branches I'd taken from the scrub pine on the edge of the cliffs. I lifted Joseph and urged him to help me to move him. I needed his cooperation as I was unable to lift him in my weakened state. He struggled to rise and fell over his own feet. Somehow I was able to place him upon the blanket.

After what seemed like hours, Joseph was resting upon the bed I'd fashioned. He coughed, wheezed, and pointed to the bundle that remained on the donkey's back. I stood and walked toward the donkey. The animal was shy and backed away from me. I supposed he'd never seen a person with so transparent a presence. Finally he allowed me to remove the pack from his back.

Joseph nodded and bid me open the bundle. Within were a clean tunic and a neatly folded packet with a few herbs in it. I took them to the Christian. Quickly he pawed through the plants. The man's eyes filled with despair.

"What's missing?" I asked.

The Holy Man shook his head sadly.

"There is no more, and it cannot be found in this land. It only grows in my homeland."

"What is it? Perhaps we have something that could substitute for your herb."

"No," he said sadly.

"Your country is much too cold a climate to grow it.

I used the last of it on Elidor to bring him from his drunken state."

"What herb could possibly serve to sober a drunk that would also heal one stricken such as you?"

"It is a special tea that possesses all manners of cures. I never travel without it. I knew I would soon have need of it, as I'd been feeling strange of late. That is why I was headed home."

Within an instant, he became quite flushed and his tongue grew thick. I could not understand a word he said. His eyes clouded over and he fell in a heap on the rough ground, flailing his arms expansively. Suddenly, the Christian lapsed into a strange sleep. His face grew even paler and he shivered as if from a deep chill.

I covered him lightly with my shawl and went to gather moss and some other curative plants. I was gone moments only, yet when I returned though his head was hot to the touch, his sweat had evaporated and he was sleeping naturally. I built a fire as dusk was fast approaching. Gathering what I harvested, I placed them in the black kettle Joseph had in his pack. From a nearby stream, I got some clear water, fashioned a rack over the fire, and then made a rich broth of the herbs. There, on the cliff above the water, the evening wind blew fiercely. The broth would warm us both.

The pungent sweet odor awakened Joseph. "Where am I? And what are you doing here? This must be far from your homeland."

"It is quite far, Joseph, but I need your assistance, and Merlin allowed me to come to you and aid you in your illness."

"And how did Merlin know I was ill?"

"Merlin knows all, Joseph, he knows all."

"While I do not doubt your veracity, I question this all knowing ability of anyone, other than God."

Fearing Merlin would still be watching, I quickly rushed to his defense. "Merlin knows all that takes place in his native land. He does not seek to usurp the power of any other entity, but in England his powers know no bounds."

I could see the Holy Man was weighing his thoughts. His convictions in his own faith were unwavering, yet out of friendship for my brother, he considered his words carefully before he spoke.

"I suppose it matters not how the wizard knew I was ill, only that he sent you to cure me. I am truly grateful."

I stood back while the Holy Man tried to stand. I did not want to give the impression I thought it too soon for him to attempt to rise on his own. He toppled as he rose too quickly. "Joseph, I think you should give yourself a little time to recoup, as you were very ill."

"You are quite right, mistress. I shall rest a bit and then try to stand a little more slowly."

I nodded my approval as he leaned back against the oak tree where he'd fallen. I wondered if he would be able to draw the same strength from the ancient tree as do the Druids. His countenance changed and it was apparent he did regain his strength.

Knowing my questions would not now anger or disturb him, I dared ask the question that burned in my heart. "Joseph of Armithea, will you reveal the ritual that will restore my daughter?"

He closed his eyes and spoke softly. "Madam, I cannot. It is a sacred rite and cannot be used upon those who do not revere the Lord and his teachings. Sorcery, wizardry, and any other forms of magic, have no place in this ceremony. It is why I left Elidor and your son, that they might pray on the matter and enlist God's help."

My concern for his feelings was not reciprocated. The man's thinking was narrower than the eye of a needle. Though I feared angering him, the truth of the matter was he had angered me. When he'd allowed me to show the Goddess the cup, he should have stated his stand against the ceremony being used to aid the swan. He had exhibited true compassion then, so why did it fail him now? I no longer knew which was the stronger of my emotions, the love for my daughter and the desire to cure her, or the anger against this Holy Man for refusing to assist me.

Only my brother's friendship with this man held my tongue. "For Elidor's sake, I will bring you to the full measure of good health, but only for my love of Elidor."

"If it were not for my friendship with your blasphemous brother, that unholy Druid, I would not have taken ill. 'Twas he who led me from my true path, the Lord's way."

He continued his rant against Elidor. "I was fooled when he declared he too would be a Christian. I should have known he was the devil in disguise. This is but one more trial I must endure for the sake of the Lord."

From what little I knew of Christians, it seemed to me he was behaving in an unchristian manner. I could not believe this Holy Man believed my brother had ever been, or could ever be, a party to malevolence of any sort.

When I knew Joseph would survive, I disappeared altogether. I found it very hard to retain my presence in the face of my anger. And I was far more incensed at this man's behavior than I had ever been. It was bad enough he would not help my daughter, but to call Elidor an instrument of evil was intolerable. I left the fool to his own devices.

***

Tag

I had always felt I was unique, one of a kind. My father had instilled in me that I could accomplish whatever I chose to do simply because God created me. Yet, here I was, certainly not one of a kind, for through whatever means, I'd been replicated countless numbers of times. Everywhere I looked, there were green-eyed foxes, hundreds of them. We, for I now felt part of some sort of team, had all been apparently captured.

Arwan seemed elated with his feat of trapping so many foxes. It was clear he'd spent little time in the country. If he knew anything about nature at all, he would have realized it was impossible to capture so many foxes on a tiny island. Each and every green eye was turned in my direction, as if they were awaiting instruction from me. I was uncertain of what action I should take. My only thought was to protect Fionna.

I fell to my side in the box trap and expelled phlegm making it appear I was foaming at the mouth. The imitators did likewise. Soon it looked as if each fox they captured suffered from rabies. Though Arwan was unfamiliar with the phenomenon, Hagga recognized the symptoms, as she'd seen sheep perish from the same malady.

Arwan slid a hand into the trap where I lay foaming on my side. I drew back my lips and growled.

Hagga reached for her brother's arm and restrained him. "Stop," she directed, "It's infected, and touching it alone can kill you."

Pheland quickly drew back his hand. "Well if it can kill me why won't it just die on its own? Can't we just leave them here in the traps to perish? Why do we need the fool thing anyhow?"

Hagga rolled her eyes in the face of her sibling's stupidity. "We can't just expect it to die. You forget one of these foaming creatures is my stepson. He's enchanted. And it's not just my enchantment that has touched dear Tag. A well-trained sorcerer has his hand in this. Probably that old fool Merlin."

Clearly impatient, Arwan pressed his sister further. "Why does it matter if he lives or dies? If he dies, you will inherit everything, won't you?"

"No, you fool," she responded. "If he dies while he is a fox, there is no way we can prove he is Rory MacTaggert. We have to determine which one is really Tag and then kill him so it looks like an accident of some sort."

"Then what are we supposed to do? Just leave them? If we do that, won't they have won? What about that wizard?"

"Enough, brother," Hagga answered, indicating she would listen to no more foolish suggestions.

From the slight crack at the edge of the box, I could see she felt the prize slipping from her grasp.

"We will leave them all, here, right where they are. If the wizard is involved, the foxes will be gone by morning. If he is not a part of this, whatever is illusion will be gone and only the true fox will remain."

Arwan appeared less convinced this would be the case. Hagga had absorbed far more witch lore from her uncle's book that her brother realized. His gaze shifted about looking at each and every fox as if he could discern which of us was of substance and which was illusion. "No, I'll not leave. I'm going to see just what happens, you can leave if you want to."

"You fool," she retorted.

"You do not give me permission. I shall leave, and you will come with me. Do you understand me?"

"But, Hagga, I'm older I should say what will be done, not you."

Hagga narrowed her eyes and glared at him, turned, and abruptly left. Arwan followed like a faithful hound.

I lay quietly for several minutes in the dark. There was no sound other than my own breathing. Suddenly a slim shaft of light peeked at the edge of the trap. A tiny pink nose edged the side of the box. A rabbit? Why on earth would a rabbit rescue a fox? There was no plausible explanation, yet it was clear the animal was there to assist me from the trap. I placed my paw next to the rabbit's nose and lifted the box. Once clear of the trap, I carefully studied the brown hare that freed me.

My boy, you've gotten yourself in quite a quandary. I knew you were in love with the girl. Hagga thought her curse would damn you forever, thankfully I was able to soften the blow.

I was dumbfounded. Could this be Da? I knew Fionna's mother was able to return from another plane, but she was a goddess, surely my father had no mystical qualities. He was a God-fearing man who attended mass each week. This could not be.

Well, Tag, aren't you even going to acknowledge your father? The rabbit's nose twitched and he moved his whiskers.

Da? How can this be? You aren't a Druid in disguise, are you?

No, Rory, I am your father. Tivannia offered me the opportunity to alter the curse of Hagga. Though you are now a fox, you will be able to once again be a man when your true love returns your affections.

My heart sank. I knew Fionna would never love me, as she believed I destroyed her trust. No other option seemed open to me. I could not have remained with her and risked her safety. I made the sacrifice and would have to live with the consequences.

Thank you, Da, for trying. However, it is too late. Fionna will not return my love as she believes I abandoned her.

Why ever would she believe that? Even I can see the depths of your love in your eyes, the rabbit said, sitting back on his haunches.

I moved to the rabbit's side and sat next to him. It was strange being with my father once again. Stranger still, as he was a rabbit and I a fox. My tears flowed profusely, though I was able to connect with my father, the two women of my heart were lost to me forever.

The brown furry creature beside me closed its eyes and softly sighed. *Rory, please trust me, you will be a man again and you will have Fionna at your side. Though she may not trust you at the moment, events will play out in order she might learn of the depth of your love. And she will return it, my boy.*

With that pronouncement, the hare stood and started hopping away. I followed as closely as I could.

Da turned to me, then said, *All will be well, my son, go to her.*

I rushed to the animal's side and begged him to remain with me. I was alone in this world, no mother, no father, no friend, and no love. How would I survive? Though the rabbit was gone, my father's words echoed back to me. *All will be well, my son, go to her.*

I turned and raced to the edge of the river where I'd last seen Fionna. Near the nest area, I heard the voices of Elidor and Tivannia.

Tivannia sat beside her stricken daughter and spoke softly. "My child, I do not know how to restore you, but I will somehow find a way."

Her brother looked up at her and said, "What do you mean, Tivannia? I thought you and Merlin found Joseph. Why did you not bring him back with you?"

Tivannia closed her eyes and rose. "I found him with Merlin's aid, but Joseph will not help us."

Elidor's eyes widened in surprise. "He won't help us? But, why? He is my friend."

Tivannia shook her head. "I don't believe he is truly your friend, Elidor. He refused to help me even after I cured him of his illness. The fool thinks you purposely used his 'tea' and tried to lead him from his God."

"But... but," Elidor replied, tears forming in his eyes, "I told him I wished to be a Christian, too. Why would he abandon me?"

Tivannia turned and sat back upon a pile of grass. Purposefully she arranged her skirt and rubbed her palms over the fine fabric. Over and over, hypnotically she brushed her hands against her garment.

I crept through the reeds until I was very nearly able to touch her.

Again she spoke, despair in her tone. "Elidor, you must bring me the Grail. We will have to do this ceremony ourselves."

I inched closer. If she were able to restore the swan with the Cup, perhaps Fionna would forgive me and once again love me.

Elidor knelt beside his sister. "It would be risky, Tivannia, if the ceremony is not perfect the transformation might not be complete. She may have a wing for an arm. Worse yet, the wrong ritual could kill her."

Kill her? I could not let this happen. Better she remain a perfect, complete swan, than to die in the attempt to become human. I slipped back into the reeds, certain I was unseen, and waited.

Tivannia grabbed at the robe of her brother. "Please, Elidor, you must save her. I lost my child once, I cannot bear it happening again. Surely, Merlin would know the ceremony. Merlin knows all."

Chapter Thirteen
Joseph of Armithea

I knew I'd disappointed the witch. It had not been my intent, but I could not allow even a friend to deter me from my course. The Lord's work is far more important than the life of a single person. My discomfort with magic and sorcerers should have provided stronger warning. I should have been more perceptive.

Now I must retrieve the grail from Elidor, as he most certainly would be tempted to use it to restore his niece. This could not happen. It would be a deed most foul.

My sturdy donkey stood munching the scrub grass near the edge of the cliffs. I could hear the water below crash against the sheer bluff. Even so far from the edge, I could feel the misty spray prickle my skin. The water was chilled, which matched the coldness within my heart. So, like Peter, I'd abandoned my God. I knew better than to place myself in temptation's way. Yet, so hungry for friendship in this far off land, I'd lost my way. I befriended a most unsuitable man. Further, I'd trusted him with the most sacred of all vessels. How could even Jesus forgive this foul sin?

Somehow, I had to bring this situation to rights. I would have to retrieve the Grail from Elidor. At one time, I was certain of the action I took placing the sacred cup in his care. His being a Druid was the reason I'd chosen him. He held no avarice and was as devoted to his faith as I was to mine. I felt he would be the perfect protector as no one was likely to believe such a vessel would be in the care of one not of the faith. When I'd felt those strange feelings, I should have paid closer attention. My Lord was directing me. I'd failed to answer his call.

My only course now was to return to the isle. Surely Elidor and his nephew would still be there. I recalled I heard someone say the Bishop was coming to marry the man Pheland and Elidor's niece. Perhaps the learned Bishop would find a solution to my dilemma.

The witch had restored me to perfect health, for that I owed her thanks.

To be indebted to a witch is most uncomfortable for me. I am sure I possess nothing that would repay the debt I owed. I could not turn my soul over to one such as this. Putting her as far from my mind as possible is my only course.

I tried to mount my mule, who seemed reluctant to allow me to do so. Each time I approached him, he shied away, just as he'd done to Tivannia. Had the witch enchanted my burro? And if she had, why?

***

Tag

I listened to Elidor and Tivannia with despair in my heart. My dream would never be realized if the Holy Man would not aid us. Wondering if the Goddess could help, I moved forward.

"Tivannia," Elidor said, "do you remember the Bishop was to come to the wedding of Arwan and Fionna?"

She hesitated, then said, "I do remember. He is an official of the sect, is he not? Perhaps he could show us the ceremony?"

Elidor responded, "I'm sure he could, but the question is, would he? If Joseph declined, what would keep the Bishop from doing the same?"

"Sometimes those with the greater station have a broader conception of situations. Perhaps he knows something your friend does not."

I knew, even the Bishop with all his learning, would not ally himself with those whose faith differed from his own. Men of high ranking within the sect dare not show compassion for one not of their faith. To do so might taint the other believers. The task was mine alone. I had to hide the grail, so that it would be lost for ages. Past my lifetime and hers. Though it meant each of us would remain as we are, I cannot not bear the thought of her being either disfigured or dead. My mind would not allow me to conceive of such an abomination.

Quickly, I raced to the rim and the area where I saw Elidor's grotto. I would have to search diligently as I was certain the Druid had hidden the vessel where no mortal would ever seek it. However, I was no longer a mortal, I was an animal. And, I would have to use all my cunning to discern the location of the sacred vessel.

I strained to remember every emotion and sense I'd used when I last saw the grotto. The gulls screaming overhead, the slight pungent smell of pine from the scrub trees at the edge of the shrine, I drew upon these and more to find the holy place. It could not be seen with the naked eye. It was a tough chore even for a clever fox. I put my nose to the ground and tilted my ears to catch each passing sound. I sniffed and caught the scent of Elidor and the smell of a sweet wine. I was in the right place, yet still I could not see it. I sat back on my haunches to give myself time to reason how I could find the cup if I could not even find the area where I knew it was housed.

If it could not be seen, I thought, why not seek the place without vision? I closed my eyes and concentrated on the sound and scent. These two became even stronger. I could hear the gull's cries reverberating within my skull, and the scent of wine spilled on a cold marble was as strong as if the wine- covered stone were beneath my nose.

Not daring to trust my sense of sight, I followed my nose. I felt my head hit something very hard. Dazed for a moment, I forgot my resolve to not use my sight. Opening my eyes, I found the vessel was before me. It was unremarkable in appearance, a simple cup for a carpenter, not a goblet for a king. Yet, I could perceive the majesty of the object. An overwhelming sense of calm came upon me. If it were not for the loss of Fionna, I would truly be at peace.

Taking the container in my teeth, I headed down from the rim. Carefully searching the beach, I found no one. I was alone. Though Fionna, her mother, and her uncle were scant feet away, I moved quietly so they would not know of my presence. I headed to the cavern that housed the underground river. Along the edges of the water the earth was hard packed. I chose a spot half hidden by the lime-covered teeth that protruded from the caves ceiling. It would be impossible for a human to get into this small alcove.

I had to dig quickly. My paws were raw, so furiously did I scrape the ground. If the Grail were discovered, Fionna would be lost. I would never know love and thus remain a fox for the remainder of my life. Though my claws were torn and bleeding, it was little sacrifice to save her. It was for her my heart beat. If I were never able to win her love, to know she would be safe because of my doing, would assuage my guilt.

The grail was hidden, and for the moment, Fionna was safe. I dared to rest for a moment only. At least that was my plan. Fatigue over took me and I fell into a profound, fitful slumber. The kind of sleep where prophetic dreams are dreamt.

I was home, in my father's house, yet not his alone. The study where I was sitting was nearly the same, yet brighter. All of Da's books were lined up properly. All his ledgers stacked neatly and it did not seem to be the dark ominous room it had been under Hagga's care. I looked up from the desk to see a beautiful woman with a tray of tea and scones. Her smile was more brilliant than the sun itself, nearly as bright as her pure white hair.

Placing the tray on a small table, she smiled and slid my chair away from the desk then planted herself in my lap. She snuggled into my arms and laid her cheek against my chest. The scent of her would captivate even the most reluctant of men. I, however, was not reluctant. I was a willing captive. She'd made a prisoner of my heart.

I drew her back and placed my lips upon hers. She returned my kiss with fervor. This was not the shy maiden I'd loved as a child. For now she was a woman, my most willing bride, my wife, my Fionna. Without restraint, she proceeded to unlace her bodice. I clasped her hands in mine.

"Perhaps we should retire to the bedroom?" I suggested. She smiled and shook her head no.

"No?" I replied, startled.

"What is the good of being married if I cannot love my husband anywhere I choose? I've nothing to be ashamed of and this is our house, after all. Why not here?"

I released her hands and she continued to remove her bodice. As she was naked from the waist up, I stroked her breasts and drew their tender tips into my mouth. Gently, yet purposefully, she drew away from me. I ached for her, yet she chose to tease me?

But it was not truly a tease, as she was preparing for a more perfect vision. There she stood, in the sunlight that shone through the high, glassed windows of the study, completely nude. Like a statue, no mark blemishing her skin, perfect in every respect. And she was mine.

I awoke with a start as I heard voices nearby. My heart and body pained with the images of the dream. Could it ever come to pass? Or was it just a dream, nothing of substance, something that would never come into being? In my heart that ached for her, I knew it would never happen. We would exist perhaps side-by-side, but never know the depth of human love and the profession of that love. We are mired forever in the marsh of our animal guises.

Chapter Fourteen
Elidor

Perhaps Tivannia was right and through some miracle, the Bishop would aid us where Joseph would not. I'd surprised myself with the success of the Summoning. Merlin was still with us, though somewhat detached. The man himself was a mystery. I was certain he was contemplating the entire situation, as great men are wont to do.

All that was on my mind was Fionna. The child had been my life, just as strongly as if I sired her myself. I'd held the sweet girl from the moment of her birth. She was as much my child as my sister's. We had to restore her.

I turned and addressed the great wizard. "Merlin, do you think the Bishop who is coming to marry Pheland to Fionna would tell us of the ritual?"

The sorcerer smiled, closed his eyes, and turned toward me. "Elidor, I've known many holy men in my lifetime, though none with the apparent ability to transverse time as is Joseph. The Bishops I've known are held within their own time, but all were great men. Do you recall the name of this particular Bishop?"

Tivannia spoke up. "I seem to recall a young fellow who visited the island when Sully was but a young boy. His father was a fisherman and he wanted even then to be a man of God. I believe his name was Adair."

"Ah, yes," Merlin replied, "I recall him. Adair Peadar, a very good man. I am confident he will aid us if it is possible."

I, too, recalled Adair Peadar. His name meant Peter the Rock, and this man was as a rock. Engaged in manual labor whenever he had the opportunity, he preferred to work the fields to feed his congregation over poring endlessly over ancient words. He was of fair complexion. Even his hair was as yellow as a summer daisy. Moreover, Adair had a reputation of respect and fairness to all he met. No task was beneath him. He would till a field or rock a baby gently in his muscular arms. Word of his reverence was well known throughout all of Scotland.

Merlin clapped his hands and then raised them high in the air. His robe fell to the elbows of his bony arms, and from his hands emanated bolts of lightning. At once, we were able to see Bishop Peadar as he arrived at the cathedral Tag's father built on the mainland.

One of us would have to leave and speak with the Bishop, but Tivannia would not be visible to Peadar and I was not confident Merlin would be able to speak to a bishop without compromising his own faith. To me, I was the obvious candidate.

"Merlin," I addressed the senior wizard, "I think it best if I leave and approach Adair."

The sorcerer turned and glared at me. His gaze was so penetrating I felt he discerned every error I'd ever made in my entire lifetime. "Elidor, you presume too much. I will determine who will ask for the Bishop's aid."

Properly contrite, I bowed to the wizard. While my head was lowered and my eyes closed, I heard snickering. Tivannia's lilting laugh was added to the snicker and I, too, joined in the mirth. Merlin was a multifaceted man and was not above playing pranks.

Then, once again, I heard the sound of tears and looked to see the swan weeping. My sister quickly forgot the amusement and rushed to her daughter's side.

Mother, my niece cried, *even if the Bishop can transform me, I will still have to marry Pheland. Please do not allow him to change me. I would rather be a swan for my lifetime than married to that cruel pig.*

My heart near to broke watching my precious Fionna gaze hopelessly at her mother. No matter her form, she was unhappy. I was no longer able to gather her in my arms and protect her from all evils.

And so it came to pass, I was the one selected to speak with the Bishop. I prayed he remembered me. We'd been friends so many years ago. Even as a child, Adair was a child of God. Many hours we spent arguing which of us would take which path. In the end, I chose to serve the gods I understood, nature, and all its majesty. Peadar chose his Lord, who could not be seen but whose presence was everywhere. Somewhere in the deep recesses of my soul I knew each of us had made the right choice and each of us had made the same choice. All Gods are the one God.

After I made certain Tivannia could reassure her daughter, somehow I would be able to make all things right, just as I had when she was a child, I left to ferry across the river.

***

Tag

As Elidor made ready the ropes on the pulleys of the ferry I snuck beneath a tarp on the deck of the vessel and lay as quietly as possible.

Elidor's arms were strong and we quickly reached the other side. He secured the barge and I eased out of my hiding place. While his back was turned, I leapt off and hid in the rushes at the riverbank.

I knew he was headed to the cathedral my father had built so many years ago. Da had hired many skilled craftsmen from the whole of Scotland. It was truly a magnificent church. The silver spires pierced the sky and the arches held the carefully handcrafted glass windows. There were fourteen windows in all, each depicting a different station of the cross. I well remembered sitting between my parents as a very young child and staring up at the multi- colored glass.

After I was certain Elidor would not notice me, I shook to rid my coat of the chilled river water. The sun was warm and quickly dried my coat. Elidor would be taking the road to the church, but I remembered a less traveled path that would lead me there faster. I scurried over the grass and stones in the graveyard adjoining the cathedral. It was here my parents were laid to rest, side-by-side, beneath a marble statue of a guardian angel.

I dared not dwell on the past any longer than a quick prayer for their souls. I needed to protect Fionna. Waiting outside the church in a large bush, I saw Elidor approach. He seemed hesitant to enter, as he looked to the high spire with the bronze cross atop it. Purposefully he stepped up onto the stair that led to the huge oak door. Though I am certain he feared rejection because of his faith, I knew he would be welcome there.

As he reached the top stair, the door opened and there before him was his friend, the Bishop Adair Peadar.

"Elidor," he exclaimed. "How wonderful to see you. It's been far too many years. Do come to my lodging and we will share a drink and talk of past times."

The Druid closed his eyes and shook his head sadly. "I dare not imbibe. Drink has led to my ruin."

"Your ruin? Elidor are you ill?"

"No, my friend, but I have created an untenable situation for my family."

"They face a cruel fate if you are unable to aid me."

"You seem certain," he responded, "The situation is of your own making, yet I am equally certain God had a hand it in as well. Elidor, whatever the case, we will examine it and determine what steps must be taken." The Bishop put his arms about the Druid's shoulders and led him down the steps to a nearby inn.

It seemed strange to me both men, each of different station, should dress similarly. Elidor, as always, was robed in a rough wool robe the color of the earth. The Bishop, whom I thought would attire himself in more splendid garments, was dressed in a wool robe of a gray hue. Father Peadar, for that was how he addressed himself, carried a leather pouch at his side. As it pressed against his side, I could see the outline of a miter. It was clear, he dressed more formally for some occasions, but his usual attire was his gray robe.

The two men entered the inn, ducking as they did so, for the doorway was short and both men were of average height. Quickly they found an empty table then signaled the innkeeper for ale and sat. While the inn's owner was distracted, I slipped in the door and hid behind a large wine cask in a darkened corner.

Elidor hung his head between his hands and said, "Adair, you remember my sister's daughter, the child I helped raise after her mother's death?"

Peadar leaned his elbows on the table and raised his hands to his chin. "I do. As I recall she was a pretty child, but her hair was stark white. I knew it would turn darker as she grew, as it does with most children."

"If only that were the only problem. It did however lead to the present situation."

The Bishop nodded. "Please go on. There must be more to this than the color of a girl's hair."

Elidor lifted his head and spoke. "Our family has fallen on hard times as the owner of the pasture where the sheep are kept in the summer passed away and his widow did not see fit to extend monies against the next year's lambing. Her husband had always paid my brother-in-law regardless of the yearly profits. With no funds, we could not make it through another year, so Portus determined to sell his daughter."

The Bishop interjected, "Elidor, I met your brother-in-law, he did not impress me as the kind of man to sell his child."

"Well, I suppose he didn't actually offer her for sale, but he did arrange for her to marry a man of means."

"That's not unheard of. Why is it such a problem?"

"The man is a snake. He told me outright he would not honor the marriage contract once he received the dowry which he believes to be the summer pasture."

"Portus thought because he was older than Fionna, he could appreciate her in spite of her unusual coloring."

"I see, but what is at stake here? As I see it, the betrothal is already broken if it is clear the man will not honor a marriage."

"If that were the extent of the problem I would agree, but my family is in financial ruin and in order to protect the girl she was changed into a swan."

The Bishop's eyes grew wide. "Elidor, is this your doing?"

"I helped. The Great Merlin, my sister Tivannia, and I all had a hand in it," Elidor responded.

I watched as a burly man sat at the table between the wine cask and the Bishop's table. I strained to hear, but the man was as loud as he was big. Carefully, I crept nearer their table. I hoped to remain unseen, but my white tail was too great a contrast and Elidor spotted me.

"Tag, what are you doing here? Don't we have enough problems without my having to explain a fox that comprehends human speech?" Elidor asked, shaking his head.

Peadar reached across the table and said, "My friend, you have created a situation unlike any other I've ever encountered. You speak to this fox as if it can understand you. Can it?"

"Yes, he can. He is the man Fionna chooses to wed, but his stepmother cast a spell on him so she could acquire his family's business."

The Bishop blanched, and his face grew as gray as his robe. "And I can help this situation in what manner? I do not understand. If the girl is a swan and the lad here is a fox, obviously they are at odds, as the two creatures are not usually compatible. While I am not truly comfortable with Druid enchantments, perhaps God's intervention will help."

"Thank the heavens. I feared I would repulse you, because my faith is different from yours."

"Friendship transcends beliefs. As your friend, and a servant of God, I am compelled to assist you in whatever manner I can," Peadar responded.

I walked around his legs and leaned into them. He reached down and petted my head. I stood on my hind legs and set my front paws on his knees. He continued to brush his hand through my fur. Gazing down on me, he smiled and scratched my ears. "Well, gentlemen, we both must seek higher powers. Elidor, do you know where this Merlin person resides?"

"Peadar, he is on the Hydon Isle as we speak. He is with my sister and niece."

The Bishop frowned. "I thought you said your sister passed away. How can she still be on the island?"

Elidor fidgeted in his seat and avoided looking at the clergyman. I knew he was hesitant to reveal his sister was a Goddess of the Hydon Isle. Peadar was a Christian and unaccustomed to unusual occurrences that Druids believe as a matter of commonalty.

Elidor struggled and finally spoke. "She did die in the manner of most mortals, but as she is also a witch, she simply passed to another plane, only making herself known to us when her daughter was in need of her."

Peadar rose and his chair fell to the floor, knocking me from his knees. I yipped as I hit the floor.

The Bishop shook his head and said, "I'm sorry, Elidor, all of this is a revelation to me. I was always aware you moved in different circles than

I and I accepted Druids are able to do things I could not understand. But, a girl is a swan, a boy is a fox, and your dead sister is not really dead, just moved to another plane?"

Elidor shrugged his shoulders and whispered softly, "It was hard for Joseph, as well, but I thought he understood. Now even he refuses to help me."

"Joseph? Joseph who? Do I know the man?" the Bishop asked, clearly exasperated.

"Joseph of Armithea, follower of Christ."

Adair's belief system had been stretched to the outermost boundaries. His mind could accept no more. I brushed against him and looked up at the cleric, begging him to understand.

"Elidor, this is virtually impossible. A man cannot live that long."

Elidor responded meekly. "I think you are right, but he has custody of the Cup. Who else could he be?"

The Bishop's eyes widened he appeared to have an epiphany. Quickly, he slammed his hands down on the flimsy inn table. "Do you know what this means, Elidor? The man is obviously a direct relative of Joseph, who was originally entrusted with the Grail. Over centuries, it has passed from descendent to descendent. Do you know where the Cup is hidden, since this man is your friend?"

"Yes, Peadar. I have the cup. He gave it to me many years ago. He believed no one would expect a Druid would have possession of the most sacred object of Christian religion."

"You have the Cup?" he asked incredulously.

"Then your problem is solved. Take me to it."

Elidor smiled, confident all wrongs could now be made right. He brushed off his robe and started toward the river's edge and the ferry he'd left at the shore.

Somehow, I felt this was not the answer. It was far too simple a solution. The Cup's seal had to be broken for the Goddess to remove the enchantment. Unless all parties were aware of the entire situation and in agreement of the solution, Fionna would be harmed beyond redemption. I'd done the right thing. She was safe if no one could find the cup. I hated to cause Elidor such grief as I knew he would feel when he discovered the vessel was no longer where he'd placed it, but I knew from the depths of my soul I had taken the proper course.

Once again, I stowed away on the barge, hidden from the two men behind a bale of hay used as seating.

***

Elidor

I felt a release from my burden as Peadar said all things wrong would once again be right. To have the child a human once more was beyond what I felt could ever happen. Yet, Peadar did not believe the situation to be without hope. I assisted him into the ferry and began tugging on the ropes to move the barge across the river. He quickly laid his own hands on the ropes and assisted me. We reached the opposite shore faster than I had ever traveled before. Peadar was a muscular man and easily set himself to pull on the rigging and accelerated our journey. As we stepped onto the narrow beach, I reached for his arm to direct him to the top of the rim.

He waved me away, saying, "It's been some time since I've climbed a cliff such as this, looks like an adventure."

I smiled. This man was unlike any other member of his sect. Then I indicated the path. "We do not have to scale the cliff face, the path is much quicker and far safer."

The Holy Man seemed somewhat disappointed, as if he were looking forward to climbing the sheer face of the cliff.

"Very well, Elidor, lead the way. I shall follow, but to scale that cliff would have been fun."

I was used to climbing to the rim, so found the journey one of little note. The Bishop seemed intrigued by the entire process. He rubbed his hands over the sharp rocks at the edge of the path and plucked flowers where he found them within his grasp. I wondered why a man so masculine in most of his pursuits would bother to gather flowers.

Finally we reached the area of the rim that housed the hidden grotto. The Bishop seemed impressed that something that was not apparent to the casual observer could have substance. I quickly swept aside the empty wineskin and indicated he was to sit at the stone table while I retrieved the Grail.

I reached into the secret place where I'd placed the cup. Moving my hand completely around the cubby I'd created for the safekeeping of the holy cup, I felt nothing. Had Merlin taken it? Would Tivannia remove it? No one else even knew of its existence. While it was precious to the Catholic Church, the item itself was of little value. A simple vessel to quench the thirst of a workingman, it was unremarkable in appearance, yet its power was infinite. And it was gone, without a single trace. How could this have happened? What now will happen to Fionna? The Church would surely punish me. And, it would be quite right in doing so. I'd failed. Failed my family and allowed this cruel fate to befall them, further I'd failed the sacred charge given me by a Christian leader.

I had to gather my courage to face the Bishop and tell him of the missing cup. Feeling a slight pressure on my legs, I looked down. A fox. I was certain it was Tag. The animal sat back on its haunches and looked up at me, curiosity in its eyes.

"What are you doing here?" I whispered. "Do you know anything about the missing chalice?"

The fox stood and exited the grotto. Without even glancing at the clergyman, I rushed to follow Tag. "Tag, come back. You must tell me where the cup is hidden. You did hide it, didn't you?" I hissed at the departing creature.

The animal ran much faster than I, and finally I had to abandon my pursuit. I slowly turned back to the grotto and the Bishop who waited there. It was a monumental burden I carried and to share it with the Bishop was an even greater load. Peadar looked at me, a question furrowed in his features. I wished I could turn away and not have to be accountable, but I had no such luxury. The music must be faced, regardless of the tune.

"Your Bishopness," I began slowly, hoping a grand thought would occur to me if I hesitated long enough, "I have something to tell you that sorely grieves me."

Though it was clear the cleric was puzzled by my demeanor, he gazed upon me kindly. I wondered how long the kindness would last, once I told him the cup was missing.

"Elidor." The Bishop smiled and continued. "I don't believe I've ever been called your Bishopness, but it does have an interesting ring to it.

However, I see by the frown on your face the news you have to impart is most dire. For heaven's sake, man, tell me and spare yourself the pain."

Though it pained me to tell him, I knew I must. No injury ever cut deeper. "Bishop Peadar, the cup is missing from where I placed it."

"Missing?" the cleric stammered. "But—but how? And who would have taken it? You are certain you told no one of its location?"

"No one, not even Joseph himself, knew where it was secreted."

The Bishop paced up and down the length of the narrow grotto. Finally he stopped and sat at the single table. Placing his hands on the table, he leaned over and said, "Let me understand this. You were entrusted with the Holy Grail because Joseph of Armithea believed no one would suspect a Druid of having a Christian relic. And you told no one of its hiding place?"

"No one," I replied, "not even Merlin, who knows all. He may have discerned the location, but I am certain he would not remove it. The cup has no value to a Druid."

Again he inquired, "Not even to your sister?"

"No, she saw it only once when she presented it to the Priestess of Avalon. Tivannia has no desire for the cup. It represents to her only the promise her daughter would be restored once the danger to her passed."

It was apparent the Bishop was confused but he did not seek to assign blame. The mantle of Bishop truly belonged on Adair's shoulders.

"Father," I said, "I think it best to return to my niece and sister. I believe the fox took the cup and he will return to Fionna. Though he probably won't reveal himself to us, he will always be close by to the swan.

"I agree, the fox did not appear to me to be mischievous, just concerned for the welfare of the woman he loved. If he's taken the cup, he must have good reason," the Bishop surmised.

Reluctantly, we headed down to the beach. There, set back hidden within the rushes, was my sister and her daughter. Both were weeping.

Chapter Fifteen
Sully

I'd dutifully followed my uncle. We'd returned from Camelot, knowing little more than we did when we started. My mother had nursed Joseph back to health, with little assistance from him. He'd turned on his friend. Though it was difficult for me to communicate with Tag, I knew he would never abandon either Fionna or me. This so-called Holy Man, did not impress me as particularly pious. He'd violated the tenets of his own religion by entrusting a Druid with his holy cup, then had abandoned his friend in an hour of need. By anything I ever learned as "holy," this man was not to be trusted. I feared he might injure my family as his cup was missing.

I was more certain than Elidor that Tag had taken the cup. The reason was as apparent to me as to him. I had heard the possible consequences if the ceremony was not properly performed and would have done the same as Rory. True, he'd taken what did not belong to him, but he'd done so to protect that which he held most dear.

Yet, I could not entirely condone the action either. I think my mother and Merlin could have used the cup in the correct fashion. They were used to ceremonies and rituals. Surely one cannot be vastly different from all others. There had to be someone in Scotland who could perform the ceremony. Why the Bishop was puzzled was more the mystery to me. He'd performed the ceremony daily all of his adult life. Why the vessel was of prime importance made little sense to me.

My duty was clear. I had to find Tag and persuade him to bring the cup to the Bishop. I knew he would resist but I must make him see reason. In our relationship since we were children, Rory was always the leader. I was clumsy and unsure of myself, thus I always followed. Tag set the course and I dogged his footsteps. This time it must be different. He would have to listen and follow my direction. If he failed, both his life and that of my sister would be lost.

I slipped unnoticed from the clearing wherein Fionna sat and headed for the mouth of the underground river. I know not what force led me in that direction, for in fact it made little sense, yet I was compelled to go to the cave.

It was dark and damp within the mouth of the river. The fall chill made the air crisp and the water cool. I tried to walk along the narrow ground at the side of the cave to no avail. My feet were too large, and I quickly fell into the cold river. No matter how uncomfortable I was, those I sought to save were far less comfortable. I had to help them.

I was now several feet within the mouth and thought I heard soft weeping. "Tag," I whispered, for I knew he would not like to have anyone know he wept. "Tag, it's me. I must talk to you. We have to save Fionna."

From a narrow ledge above the water, the fox emerged. There were tears on his muzzle. He turned his head and wiped them away with his head against his shoulder. Then he looked, clear-eyed, directly at me. As before, I could discern his thoughts, so I tried to project mine to him. Apparently it worked as he nodded.

The Bishop is with Fionna. He knows the ritual but he must have the cup.

You must return it, I begged.

I cannot. If the ceremony is not performed by Joseph and the Lady of Avalon, she could be maimed or killed. I will not risk it.

But, Tag, the Bishop is a man of high stature within his faith, surely he would not seek to do harm.

Tag sat back firmly on his haunches and shook his head. It would be no easy task to make the stubborn fox see reason. I knelt beside him and stroked his coat. He shrugged and glared at me.

Sully, you have no idea what evil forces are at work here. Hagga is truly a witch, and I have no idea what animosity Joseph feels against your family.

I felt his logic rage against the confines of my skull. Too much thinking was giving me a headache. Once again I sat beside the fox. This time I petted him to give him reassurance I meant him no harm, but then tightly closed my arms about him. He wriggled and twisted against me, but I would not release him.

Tag, as much as you want Fionna unharmed, I want her restored. If you just show me the location of the cup, we may restore her and you as well.

I felt the animal relax yet I dared not release him until he'd given his word. How I held my family's future in my embrace both amazed and frightened me. He had to see reason. Rory was usually a reasonable man, an astute business man and fiercely loyal to those who trusted him. I knew he would not betray my trust. The fox firmly nodded his assent.

After I placed him on the ground, he barked sharply and headed further into the narrow cavern. I followed and saw him furiously digging at the river's edge. I moved to his side to assist him. Together, we excavated a rather large hole. Though there was little illumination, the cup seemed to have a light of its own. Patting Tag's head with my right hand, I removed the vessel with my left. It was probably the most beautiful thing I'd ever seen. It was not ornate, but the beauty lay in the simplicity and purity.

I brushed it free of the dirt and shined it against my tunic.

Projecting my thoughts to my friend I said, *Thank you, old friend, you've done the right thing. I am certain all will be made right as soon as we turn the cup over to the Bishop. He seems a kind and reasonable man and he will aid us.*

I can only pray you are right. I fear even if Fionna is restored, we will be faced with the same problem that got us into this in the first place.

I understood his feelings. The most important thing was his love for Fionna. In truth, my sister was a fortunate woman to have such a man so deeply in love with her. I cannot allow myself to think after all we'd endured, the Gods would still rail against us. We'd done our penitence. These dark times would soon give way to the light. Arwan Pheland would never be a part of our family.

Tag led us out onto the narrow beach. We, at the mouth of the river, were mere paces away from my mother and sister. Tag, using his acute sense of smell, located them quickly. He stuck his muzzle between the reeds and gazed upon his selected mate. The swan was weeping convulsively, barely able to breathe she cried so violently.

I entered the circle and knelt beside her.

"Fionna," I said, for I was uncertain how she communicated, "we have the cup and the Bishop knows the ritual. You will soon be made whole."

The swan looked up at Mother with tear-swollen eyes as if she implored Tivannia to understand.

"You can speak to her directly, Sully, just as you do with the fox. Use your mind."

I was relieved I would need no translator to speak with my sister, yet I feared her despair would render such communication useless. She still held to the belief she must honor Father's betrothal promise. Though I am certain within her heart she knew Father would never place her in such a position. Portus Sullivan was a man of honor and strong conviction, but he would not compromise his own daughter, not for any amount of money. Like most shepherds, he was close to his animals, and even now, unaware of his daughter's plight, he tended his sheep.

Chapter Sixteen
Bishop Adair Peadar

Often my faith was my refuge in times I did not fully comprehend. When my dear mother died, I thought the Lord had abandoned me. I was wrong when I could not interpret His will. My faith was such that I knew He would protect me at all times. Whenever I was faced with a circumstance I did not understand, He sustained me. Though I wept for my mother, I knew my God was with her and she would suffer hurt no more.

Though I was not Fionna's brother, I felt her pain just as profoundly as did Sully. Whatever the Lord had in store for her, I would help her see it through.

I observed my friend and his family as they clung together like frightened sheep, each trying to draw comfort from the others. Quietly, I knelt beside the woman who was obviously the swan's mother. She had a transparency about her, a presence so faint I was not certain if the woman was actually present. As I prayed for the girl's safe return from her animal guise, the woman touched my arm and murmured her thanks.

Placing my hand over hers, I assured her I would aid her in any fashion I was able.

Her brother had been a friend of mine for many years and, though we were of different sects, we both revered life.

"Elidor," I asked, "how can I be of service?"

The Druid looked down upon me and his sister as we knelt beside the swan. He extended his hand to assist his sister from her knees.

I, too, rose. The terror in his eyes frightened me. I'd never before even heard of a situation where humans become animals and was thus at a loss as to how to assist my friend.

"Father Peadar, do you know the ritual that uses the cup?"

"The cup? Do you mean the grail cup?"

Elidor nodded almost imperceptivity, as if he felt saying the words would somehow cancel the force of Christ's cup.

I returned his nod. I'd never hoped to use the actual cup of the Lord in a daily communion, and it was a great honor my friend offered me.

"Will you help us, then?" Elidor asked.

"I will. What is it you would have me do?" I inquired. Did he wish the entire mass or merely the sacrament of communion?

Taking my arm he led me to an even area among the rushes, where the grasses were trampled flat. Therein was a boulder, flat surfaced and smooth, which seemed to serve as a table.

At the edge of the stone table sat the fox and Fionna's brother. The fox held between his teeth the Holy Grail. Though simple in design, its majesty was awe-inspiring. I extended my hands, and the animal dropped the cup into my palms.

At once, a white-bearded man appeared beside me. I believed him to be Merlin, a man of vast reputation some thought to be a myth. Though I respected Elidor and his faith, I was not certain I could condone a wizard's presence at Catholic communion. Though my faith was strong, I feared compromising it. How would the Lord feel about sharing such a sacred ritual with a non-believer?

The bearded man extended his arm and placed it about my shoulders, saying, "Though you may not recall, we are well acquainted. I've many friends among your sect. I will do nothing to compromise or impugn your faith. It is the force of the belief that has the power not the basic tenets."

I nodded, so relieved that I was for a moment unable to speak. Extending my hand, I shook the elderly gentleman's frail hand in my own. The man seemed so delicate, it seemed his power was failing him. Regaining my voice, I said, "Master Merlin, you are Merlin, are you not?" He nodded, and I continued. "What is it you would have me do? How many I help you and this poor child?"

The man paused and stroked his beard. He then raised his arms high in the air, his sleeves falling to his elbows. Closing his eyes, he began to chant in some tongue I'd never, in all my travels, heard before.

The entire area of flattened grasses was at once fused with a soft green light that grew whiter as it encompassed the Wizard. Within the lighter beam, a wind swiftly blew. Merlin's cloak whipped close to his body and his beard nearly encompassed his head. He was oblivious to the phenomenon, as if it were something he'd experienced many times before this. He continued his chant.

Ydal fo Nolava emoc Ot llifluf ruoy esimorp Raeh em dna emoc

Over and over, he said the words. No one seemed able to understand the dialect, if, in fact it was a dialect of known speech. It seemed foreign, yet the words appeared to give comfort. The child's mother sat beside her daughter, tears flowing freely down her translucent cheeks. The fox somehow appeared less comforted. What dwelt in this sleek animal's heart, I could not discern.

Tivannia grasped the hand of her brother and that of Merlin. They formed a triangle around the swan. Merlin again repeated the chant, and Tivannia and Elidor took up the strange tongue, as if they were born to it. Yet, only moments before they appeared as confused as I. This was surely magic or sorcery. *Did I dare keep my word to aid my friend?*

Just as I was contemplating my role in this pageant, I raised my face to the center of the triangle above the heads of the Druid, the witch, and Merlin. There, suspended in midair, was a woman of the same translucency of Tivannia. Every shade ever seen in a forest graced her voluminous gown. The cloth seemed to shimmer like the scales of a fish in a clear stream. She was beautiful beyond compare. Were I not a man of God, she could have easily tempted me. Though I knew the woman did not appear to tempt me, she was here to aid the girl and her family.

The Priestess, for I assumed she was of the same sect as Elidor, extended her hands over the swan. She closed her eyes then raised her arms and said, "I have given my word this child would be restored to her former shape and being. The cup must be placed in my hand."

She looked directly at me, ordering me to hand over the sacred relic. I hesitated, and at once, the swan grew faint with the same translucency as the Goddess herself. Though I wanted to help, my fear of doing something against God's will paralyzed me. I could not move and felt the ground beneath my feet grow soft. The earth was as a quagmire, brown oozing mud. The swan fell to its side, laying its neck in the softened earth. Its neck appeared as a white snake, flecked with brown scales. Slowly, it raised its head, becoming like the hood of a cobra.

I cowered in fear and tried to hide the cup. Snakes were considered evil within my faith, and I took its appearance as a warning.

The Priestess pointed a long slender finger at me and the cup moved from my tunic as surely as if it were a lamb seeking its mother. There, between us, the cup was suspended in the air surrounded by a white, nearly blinding, light. The light and the cup moved and the Lady bid the swan to follow. The large bird, whose head was now that of a swan, once again stood and followed the moving cup. The brighter the light became, the more of substance did the bird become. It shook its body and flapped its huge wings. As she did, she took on the substance of a woman.

***

Joseph of Armithea

I could scarce believe my eyes, so foul was the abomination I beheld. Knowing Elidor would return to his family and most probably would use the grail to save them, I, too, went back to the island in the river. Perhaps I should have advanced more quietly, that I might learn more of the heinous action. However, I knew the Lord was with me and nothing could injure me.

I entered the area of the flattened grasses and there stood a woman, naked as on the day of her birth. And, all about her were witches, wizards, and beasts. This truly must be some pagan festival. So intent was I upon finding evil, I nearly failed to see one of the Church's most venerated bishops. Why would a revered clergyman be present at such a ritual? My father and his father, and the father before him had each handed down the protection of the grail. I knew of all these great men, I was the only failure among them. Perhaps the Bishop was here to rebuke me? But how would he know of my presence? Of course, Merlin knows all. He must have told of my wanderings to Rome. And no doubt the Pope dispatched his most trusted bishop to regain the Cup of Christ.

Boldly I stepped forward and fixed the blame for the missing cup upon the shoulders of the Druid Elidor.

The bishop turned and glared at me. "How dare you interrupt this proceeding?" he demanded.

I was at a loss I could not truly give an answer. Certainly I was not invited to this meeting.

I stammered, "I—I am on a mission to regain the Grail cup. The man I trusted has befouled the sacred relic."

Turning completely around so his hands were in my view, I saw there, upon his palms, the holy vessel. "You've found it, then? Thank the heavens. I truly feared the cup would be missing forever."

The bishop then turned back to the apparition that was suspended above the naked woman. "Mistress, I present to you the cup which was used to secure the safety of Fionna Sullivan. Please insure the woman will always be as we now see her, and shall never again fly the skies as a swan."

The woman reached out and lightly touched the cup. "As you have said, so shall it be done," she said, then vanished without a trace.

Merlin removed a heavy shawl from his shoulders and placed it about the naked girl. She was very fair of face and moved with a striking grace. Gathering the shawl about her shoulders, she smiled at the remaining woman, who was also as translucent as the woman who vanished and said, "Thank you, Mother."

Out of the corner of my eye, I noticed a fox scurrying from the clearing, as if the very devil were on his tail. Elidor's nephew hurried after him.

Would the Bishop again turn over the protection of the grail to me? Though I'd failed, the cup had been handed down for generations thorough the line of Joseph of Armithea. It was as God intended. Surely the Bishop would recognize that. I approached the clergyman with extended hands.

"Bishop, may I have the cup? It has been in my family for generations and I believe it to be God's will that it remain with me."

The bishop nodded and sat on the ground, dirtying his robe on the mire at the river's edge. He rubbed the side of the vessel over and over. "Joseph, for that is who I believe you are, I feel you have lost your way. Your zeal for the cup is overshadowing your true mission, which is to spread the word of God."

"But—but"—I gasped for words—"I entrusted the cup to a man whose sect is to revere life and all it represents. He befouled my trust. It is his fault, "I lost my way."

"Assigning blame is not the Lord's work," Father Peadar explained. "You may have the cup, but you are directed to place it in the hands of the man who once held it."

"No," I cried, "he's used it for witchcraft and sorcery."

The Bishop stood and brushed his robe free of the caked dirt and said, "No, Joseph, what has transpired here is part of the Lord's will. Just because we cannot understand all that takes place in the world is no reason to believe God cannot."

"But magic was used to transform this young woman from a swan. Surely her beauty is the temptation of the devil," I replied.

"And you do not believe anything beautiful to be the work of the Lord?"

"No, I mean yes," I mumbled. No matter what I said, it would be wrong. Could I ever regain the love of God?

Merlin held the two women in his embrace and answered my unspoken thought. "It is my understanding your God never withholds His love. Those who seek darkness are condemned to find it."

"How," I asked, "Can you know what I am thinking?" I was certain I was falling further and further down the path to perdition.

"It is a skill. All men have the ability. It simply takes years of practice. That is the part of my sect you seem unable to comprehend. We seek to do no harm and to aid, through whatever means at our disposal, those in need of protection."

Elidor said, "Joseph, I never revealed the cup to a living soul. The fox was able to find it only because it was needed to protect his love. Love is the all-powerful force. The teachings of your faith as well as mine understand this principle."

"That is quite so," Bishop Adair replied. "Now we must find the young lad who suffered so much for his love."

The young lady turned and shook her head. "No, Father, he does not love me. He abandoned me in my hour of need. I have no need of his love."

Arwan Pheland

This must be the day of my delivery. I'd found her, and she can no longer become a swan. Slowly, I crept through the reeds that hid me. All I had to do was wait until the girl was alone. Now that they believed her protected, surely they will allow her to return to her own hearth. Her brother may follow her, but he is a simpleton, no more than a clumsy oaf. I could easily best him. Moreover, I would not try to capture her myself. I would employ my sister's craft to bind her to me, so I might own the entire island, as is my due.

So fiercely did I concentrate on the tableau before me, I failed to notice my sister, who crept through the grasses to join me.

"What are you looking at?" she hissed.

I turned and said, "Our future lies before us. They have turned her back to a human and have decreed she can never again become a bird. When they leave, we will capture her and take her to her father's house to claim the dowry."

Hagga sighed. "How do you plan on capturing her? Her uncle and her brother will not allow her from their sight."

I sat back upon the damp grasses and thought. I knew she was different from most women, yet she might still be frightened of rodents as were many ladies. "Sister, you will turn us into rodents and we will chase her from the protection of the others."

Hagga looked skeptical. "Yes, but not mice, they are too slow. We shall become as shrews. And not just two shrews, we will be as thousands. One or two might not frighten her, but a sea of them will."

Fionna, the bishop, and her uncle left the clearing and headed for the Sullivan home. Tivannia and Merlin seemed to step into midair and vanished, leaving only a sliver of silver smoke in their wake.

We followed the girl and her two male companions. To separate them would be the best tact.

THE FOX AND THE SWAN

***

Sully

I was the only one who noticed the fox as he took his leave. Tag ran away swiftly and it would take a great effort to find him. But find him I must. Though not schooled in either faith, it did not take a scholar to realize the greatest power is love. I could not let my sister and my best friend suffer its loss. They were both far too dear.

Quickly, I hurried after him. He would be able to easily run over the grasses in the marsh but my weight would prohibit me from the same route. I sensed deep in my heart he would seek his only refuge, his father's study. Whenever Tag was troubled he sought the silence of the only room in the house untouched by Hagga. There, he could remember the long hours he and his da had spent talking of the business and his mother.

I headed for the ferry and noticed the fox swimming far ahead of me. Though I was strong, the animal swam faster than I could pull the rope. He would arrive on the opposite shore well ahead of me.

Tag never looked back, though I am certain he knew I was following. He seemed determined to put everything behind him, even our friendship. I could not allow him to do that. Securing the ferry to the riverbank, I ran after him. I don't know how, but suddenly I was surefooted, not my usual bumbling self.

The MacTaggert mansion was not far from the river's edge and I soon arrived at the door. It was locked securely, but the window near the entrance was open, just wide enough for a fox to slip through it. I pushed against the opening to increase the size that I might enter. The house was quiet, the furniture draped with sheets, dust over every surface. Tag had been too long from his home. With no one to care, the residence was falling into disrepair.

As I slipped over the sill, I thought I heard a soft whimpering from Mr. MacTaggert's study. The door was ajar, I pushed it open and found Tag curled up on his father's chair. He heard me and turned with a growl. I think for a moment he'd thought me to be the witch.

What are you doing here? Go to your sister. She needs you.

Tag, what Fionna needs is not me, but you. She loves you. She just doesn't know it yet.

The fox raised a critical brow, giving his face a comic appearance. *How can she deny love? I know I cannot, even though it will never be returned.*

Tag, you must come with me. She is still in danger. If Pheland discovers she is human again, he will demand the betrothal be honored.

Tag agreed, as he well knew the truth I'd spoken. Together, we headed once again for the river ferry.

Arwan Pheland

My sister was a genius. One tiny creature would not frighten anyone, but a multitude is cause for horror. We followed as close as we dared to avoid being seen. When they reached the Sullivan home, the uncle and the priest left the girl as she went to her quarters. The two men remained on the first floor and the girl went up the stairs. I climbed the tree outside of her window, with Hagga close behind me. Of course, Hagga did not climb; she ascended in midair. What a joy it was to be allied so intimately with such power.

"Listen closely," Hagga directed. "I want you to go to the branch closest to the window, kneel down, and then quickly spring to the window ledge when I change you. You must not hesitate or you will fall. And after you will come hundreds. I will be at the end of the shrews and before me will come thousands. We will swarm as a single unit, a unit with a multitude of disgusting rodents."

I wondered what Fionna's fear would gain us, but I knew Hagga was well prepared to achieve us our goal. Before I could waste any more thought on the matter, I felt my body shrink. As soon as I had four feet I sprang from the branch to the windowsill. At once, I was pushed to the floor by hundreds like me. The girl lay sleeping on her bed. I leapt up and landed on her leg.

She let out a scream that would wake the dead. The terror in her eyes was a treat for me. How I wanted her to cower. My companions flowed over her entire body. Shrews have tiny, razor-sharp teeth and we each set to gnawing on her flesh.

The men on the floor below heard her cries and rushed to her aid. Elidor was the first to arrive and swept at the rodent mass with a broad hand. The wave of shrews moved only slightly and as soon as the hand was withdrawn they returned to their feast.

The Bishop recognized the mass as evil and held the Cup of Christ before him. Offering up a litany of prayers over and over, he held us at bay.

Hagga saw him and ordered us to retreat.

"We shall not waste our time and talent against the Bishop, his force is greater than ours. Waiting until they feel the danger is past is our best chance. Then they will relax their vigilance and believe she is again safe."

***

Tag

We approached the simple country home of the Sullivan's and heard a horrendous cry. At once I knew it was Fionna. I raced ahead and bounded up the narrow staircase. Sully was close behind at my heels. I'd never known a brother and sister closer than Sully and Fionna. Whatever it took, Sully would protect his sister. I would do no less.

As I entered Fionna's room, the Bishop was sitting in a chair alongside her bed. He was sweating profusely, and his hands shook as he cradled the grail in his hands.

I brushed against his legs and nosed the cup. He reached down and scratched me behind my ears.

Sully burst in and demanded, "What's happened here? Fionna, why did you cry out in such a fashion? One would think you were being murdered."

"What befell me was far more heinous than murder. Truly death would be preferable to being covered with dirty disgusting rodents."

"Rodents? You mean mice?"

Fionna replied vehemently, "No, not merely mice, far worse. Hordes of tiny shrews, each of them chewing on my flesh."

Her words filled me with loathing and disgust for the witch who'd so afflicted her. I knew she would never forgive my leaving her, but somehow I would make certain Hagga paid dearly for her misdeeds.

Her uncle tried to comfort her. "Be still, my child, you are safe now. The Bishop will remain until we can be certain no further harm will come to you."

Elidor's words were no more than out of his mouth than she relaxed and fell back on the bed.

Perhaps I should have been comforted by her peaceful attitude, yet something told me this was not a usual sleep. She rolled to her side and drew her legs and arms into the position of a small babe. I went to the edge of the bed and grabbed the bedclothes in my teeth. Pulling against them, I hoped to rouse her. To no avail. This was a slumber that would not be disturbed.

I looked to the Bishop who was still shaking. He nodded solemnly. He, too, knew something was not as it should be. Taking Fionna's shoulder, he shook her gently. She did not awaken. The clergyman would keep vigil and pray for her safety.

Certain the Bishop's cup would protect her, I felt it was safe to seek out and destroy the root evil of this situation. I had been snooping around the Pheland home, so knew the direction I must take to find the heinous duo. I'd gone only a short way when I noticed a strange, yet very pleasant smell. The same scent that had hovered in the air when the goddess was present.

The aroma grew headier as I approached the massive stone edifice that was the Pheland manor. The windows were dark, a curtain drawn at every opening. The structure truly reflected the personality of the people who resided there. Cold, dark, and unwelcoming.

A window was open a crack, just enough to let out the sound of an argument. Hagga was berating her brother, just as she had done with my father. However, Arwan was not about to capitulate as easily as did Da.

"Just because I allowed you to take over this situation with the shrews does not mean you will have a say in every matter. I am the man, and I am also older. My word will be the final say."

Hagga narrowed her eyes to ominous slits and said to her sibling, "You fool, I am the witch, not you. I have skills you can only imagine.

It is you, who will do as I say." Meekly as a chastised child, he hung his head and nodded.

Again, I drew in that strange, yet familiar perfume. Was the goddess here and would she help me? Somehow, I do not believe a Lady of Avalon would engage in a matter of revenge. Yet, I was compelled to avenge the woman I love. I would have to make certain that he could no longer harm Fionna or any other woman. The air grew thick with the Lady's scent. Had she returned unbidden?

I have, young Tag.

She spoke to me in the same manner as Sully. My mind was as an open book to her, though I was unable to perceive her presence. I could not hide either my feelings or my doubts. The Lady was as all-knowing as Merlin.

And how can I aid you? The girl is no longer a swan, but the evil pair who live here, intend her harm. I cannot allow one so protected by Avalon to be compromised, even if the seal has been broken.

This was more than I'd dared hope. Even the ladies of Avalon still sought to protect her. If I could outwit Hagga and her brother and they could no longer pose a threat to Fionna or the island, though I must remain a fox for the rest of my days, it would be well worth the sacrifice. The sounds from within the manor grew louder.

"Hagga, I will not again become a disgusting rodent. Surely you can think of something better. It's bad enough her hair is so damned ugly. At least she was somewhat comely before the shrews gnawed upon her. Her face looks like raw meat. I cannot have a disfigured wife. It would place me beneath my station. I will not do it."

Hagga stamped her foot, a gesture I well remembered. She would not be thwarted. But I could judge from her tone she had another plan.

The scent of the priestess grew stronger, and then I spotted her above my head in a tall oak tree. A soft green light shone all about her. She was as at home in the tall oak as she would have been in her own sanctuary. Quietly she placed a finger to her lips and pointed to the arguing pair.

Hagga was pacing back and forth over the ornate rug in the parlor. She stopped in the center over a pattern in the rug that resembled a star. "We will trap the girl into believing we will save her family from financial ruin."

Her brother interjected, "You stupid witch, that is why I am marrying her. Or have you forgotten? With her comes the land and the island."

"Of course I remember, you simpleton. That is to improve our situation, not hers. She must believe her father, brother and even her uncle will never want for anything."

"And, dear sister, how do you plan to accomplish this? What are you going to do, give her a dowry?"

Hagga stopped abruptly and turned to face her brother. "Precisely, Arwan, we will assure the Sullivans that with our protection they shall never again fear hordes of rodents that invade their home and frighten their sheep."

This I knew to be an outright lie. The green goddess was aware as well. A steam seemed to rise about her, giving evidence to her anger, though nothing in her tone indicated her ire. I leapt forward, my anger so intense I could have slain the pair in the blink of an eye.

No, Tag, she said, halting my assault with a beam of green light.

The light was unlike the one that surrounded her. It was green, but not a green of the forest. This shaft of light was as the foam on an angry sea. So like the sea, I could almost taste the salt. I could not move from its illumination.

The Goddess spoke, directing me. *Tag, this is your task. You must make certain no matter the enticement, the Sullivans must never ally with the Phelands.*

The lady could tell I was in the depths of despair. She smiled and drew her arms wide. The folds of her robe grew transparent. Raising her arms higher, she showed me a tableau of what my life could be if I only dared to hope Fionna would forgive me. It was like a dream, one that tells of prophecy, that which will occur.

Strangely, I was still a fox. One would think in a dream everything would be made right and I would once again be a man. But, such was not the case. I was walking along the bank of the Hydon River, deep within the chamber that housed the underground river.

There before me was the swan. A white so dazzling it illuminated the entire cavern. It was as bright as noon on a summer day. The swan approached the bank, extended its majestic wings, and stepped from the water. At once, feathers fell from those wings and there stood Fionna, as she'd been on the day she was born. No clothing or adornment to enhance the eye. She needed none, for she was perfect in form and grace.

I tried to hide from her, knowing my affection would never be returned. Yet she walked toward me, her arms extended. As she grew nearer, I felt my fur fall away and I was once again a man. A naked man, whose desire was obvious. I wanted this woman for all time.

I raced toward her and took her in my arms. Drawing in the scent of her, I nuzzled her throat.

She arched against me and murmured, "I love you."

This pronouncement was of greater importance than the coronation of a king. She loved me, and nothing else could matter in the great scheme of life. I felt her arms around me, her warm flesh pressing against mine. Then she was gone, and I was once again a fox.

How, Goddess, can I make this pageant a reality? What must I do to be once again a man?

The Lady of Avalon smiled. *For you, Fionna, and Scotland as well, we must stamp out the evil that festers this land like an infected boil.*

How? My Lady, I shall do whatever you bid. But I have no plan that would eradicate them. I cannot kill them, though they would not hesitate to slay me.

I am well pleased you feel you cannot slay them. To do so would only perpetuate their evil. Evil begets more of the same. They will be dealt with in the proper manner. The Lady appeared to sit within the branches and gave me further instructions.

Nodding my agreement, I headed back for the cottage. The priestess of Avalon vanished, and I was once again alone. As I approached the home of the woman I love, I noted Sully sitting on a bench outside the narrow door. His head was bowed and held in his hands. I yipped, and he looked up at me.

Where have you been, Tag? Still she sleeps. None of us can wake her. Not even my uncle, who is a Druid and should have the power to save his niece. Once again, Sully returned his head to his hands. I nudged him with my snout.

He opened his eyes and looked down at me. The longing for the answer was reflected in his eyes.

Sully, tell your Uncle Elidor to summon his sister and Merlin. You and I must find Joseph. Only if all parties are present can we save Fionna, I directed.

And you know this how? Why is Joseph important? He played my uncle false. I don't trust him.

But somehow he is part of this, this situation. It as the Goddess directed. She has the greater wisdom. For my part, I will do as she instructs.

I agree, my friend replied. *I will ask the Bishop, to remain with my sister and tell him we seek Joseph.*

Quickly, Sully entered the cottage. He was gone only moments and emerged carrying a bundle and a staff. He held them out to me. *I've food for our journey and my staff will aid me wherever we find the missing Holy Man.* I ran at my friend and butted him with my head. This would be just another adventure for us. It had been a long time since we were together as companions with a single goal.

Sully laughed heartily and said, *If this were not so dire a venture, it would be as it was when we were boys.*

Nodding, I headed toward the river.

Sully called after me, *Why are we going there? Do you know something you've not told me?*

I know little more than I did when I left. But, in truth, it is simply my belief Joseph will head for the only place he can find solace. Where he feels protected. The church.

Sully shook his head thoughtfully and followed me to the water's edge. There, among the reeds, was the barge that made the same crossing so many times previously. I leapt on and Sully followed, not quite as gracefully.

He grasped the rope and gave it a mighty tug. The barge eased off the muddy riverbank and into the cold water.

It was dusk and the church could not be seen from the river. As we got closer, I noted the structure was completely dark. An unusual circumstance, for even if the Bishop were not in residence, surely the parish priest would be. Why was the imposing structure without even a single candle?

Sully guided the barge to shore, and I bounded ahead of him.

Wait, he called. *Aren't you going the wrong way? The church is this direction.*

I shook my head vehemently and raced on. He followed and soon we were at the entrance of the church. Many hours I'd spent in that church and knew every pew. We approached the altar with Sully hanging on to my tail for guidance. I lifted my head and turned my large ears in every direction to catch some sound, indicating someone was here. Though it was very faint, I heard what seemed to be crying. It came from behind the altar, in the sacristy. Cautiously we ventured forth.

There, sitting on the floor was Joseph. Crying. Huge copious tears flowed unfettered from his eyes. In his hand, he held a communion wafer.

Sully approached him and was able to see him more clearly as the evening stars shone brightly into the small room. "What are you doing, Joseph? What is cause for your weeping?"

The Holy Man closed his eyes and lamented further. "I've failed, I've failed, both my God and my mission. Who would turn to Christ on my word, when I am not certain if the words I know are, in fact, those of the Lord?"

I was growing impatient with the man. It did not seem to me he was exhibiting any wisdom at all. To wallow in one's own sorrow with no thought for others seemed to be a foolish endeavor. I barked sharply at him. The sound startled him and he rose, holding the wafer high in the air. He began to chant the ritual I'd heard countless times as I sat between my mother and father in the same church.

"*Corpus Christi, Corpus Christi, Corpus Christi, Corpus Christi.*"

My friend, who had not been indoctrinated in the church in the same manner as I, grabbed at the man's robe and shook him.

Joseph ceased his chant and dropped the wafer. Sully, who did not feel anything was amiss, shook him further. Though I was an animal, my Catholic upbringing would not allow the Body of Christ to fall to the floor. Deftly I caught the falling host and held it gently in my teeth.

This action seemed to stun Joseph out of his stupor. His eyes widened more than I would have believed possible and he stared at me. He must have experienced an epiphany as his demeanor changed at once.

"Oh, my Lord," he wailed. "I've wandered so far from my God even a woodland creature treats You with more respect."

He continued ranting and beating his breast, until I again softly growled at him. A yip may have been more appropriate, but I could not do so with my teeth clenched.

Joseph was not really a complicated man. He approached all problems attempting to do the will of his God. He reached down and took the wafer from my teeth. After he placed it into a golden container he'd extracted from the folds of his robe, he petted my head. I was not really comfortable being petted, but allowed him to rub his hand over my fur rather than nip him as I wanted.

"Young Sullivan," he replied, "Whatever you would have me do, I am prepared to undertake."

Sully nodded and took the Holy Man by the arm and directed him to the river's edge. Still somewhat confused, Joseph clung tightly to Sully as they walked the short distance to the barge. I raced ahead of them and leapt onto the vessel causing it to wave off balance. Joseph, looking intimidated, reached out with his foot hesitatingly. Sully held him firm and he dared step onto the low-slung boat. He found a seat and clung to it as Sully pushed the vessel from shore.

The mid-day sun beat down on us as we crossed the chill waters of the Hydon River. Joseph, sitting in the rear of the vessel, dipped his hand in the water and trailed his fingers along the wake. As he did so, a tiny white duck swam alongside the barge. Soon there were several ducks surrounding us. They paddled silently always keeping abreast of the raft.

We were nearly to the opposite shore when the birds took flight. At once they became as doves, each flying to the peak of the Sullivan home. As they sat on the ridge board, they softly cooed. Joseph watched them in awe, his mouth hung open as a single feather fell into a shaft of sunlight.

"This must truly be the work of the Lord. Our Father used the dove to signify the Holy Spirit, so this must be a sign I am to do as you direct," Joseph said, his face as angelic as a newborn.

I watched as Tivannia and Merlin descended over the roof of the cottage. Merlin set himself gently on the lawn as he, too, marveled at the spectacle of the doves.

"Tivannia, is this your doing?" the sorcerer asked.

"Great Merlin, though birds are a particular favorite of mine, I have no hand in this. Nor do I believe has Elidor."

Tivannia landed on the lawn beside her son and asked him, "Son, what have you and Tag done? Are you courting evil?"

Sully looked at his mother, horror in his eyes. "Mother, surely you know though I would dare most anything to save Fionna, I would never entertain the dark forces. I've seen enough evil to last a lifetime."

Joseph interjected, "Madam, this is no manifestation of malevolence. The doves are a symbol of God's grace."

The Bishop, who had heard the commotion on the lawn, emerged from the house. "Sully, who are all these people, and why are they here?"

Before Sully was able to open his mouth to speak, Joseph rushed to face the Bishop and offer his explanation. "Your Lordship, we are all here to do the will of God."

"Well, sir, that is admirable. And, how are you all doing the will of God?"

Tivannia placed a restraining hand on Joseph's arm. "Truly, Bishop, the circumstance we all find ourselves in is not the usual place to perform the will of God, but in order to save my country, my family and my daughter, He has most graciously shown us the way to that salvation."

"I understand, dear lady, your feelings for your child, family and country. But how can we be certain this is what Our Lord wishes?"

Joseph pushed forward and said, "Bishop Peadar, I, too, was skeptical, but He has given us a sign, one that cannot be ignored. See," he said, pointing to the rooftop.

The clergyman raised his eyes and saw the bevy of doves on the ridge board. He smiled and said, "Quite so."

Chapter Seventeen
Tivannia

Through all the tumult, I had to remain steadfast and not allow any faint hope to deter me from what I must do. Though the Catholics seemed bent on helping us, I was not certain of a selfless motive. I'd seen too little of it in my lifetime. As a priestess of Hydon, of course, I'd experienced such altruistic behavior. However, people of other realms do not often exhibit concern for others.

From the corner of my eye, I saw Tag sneak to the river's edge. Here was one who displayed true sacrifice for the love of another. Even now, he was leaving to protect the woman he loved. It mattered not to him that he would not experience the love returned, as long as Fionna was safe.

I watched the fox for several moments, unsure if I should call out to him or allow him to leave. It was then I saw my dear Portus. Though I'd seen him each day since I passed from his reality, I'd never allowed him to view me. I felt it would cause him too great a pain. Fionna had never inquired about me to him, preferring Elidor tell her the tales of our youth. Portus was the dearest man God had ever placed on this earth. He dragged the flat-bottomed punt alongside the barge. Reaching back into the vessel, he took out a small, dirty lamb. The creature was covered in mud and bleating loudly. Portus petted the lamb with his large calloused hand. Well I remembered those hands so toil worn and rough, yet tender in every touch.

He walked the few feet from the water's edge carrying the tiny sheep and noted the group of us in front of his cottage.

"Elidor," he cried out, "Who are all these people? My God, is that Tivannia I see before me?"

I rushed to his side and held out my hand. Though he wouldn't feel my touch, I most certainly could feel his. As our fingertips touched, I noted a single tear slide down the face of the only man I would ever love.

"Tivannia, how long have you been able to pass back from wherever you went?" he asked.

"Portus, do not trouble yourself about that now. We must save our daughter."

"Save her? From what? Is she in some sort of danger? Sully, why did you not tell me your sister needed aid?"

"Papa, I knew you would not listen. You had already made up your mind. You have never backed down from a bargain once it was struck. I did not believe you would do so in this case."

"What bargain?" my husband asked. "No matter the commitment, I would not have my daughter harmed. Where is she?"

Elidor stepped to Portus' side and placed an arm about his shoulders. "She's sleeping in her room. It is a very deep sleep and we are unable to awaken her."

Merlin entered the conversation and said, "Laird Sullivan, your daughter and the son of your former employer have become part of an Ordination cast by the Ancient Druids to protect the Hydon Isle. Here your wife protects the Old Ways.

"And how has my bargain placed the Old Ways in jeopardy? Furthermore, what commitment are you referring to? I've not entered into any negotiations that would harm this island."

I could see Merlin was becoming impatient with Portus' lack of understanding of the situation. As all-knowing as he is, I realize it is difficult for him to realize all peoples do not have that capability. Gently, I placed my hand on the sorcerer's arm.

"Please, Great Merlin, explain to Portus how our daughter is in danger because of the alliance he's entered with Pheland."

Portus turned abruptly and asked his son, "Sully, are you telling me all this is because of the betrothal to Arwan Pheland?"

Both my brother and my son nodded vigorously. "Yes, yes," they both replied.

I glanced a warning to them. They should not reveal she might never awaken. It would have been too much for Portus to understand. He loved me and accepted my brother was a Druid, but if he thought his actions would cause our daughter harm, he would be desolate.

"Well, if this be the case, I believe we should have Fionna tell me if she's been compromised by this alliance." He turned to me, tears in his eyes. "Tivannia, would that you would have come to me sooner."

It was apparent the Bishop would have to ally himself with Merlin in order for Portus to comprehend all that had transpired. "Laird Sullivan," Peador said, "do come into your humble home. I thank you for your hospitality. I've made myself quite at home here. There is tea ready. Let us have a cup and see if we can understand what has occurred and what can be done about it."

Portus nodded and carried the lamb into the kitchen. He placed it onto a soft blanket next to the hearth. The poor animal had been shivering and welcomed the warmth. He washed his muddy hands and then sat at the narrow table with the rest of us clustered together on two small benches.

I was growing weaker by the moment. It was time I left this plane. My strength had been tried to the limits. I would have to return to my sanctuary to renew my vigor. Though I would love to remain with my family, maintaining a presence is very tiring. The Bishop would impart all the information Portus would need, and Elidor would explain why I could not remain. I stood behind the man who was the keeper of my heart and allowed myself to move to the other plane.

As I drifted away from my family, I truly wondered if the path I'd chosen was correct. My spirit was so thin I barely made it back to my home. When I arrived, the Lady was waiting for me. Her hands were extended over the small fire and her feet propped against the hearth. The winters within the Hydon Valley were harsh and the Lady was unaccustomed to such mean conditions. My priestesses were trained to endure the climate, but Avalon was vastly different from this tiny sanctuary and the Lady would truly suffer if she remained long in my home.

I fetched a warm woolen blanket and placed it about her shoulders. She thanked me and hugged the warmth tighter about her body.

"Tivannia, we must rid this land of its malevolence or all of Scotland will fall prey to the forces of evil."

"How, Goddess, can I do this?" I was certain she had a plan but at the moment it was not obvious to me.

"You alone cannot, we must unite our power and faith. Right will overcome wrong only if we combine to rout this pestilence from Scotland," she replied, as she briskly rubbed her hands in front of the fire. "How do you manage to bear this dampness? It seeps into the very marrow of my bones."

I was truly upset she was so uncomfortable, but learning to endure the climate was part of the reason I was allowed to remain in my own country. "Please, Goddess, allow me to fetch you a warmer garment."

She waved me aside and stood. "It matters not, as I will not remain long in your country."

"Will we be able to rid Scotland of the evil of the Phelands so quickly you will not require warmth?"

She turned her head to the side and placed a finger on her cheek. "Perhaps you are right. The deed will take some doing and there is no sense in making it more difficult by fighting the elements as well as the evil."

"I bow to the Goddess' wisdom," I said, smiling. I went to my closet and removed a warm dress crafted from my family's wool. It was my favorite, but at this time of the year was far too warm for me. I presented it to the Lady. She stroked the garment softly. I could tell she was impressed by the quality of the fiber.

"Tivannia, is this the wool that is famed to keep the wearer dry even in this incessant dampness?"

"It is, my Lady. It will surely warm you, right to the marrow."

She turned from me and removed her light gossamer shift and at once donned the wool dress. "Now, Tivannia, we must be about the work of the Ordination."

"How does the Ordination effect the removal of the Phelands?"

"My dear little priestess, if the Ordination is blocked by evil, anything that serves to remove that block is part of the Ordination. The Druids care not how we deal with the evil that bars the completion of their work, only that we do so with dispatch."

"I am here to serve you, Goddess. Whatever you bid, I will undertake," I said solemnly.

The Lady of Avalon opened her arms and drew me into an embrace. "Be still," she directed as she held me fast. "We must revisit their most terrible act."

I prayed my daughter would not have to relive the incident as well. "My Lady, will Fionna suffer the same hurt as before? I fear it is more than either she or I can bear."

"Have no fear, only you and I will view the terror, so we can defeat their foulness at its peak," she explained.

Within the arms of the Lady, I felt us transported to another time and place.

We landed in front of my former cottage, though none of the people I'd left were present. The window of my daughter's room was open, the curtains fluttering out. At once I saw them, hoards of them. The shrews scaled the wall of the house and poured into the second floor. The Goddess and I followed, hovering above the despicable rodents. We entered the room and saw Fionna's shell lying where she was first attacked. The shrews were similar in color, save two. I pointed to those mismatched ones and asked, "My Lady, these have different colored pelts, are they the font of evil?"

"They are, Tivannia. Once we quell these black ones, the rest will dissipate. They have no real substance without the perpetrators of this wickedness." She extended her left hand to me.

"Face me and give me your left hand." I did as I was bid.

She then drew herself close to me and we elevated over the darkest of the shrews. She held her right hand high in the air and I did the same. "Now," she cried and we came down upon the creatures with the force of a mighty rock and crushed the pair.

The Lady of Avalon released me and we both landed gently on the floor. The shrews, other than the two we'd crushed, vanished without a trace. The larger of the two seemed to have some life left and the Goddess crushed him beneath her heel. I knew for her to harm any life in any form was abhorrent to her, yet she'd rescued my family without hesitation. I would be eternally grateful.

She came close and once again embraced me. "My dear Tivannia, for your devotion and courage you have earned the right to address me by name. I am Aoife, the giver of life."

To be allowed to address the goddess by name was an honor not often given. Overwhelmed, I broke into tears.

She held me close and soothed me, patting my back as I hiccupped my gratitude. "Now, we have one task remaining," she said.

I was startled from my crying and puzzled by her statement. "What further task is yet undone? They are dead."

"Yes, they may be dead, but unless they are sealed away from all mankind, the evil may escape their bodies and once again plague the innocents."

Her pronouncement struck fear in my heart once again. Would Fionna be in danger, until we contained the evil?

"Yes, my dear," Aoife said, having discerned my thought. "We must return to present time and protect her until the Phelands are dealt with."

The goddess reached out for me and held me once again within her embrace. We lifted soundlessly and went again to the present time and place.

***

Elidor

It seemed like eons since my sister left us. I knew she needed to renew her strength, but I thought she would return immediately once she was restored. It had been far too long. And I was beginning to fear for her safety.

The Bishop remained at Fionna's bedside. Though his trembling ceased, his face remained ashen.

I went to his side to relieve him of his duty that he might eat. He waved me away.

"No," he said, "I will remain with her until the evil is thwarted."

"Your Lordship, you must eat, else you, too, will lose your strength. I will stay by Fionna until my sister returns. Go and dine with Joseph. He finally sees the truth."

The Bishop lifted his gaze to mine and nodded slightly. Handing over the cup, he said, "Watch her closely and hold the vessel securely. For the moment, it is her only protection."

Reluctantly, Bishop Peadar went down the narrow stair. I heard the scrape of the chair as he drew it to the table.

I slid the seat in Fionna's room closer to the bed then took her hand in my own and marveled at the smoothness of her flesh. As hard as she'd worked with the sheep, somehow she'd never developed the calluses that plague most shepherds. As I watched, her body seemed to be losing substance. She was becoming like Tivannia, nearly transparent. Did this mean she, too, would pass from this plane? I knew Tag would be the one to suffer most if this were the case. Somehow, she had to remain here with a happiness to which she was entitled.

Below me, I could hear the conversations of the others. It grew apparent Joseph had finally realized the right of the situation. He could now accept that the two religions could exist side-by-side.

Someone went to the door as I heard it creak open. Merlin addressed the guest. "Ah, Tivannia, you've returned and brought the Goddess with you."

"I have," she replied, and I perceived the closing door.

I knew it would be scant moments before she stood at my side next to her stricken daughter.

While listening for my sister, I'd turned away from Fionna for moments only. When I looked once again upon the comatose girl, there existed the indentation of her body but only a translucent form remained where the girl should have been.

I cried out, "My God, she's dying, she's dying!"

The words had no more than escaped my mouth than the girl's room was filled with her family, the Bishop, the Goddess, and Merlin. I placed my head in my hands and cried great heaving sobs. For all my training and my attention to the healing arts, I could not save her. My niece was as much a part of me as she was of my sister. I loved her as if I had sired her instead of Portus.

Her father pushed his way to the side of the bed and knelt beside his daughter's bed. "Fionna, you must forgive me. I would never have placed you in this danger if I knew your true feelings. Please, child, come back to me. You are so like your mother. I've lived a lonely life since she died, but without you and your brother, life would have little meaning for me. Please, child."

The Lady of Avalon approached and laid her hand gently on the forehead of my niece. Slowly, she seemed to gain more substance, yet instead of a woman near death, she became as a healthy swan. She extended her broad wings and flapped them as she extended her long neck.

My sister's face blanched. "Goddess," she pleaded, "you said she would not again become a swan. Is this more of the Pheland evil?"

"No, Tivannia, I have given her this form only until the danger is contained, then she will once again be as a woman. We must make certain the Phelands are punished and sealed away so they may never harm another."

I grew impatient. "Goddess, how do you intend to do this? Surely, you have it within your power to completely destroy them?"

Merlin interjected, "Elidor, of course she has the skill, but in this instance her power is not sufficient. She must work in tandem with the Bishop and Joseph.

I'd learned long ago one does not question the Great Merlin. The wizard had the power to see the whole of an issue and was considering more than one solution to the problem. I would wait, sure in the knowledge all would be made aright. Though in one very tiny corner of my heart, I still doubted.

***

Tag

When I heard that great flapping, I feared Fionna was once again a swan. There could be no happing ending to this tale. She'd lost so much and now I feared she would never again regain her true form. This was the way of the Druids, and I would have to accept it. I wandered aimlessly along the riverbank. There at the edge of the shore were two shrews. They were darker in color than any other I'd seen. The animals were apparently dead, yet something gave me pause. The largest of the pair moved his hind legs convulsively. The smaller remained motionless, but its eyes darted all about the shore. I grabbed them both up and held them tightly between my clenched teeth. Though I was hungry, something told me not to consume them. Unused to following directives from questionable sources, I raced back to the cottage to show Sully of my find.

He was sitting on a long narrow bench at the side of the front door. Tears streaked down his cheeks and his shoulders rose and fell with each heaving sob. He, too, had come to the conclusion all was lost. Fionna would never again be the smart beautiful woman we both loved. Never had I known a closer brother and sister. This wounded Sully more than any other fear he'd ever entertained. They were a family, their ties closer than a tightly woven tapestry. And this family meant more to me than I'd believed possible. Deep within my soul, I needed this family to be whole, that I could be a part of that whole.

Sully lifted his head to wipe the tears from his face with his sleeve. He caught sight of me and rose. *What have you there, Tag?* He spoke again using his mind to communicate with me.

I told him I believed the shrews were, in fact, Arwan and Hagga. His eyes grew wide, and he gasped. Reaching down, he grabbed me and said, *Don't you dare let those ugly things loose. Mother and the Goddess will know what to do with them.*

He held me to his chest and entered the cottage. He bounded up the stair and into his sister's room.

There, in the center of her bed, sat a swan, its snow-white feathers a stark contrast to the dark gloom of the room. The bird rose slightly and adjusted its position, then settled back down on the bedding.

Tivannia was beside the swan stroking its slender neck. The Lady of Avalon held her hand to Fionna's bill. All sound suspended. Not a soul within the room spoke or even dared to breathe. I held the shrews tightly in my teeth.

The swan once again slipped to transparency, its very form giving away to a velvet mist. I forced myself to concentrate. I knew whatever was happening would affect not only the Sullivans, but me as well. Here was the woman who held the key to my soul, even though the love I felt would never be returned.

Joseph of Armithea had remained in the kitchen and only now decided to make an appearance as he stepped from the stair and into my beloved's room. He carried with him the Cup of Christ.

The Bishop moved to his side and saw me standing by Sully's legs. He addressed my life-long friend and said, "Young man, we have within our power the ability to restore these two people to the love that the Druids ordained."

Sully stammered, "W—we do?"

The Priestess of the Hydon Isle patted my head. My mouth opened in awe and I released the rodents into her palm. She took them to the

Avalon Priestess and turned them over to her. At once, the room was filled with brilliance unlike any I'd ever witnessed. The light seemed to fuse with power and we were all held transfixed. All save my Fionna, the Fionna I thought lost to me forever, Fionna, the good, the wise, and the brave.

Her soft, sweet voice seemed to come from the swan then the bird began to molt. Feathers slid to the floor in an ever-increasing torrent. The boards were covered, and from the discarded feathers stepped my Fionna.

She spoke softly, yet confidently. Addressing me, she blushed, as she was naked, a little shy, but not ashamed.

"Tag, I have wronged you. I now realize you did not abandon me. You only left to protect me."

I shook my head furiously as Sully held me. She reached out and took me from his arms. Eagerly I licked her cheek as she softly stroked my fur.

The Lady of Avalon then took me in the crook of her arm and Fionna by the hand. "Come with me," she directed.

Fionna seemed more like herself. The woman I'd fallen in love with no longer timid or afraid. She easily kept pace with the Goddess and was decisive in her action. As we hurried along the beach, I wondered where the Lady of Avalon was taking us. It would seem that since she did not reside here, she would not know where things might be on this isle. Yet, she proceeded with the confidence of one well acquainted with the terrain.

There, just ahead of us sat an ornate shrine. I'd lived all my life near this island and it was a structure I'd never seen before. It was cut into the cliffs that rose to the top of the rim. There were steps cut into the stone and a waterfall fell down upon them. At the very base of this shrine was a glistening pool. The water so clear and the surface so smooth, one would doubt it was actually fluid. Fionna knelt beside the pool and studied her reflection. The priestess eased me onto the ground, and I sat beside my love.

"What are we to do, my Lady?" Fionna asked.

I, too, wondered what would be our course of action and I looked to the goddess for instruction.

She smiled, reached down, and petted my head. I disliked being petted, but the goddess's touch was pleasing.

"All in due time. We will keep a vigil until the others arrive."

Chapter Eighteen
Portus Sullivan

I've long known my beloved wife was a priestess, but the fact never troubled me. Her presence was a treasure to me, and I savored every moment with her. When she died, I felt the world had come to an end. But then I remembered the two beautiful children she'd given me and was able to go on for their sakes.

Tivannia's reappearance startled me, to say the least. Had I known I could speak with her through these troubled times perhaps I would have come to a better solution for our daughter. However, I had not that insight and had done what I felt was best for our family. And I was wrong, horribly wrong. It is time for me to take action.

"Gentlemen," I said, addressing Joseph, Merlin, the Bishop, and my son. "The time has come."

From around the table four sets of eyes focused on me. I stood and pushed the chair firmly back in place. The others did the same.

"Elidor," I asked, "does this man Joseph have the approval of the church for whatever he is compelled to do in this matter? That Tivannia is a witch and you are a Druid has never given me pause, as I know there is room for all faiths. But we must not compromise Fionna on any quarter."

The short, muscular Bishop reached into his robe and withdrew his miter saying, "All that truly concerns the church is this Druid Pair must be married both to honor their faith and fulfill the Ordination of the Druids. We must find Tivannia and the goddess."

Sully grabbed a warm cloak and placed it about my shoulders. I'd been so centered on helping Fionna, I'd failed to consider comfort. My son had made certain all were protected from the damp in our search for the Priestess of Avalon. We all went outside and I noticed Elidor was not with us. I called back into the house.

"Elidor, are you not joining us in our search?"

He stuck his head out the window and called out, "I believe we must bring Fionna's finest gown with us as there can be no delay in marrying them once we find Tivannia and the goddess."

I found no fault in his conclusion and advised the others to wait.

Joseph came to me and said, "Laird Sullivan, I fear I've misjudged you and your family. I most humbly beg your pardon."

"I forgive you. Faith is a tenuous thing and must be protected at all costs. I believed I was doing the best for my family. When we realize we are mistaken, we must take steps to right the situation."

Joseph smiled and nodded. The Bishop then approached me saying, "Portus, this very day I will marry the pair, and I assure you, your fault will fall away with the joy of this union."

I had no idea how Bishop Peadar felt so confident, but it was contagious, I could see the confidence swell in the breasts of all of us. Dare I hope all will be well?

Elidor came from the cottage and enlisted Sully to carry Fionna's finery.

Merlin stood and closed his eyes. It was as if he'd left us and was conversing with another person. He spoke softly in a tongue I'd never heard before, the same phrase over and over. From the misty sky a light shone down upon us all, from that beam stepped the Lady of Avalon. She seemed to have more substance than when I last saw her.

"Gentlemen, what you are planning is right and in time it will be done, however we have a far more pressing problem. We must rid this isle forever of the malevolence of the Phelands. Though Tivannia and I have killed them, their evil can escape their broken bodies and find a willing host in another person of avarice."

Bishop Peadar nodded, bowed, and removed the golden miter from his head. "The cup. We must employ the graces of Christ to eradicate this iniquity."

Joseph reluctantly handed the grail cup to Peadar and bowed slightly over it. This must have been the response the goddess sought, as she rose within the beam and directed us to follow her.

We could barely see her when I shouted out to her. "Where is my daughter? You took her away. I greatly fear for her safety."

"Have no fear, dear Portus, I have the lass, and I will protect her."

Tivannia

I watched as Tag paced back and forth in my small kitchen. *When is the goddess coming back?* he asked. *Will she be able to make it right? Can Fionna and I have a life with one another?*

Though the goddess's ways were incomprehensible to the fox, it was apparent he was certain some action, perhaps at the hand of the Lady or Merlin, would right all wrongs. He sat back on his haunches then lowered his body to the floor in front of the fire. My daughter slept on a nearby cot. She was tired from all the strange things that happened to her. It was a far greater trial than most women endure.

The goddess previously placed the dead shrews in the heavy iron pot that hung over the fire. Tag seemed to be dozing when suddenly he raised his head and sniffed the air. I glanced toward the pot and noted a thick, dark, choking smoke pushing up the cover on the pot. Tag began barking. He nipped against my skirts and dragged me from the kitchen.

I tried to retrieve my skirt from his mouth, but he held me fast. *Tag, we must contain the evil in that pot. We have to go back in.*

He dropped the hem of my gown. I tried to rush to the door, but he growled at me. I feared the evil had already seeped into the fox. He sneezed, held his breath, and stormed the kitchen. He lifted Fionna from the cot and dragged her to me. At once, he raced back into the smoke-filled room. Through the crack in the opening of the kitchen, I saw the most courageous act. The fox inhaled all of the smoke and held it within his own body. He rushed along the narrow beach and up the steep grade to the rim. I was certain he would be unable to hold the smoke and run. Surely he would soon need to take a breath of fresh air else he would perish.

I summoned every ounce of my strength and followed him, leaving a confused Fionna outside my tiny sanctuary. She would be safe, and I dared to leave her.

Though his lungs were fair to bursting, he forged onward. I tagged closely, as I knew if he were to fail in whatever plan he was employing, I would have to kill him. There was no other alternative.

Within moments, we were outside the Pheland mansion. The fox leaped up to an open window and slipped inside. I watched, helpless, as he appeared to be searching for something in particular. He found an ancient spell book that was open on the library table. As he looked for my aid, I went in and stood beside the open book.

Expelling the rancid smoke from his lungs and throat, he spewed the evil into the book. When every part was purged from his body, I slammed the book shut firmly.

He fell to the floor and I started toward him. *No,* he screamed. *If you remove your hand, they will escape.*

I held the book shut tightly, clutching it against my breast. *How can we contain them for all time?* I asked.

Come with me, Tag directed and started down a long dark hallway. He stopped at a supporting pillar in the wide hall. A panel high within the support column was open. I could not reach it without levitating. I prayed I had the strength to hold the book and rise as well. Deliberately I placed the book in the column and slammed shut the panel.

Tag sat on the floor inhaling deeply. He closed his eyes and fell quickly asleep. I watched over the lad, as near a son to me as my own. He possessed every good quality a woman could want in a son-in-law. Now, if only the fates would be kind and make it a reality.

Just as I was near to nodding off myself, as I had expended much energy in containing the evil, the room fused with a dancing light. There, above us, suspended the Lady of Avalon herself, attired in her finest garment. The fabric was flowing and light. Her skirt danced about her body as joyously as children around a maypole.

"Come, my little priestess, today you are to attend a wedding."

"A wedding?" I stammered.

"Whose? I am certainly not dressed for a service. I must tell you what happened here."

The goddess smiled. "I know well what transpired, Tivannia. The boy vanquished the evil."

"Boy? No, the lad is still a fox."

She pointed to the hearth and threw a beam of light upon the sleeping fox. "I think not," she replied.

At once, the fur fell from the animal and a very handsome Rory MacTaggert stepped from the discarded pelt.

Chapter Epilogue
Rory "Tag" MacTaggert

I could not believe I was once again a man. Rather than offend the Goddess and Tivannia, I grabbed a tartan from the bed and wrapped it around me. I grabbed another tartan and wrapped it around my shoulders as we ran back to the cottage. There, Tivannia moved to the bed and took the larger cloth from my shoulders and covered her daughter with a matching piece.

Fionna drew the blanket up and secured it tightly around her bust then rose and came toward me. Never in this or any other of the known worlds was there a creature so perfect. Her skin was flawless, her hair shone like white silk. But it was her eyes that drew me most, the spark I'd thought long gone twinkled within them.

She laughed and said, "Now that we are restored, are we free to marry and not bartered for coin?"

I heard a sharp intake of breath and quickly turned to see the group of men we left at the cottage standing in the doorway of Tivannia's sanctuary.

One man was sobbing.

Sully embraced his father and said, "She knows, Papa, that you would never willingly cause her harm. She knows and loves you still."

Portus embraced his son and then moved forward to embrace his daughter. "I'm so sorry, my dear child, I should have gone directly to Tag when I realized we were going to suffer at the hands of his stepmother. He's a smart lad, he'd have found a way."

I crossed the room and placed an arm about the old man's shoulders. "I should have told you straight away I loved your daughter and could provide for all of us, but I did not. Sully told me there was no way to compromise your bargain. I thought I was respecting you. You were too proud to accept my charity."

"This is how men fall into folly believing they understand another's motives," Portus replied sadly.

Bishop Peadar stepped up and said, "Gentlemen, gentlemen, none of 'what might have been' matters. We have a wedding to perform." He extracted his miter from his robe and then addressed Joseph. "Joseph of the line of Armithea, please entrust to me the Cup of Christ."

Joseph smiled widely and removed the chalice from the pouch at his waist. Holding it briefly, he rubbed the surface until it shone like the sun.

Portus was confused. Of course he had no knowledge of the journey he'd taken to get here, nor did he understand how a woman could become a swan or a man a fox. His credulity was being tested.

Tivannia's intimate sanctuary seemed to grow. The ceiling rose high, like those in a cathedral. Sunlight flooded in through the intricately decorated glass windows that moments before had not existed. Finely crafted pews formed facing the hearth. The simple wooden table in front of the fireplace became as a marble altar.

Robed in the finest vestments seen outside of Rome, the muscular Bishop approached the altar with the Holy Cup and placed it centrally on the marble. When he placed the miter on his head, all evidence of crumpling faded. The headpiece was unblemished.

The decorations, flowers, and other embellishments were fit for a coronation. It was as formal an occasion as I ever expected to be part of. I stood nervously as any groom at the end of the long red carpet leading to the altar. There, at the farther end, stood Fionna on her father's arm. The gown Sully had fetched for her was replaced with a creation that might have come from the finest dressmaker in France. Her skirt billowed like a frothy cloud. On the bodice were embroidered thistles. I'm certain a woman would understand all the intricacies of her dress, but for me all I truly noticed was the beautiful woman wearing it.

I swallowed hard and drew in a sharp breath. She would be mine and mine alone within a few moments.

I was certain Portus had never worn such fine garments. He seemed almost uncomfortable, but the pride shining in his eyes overshadowed the tight collar. Sully stood by my side in front of the altar nervously picking nonexistent lint from his sleeve.

The Lady of Avalon served as Fionna's maid of honor, and preceded her down the green velvet carpet.

Once again, I looked down the emerald rug and saw a vision I knew for a certainty I would never see. On the arm of the old wizard Merlin was my mother. She appeared translucent in a gown of flowing yellow, so like the ones she wore when I was a child and we skipped down the halls. The sorcerer seated her and moved to sit next to her when his place was usurped by a brown rabbit. No one had seen the animal enter yet there he was. My mother gazed down upon him, smiled, and allowed him to rest in her lap. Merlin again went to the beginning of the carpet and brought another translucent lady to the proceedings.

Tivannia was of more substance than I'd seen her in many years. Merlin led her to the pew next to the altar. Portus beamed, and his smile lit the entire area. He slid along the pew easing his way to his wife's side. He took her hand in his own and appeared more content than I'd ever seen him.

Bishop Peadar held the cup of Christ high in the air. Light streamed through the glass windows reflecting off the splendid chalice.

Fionna and I faced the altar as Bishop Peadar offered each of us a communion wafer. We accepted, then turned to Merlin, who extended the holy cup filled with a subtle red wine.

I swirled the sweet-tasting wine around my mouth dissolving the wafer as I'd done so many times. I felt the protection of the Christ and the seal of the Druids upon my shoulders. Fionna and I exchanged our vows and were pronounced man and wife. Once the service finished, the bishop returned the grail cup to Joseph. He, in turn, passed it back to Elidor, saying as he did so, "My thoughts were correct when I appointed you to safeguard the cup. It is safest in your care."

Elidor took the cup and left the sanctuary to return the cup from whence it came.

As we started back down the isle, the rabbit leapt from Mother's lap and raced ahead of us.

He stopped, turned, and said, *All will be well, my son. Stay with her.* And then he hopped away.

Also by **Dee Carey**

THE CRIMSON VIXEN

The preordained couple meet when Leigh discovers an orphaned fox and keeps her as a secret companion. In time it is revealed his Kit is also a fierce female pirate. The Druids determine the pair are destined to rule Ireland. As a fox she is clever. As a woman she is enchanting. Can Leigh set aside his devotion to King Arthur to be with the woman of his dreams?

Available now on Amazon.

Meet Dee Carey

Dee Carey started writing before she knew how to form words. She lived in Upstate New York with her husband of 48 years. Now widowed she lives with her memories. She has two daughters and two grandsons.

Dee writes fantasy because "All my fantasies have been realized, I lead a wonderful life, my reality is perfect, therefore I write fantasy to inflame the hearts of those who are not as blessed as I am."

All of her stories feature a fox as either the hero or heroine. A long-time King Arthur fan, she uses just a touch of his legend.

www.ingramcontent.com/pod-product-compliance
Lightning Source LLC
LaVergne TN
LVHW091530060526
838200LV00036B/557